"So dancing with me pleasures you, sweet Brigitta?"

Even through Devon's gloved hand, she could feel his warmth, and it was impossible to ignore how easily their bodies slipped into the same rhythm.

"Certainly not!" she quickly replied.

"No matter," he said, guiding her expertly around the floor. "It is my intent to let it be known I have laid claim to you—"

"No man lays claim to me," she retorted forcefully, making a motion to step away from him, but Devon would not release her, not just yet.

"Then prepare yourself for battle, sweet Brigitta."

* * *

"*Two Hearts Too Wild* reads like a wondrous fairy tale. Get ready to be swept off your feet and into a magical realm of mystery, adventure, deception, and timeless romance."

—*Romantic Times*

* * *

TWO HEARTS TOO WILD

LINDSAY RANDALL

PAGEANT BOOKS

PAGEANT BOOKS
225 Park Avenue South
New York, New York 10003

PAGEANT and colophon are trademarks of the publisher

Cover artwork by Sharon Spiak

Printed in the U.S.A.

First Pageant Books printing: November, 1988

10 9 8 7 6 5 4 3 2 1

For my grandmother, Genevieve Augusta Kindblom,
with deep love and affection

My sincere thanks to Gudrun Friberg
of Gislaved, Sweden,
for all the assistance she so unselfishly gave.

TWO HEARTS TOO WILD

BOOK I

The Innocent

Chapter One

SWEDEN, 1650

A FULL MOON rode high in the night sky, casting iridescent reflections on the hushed winter landscape below. A lone rider appeared on the crest of the dunelike drifts of snow and reined in his mount while sweeping his gaze across the seaside lands he had once known so well. In the distance, beyond the silvery waves of snow, stood a solitary castle, the home of Erik Bjord and the final destination of a determined traveler. Spurring his horse suddenly, the rider plunged onward, anxious to reach the castle before the first hints of daybreak.

He gained the castle within minutes and wound his way into the sheltered yard. There, the figure dismounted and his ebony stallion snorted clouds of breath as it lifted its front hooves alternately from the ground, the only sign of its impatience to be in a warm stall. The man patted the great beast's

3

neck affectionately, running a hand along the sleek blackness of the magnificent animal. His hands were gloved in the finest leather, tasseled and fringed, the gauntlets made of stiffened silk. He was silent as he looked up to the forbidding castle of Vardighet. The structure was tall and imposing, an ominous presence in the halo-hued night. The mere sight of the huge rounded towers rising up toward the sky brought back a rush of childhood memories. Memories the man wished he could forget.

A young lad, his low status apparent from his shabby clothing and half-witted manner, came toward the man and took the stallion, leading the beast away from the main entrance of Vardighet. The man, once again alone, scanned the silent stone steps of the castle, his movements as cautious and predatory as a wolf. His eyes were black as coal, mysterious and piercing—alien in this Nordic land of blue-eyed people. They had the look of seeing all, seeing through. He exhaled deeply and took the last few steps over the snow-packed ground with a confident stride. His feet were booted and spurred, and he wore a sheathed sword at his hip, a military jerkin about his broad chest. Over his shoulders was a fur-lined cloak which he unfastened and set at a calculatedly careless angle about him. He ignored the cold that assaulted his exertion-warmed body. This night his mind centered solely on his purpose in Sweden.

Above his hair, which was black as a moonless night and fell loosely below the line of his shoulders, was an ebony hat now cocked at an acclivous angle that gave him the look of a gentleman-adventurer. Encircling the band were feathers of red giving the only bit of color to his dark outer attire, and the contrast was great, the effect startling.

With a deceptively calm, purposeful stride, he entered the castle of Vardighet. The passage of years had not altered the structure, he noted. But what about the castle's occupants? Would the people of Vardighet be the same as when he had left those many years ago? Was the master at home? Or was the building inhabited only by the young Princess Thora-Lisa, soon-to-be bride of General Bjord?

The darkness enveloped him as he passed into the cool entry hall. No hissing flames of a torch shed light upon the narrow stairs, no soft familiar voice welcomed him. There was nothing but bone-chilling air and the empty echo of his own footsteps as he made his way toward a secret passage, avoiding the castle guard. Almost by instinct he navigated the same well of hidden stairs he had been brutally shoved down when he'd been a child of twelve. Even now he could hear the screams of his mother as she urged him to run with his life. But Devon had not run. He'd held his ground and attempted to fight the intruders who dared harm his mother.

Time had taken much from Devon Courtenay since then—but never the memories of that dreadful night, and he was suddenly glad no flame lit his way, for he did not want to view the stains of his dear mother's blood—stains that surely must still be dripping on the walls.

Devon paused on the last step with his hand atop the latch of the hidden door to Princess Thora-Lisa's private chambers. Should he enter? If he made his presence known to the princess now, he could very well be putting his own life in jeopardy. But if he didn't speak with the young woman who held the answers to his most burning questions, his sixteen-year quest would see no end.

He had no choice. He had come this far without second thought.

Lifting the latch, he cautiously pushed the portal open and stepped inside.

A warm rush of air laced with a heady fragrance bathed his face as he stood behind a carved wooden partition covering the hidden door. A shadow with gentle curves passed before his eyes, moving briefly into his line of vision and then retreating to a part of the chamber that was obscured from his view. Waiting for his eyes to adjust to the golden light cast by a few candles and a fire in the hearth, he closed the door soundlessly behind him and then stepped to the opening of the partition, watching the slender, yet womanly figure before him.

Ah, Lisa, he thought to himself, *how you've blossomed from a small child to a beautiful woman. You are not the young girl I remember.*

The woman seemed enthralled by a dish of jewelry on a wooden stand and did not hear his entrance. Laughing softly to herself, she scooped up a heavy strand of pearls from the decorative wooden dish, then looped the necklace about her slim throat—once, twice, and then a third time—not bothering to pull the lustrous waves of her Nordic blond hair from beneath the gentle burden of the exquisite pearls. Eagerly, she shoved her tiny hands deep into the overflowing dish of jewelry, and joyously began pulling out all sorts of queenly trinkets: an ivory brooch, a ruby brooch, pearl earbobs, silver bracelets. One after the other she admired them, then quickly cast each piece aside and dug deeper into the collection for more.

Such childish glee, he thought to himself, still watching. The Thora-Lisa he remembered had been quiet and thoughtful—even given to moods of sullenness or uncontrollable grief. This vision before him contrasted sharply with his memories. Dressed in a navy skirt with a decorative but peasantlike red and black apron secured tightly above it and a common white blouse beneath a simple laced bodice, this woman certainly did not appear to be a princess. Perhaps, he thought to himself, the princess's chambers had been moved since the last time he'd been within these walls. But no, his reason argued, the jewels on the stand, the intricately woven tapestries covering the wall, the elegantly embroidered sitting chairs, the huge four-poster bed with its heavy draperies opened, revealing rich furs across the bed, all told him this was indeed a suite for royalty. What could possess Thora-Lisa to don the clothes of a peasant? Even as a child of four, she had been attracted by elegant things.

So many years . . . could this young woman before him even recall the time they'd spent together?

"Lisa," he murmured softly.

Her hands freezing in midair, the woman whirled toward him. As she did, the man felt his heart fall to the pit of his stomach.

"You are not Lisa!" he breathed. Incredulously,

he gazed into a tiny heart-shaped face with blue eyes the color of summer skies, a tiny upturned nose, and lips full and tinted a delicate shell pink. No, certainly not Lisa!

The girl's mouth was too full, too alluring . . . too perfect. Lisa would never go about with her face uncovered. No, this woman was not Thora-Lisa, not with those gorgeous lips and smooth skin.

"Thief!" he accused, as the memory of his gentle friend became tarnished by this girl's wanton actions. In a passion, he unsheathed his sword. "You are a thief!"

Brigitta Lind gasped. The tip of the sword caught the firelight and dazzled her in an instant as the bracelets fell from her nerveless fingers and clattered to the floor.

Sweet Lord! Who was this man who appeared from nowhere and branded her a thief? The dark figure stepped from the shadows and took two great strides toward her, the tip of his blade heading straight for her throat. Stifling a scream, Brigitta lunged for the door. Escape stood only a few feet away but it might have been a league's distance from her.

"You go nowhere!" the intruder ordered as he latched on to her mane of hair and halted Brigitta in her wild dash for safety.

She cried out with pain. Roughly, he yanked her back against his solid frame.

"No!" She struggled wildly in his imprisoning grip. "I'm no thief! Let me go!"

The man brought his sword flat against her throat, pressing the icy cold blade to her suddenly burning skin. She ceased her struggles instantly. A horrible vision appeared in her mind's eye—that same blade could turn and effortlessly slice her head from the rest of her body!

"Who are you?" the man demanded, his voice a rasp in her ear. "What are you doing in the princess's chambers fondling her jewels?"

Brigitta's heart thumped in her chest. She felt sick with fear. True, she had every right to be in these chambers but she'd had no license to scoop up the princess's precious gems and lace them around her own slender neck. Trying on the jewelry had been an impulsive act, something she'd done without considering the consequences. But she couldn't help the excitement she'd felt upon first entering the princess's rooms. The glitter of wealth awed Brigitta. A peasant's daughter, she had been swept away by just the sight of such riches.

The once-cool blade at her throat had warmed with her own body heat. "I'm no thief," she whispered again.

The man gave a low, dangerous chuckle. He held one arm around her waist with the fingers splayed and intimately covered her right hip as his sword pressed against her neck. "Then what is this?" he asked, lifting with the edge of his sword the string of pearls draped down the front of her chest. "Do these not belong to Thora-Lisa?"

With a blade at her throat, Brigitta had no choice but to answer the man. "Y—yes, the pearls belong to the princess," she said, then added quickly, "but

I had no intention of stealing them!" Bravely, she raised her voice. "Now take your hands from me before I call the guard!"

He gave a short laugh and she felt the sound of it rumble in his chest. "Will you now?" he asked softly. "I'm very handy with a blade, you know. I've fought off as many as five armed men at once before. Do not be fooled in believing anyone can overtake me easily."

"You speak brave words, stranger," Brigitta replied, struggling to keep the tremor of fear from her voice. "Perhaps I'll shout for a guard and let you prove your prowess with your sword!"

"Ah, but I could prove my prowess to you right here," he whispered, his breath lifting a few wisps of hair near her ear. "We need not the watchful eyes of your highness's service. In fact, my performance would be much better should we remain alone."

Brigitta froze as he lifted the strands of pearls and then let them fall gently back against her trembling breasts. Acutely aware of the lean, hard body behind her and how the man's left hand roughly caressed her hip, Brigitta's fear for her life became overpowered by worry for her virtue. She'd been warned of such goings-on within these walls. Innocent maids were often taken by unknown assailants. But Brigitta never believed she would be a victim! Could this intruder be such a madman? God in heaven! After just one day at Vardighet, she'd never live to tell her family of the wonders she'd seen!

The stubble of whiskers on his face roughly scratched Brigitta's delicate facial skin. She felt her knees beginning to buckle beneath her as her body tingled with odd sensations that began exactly beneath the point where the man's left hand rested on her hip. Slowly, his fingers moved over the coarse material of her skirt.

"If you are not guilty, then relax; you've nothing to fear," the intruder whispered.

Nothing to fear but debauchery! In one swift movement, Brigitta pushed the sword from her way. But the man behind her was quicker. With fluid ease, he captured her by wrapping his left arm tightly around her body. Her arms trapped, he could have easily flicked her tender skin with the blade, but he held the sword just inches from her neck and paused. Brigitta no longer felt its piercing prick.

"Easy now," the man crooned, tormenting her. "I told you you've nothing to fear—if indeed you are not a thief."

Anger bubbling over, Brigitta declared, "I'm not a thief!"

"Very well, calm yourself and then explain to me what you are doing in the princess's private chambers."

"Calm myself? How can I relax with a blade at my throat?" Brigitta struggled once more in his hold, determined not to do anything he demanded. "And what are *you* doing in the princess's chambers? You ruffian!"

To her surprise, the man laughed and his tight hold slackened. "Ah, a spitfire, are you? *Bravo.* I was beginning to wonder if all Swede women were as cold as the Baltic in winter. Thus far, my welcome in Vardighet has been as chilling as the northern winds that sweep across your country."

"If you brandish your sword at every person you encounter, I shouldn't wonder why!"

Chuckling, the intruder dropped his arms to his sides, releasing her, and Brigitta immediately took two giant steps forward then whirled toward him.

A gasp caught in her throat as she glared at the rough stranger. *This was not the madman she had expected to see.* Attired in a fur-lined cloak fastened only at the neck and swept back in a furl of blackened folds, he appeared anything *but* a madman. His powerful chest was encased in a yellowish-colored leather jerkin over a white shirt with paned sleeves, and he wore black breeches that gave way to dark, wide-topped, spurred boots. He stood boldly across from her, legs braced wide, fists on his hips, and a jaunty smile on his lips.

"Who are you?" she asked, forcing her eyes to travel up to the man's face. Never before had she seen a person of such dark coloring. His hair, the color of a raven, appeared blue-black as the light from the fire played upon it, and it was long and straight, pushed back from his clean-shaven countenance. His eyebrows, above ebony eyes, were thick and now pulled together as he scrutinized her as openly as she did him. His cheekbones, broad and flat, appeared nearly chiseled as the skin covering them joined a strong jawline so expertly squared it exuded an aura of strength and unlimited physical abilities. Giving her a mocking grin, he tipped back the broad-brimmed hat atop his head and peered intently at her. Brigitta felt herself shiver inwardly. Those eyes—they were more piercing than the tip of his sword.

"Who am I?" the stranger repeated, cutting into

her thoughts. "I believe I asked you first." He looked casually predacious standing there leaning slightly on the hilt of his sword. He also appeared alarmingly in control; something Brigitta did not feel at all.

"I—I am Brigitta. Brigitta Lind."

"And what are you doing in these chambers . . . Brigitta Lind?" Her name passed through his lips like a caressing breeze over a field of flowers, and although he spoke her native tongue, Brigitta could discern a foreign accent draping his words.

Giving a challenging lift to her chin, she responded, "I have every right to be in the princess's chambers. She has requested my presence and I await her arrival. But you—I doubt the princess has requested *your* presence. She would not deal with such a barbarian!"

"A barbarian, am I?" He laughed at her choice of words as his black eyes shone. "Yes, there are those who would call me a barbarian. But I don't recall a woman ever saying such a thing."

He gave her a thoroughly disarming grin as he resheathed his sword. He was indeed a rogue, Brigitta decided, altogether too sure of his charms where the fairer sex was concerned. Now that she had a moment to view him and he wasn't staring at her with murder in his eyes, Brigitta could see the spark of mischief in his black gaze, the fine laugh lines near the corners of his eyes and the natural upward curve of his smooth lips. Her grandmother had warned her about such men, telling her they were nothing but trouble for any young woman with a tender heart. But Brigitta guessed her grandmother had never met the likes of this stranger.

And though her experience was small, she knew it was not every day a woman encountered such a man: dangerous, mercurial, able to charm as easily as threaten. In spite of herself, Brigitta felt a thrill of anticipation course through her.

"And what are you, sweet Brigitta, if not a thief?" he asked, interrupting her train of thought. He motioned to the pearls draped across her bosom. "You wear the spoils even as we speak." His ebony eyes had a mischievous light in them, yet his tone bordered on serious. Brigitta fidgeted, then averted her eyes.

"I—I told you," she said in almost a whisper. "The princess has summoned me and I only await her arrival." A horrid thought of the stranger revealing her actions to the princess winged through her mind. Would she be flogged for touching the jewels? Or worse yet, sent back to her family in disgrace? "Please," she continued, finally bringing her eyes to meet his. "I meant no disrespect. I—it is only that I've never seen such wealth."

"Ah, yes, the lure of gems and gold. Men have killed for less." He moved toward the stand and casually dipped his hands into the dish Brigitta had been emptying minutes before. He lifted one sapphire brooch from the pile, running his well-shaped fingers over the smooth stone. "I see I am not the only one to succumb to the glittering treasures within the walls of Vardighet," he replied cryptically. In a swift movement, he tossed the brooch toward Brigitta and she instinctively reached her hands out to catch it. "Keep it," he said. "I am sure Thora-Lisa will not miss the bauble."

Brigitta stared at him in shocked amazement.

Did he actually think she could take something so valuable from her princess, or anyone for that matter. Who was this man? she wondered. He had used the princess's given name and he had entered into the chambers through a door Brigitta could not even see. And what had he meant when he'd said he'd been lured by the riches within Vardighet? Was *he* a thief! If so, it was Brigitta's duty to inform Princess Thora-Lisa of his presence! "I don't want it," she said, her eyes flashing fire. "And I intend to tell the princess of your intent!"

His black brows lifted. "Oh?" he asked, and then smiled. "Tell Lisa what you will. I've no fear." He brought the great folds of his cloak around him, obviously preparing to exit the way he'd come.

Brigitta searched her brain for some way to detain him, but nothing came to mind but some castle gossip she'd overheard earlier. Hurriedly, she announced, "Then perhaps news that General Bjord is on his way to Vardighet will give you some food for thought. I am sure the general would not hesitate to give the likes of you your due!"

A flicker of interest lit the man's black gaze, and Brigitta momentarily felt triumphant. But in the next instant, the glimmer vanished and his eyes once again took on their cold aspect. "Erik is returning to Vardighet?" he asked. "When?"

Aha, she'd struck a sensitive chord! Although she knew nothing more, she pressed her advantage, threatening, "I'll tell the general of your intent and he will personally see you are—"

"When?" the stranger demanded, taking a step toward her, his right hand instinctively touching the hilt of his sword.

The man was much too eager to draw his weapon! Quickly, Brigitta said, "Soon. Today!" It was an outright lie and she instantly prayed for forgiveness. For all she knew Erik Bjord wouldn't be home for a fortnight! The general had taken his vast army out on one of his long marches and who knew when the brave man would see fit to bring his troops home.

"Today? Are you certain?" His features hardened at the news.

Brigitta nodded swiftly. "Yes! And I'll tell him what has happened this day!"

"Hmm," the man murmured, clearly not in the least disturbed by her threats. "That information changes my plans."

"That is a relief! Judging by your quick use of that sword, you're here for nefarious purposes!"

The intruder stared at her for long moments, but his thoughts were with the news she'd just given him. Quite suddenly however, he refastened his cloak and smiled. "What exactly will you tell Erik, Brigitta? That I found you with your hands elbow-deep in Thora-Lisa's jewels?" He shook his head, giving her a self-assured smile. "No, sweet Brigitta, you'll be telling no one about our encounter."

Cheeks aflame and her heart beating much too fast for comfort, Brigitta attempted to deny his allegation, but when she opened her mouth no words came out. Just then, the sounds of footsteps from beyond the huge door came to their ears.

"It is the princess," Brigitta declared, watching the man for his reaction. She was disappointed to see no sign of fear but only a look of longing pass over the man's handsome features. Could he perhaps be in love with the princess, she wondered? Her back against the door, Brigitta closed her hands over the latch and lifted it. "Or perhaps it is the general approaching, and when he sees you in the princess's private chambers he will take action, of that I am certain!"

Mischief still lighting his eyes, he said, "Erik will not find me here. And if you know what is best for you, you will tell no one I was here." With that, he lowered his hat to a jaunty angle over his forehead and gave her a long, hard look. Brigitta felt his black gaze all the way to her toes. "I suspect we'll meet again, sweet Brigitta," he said softly, and with those words he sketched a sweeping bow to her, then turned and made a silent exit by the way he had come.

Chapter Two

STARING AFTER THE man who disappeared like a phantom, Brigitta considered raising an alarm. But just as quickly she realized she would appear foolish to the princess if she bolted from the room, screeching about a sword-wielding intruder. She wanted to impress Princess Thora-Lisa in their first meeting, and quivering while relaying a wild tale would never do. Why, Brigitta even still wore the princess's pearls draped over her bosom! How to explain *that?*

Panicking, she whipped the precious gems from around her neck and replaced them in the decorative dish. She had only enough time to scoop up the fallen bracelets before the doors opened and the princess and her lady-in-waiting entered the chambers. Dropping the silver things onto the table beside her, Brigitta straightened and immediately began fumbling with the strings of her bodice that had been sliced when the man had lifted the pearls with the tip of his sword.

No use. The stranger's blade had irreparably severed them. Brigitta felt like a naughty child caught playing forbidden games. Her hopes of making a good first impression on the princess vanished, and Brigitta averted her eyes from the two figures entering the room.

Her shame was immediately overridden by curiosity, however. The princess was almost a mythical figure in this country. All Brigitta knew of Princess Thora-Lisa was that the woman was ugly beyond belief and very lucky indeed to have a man as brave and handsome as Erik Bjord request her hand in marriage. Exactly what did the princess look like?

Rumors of the princess's unsightliness ran rampant across the lands. Brigitta had heard numerous stories, all varying greatly. Brigitta's grandmother had once told her the princess had a hunched back and brittle, broken skin, a horrid face, and hands that could pick up nothing because they were so twisted and deformed. Some villagers even said the princess was a witch who had lost favor with other witches. A spell had been cast upon her that caused the princess to grow uglier with every passing year, and anyone who touched the princess fell prey to the same spell! Brigitta shivered as she remembered the lurid stories. Surely just touching the princess's jewels would not cause the spell to work its evil on her, would it?

Brigitta dropped into a deep curtsy, keeping her head lowered as she awaited her instructions from the princess. Whatever the princess's reaction to seeing her jewels tampered with, Brigitta decided to be brave and take responsibility for her reckless actions.

"Welcome, Brigitta Lind," said a cultured voice, soft yet ringing as a bedside bell might peal. "Arise. I have been awaiting your arrival with pleasure."

Hearing the soft loveliness of the voice, Brigitta lifted her gaze slowly over the woman opposite her. The woman's voice was soft as falling snow and clear as cool forest air.

Dainty satin slippers peeped beneath full skirts that belled out gracefully from a belted waistline decorated with a large deep blue rosette. The dress the princess wore was of fur-lined ice-blue satin and had full sleeves that were tied around between shoulder and elbow with a rosetted ribbon in a deeper shade of blue, with the sleeves ending in crisp, white cuffs. The neckline of the dress left the princess's shoulders bare and was adorned by a brooch clustered with pearls and one solitary sapphire. Her hands were concealed in fringed gloves of the softest leather but the shape of her fingers looked normal enough to Brigitta. They held lightly on to a white ermine muff, a sign that the princess felt calm about her first appearance before a peasant girl.

Slowly, Brigitta looked to the young woman's

face and there, covering all but her blue eyes, was a veil. More than one layer of gauzy fabric was draped pleasingly across the princess's lower face and fastened to an elaborate head covering. Her small, stiffly curled blonde locks escaped from beneath the turbanlike covering decorated with tiny seed pearls and two jeweled clasps with sapphires that held the veils in place. Not even the woman's nose showed—just her eyes, and these were a pale, watery blue.

Brigitta held back a gasp, startled by the sight of a young woman hiding behind a mask. The rumors she'd heard must be true! Brigitta's eyes must have shown her shock, but the princess had immediately turned away from her, as though she were giving Brigitta time to compose herself. Hastily, Brigitta wiped any expression off her face and stood rooted to her spot, unsure of what her next movement should be.

"Shall I bring another fur for your bed, Your Highness?" the princess's lady-in-waiting asked, obviously trying to smooth over the uneasy moment.

Brigitta glanced at the older woman and gave her a thankful smile. The woman wore a pleated, multicolored, vertical striped skirt, a white apron decorated with lace, and an off-white blouse with a turned-down collar. Atop her gray hair, which was plaited and wound into a bun, was a small white cap. To Brigitta, the woman dressed as though she belonged in some small peasant village, not the castle of Vardighet.

The woman did not return the smile. Instead she pursed her weathered lips into a disapproving pucker and stared directly at the severed strings of

Brigitta's bodice. Brigitta once again nervously fumbled with her lacings.

"No, thank you, Marta," said the princess from the opposite end of the huge chamber. "I will be warm enough this night. You may leave now. I wish to be alone with Brigitta."

"Yes, Your Highness," Marta replied coolly, curtsying. After giving Brigitta another disapproving glance, the woman left the chambers through the huge double doors leading to the outer hall.

"Do not mind Marta's way," the princess said from her spot near the huge four-poster bed. "She is old and worries overly much about my feelings. After all these years, Marta is still not used to people's reactions to . . . to my appearance."

Brigitta felt a fool. "I—I am sorry, gracious Princess. I did not mean to offend in any way. I only—"

The princess raised one gloved hand and waved gracefully at the air. "I understand," she interrupted, "you did not know what to expect, I am sure. Rumors of my disfigurement and—and my sickness travel through every village. I've no doubt you were most curious about what you might find within these walls. But," she said, and paused, her pale blue eyes staring directly into Brigitta's, "I do hope I am not as hideous as you expected."

"I find nothing hideous about you, Your Highness!" Brigitta's reply was quick, but her heart raced. Perhaps a childish part of herself feared that the princess would rip off the veils and reveal a ghoulish face more terrifying than any nightmarish apparition.

The princess nodded brusquely, ending their

current conversation. She dropped her ermine muff atop the dark furs of her bed and then removed her gloves, tossing them after the muff.

Brigitta could not help but watch the princess's actions closely. She was relieved to see not twisted, knotted fingers, but long and graceful ones instead. They were frail hands, yes, but far from deformed.

"I am sure you are curious to know the reason I have summoned you to Vardighet," the princess said.

"Yes, Your Highness, I am."

The princess's eyes seemed to smile. "Please, call me Lisa," she urged gently. "We will soon be friends, I think."

"But, Your Highness," Brigitta began, aghast at the suggestion. "I—"

" 'Your Highness' sounds much too formal," the princess interrupted. "Even though I am in line to the throne, it is no secret I have no wish to be sovereign of Sweden. My distant cousin, Queen Christina, will maintain that position a long time, I am sure. Soon a male heir will continue the Vasa Dynasty, and then perhaps the nobles of the court will discontinue glancing in my direction."

Brigitta only nodded, surprised the princess would deign to speak to her of such important matters.

The princess sat on the edge of the bed and turned her attention to Brigitta. "I hope your journey to Vardighet was not too arduous for you."

"No, Your—Lisa, it was not," Brigitta answered politely. "With the snow, my journey was lengthened, but no more than a day or two."

"I see. And your family, were they overly saddened by your leaving?"

"Y—yes," Brigitta answered. "Very sad." She remembered back to the day she had left the small village, or *byalag*, she had been born and raised in. Never in all her sixteen years had she been away from her family. She had at first been hesitant to leave her parents, grandmother, four brothers, and three sisters behind, but her mother and father had been adamant. They wanted their daughter to have a better life, and going to the castle to serve a princess was beyond their wildest hopes for their eldest daughter. The whole village had been proud to hear Brigitta had been summoned by Thora-Lisa.

Being uneducated and of peasant rank, Brigitta had had no other ambitions than to marry and produce healthy children. But as she had ridden away from the *byalag* in the rickety wagon Thora-Lisa had sent, waving to her family until they became specks on the horizon, Brigitta's thoughts turned to her bright future and her excitement at her new appointment swept away any doubts.

Thora-Lisa watched Brigitta closely, and then said softly, "If you ever find yourself lonesome for home, tell me. There is no reason you cannot return to visit. Or they could even visit you here, if you wish."

Brigitta was stunned that the princess should show such concern and generosity. *"Varmt tack,"* Brigitta responded, thanking her. "My family is very proud to have me at Vardighet. To serve you is a great honor. I will do my very best, Your High—Lisa."

Thora-Lisa gave a slight smile that could be seen only in her pale blue eyes. "Service is not what I desire from you, Brigitta. I have requested you because I want a companion. A—a friend. I—my days are very lonely. Few people have time to spend with an ailing princess." The princess's lonely voice caught, but she controlled the tremor and continued. "You see, not only was I born with a marred face, but I have—I have illnesses which plague me frequently. I am sometimes bedridden for weeks and the only person I see is Marta. She is a good friend, but I need someone closer to my own age. This is why I have summoned you, Brigitta. Your only duty will be to keep me company."

As Brigitta listened to the princess's gentle voice, she began to relax a little; her job would not be difficult. Why had Thora-Lisa chosen *her*, though? Was there not some young woman in the castle who could become a suitable companion? Need Thora-Lisa have searched as far away as Brigitta's *byalag*, which was leagues from Vardighet? Brigitta sensed there was a more specific reason Thora-Lisa had chosen her, and yet the princess was hesitant to inform Brigitta of that reason.

"I will keep you company, Lisa," Brigitta assured her, willing herself not to pose a dozen questions. "I will do whatever you ask of me."

Thora-Lisa's watery blue eyes wavered slightly. She folded her birdlike hands and nervously twisted them together. Then she caught herself and stopped. "I hope you will, Brigitta," she said quietly. Then, her mood lightening, she stood up and moved toward the stand draped with the jewels Brigitta had haphazardly cast there. "I see you've acquainted yourself with some of my nicer jewels," she said calmly, but her eyes sparkled as she glanced at Brigitta.

Brigitta's cheeks flamed. What was there to say? She'd been trying on jewelry that was not her own—jewelry that belonged to a princess, no less! An apology was not what Thora-Lisa would want to hear from her, she was certain. "Yes, I have," she said miserably. "The pearls are—are quite beautiful."

Thora-Lisa scooped the strand of pearls from the dish and handed them to Brigitta. "You may have them." When Brigitta did not reach for the strand, she laughed and insisted. "Please. Take them! They would look lovely on you. You have such a fair face and a pretty neck." In spite of her good humor, she spoke the words longingly. "They will suit your beauty nicely, Brigitta."

Brigitta felt a wave of sympathy for the princess wash over her. Thora-Lisa was such a gentle and generous creature. It was not fair that she should be burdened with ugly features and a sickly body.

"Varmt tack," she murmured, accepting the gift. The necklace felt warm in her fingers. Only moments ago the dark-haired stranger had lifted these same pearls from her breast, and Brigitta knew she would not be able to wear them without remembering the dashing intruder.

"Do you see anything else you like?" Thora-Lisa asked, not noticing Brigitta's thoughtful frown. She replaced the silver bracelets Brigitta had fumbled with just as she'd entered.

"N—no, nothing else," Brigitta begged. "You've been much too generous already, Lisa."

"A gift exchanged between friends can not be too generous," the princess said lightly. She turned and said with more emphasis, "I want you to be my friend, Brigitta. I desperately need a friend."

Brigitta heard the words—and the plea within them—and although her heart went out to this kind and sweet young woman, Brigitta knew somehow that Thora-Lisa had an ulterior motive for requesting her presence. Could Thora-Lisa be so lonely she'd have to *summon* a friend? Or was there another reason a country girl had been plucked from her home and brought to this curious place?

As she watched the princess straighten the cluttered jewelry on the stand, her hiding veils fluttering slightly with the movements, Brigitta didn't know what to think about her new position. She was suspicious, but also saddened somehow. Maybe Thora-Lisa *was* truly lonesome. Many of the villagers snickered about the princess's ugliness. Perhaps many of the castle dwellers did, too.

"I *will* be your friend, Lisa," she answered, truly meaning the words. Her reward was a twinkle of pleasure in Thora-Lisa's eyes. Had the veils not covered her face, Brigitta was certain she would have seen Thora-Lisa smile.

"I will have Marta show you to your room," the princess said triumphantly. Then, she led the way to the double doors of the chamber.

Brigitta followed in the princess's wake, her mind brimming with thoughts of all that had happened to her this day. Her *own* room? She'd never had such a luxury! Perhaps living at Vardighet and serving Thora-Lisa would not be so terrible. . . .

*   *   *

Thora-Lisa hurried along the familiar garden path, glad to be alone to think. A brisk wind blowing in from the frozen Baltic lifted her cloak and skirt hems as she walked along the inlaid stones. Packed snow crunched beneath her pattened feet and she nearly lost her footing as she skidded over a patch of ice hidden under a dusting of snow that had fallen through the night. The winter white world around her sparkled in the bright sunshine, and even though her breath made little cloud puffs when she breathed out, Thora-Lisa barely felt the cold air. She was tired of staying within the castle walls and the minute she'd stepped outside and started toward her own private gardens, she'd felt her spirits soar.

She longed to remove her hiding veils and breathe in some fresh air. For too many months the physicians had ordered her to stay cooped up in her rooms. If they didn't bleed her in hopes of purging the poison from her system they were forcing her to drink vile concoctions. Thora-Lisa never felt well after their ministrations. In fact, she often felt worse. Even physicians from as far away as Italy could do no better. But today Thora-Lisa would do as she pleased.

Coming to a stop near a row of snow-covered hedges, she reached up and undid the veils covering her face. Surely no one would see. Cold air slapped her marred features and she let out a sigh of contentment at the invigorating sensation. How nice to have something other than her horrid veils touch her face! How wonderful to be able to breathe freely and to experience the caress of warm sunlight upon her cheeks.

If only I were as beautiful as Brigitta, she thought to herself. Lisa tried not to dwell on her disfigurement, but the interview with her new companion brought her own appearance sharply into focus. Brigitta was lovely—her face full of energy and spirit. What did it feel like to be so pleasing to look at? How would it feel to walk into the court of Sweden without having to hide behind layers of material? What would Erik Bjord think of her if she were not the pathetic being that she was?

Erik, her intended spouse since birth, always behaved with kindness to her, but Thora-Lisa knew the general secretly wished he would not have to marry her. How could she not know the truth?

The man was a great general, having served under Queen Christina's father, Gustavus Adolphus. Erik had marched with Gustavus to Lützen in 1632 and had been beside the king when he was killed during that battle. And it was Erik who had helped lead the soldiers home bearing the body of Gustavus, one of Sweden's greatest monarchs. Since that time, Erik Bjord had led many successful campaigns in ensuring Sweden's safety, most of them against the hated Danes of the South. It was no secret that Erik and Jorgen, a Danish general, were sworn enemies. Both men waged war against the other whenever possible, and such actions took Erik away from Vardighet quite often. So, also, did Erik's interest in mercantile trade. If not on the battlefield, Erik could be found in the ports of Göteborg or Stockholm, conversing with the wealthy burgher shipowners. Consequently, Erik Bjord had time enough to care about battles, foreign trade, and drink—yet not the princess who loved him more than her own life.

But now, Erik was coming home and Thora-Lisa looked forward to his return. She knew he did not reciprocate her undying love, but she was thankful enough that he still considered marrying her.

Ah, Erik, she thought. *If only you could have someone as healthy and beautiful as Brigitta.*

Thora-Lisa felt great guilt at being born hideous, and it was also the reason she had summoned Brigitta to Vardighet. Lisa had exerted much energy searching for just the right young woman to serve as her companion. Her quest had taken her to the many small *byalags* throughout the country, jaunts that had taxed Thora-Lisa's health greatly. But when Lisa had laid eyes on Brigitta from afar, the princess knew then her efforts had not been in vain.

If not for Lisa's thinning hair, her extreme thinness, and of course her deformed face, she and Brigitta Lind could have easily been related. There was a definite resemblance between them. And Thora-Lisa intended to make use of this likeness.

Again, she was sharply reminded of the burdens her deformity placed upon her. If only others could accept her face and treat her normally, Thora-Lisa knew she would be the happiest person alive. But the people of Sweden were superstitious—especially the villagers—and the long, dark winter nights coupled with the abundance of deep forests added to their immersion in such beliefs. Thora-Lisa had been branded a witch since the day she was born, and the only reason she was given any respect was because she was of royal blood.

Thora-Lisa tried to clear her mind of her troubling thoughts. Turning her face skyward, she let herself bask in the rays of weak sunlight a moment longer.

Suddenly, from a short distance in front of her, she heard voices. There were people coming!

Thora-Lisa panicked—she couldn't be seen without her veils! Fearful that someone would catch her unmasked, Thora-Lisa quickly shook out her veils and attempted to reattach them to her headcovering. But her fingers were stiff from the cold air and she dropped the filmy cloths to the ground.

She gasped and bent hastily to retrieve the material. The voices along with the sound of footsteps were getting closer. Suddenly sick inside, Thora-Lisa knew she would never get her veils attached in time.

She fumbled with the sapphire clasps of her headdress, nearly weeping with fear. She could see the shadows of the approaching people as they rounded the slight bend in the path. Tears filled her eyes and she turned her back, ashamed that a princess should have to cower as she was doing now. Her limbs began to shake, her fingers trembling so that she'd never do her clasps properly. It was no use. She had been caught without her veils and now she had to suffer the consequences.

Clutching her veils in her right hand, she lunged toward the farthest recesses of the garden just as she heard the people behind her round the bend. She wasn't going to escape. Thora-Lisa rushed forward and tripped over her own clumsy feet. As if in a dream, she saw nothing but the snowy ground coming up in front of her face.

Suddenly, from somewhere behind the row of hedges, strong arms reached out, grasping firmly onto Lisa's falling body. Her savior yanked her quickly behind the cover of snow-laden branches and Lisa landed softly on the cold ground.

"Oh—" she began.

"Hush," replied an oddly familiar voice. "They'll hear us if you speak."

Thora-Lisa didn't dare look up to see the face of the person who'd spared her from exposure. Instead, she kept her eyes on the ground, watching as the snow from the disturbed branches sprinkled the area. The voices she'd heard became louder as two women walked past the spot where she crouched in the shrubbery. Lisa dared not even breathe until those voices died away. Even then, she stayed motionless, wondering what her fate would be now that she was alone with the person who so daringly dragged her between the hedges.

"Cover your face," the man behind her said.

"Wh—who are you?" she asked, hurriedly trying to obey. Her hands trembled as she fumbled with the sapphire clasps of her headdress, but she managed this time. She got to her feet, keeping her back turned.

The man chuckled. "A friend. Now if you hurry with your veils you can turn and greet me properly."

Thora-Lisa fastened the last clasp and moved herself a few inches away from the stranger before whirling toward him. "Devon!" she gasped. "Devon Courtenay? Is it really you?"

Devon gave her a broad smile as he stood and reached out a hand to her. "It is me, Lisa."

"Oh, Devon, how I've missed you!" Immediately, Thora-Lisa threw herself into his arms and hugged his neck. Her frail body trembled and tears of happiness filled her eyes. But in the next instant, she recovered herself, stepping sheepishly out of his embrace. Nervously, she dusted the snow from her deep blue cape. "I—I'm sorry," she said. "I shouldn't have done that."

Devon allowed his childhood friend to be embarrassed for only a moment. "And why shouldn't you have hugged me, Lisa? We are old friends and I have thought of you often these past years."

"But . . . we're older now, no longer children. You—you've grown to be a man." And a handsome man at that! He was dashing as a soldier, but the old flash of fire in his eyes lent a rakish air of danger to his appearance. Surely women everywhere flung themselves at his feet!

Devon gave her a fond smile. "And you have become a beautiful young woman, my old friend." At this, Lisa turned her head away, uncomfortable with his compliment. Devon touched her veiled cheek with his fingertips, gently turning her gaze back to his. "Come now, Lisa, don't be shy or nervous with me. We shared a great deal in our childhood years. I love you like a sister and I hate to think that the mere passing of years could destroy our love and friendship. I hope what we have is stronger than that."

Her pale blue eyes became moist with tears. "Oh, Devon," she exclaimed taking his gloved hands in hers. "It is, my friend. My love for you has never died—it is just that I thought all your travels would have lessened what you feel for me.

Where have you been all these many years?" A rush of questions spilled from her. "Has life treated you kindly? And your mother, how is Augusta?"

"Now this is the Lisa I remember," he said with a laugh, "always worrying for others instead of herself. Augusta is—she sends you her love."

Thora-Lisa detected his hesitation. "Is she not well? Devon, please, do not keep anything from me."

The sparkle in Devon's black eyes clouded over. "I'm afraid I have bad news, Lisa. Augusta is dying. That is the reason I have returned to Vardighet."

"Dying?" she exclaimed. "Oh, Devon, I am so sorry! But maybe I can help. I know a very skilled physician. He is in Italy, but I will send word for him at once. I will send this physician to her."

"No, Lisa, no physician can help her. Augusta's heart is delicate. She had wished to die in Sweden, her homeland, but the journey is too strenuous for her. She is in England living in a small cottage in Dover. I have come on her behalf. She deserves to—well, she is an honorable woman and deserves to live out her final days with her head held high."

Thora-Lisa nodded in understanding. Augusta Courtenay had lived her life labeled as an adulteress. "You mean the documents of her marriage, don't you? Do you truly believe they exist?"

Devon nodded, his features grave. "If she says there are papers documenting her marriage to Michael Courtenay, then I believe her."

Thora-Lisa knew the story well. Years ago, Augusta, then a servant to Thora-Lisa's young mother, had had a shocking affair with Michael Courtenay, then a pirate of the high seas for King James of

England. Augusta's family had shunned her and none believed Augusta's story that Michael had married her just before setting sail for England. Their suspicions were confirmed when Michael Courtenay never returned for the Swedish woman and she was left alone to bear her illegitimate son. What the people of Vardighet did not know was that the famous pirate favored by King James had been thrown into prison by the petty new king, Charles. Although Augusta had given Devon his father's name, all believed the boy illegitimate and had ostracized the pair. Only Thora-Lisa, then a small child, and her mother had been kind to the two.

"But Devon, that was such a long time ago. Where do you think these documents are?"

"I have an idea, but I don't want to voice it until I am certain." He stared off into the snowy distance for a moment, then returned his gaze to her, the clouds in his dark eyes gone. His tender smile returned. "But enough of me. I want to hear about you, Lisa. Has life been kind to you?"

"It has," Lisa replied, glad to have her dearest friend once again with her. "I have good news, Devon. You probably have heard. Erik and I are to be married soon."

"Yes, I have heard." Devon's expression changed. Suddenly, he was stony-faced. "That is another reason why I've chosen now to return to Vardighet, Lisa . . . you cannot marry Erik."

Thora-Lisa could only stare at Devon. "What do you mean?" she breathed. "I thought you would be happy to hear this news! The three of us were such close friends when we were children. You know I've always loved Erik! How can you not be happy for me?"

Devon turned away from her, lifting branches from their path and motioning for Lisa to lead the way out of the hedges. "Erik and I were never close friends, Lisa, and you know it. You only *wished* we were friends. Erik hated me—I've no doubt he still does."

"But why do you tell me I cannot marry him? I do not understand."

To quiet her agitation, Devon took her hand. Together they strolled along the path toward the entrance to Thora-Lisa's apartments. Devon remained silent. She had never liked this side of Devon—his harsh silences and stubborn declarations. She remembered how frightened she used to be when, as a child, Devon would suddenly become moody and withdraw from the people around him.

"Devon," she pressed. "I don't understand why you do not want me to marry Erik."

Devon came to a halt. The brim of his black hat very nearly covered his eyes but Thora-Lisa could feel their penetrating stare. "There is no easy way to tell you this, Lisa. So I'll just come right out with it. My father, Michael Courtenay, was murdered some time ago. I believe Erik might have had a hand in that murder, and I've come to see justice done."

Thora-Lisa felt her world fall from beneath her. Of all the things Devon could have said nothing could have shocked her more. "No," she exclaimed. "You must be mistaken! Erik would never murder a man—*your* father—for no reason." She wrenched her hand from his. "He—he only kills in battle, to protect our country. You are wrong, Devon! How can you say such things to me!"

"Lisa, I say these things because you must know what type of man Erik is. For too long you've held Erik on some pedestal. He is not worthy of you." Fiercely, Devon said, "He will never be able to give you the love you need. Oh, my dear Lisa, you deserve better."

Thora-Lisa stepped away from him as though he'd slapped her. "No! I do not believe you. Erik would not kill a man outside of war. I will not allow you to talk of him in such a way! I love him!"

"Please, Lisa, take heed of what I'm saying," Devon begged. "Erik Bjord is a murderer. He's cold and heartless. He is only marrying you for your wealth and position."

Thora-Lisa let out a stifled cry. "It is you who are cold and heartless! You are saying no man would want me for the woman I am! Are you saying Erik couldn't possibly love a woman as ugly as me?" Her voice rose, and when Devon stepped toward her and tried to comfort her, she brushed his hands away. "No! Do not touch me. I don't want your sympathy!"

"Lisa, please, you know that is not what I meant." Trying to speak calmly, Devon said, "You are a lovely woman. Any man would be proud to take you to wife. But Erik is not the man for you. He will only make you miserable. My God, Lisa, he helped murder my father!"

Thora-Lisa shook her head, tears pouring out of her pale eyes. "Have you any proof for your wild accusations?"

"I—no, I do not. But soon I will."

Lisa collected her wits, reminding herself this was no way for a princess to behave. Heavily, she whispered, "How could you do this, Devon? I thought you to be my truest friend and now you are destroying the one dream that has kept me living these many years. You have cast a dark cloud over my coming wedding when all I wanted was your blessing—"

"Lisa—" He tried to interrupt, but she would not let him.

"You of all people should know how very little I ask of life, and yet you're telling me I cannot have the one thing I want most!" She sobbed openly then, her veils fluttering with her ragged breath.

"Lisa, please, do not upset yourself. I know my words sound cruel to you now, but think on them." Urgently, he added, "Learn of the true Erik before you give your hand in marriage."

"No! I am going to marry Erik and there is nothing you can do to stop me!" With her words ringing in the cold air, Thora-Lisa lifted her skirts and ran toward her private entrance.

Devon watched her leave, his heart feeling as though it had been wrenched from his chest. He hadn't meant to upset Lisa. She was his oldest and dearest friend. He'd only meant to save her from a life of hell as Erik Bjord's wife, but all he'd managed to do was make her cry. He should have been able to manage it better. He knew how frail of health Thora-Lisa was, and he cursed himself for upsetting her.

"I'll find the proof that Erik had a hand in my father's death," he said aloud. "I'll prove to you Erik is not the man you think he is . . . and then I'll find a man who is both noble and decent enough to be your husband, one who is worthy." With that vow, he too headed toward the castle, his spurs jingling as his booted feet crunched down the snow upon the ground.

Chapter Three

BRIGITTA'S FIRST DAY at Vardighet went by quickly. She was measured for numerous outfits befitting her relationship to the princess. A fussy German tailor had been employed to sew her garments, and although most of the clothes were made of the plain Swedish linen, a great many were to be fashioned out of beautiful woolen cloth in rich colors imported from England and Germany. She was even given a pair of pattens for her feet that were fashioned of poplar and raised off the ground by an iron ring. A pair of wooden clogs covered with moss green silk with matching slippers completed her footwear wardrobe.

And her room, it was grand indeed! Situated in the princess's royal apartments, only three doors away from Lisa's private chambers, Brigitta's room had three deep-set windows that overlooked the princess's gardens. These and the walls were clad with wooden panels inlaid with various colored woods that depicted scenes of castle life and the arms of Vardighet. Even the ceiling was of carved wood and decorated with painted floral ornamentation. The bed was covered with a rich blue counterpane and set upon a dais, and a small stand holding a huge pitcher and bowl stood to the right of the bed. The only other furniture was a round stool situated beside a medium-sized hearth and a cedar wardrobe whose fresh scent filled the chamber, clinging even to the bed linen.

Gazing at the room that was to be her very own, Brigitta decided she would indeed enjoy living at Vardighet.

It was also on that very first day that Brigitta began to realize the seriousness of the princess's illness. Thora-Lisa fell ill that very afternoon, and she kept herself closeted in her rooms, not even emerging for the meal hours. The next day, the princess was too weak to leave her bed.

Brigitta wondered at the princess's illness, which caused her to become sick so quickly and without apparent provocation.

"I do not understand why you have become so weak," Brigitta remarked as she sat beside Thora-Lisa's huge bed while the princess rested. Already she felt quite close to the princess and was worried about her. "On the day of my arrival you appeared quite healthy. Does your illness always come upon you so rapidly, or has something happened to upset you?"

Thora-Lisa, dressed in a nightdress of eggshell white and snuggled beneath three furs, did not answer immediately. She wore no headcovering this day, only a white veil attached with clasps to her thin blond hair. Within the mammoth bed, she looked like a fragile bird. "Nothing has happened," she whispered dully.

"I think something *has* happened," Brigitta declared, reaching for the vessel of snow she'd brought in for Lisa earlier. Half of the snow had melted and Brigitta now poured the princess a cup of water. "Here, drink this and then tell me what is troubling you. I cannot help you if you are not honest with me."

Thora-Lisa's eyes crinkled at the sides in a weak smile. "You are boldly disrespectful to your princess, Brigitta, and I love you for it. No one has ever cared enough to inquire about me; everyone assumes I am ill and will recover on my own. But even a princess is human."

"Then tell me, Lisa. Let me share the burden of your troubles."

Thora-Lisa blinked her eyes rapidly, clearly trying to fight the tears that threatened to overwhelm her. "You are too kind, Brigitta. Yes, I will tell you. A—a dear friend of mine has returned to Vardighet. His mission here is a grave one and if he succeeds with his plans, he—he will destroy my dreams of a happy future."

Brigitta listened in silence. Was it possible Lisa meant the mysterious man in black?

"I asked him to reconsider his course of actions, but he refused and we—*I* spoke hateful words to him." Lisa's voice, as she paused to clasp her hands tightly together, quivered slightly. "It—it saddens me that after all these years my friend and I have come to be on opposite sides."

"Will this man not change his mind?" Brigitta asked. "Perhaps if he's given time—"

"No," Thora-Lisa interrupted. "He will not alter his plans, of that I am certain."

"Then you must not worry about his feelings," Brigitta said stoutly. "You deserve your own happiness."

Wiping away her tears with one thin hand, Thora-Lisa nodded. "Perhaps you are right. But I fear doing so will take all of my strength."

"I will help you," Brigitta said, and her words seemed to echo in the empty chamber.

Lisa did not respond.

Seated beside Lisa's huge bed with the red fire sputtering in the hearth and no other illumination, Brigitta suddenly felt uneasy. She watched the light play eerily over Thora-Lisa's veil and saw Lisa's frail body inhale and exhale shallowly. Thora-Lisa no longer appeared to be a royal princess, but rather just a shadow of some sickly, tortured being. Affected by the flickering firelight and the oppressive air that suddenly smelled of illness and suffering, Brigitta's imagination wandered.

Perhaps Thora-Lisa *was* a witch. Perhaps the princess's illness would soon inflict Brigitta! Perhaps Thora-Lisa's "dear friend" was a warlock and was attempting to override Lisa's powers with his own unholy ones! Time stood sickeningly still and Brigitta felt horribly alone in a bizarre world. The room suddenly smelled of sickness and evil powers. . . .

Brigitta sat back on her stool, taking in a deep breath as she tried to calm herself. Of course Lisa wasn't a witch! She was too kind, too sweet. Brigitta chided herself for her foolish thoughts and when she glanced over at Thora-Lisa, she noticed the princess was fast asleep. Brigitta's momentary fright left her and she passed the hours of the night keeping close vigil on the princess.

Just before the gray dawn broke, Thora-Lisa awoke with a weak cry, and Brigitta, who had stayed awake throughout the night feeding the fire and pacing the chambers, quickly rushed to Lisa's bedside.

"Lisa! What is it? What is the matter? Are you in pain? Should I summon Marta?"

Thora-Lisa's eyes flew open, fear-filled, and she stared blindly at the ceiling. "Brigitta?" she whispered hoarsely. "Is that you?"

"Yes, Lisa, I am here. You must have had a nightmare. All is well. Go back to sleep."

"No! It was no nightmare." Thora-Lisa blinked and drew a ragged breath. In a moment she spoke again but her voice sounded dull. "I am very ill, Brigitta. I—I fear I will not live to see the home-coming of my beloved Erik. I am afraid I will not live to marry him as I have longed all my life to do."

Gently, Brigitta touched Thora-Lisa's pale and sweating forehead. "I shall summon the physician, if you wish. Tell me, how can I help you? Let me remove some furs."

"No!" Thora-Lisa said excitedly, then she rasped, "I—I am cold. I cannot stop trembling."

Brigitta immediately straightened, sick inside at the sight of Thora-Lisa trembling uncontrollably beneath the furs.

"Then what can I do for you?" she begged,

frightened by the intensity of the princess's suffering.

Thora-Lisa blinked her blue eyes once, painfully, then in a whisper said, "There are two things you can do for me, Brigitta."

"You have only to ask."

Thora-Lisa attempted to laugh but the sound passed from her lips as a gasp. "You are too quick to reply, my friend. It is a great request."

"I will do it!" Brigitta cried, anxious to help her mistress.

After a long silence, Thora-Lisa finally said, "I wish for you to go secretly to a nearby village and bring to me the medicines of an old seer-woman who lives there."

"Is she a physician with a physician's powers?"

Thora-Lisa shook her veiled head. "No, but her medicines help me. You may find her senile, Brigitta, but she is my only solace in the constant search for a cure to my illnesses."

"If she has the power to cure you why don't you summon her to the castle? Why isn't she by your side when you need her most?"

"Because," the princess began slowly, "she is an outcast among her own people. They think her evil and crazy—as do the people of Vardighet—but her potions give me ease—much more than the bleedings the physicians call for."

Brigitta nodded, willing to do anything for her frighteningly ill friend. "If this woman has the power to help you, then I will go to her."

Thora-Lisa's eyes closed slowly. "Thank you. I prayed you would do this for me . . . but there is one other thing, and it is a great request."

Brigitta leaned forward, so intense was Thora-Lisa's raspy voice. "What is it, Lisa? What else can I do to help you?"

Thora-Lisa paused a moment, taking in a ragged breath. "What I will ask of you is the most important reason, the reason I chose you to serve me. . . ."

"I will do anything you ask, Lisa!" Brigitta replied quickly. Every moment they spent talking delayed her from bringing to Thora-Lisa the potion she'd requested. "Whatever you wish, Lisa, I will do, you know that. But for the moment, I want you to rest. Do not overtax yourself with words. We will speak later . . . when you have the potion and are feeling well again."

Thora-Lisa, as if having a great weight lifted from her delicate shoulders, closed her eyes and let out a deep sigh. "Yes, I will rest, but only after you are well on your way to the old seer-woman's cottage. Summon Marta for me. I wish to speak with her and when we are finished, you may rejoin me here."

Brigitta, reluctant to leave Thora-Lisa in her confused state, could only nod. "Yes, I will find Marta for you. Will there be anything else?"

Thora-Lisa shook her head and Brigitta left the darksome chambers in search of the princess's lady-in-waiting. She found Marta in her own chamber.

The old woman, at first brusque with Brigitta, went quickly to Thora-Lisa's apartments when she learned Lisa was ill and was asking for her. Brigitta was left standing in the cool, cavernous hall outside Thora-Lisa's rooms for only a moment before she was summoned back inside. To her surprise, Marta was nowhere to be seen.

"Marta knows I need the medicine of the old seer-woman," Thora-Lisa explained from beneath her furs. "She is bringing a friend who will escort you to Darlana's village. You would never be able to find Darlana's cottage on your own. You will need a guide. My friend will be that guide. Also, Darlana will speak to no man."

"Man? Am I to ride alone to this woman with a man I do not know?" Brigitta asked, uneasy with the idea.

"Yes, but Devon is a man you can trust. Devon Courtenay is a childhood friend of mine. As children, we used to go to Darlana's cottage together. Darlana does not mind speaking to male children—it is grown men she does not trust."

At that moment, two figures stepped from behind the partition hiding the secret passage the dark intruder had used to slip into Thora-Lisa's chambers. Brigitta was now glad she hadn't mentioned the intruder to Thora-Lisa. For the man who stood before her, his black gaze passing insolently over her, was the sword-waving barbarian.

Devon took in the sight before him: Lisa lying pale upon her bed, and the radiant Brigitta Lind keeping watch over her princess. Brigitta looked like a bright and beautiful angel of the morning, and it was with great effort he pushed thoughts of her beauty—along with regrets that he hadn't met her at another place and time—from his mind. Thora-Lisa needed him.

At sight of Devon Courtenay, Brigitta stiffened. He looked just as dangerous as before. Dressed casually in brown breeches tucked into wide-topped, spurred boots; a dark-colored jerkin laced across his well-defined chest with leather strips braided down the outer sides of his puffy-sleeved, buff-colored shirt beneath, he appeared as frighteningly in command as he had the first time she'd seen him in these very rooms. He let his gaze linger on her for only a moment before focusing all of his attention on Thora-Lisa.

Crossing the room in several great strides, the man knelt at the opposite side of Thora-Lisa's bed. He reached for her frail hand.

"Dear, Lisa, what has happened to you?" His teeth were clenched as if he held back great emotion. "Marta tells me you have taken ill again. Has my arrival at Vardighet caused this?"

Thora-Lisa turned her veiled face toward him. "Devon," she breathed. "I need Darlana's potions. Will you take my companion to Darlana's village?"

Devon did not glance up at Brigitta. "You know I will," he answered. "But can Darlana cure you? Should you not have a physician examine you as well?"

She shook her head. "No. I trust only Darlana." She turned her pale gaze to Brigitta then and summoned her remaining strength. "This is Brigitta Lind, Devon. She is my companion and friend. She will speak with Darlana and get the potion I need. Please, the two of you must hurry. I—I grow weaker by the moment. And Devon . . . once you return Brigitta to Vardighet, do not accompany her to this chamber. It is far too risky for you to be with me. I would rest easier if—if you were not here."

A taut muscle twitched along his jawline as his

ebony eyes gazed down at his friend. "As you wish," he whispered. "But should your condition worsen, summon me. You should not have to suffer alone, Lisa." In an instant he was on his feet and motioning Brigitta to follow him. He whirled away from the bed, and after a quick order to Marta to care for Lisa in his absence, he said to Brigitta, "Come. We've miles to travel this day."

Brigitta longed to tell him to travel those miles alone, but her sense of responsibility to Lisa was great, and so she nodded and started after him.

"Wait," Thora-Lisa said weakly. "Brigitta, the day is cold. Take one of my cloaks." She motioned for Marta to retrieve an ermine-lined blue cloak from her wardrobe, and once Brigitta had the inner cords of the garment secured, she whispered, "Godspeed. Hurry back to me, my friends."

Brigitta did not even have time to bid her princess good-bye. The man called Devon ushered her to the dark recesses of the room, pushing her behind the partition and through the opened door. Complete darkness enveloped them as the man pulled the door panel shut behind them, and Brigitta stood rooted to her spot, afraid she might step off the end of the earth. She had no clue what lay in front of her in the inky blackness.

Devon felt her hesitation, and it was with concentrated effort that he kept his hands to himself. She was even more beautiful than he remembered, and there still remained in him the unchivalrous desire to pull her svelte body to his in a tight embrace. Devon shook such thoughts away. Angry that he could be so diverted from his task, he said, more sharply than necessary, "Turn to the left.

There is a small landing and then a flight of narrow stairs."

Brigitta took a hesitant step forward and then another. "I—I can't see a thing," she muttered softly. "Must we sneak in and out of the castle like thieves? Lisa is a princess! Surely we can exit through a different passage." She came to an abrupt stop, ready to turn and leave the castle via another route.

Her sudden halt caught Devon unaware, and he ran directly into her soft body. With a muttered curse, he reached out to prevent her from falling and in so doing wrapped an arm about her waist. He could feel the gentle curve of her hip and the warmth of her body. Impatient with himself, he released his hold and stepped around her.

"I'll lead the way. Here, take my hand." With none of the gentleness she'd seen him display with Thora-Lisa, Devon grabbed her ungloved hand and pulled her forward.

Incensed that he should treat her so roughly— and also remembering how he'd held a sword to her neck—Brigitta pulled her hand free from his tight hold. "I will not!" she exclaimed. "I am capable of following you on my own."

He muttered something she didn't hear and started down the passage. "Have it your way. I don't know why Lisa ordered you to Darlana's. Marta knows her way through this passage. She and I could have been outside the castle walls by now." *And with Marta, my mind would doubtless be on my duty to Lisa and not on what charms you hold*, he added to himself.

"Marta is old, and *I* can do this task for the

princess," Brigitta shot back. "Lisa has faith in me."

Devon made no response. He plunged forward with a jingle of spurs, and the sound of his boots hitting the cold stone of the stairs echoed in the gloomy passage. "Watch your step," he commanded, nearly racing down the pitch black stairwell.

She scurried after him, staying close to his heels. Even though she had to hold her skirts high, her slippered feet were sure as a cat's on the narrowly cut stone. Her confidence rose. A pox on him for attempting to make her feel like a child!

"You are slowing," she taunted. "If *I* knew this passage as well as you, I could have reached the end by now." She boldly took a step to the right, attempting to pass him and lead the way. But where the next step should have been was nothing but crumbled stone, and with a small scream escaping her, she tumbled forward as more stone gave way beneath her. With jarring force she fell against the man's solid frame.

Devon's right arm went immediately around her waist, lifting her body in the air. He did not even break his stride. Holding her beneath one powerful arm like an errant child, he continued his mad pace down the stairs.

"Unhand me!" Brigitta yelled, struggling in his hold. Her right hip brushed roughly against the stone wall and she cried out in pain.

"Put you down and let you break your fool neck? I will not. The princess is perhaps on the verge of death, and you are wasting time with childish pranks." He clutched her even tighter to his side.

Fortunately, the remaining length of the passage was short, and Brigitta silently endured his ruthless hold until the stairs were behind them. They emerged into a long hall, where Devon set her on her feet. She stumbled back and watched as he pushed against what looked to be only a stone wall. To her amazement, the mortar gave way and the gray light of morning streamed in.

"Come," he said, and led the way through the small opening only wide enough to accommodate his body turned sideways.

Brigitta found herself standing behind a huge clump of snow-covered shrubbery. As Devon closed the passage behind them, she surveyed the area and recognized it to be part of the princess's private gardens. A huge black steed stood tethered to the shrubbery, saddled and ready to be ridden. It gave a snort at sight of them and pranced lightly on his powerful feet. The rich material beneath the saddle was intricately embroidered with blazing reds and cool blues, and the reins were grandly ornamented with tassels.

Devon glanced back to appraise her as she stood in a weak ray of sunshine. A gentle snow fell from the gray sky, the huge flakes covering her lashes and clinging to her hair. She looked a vision standing there nestled in Lisa's cloak.

Brigitta shivered as her slippered feet sank into the deep snow. With the cold wind swirling about her and her feet getting wet, she felt miserable. And now, of all things, it was apparent she'd have to ride atop a horse with this man.

"I do hope you've ridden before," Devon commented as he unlooped the reins from a branch of shrubbery.

"I have," Brigitta replied. She tried not to eye the horse suspiciously. She was glad Devon hadn't asked how many times she'd ridden since she'd only climbed atop a horse once and the skittish thing had thrown her to the ground. Since that day she had avoided any animal larger than a hound.

Devon drew on this leather gloves, whipped his cloak over his broad shoulders, and easily mounted the steed. "You'll have to ride in front of me."

Brigitta nodded, absently wondering why he always spoke to her so coldly. Even though Brigitta stood only a few feet from him, she felt they were worlds apart. He reached out a hand and waited for her to take hold of it.

Placing her bare hand in his gloved one, she allowed him to help her atop the saddle. He jerked her arm so roughly, she almost flew to the other side of the horse. Once securely in the saddle, she dared not look down at the ground, but grasped tightly on to the saddle and closed her eyes as Devon wheeled the animal around and spurred it into a run.

Bitter air stung her unprotected face and hands as they galloped away from the protective walls of the castle. The man behind her was sure in the saddle, almost at one with the beast beneath him. His hands held the reins loosely and he commanded the horse not with the pressure of his legs but with his voice, using the English language. They rode at such a maddening pace that Brigitta leaned back against him in fear. His arms on either side of her held her steady on the saddle and his cheek touched the edge of her hood. Brigitta prayed the ride would be short.

"Is it far to Darlana's village?" she asked, her voice almost being carried away with the rushing wind.

"It is a good distance. I don't expect to be back to Lisa before nightfall."

"Nightfall!" she exclaimed. "I do not think Lisa can wait that long!"

"Nor do I," he said, his voice grave. "But we must try."

Some awkward note in his voice caused Brigitta to turn and look at him. His hat, despite the wind, was still affixed firmly atop his head, and he squinted his eyes against the wind and reflection of light on snow; the blackness of his gaze was hidden from her view. He appeared to be greatly troubled and . . . and guilty.

Suddenly, the cause of Thora-Lisa's illness became clear: *this* man was the person Lisa had had words with. Devon Courtenay was the one whose purpose at Vardighet could destroy all of Lisa's dreams!

"*You* are the reason Lisa is so ill," she breathed. "Lisa told me of your conversation! She is fighting for her life this very minute, and you are the cause of her illness!"

Devon's lips thinned into a straight line. "You know nothing of the situation."

Brigitta looked away and fixed her glare on the horizon. "But you have known Lisa since childhood!" she insisted. "You know how delicate she is.

I knew I should have called the guards the first night I saw you. I knew then you would be trouble!"

Devon ignored her angry words, urging the beast on to an even greater pace. The horse shot forward and Brigitta was thrust back hard against Devon with the surge of power. Devon instinctively steadied her with his left arm, holding intimately on to her waist. To her discomfort, he did not release her.

"Perhaps you should have called the princess's guard that night," he said ominously against her hood-covered head. "But I am here and I'm not soon to be leaving."

Chapter Four

THE JOURNEY TO Darlana's village went by in a blur. Brigitta could think of nothing but Thora-Lisa lying ill upon her great bed—and that Devon was the cause of Lisa's illness. Filled with anger that anyone should speak even one unkind word to her princess, Brigitta's dislike for Devon Courtenay grew more intense by the minute.

The gray dawn broke and gave way to a bright day with a few sailing clouds. The sun's rays were warming and the air was sharp, invigorating. Not once did Devon let his mount slow but kept up its rapid pace, and by the time they reached the small *byalag* where Darlana lived, the animal was lathered and worn. The *byalag* was nothing more than a small grouping of crudely built homes with the smell of inside burning fires in the air. The village was similar to the one Brigitta had been raised in, only the faces of the many people they passed were unfamiliar.

Once they passed the heart of the village, the horse found the going more difficult as the road they traveled became nothing more than a snow-covered footpath. Darlana chose to live alone, away from other humans.

Finally bringing the horse to halt in front of a lone cottage, Devon jumped down to the ground and reached up to help Brigitta slide off the saddle. Her fingers, nearly numb from the long ride, could barely latch on to his arms, but Brigitta uttered no complaint. She was intent upon obtaining Darlana's medicine for Lisa. Without a word to Devon, Brigitta made her way to the door of the cottage, her wet, slippered feet sinking into the cold snow.

The small structure was of laft construction; reddish colored wood logs placed one upon the other with the ends cut for dovetailing. Although the building was in disrepair, it contrasted prettily with the winter white. Long icicles, thick at the base then tapering nearer to the fragile crystalline tips, hung from the roof of the cottage, catching the sunlight and splitting it into prismed hues of red, yellow, indigo, and blue. High above, the northern wind whirred through the branches of the tall firs that surrounded the small home. They stood sentinellike, yet serene and majestic, the boughs hooped with the heavy pristine blanket of winter.

Brigitta could smell the burning logs of the open fireplace within, and as she stood in front of the door she felt a brief bit of nostalgia. The cottage, the smells, indeed everything about this *byalag* reminded her of the village she had grown up in.

But her nostalgic thoughts were quickly banished when the door flew open and a voice from deep within demanded, "What do you want from me?"

Brigitta couldn't help the involuntary quiver of her body, for the voice was brittle with no notes of softness. She was speechless for a moment as she peered intently into the Cimmerian darkness of the interior before her. The room seemed to be filled with mist and gloom. She dared not enter.

"Speak, child! The draft is chilling my old bones!"

"I—I have been sent by the princess, Thora-Lisa, she—"

"Darlana knows what the princess wants! Come in and shut the door."

Brigitta looked hesitantly into the room then quickly back over her shoulder, wishing she could have some help. A ray of sunshine shone down on Devon as he rubbed the haunches of his mount. For an instant, Brigitta thought she would rather face *him* than the dark room in front of her.

"Come in or leave!" Darlana thundered from somewhere within the cottage, spurring Brigitta into action. Without another qualm, she walked into the cottage and quickly shut the door.

Inside, Brigitta blinked her eyes to get accustomed to the gloom. The old woman hobbled to the darkest corner and sat down. The open fireplace in the middle of the room flickered weakly in the windowless cottage. The framework of the hearth was formed of thin, upright flat stones placed on a slightly higher level than the floor. Upon these stones stood one medium-sized kettle and from its depths rose a gray cloud that wafted about the room like a light mist. Its vile smell told Brigitta that the contents of the pot were volatile. She could put no name to the foreign smell but it made her eyes water.

"My medicines have not been readied yet. Thou must wait for them," the old woman said.

Brigitta turned her gaze away from the small fire to the darksome corner, and there, seated in a crude wooden chair, was an ancient woman. Darlana. She was decidedly hunchbacked, with hair the color of snow and a face so wrinkled she must have endured many a hardship. Slowly, stiffly, she raised her weathered body from the chair, leaning her weight onto a crude wooden staff. Her eyes, however, gleamed with an odd intensity.

"I will wait," Brigitta replied, fighting her fear. "But you must hurry." Despite her unease, she felt a flood of pity for the deformed old woman.

Darlana seemed to sense this pity, for as she hobbled toward the pot near the fire, she cackled. "This is what happens when the body has lived too long a life, young one!" She held up one gnarled hand, the fingers of which were crooked and knotted from age. She pointed one long, twisted finger in Brigitta's direction. "If you are lucky, you will die young!"

Brigitta did not respond. Instead, she took a seat uneasily on the boxlike wooden bench near her. She knew the bench was filled with earth and was constructed for the purpose of keeping the cold from penetrating the dwelling.

She watched with frightened interest as the old woman knelt on the floor near the fire and stirred the contents of the kettle. The woman's eyes were a faded blue, as if the artist had had more water than paint on his brush when he created them. Her nose was hooked and long, and her lips were just a colorless slash on this portrait of age.

"What is your name, young one?" she asked with her quavering voice.

Brigitta loosened the strings of her cloak. She had finally become accustomed to the dim light and strong odor. "Brigitta Lind."

"Brigitta," the old woman repeated, as if marking it in her mind. "The medicine will be ready in long minutes. It cannot be prepared and saved; it must be fresh. The princess knows this. Is she very ill?"

"Yes." Brigitta did not trust this odd woman but decided to discover as much as she could about her and her cures. "Lisa's wedding day draws near. Will your potion cure her?"

Darlana straightened her bent body as best she could, and her white-haired head shot up. "Darlana *knows* her medicine is effective, she needs no proof from some errand girl!"

Brigitta became indignant. "Errand girl? Hardly that! I am companion to the princess!" She said the words with great pride and she was astonished to see the old woman crack her cragged face into a smile. Darlana began to laugh—a cackling sound that filled the dim room as she stirred her brew.

"Darlana *knows*," the old woman said suddenly in a queer voice as she tilted her small head to the side and peered with watery eyes into Brigitta's very soul—or so it seemed. She pointed her stirring utensil, wagging it, and said again, "Darlana *knows*."

"What do you know?" Brigitta questioned.

"About you—about Brigitta Lind who is not Brigitta Lind."

"You speak in riddles, Darlana," said Brigitta, increasingly uneasy. "Please, give me the medicine and I will leave."

Darlana shook her head and hobbled away from the fire, back to her crude chair in the corner. The fire hissed and popped, but Darlana continued to laugh. "Darlana knows many things."

Brigitta felt fear, a fear that pricked her spine and sped her heart to a racing beat.

The old woman leaned back in her chair, staring at the darkness of the low ceiling as if images danced there for her amusement. "I know," she repeated, her voice turning raspy. "I have visions . . . they tell me."

Brigitta sat still at these words. Had not Thora-Lisa called Darlana an old "seer-woman"? Could Darlana actually see things others could not?

"Last night, I had a vision—about Brigitta Lind."

Brigitta felt her heart stop beating for a flash of a second. "N—no. I—I do not want to know."

The old woman didn't move, she kept her gaze on the darkness above them. "I *will* tell you."

"No, I—"

"*I will tell you!*" the woman said with fierceness in her aged voice. "You *must* be told. The visions have indicated that you must be told."

Darlana took in a deep breath, then exhaled as

she laid her staff to the floor beside her. She began, in almost a chant, "I saw you, Brigitta Lind. You walked in great sunshine and the air was warm . . . so warm. I could feel happiness when I saw you but then something came. Slowly at first, so slow you didn't notice until it was upon you."

"What? What came?"

"The darkness came. It surrounded you and I could feel a cold chill. A man—I see a man. Do not trust him, Brigitta who is not Brigitta. He is not as he appears." Silent for long moments, the woman began rocking back and forth in the chair. Her head fell forward and her lips quivered as she began to sob softly.

"Darlana!" Brigitta exclaimed, moving to the edge of the bench. "Darlana, what is the matter? Stop this! You—you are frightening me!"

But the old woman did not appear to have heard her. "The vision—it is changing before my eyes!" she said between sobs. Her voice dropped in pitch. "There are two of you, Brigitta, and one weeps for the other. This man—he will take from both and give to only one."

"What man?" Brigitta asked, caught up in the prophecy. "What do you mean two of me? Is this true?"

"*Ja*, the vision will be true," Darlana replied weakly. "You are the daughter light, Brigitta. But darkness pursues you. I see flames—wings of flame. These flames giveth and they taketh. I see your mouth move and off of your tongue roll lies. Why do you lie, young Brigitta?"

"I do not lie!" Brigitta responded fiercely.

Darlana ignored her. "You are young—but you

are going to die. . . . Again I see the flames . . . ,"
her voice drifted off and then Darlana opened her
eyes. "The vision is gone now."

Brigitta sat in stunned silence, trying desperately
to calm her nerves. "I—I cannot believe this could
be true!"

"For you, Brigitta Lind, daughter of light, my
visions will be true."

"Wh—why do you tell me this?" Brigitta blus-
tered, not wanting to believe the prophecy. "Why
do you frighten me with your idle dreams?"

"They are not dreams. They are *visions*." The old
woman seemed to rouse herself from the brief
trance. She rose from her chair, once again going to
the kettle and stirring the contents. "You must be
warned. It is so, Brigitta . . . beware the darkness
and be cautious when the darkness comes to you
on wings of flame!"

The fire sputtered once more and Brigitta
jumped. She was annoyed—both with the silly old
woman and with herself for getting caught up in
such nonsense. Prepared to ask Devon to fetch the
medicine, she got to her feet, but the old woman
was quickly beside her, surprising Brigitta with
both her agility and the strong grip of her gnarled
hand.

"You were sent here for a reason," said the
woman. "Fate has sent you here for me to tell you
of my vision! Beware, Brigitta. Heed my warn-
ings!"

Brigitta broke free of Darlana's grip and opened
the door. She stepped into the glaring sunlight and
strode toward Devon and his mount.

Devon straightened from the task of rubbing

down the right leg of his mount. "Brigitta, what is the matter?" he asked as he saw her face. "You look as if you've seen a goblin."

Brigitta stopped beside him, shivering as she wrapped her arms around her waist. The deep snow covered her ankles and her teeth began to rattle. "Nothing is the matter," she snapped, angry with herself that she would let a senile old woman frighten her. "I am worried for Lisa, that is all. I do not believe Darlana has the powers to cure the princess. We should not have come here."

"Do you have the medicine?"

"Darlana will bring it out when she has finished preparing it."

Devon pushed his hat back on his head, his black eyes appraising Brigitta as she paced fretfully. He had not wanted to come to Darlana's, but since Thora-Lisa had asked, he could not have stayed away. That Brigitta had had to endure the old woman's odd humors was something he greatly regretted. He should have at least warned her about Darlana. Removing his gauntlets one at a time, he said, "I have known Darlana since I was a young boy. She talks much and enjoys disturbing her guests. Whatever she has said to you, forget it. I only agreed to bring you here because Lisa truly believes in Darlana's powers. Believing can be a powerful weapon in itself."

Brigitta felt a twinge of guilt, for her thoughts had been about herself, not Lisa's suffering. It was absurd to put faith in Darlana's words—the woman was crazy. But . . . what if Darlana truly did have an eye for the unseen?

"Here," Devon said gruffly, breaking her train of

thought. "Put these on. You are going to catch
your death if you stand any longer in this deep
snow." He handed her his gloves, waiting as she
slipped them on her tiny hands.

Brigitta put them on. They were large on her
hands, warm on the inside. The feel of them was
intimate.

Stepping toward her, Devon lifted her out of the
snow and up onto the saddle where her feet might
stay drier. His hold on her waist was rough, for
just to touch her caused his blood to boil. He turned
away and began to pace irritably, leaving Brigitta
alone.

In a few minutes Darlana appeared with a vial.
She ignored Devon as if he were invisible and
handed the potion up to Brigitta. With only a single meaningful glance into Brigitta's face, she
wordlessly returned to her cottage and slammed
the door. In the next instant, Devon swung aboard
the great horse, and they were off again.

The ride back to Vardighet seemed endless. The
sun lowered in the sky and the air turned bitter
cold as the horse galloped on through the countryside. They shared Devon's gloves, he wearing
them for a time and then Brigitta putting them on
her own hands. And for the entire ride, Devon
held her steady on the saddle, even enfolding her
with his own cloak when her shivers became too
great.

They remained silent throughout the wild
ride, each lost in their own troubled thoughts.
When they finally reached their destination,
Devon deposited Brigitta in front of the hidden

passage they had taken earlier, but he did not follow her up the dark stairs.

"Tell Lisa I will have an audience with her soon," he said before Brigitta made her way into the pitch black corridor, the tone of his voice telling her he wished Thora-Lisa had not banned him from her chamber.

She wanted to turn around and ask him to lead her up the stairs, but the sound of stone scraping against stone filled her ears and she knew Devon was gone. Alone, she found her way back to Lisa's private chambers and the sight she found there tore at her heart. Once again, Brigitta became angry at Devon Courtenay's role in her illness.

"Brigitta," Thora-Lisa said weakly from across the room. "Do you have the medicine?"

Hesitantly, Brigitta crossed the space to Lisa's great bed. The princess was alone. "Yes," Brigitta replied. "I have it."

"Good. Quickly, let me drink it."

Reluctantly, Brigitta held out the crude vial, and Thora-Lisa snatched it quickly from her fingers. Before she could say a word of warning, Thora-Lisa had drunk half of the thick substance. Brigitta watched in horrified silence as the young princess brought the near empty vial from beneath her mask and handed it back to her. Then she sank back into the bedclothes.

"Is that too much?" Brigitta asked in alarm.

Thora-Lisa closed her eyes momentarily, as if just finding a great wave of contentment. "No," she whispered. "It is never enough. Now, please, let me rest while the medicine works its wonders. In a few hours I should feel better."

"I want to sit with you. I—I do not trust this medicine."

"Please, Brigitta, leave me alone," the princess replied soothingly. "I will be fine. Already I feel much better."

Thora-Lisa's appearance *had* improved, Brigitta decided. But that could not be from Darlana's potion, surely. Thora-Lisa had just taken it!

The princess closed her eyes again and as she did so, she let out a long, light sigh, as if the weight of the world had just been lifted from her delicate shoulders. Perhaps Devon was right. It was a comfort to Thora-Lisa just to have taken the medicine. Any of the medicine's restorative powers lay in her mind and not in Darlana's brew. As Devon had said, believing could be its own healer.

Brigitta gave a squeeze to Thora-Lisa's hand. "I will let you rest, but I will be back. You will not be able to chase me from your side!"

If Thora-Lisa's veil had not been there, Brigitta was sure she would have seen a smile upon the princess's face. "You are indeed a good friend, Brigitta," Thora-Lisa murmured. She looked as frail as a sparrow upon the huge bed and Brigitta wished she could give to the princess some of her own strength. "I love you, Brigitta. I love you as a sister. Thank you for bringing Darlana's medicine to me."

With those words, Thora-Lisa slipped quietly into a restful sleep. With a whispered good-bye, Brigitta turned from the canopied bed and made her way to the door. With her hand on the latch, she turned to gaze once again at Thora-Lisa. The woman's veils fluttered with her slight breathing and Brigitta said a quick prayer of thanks that Lisa had not passed away in her absence.

It was well after midnight when Brigitta heard the urgent pounding on her door. She awoke with a start, pushing the heavy counterpane aside and searching for her robe.

"Brigitta! Brigitta!" the voice cried from beyond her chamber.

Brigitta scrambled from her warm cocoon of blankets, wincing as her feet touched the cold floor. Her fear bubbled over inside. Had the princess died? "Yes, do come in!" she called, snatching her robe at the foot of her bed, beneath the covers.

Marta entered the room, her wrinkled face etched with worry. The long braid of gray hair that hung down her back was untidy with bits of hair straying from the bands. "It is the princess!" she breathed urgently. "She calls for you."

"She is alive then?"

"Yes, yes, of course! I try to reason with her, to urge her to let me summon her physician, but she insists that I call only you!"

Brigitta was instantly awake, forgetting her previous warmth and slumber. The only thing that mattered now was to see to the princess. Brigitta hurried to the stool where she had tossed her skirt. In the pocket of the garment she dug for the half-full vial of Darlana's potion.

Frantically, Marta chattered on. "She has been ill all through the night but only now will she let me bring you to her. You must reason with her, tell her she needs her physician! General Bjord is due home in two days' time—he will be most upset that his wife-to-be is so ill."

Already halfway out the door, Brigitta asked, "He's arriving in two days?"

"Yes, yes! I have not told the princess about the general's arrival. I thought the news might upset her even more. Please, Brigitta, you must see that she gets well before General Bjord arrives. She needs a physician!"

Brigitta dropped the vial into her gown pocket and the two quickly sped down the dim, cold corridor together, Marta murmuring her concerns, Brigitta not saying a word.

At the rough-hewn door of the princess's chambers, Brigitta entered without knocking and went quickly to Thora-Lisa's side. The princess appeared more fragile than seemed possible. Her thin body lay immobile within the warm covers and furs, her silky veils hanging limply over her face. Only her eyes were visible in the waning firelight and they were closed, the lids shadowed deeply.

"Lisa," Brigitta said softly, finding the princess's hand among the bedclothes. "Can you hear me?"

"Brigitta? Is that you?"

"Yes, it is me, gracious Princess."

Slowly, and with great effort, Thora-Lisa opened her eyes. "Brigitta, I . . . I need more medicine."

Brigitta felt the weight of the half-full vial in her pocket, but she was loathe to withdraw it. She did not trust the medicine she had traveled so far to get. With a dismissing nod, Brigitta looked toward Marta. The older woman bowed her head and left the chambers, leaving Brigitta alone with the princess.

"I do not think this medicine helps you, Lisa. I will not give you any more. Your lady tells me you have been ill all the night through. This medicine is no medicine! It has made you more ill than before!"

Thora-Lisa's eyes grew wide. "Brigitta," she weakly gasped. "I *must* have it! Please . . . please, Brigitta, it is the only thing that makes me feel better."

"But look at you!" Brigitta exclaimed, tears forming in her eyes. "You are so very weak!"

"No . . . no!" Thora-Lisa said, a sob breaking from her throat and sounding pathetically weak. "I did feel better today only . . . only now, the effects of the medicine are gone. I need more. Please, Brigitta, give me the medicine."

Brigitta looked at Thora-Lisa's hand, and its fragility within her own sturdy grasp caused her heart to constrict. "Oh, Lisa, I want only what is best for you. This medicine—"

"Please!"

So heartrending was the plea that Brigitta felt her body move, felt her hand reach into her robe pocket and withdraw the vial, as she heard her voice say, "Here, my princess, here is your draft."

Thora-Lisa swept the vial from Brigitta's hands, bringing the small vessel beneath her veil and drinking its contents. When she had finished and handed the empty thing back to Brigitta, she said, "You must go back to Darlana and get me more. You must promise to go see Darlana tomorrow."

Go back to that horrid little cottage? Brigitta trembled at just the mere thought of seeing Darlana again—but if Lisa wanted her to go, Brigitta could not deny her. "I—I will go," Brigitta responded automatically, despite her rising fear. She would do anything for her princess. Perhaps Darlana would show her how to make the brew and then Brigitta would never have to see Darlana again. Brigitta would ask Darlana to teach her, but in the meantime, Brigitta knew she must help Lisa get well. Perhaps mention of Erik's arrival would give Lisa something to look forward to.

"Lisa," Brigitta ventured. "Have you heard the news? The news of General Bjord?"

Thora-Lisa immediately stirred in her bed, and Brigitta could see the pain the quick movement caused the princess, although her eyes were suddenly sharp and alert. "What—what news? Oh, tell me, Brigitta! Has something happened to Erik?"

Brigitta was quick to comfort Thora-Lisa. "No, not at all. He is well . . . and coming home to you. Soon."

"Home?" Thora-Lisa asked in a whisper. "He is coming home?" Slowly, she fell back against her pillows, a dreamy look in her watery blue eyes. "My Erik is coming home? Oh, Brigitta, are you certain of this?"

"Yes," Brigitta assured her. "I am certain. He should be here in two days' time."

"Erik. Coming home! Oh, Brigitta, my elation is great! We must plan a celebration. A costume ball, perhaps. Yes, that is it! We shall celebrate Erik's arrival with a costume ball."

Brigitta watched in amazement as Thora-Lisa slowly pushed the furs from her thin body and pulled herself to an upright position in bed. Like a moth changing to a butterfly, Thora-Lisa slowly began to metamorphose from a sickly creature into a healthy being.

"Bring me my dish of jewelry, Brigitta," Lisa ordered. When Brigitta handed her the tiny decorative dish, Thora-Lisa added, "We shall plan a ball—a ball where everyone will be masked. Will it not be wonderful? I will be able to relax knowing I will not be the only person with a veiled face. I will be able to *enjoy* myself, Brigitta."

"It—it sounds like a lovely idea, Lisa," Brigitta replied, wondering at the change in Thora-Lisa. Every day should be a homecoming for Erik Bjord if this is what Lisa's reactions would be.

"Devon will be able to walk freely about the castle then, too. If he is masked, none will know who he is," Lisa continued, although on a softer note, as though talking to herself. "If Devon can see how in love Erik and I are, then he will abandon his foolish plans . . . yes, a costume ball it shall be, and a grand time will be had by all."

Instantly alert at mention of Devon Courtenay, Brigitta shifted on her small stool. "Plans?" she asked. "What plans, Lisa? Why has Devon Courtenay come to Vardighet?"

Thora-Lisa's blue eyes lost a bit of their sudden sparkle and her exuberance ebbed somewhat. "His purpose here does not concern you, Brigitta. Forget I mentioned his name," she said sternly. Suddenly, Thora-Lisa was very much a princess, the royal descendant of generations of Sweden's ruling class. Despite her weakness, she commanded with a noble air that forbade disobedience.

Brigitta fell silent, knowing better than to question Thora-Lisa further. But as they made preparations for the costume ball, Brigitta felt a wave of premonition wash over her and she had to wonder just how wonderful Erik's homecoming would be.

Chapter Five

TWO DAYS LATER, just an hour before the ball in Erik's honor was to begin, Brigitta Lind scurried through the cavernous, flame-lit private passages near Thora-Lisa's apartments. Clad only in a paper-thin chemise—for she hadn't a moment to dress in her own costume—Brigitta hurriedly made her way toward the small chamber used to store Thora-Lisa's outfits. In the haste of preparing for the costume ball, Thora-Lisa had decided that her powder blue slippers would be more appropriate for the occasion than her black ones. She had commanded Brigitta to run down the passage and get the things for her. No matter Brigitta was half-dressed; Thora-Lisa's thoughts centered solely on Erik's homecoming. Brigitta didn't mind. She was delighted to have Thora-Lisa back in good health again.

Erik and his vast army had arrived in the early hours of the morning and the castle of Vardighet had been in a state of confusion ever since. Even now, Brigitta could hear loud voices and music floating up from downstairs. Erik and his men had warded off a Danish attack along the coast, and from the minute they had stepped inside the castle walls, a celebration had begun—one that would last for several days at least.

Brigitta rounded the small bend in the hall and attempted to push the portal of the vacant room open. It wouldn't budge. "The key!" she cried aloud, frustrated at her own lack of foresight. "I forgot to get the key!"

"So you have," said a lazy male voice.

Brigitta swung toward that sound, trying to shield the view of her near-naked body as she did so. A tall and imposing blond-haired man stood surveying the picture she created.

"Shall I open the door for you?" the man queried, pulling a sturdy-handled dagger from the belt hugging his tapered waist. Tall, definitely over six feet, the man wore a dark military jerkin, breeches, and enormously spurred boots. The shirt beneath his jerkin was sweat-stained and filthy, and his blond beard and mustache needed a trimming. The low-crowned hat atop his head was worn, the plumes limp, and the dull-colored boothose showing atop his boots were torn in spots and spattered with dried mud.

Instinctively, Brigitta knew the man must be Erik Bjord. He appeared larger than life and his smile was charming. No wonder Thora-Lisa could not wait for his return! His great strength was tangible—as one would feel a raging snow storm or a fragrant summer day. He was rage and gentleness, godlike and devillike all in one—simply commanding.

"General Bjord," she sputtered, sketching a belated curtsy. "I—forgive me, I am just running an errand for the princess. I—I will go now and tell her you are here."

"No need for that," he drawled, stepping forward and perhaps inadvertently blocking her way of escape. "My rejoining with Lisa can wait until later." His eyes, blue as the Baltic in summer, were somewhat bloodshot and his lids drooped lazily over them, as if he had just awakened from a long slumber—or had just downed a tankard or two of potent ale.

Brigitta decided the latter was the case. The man reeked of strong drink. Bracing his left arm against the wall, Erik Bjord leaned toward Brigitta, his lips curling upward into a deeper smile. His teeth were strong and straight, white against his ruddy-colored features, and the laugh lines along the corners of his eyes made him appear boyish. But the gleam in his eyes was anything but carefree. No youth could ever know of the things his gaze seemed to speak of.

"And who do we have here?" he asked, his words slurring slightly together.

Brigitta wanted to bolt from this man's reach, but she knew the consequences of such an action. Erik Bjord was a nobleman and she was merely a peasant. To dart away from him now would bring his wrath upon her.

"I am Brigitta Lind," she answered in a nervous whisper, sidling away from his enormous frame. "I—I am companion to Princess Thora-Lisa."

"I see. She does require companionship now and then, does she not?" He gave a small chuckle but his eyes raked over Brigitta's improperly clad form without any amusement.

"I—I must go to her now." Brigitta attempted to slip around him, as just his gaze could make her feel impure. "The princess is now preparing for the costume ball and needs my assistance."

Erik Bjord lifted his right hand to stay her escape and touched her cheek. "Will *you* be at the costume ball?" he asked, his roughened, ungloved fingertips brushing against the soft skin of her face. "If Lisa has not already given you leave to be there, I am doing so now."

"Yes," Brigitta said unsteadily. "I will be there . . . by Lisa's side."

"You may leave Lisa's side if you wish," he offered suggestively, his gaze telling her exactly what he was implying.

"I am sure I will have no wish to leave Lisa's side."

"But if the urge seizes you . . ." He let his words trail off, his eyelids closing over his eyes and his face lowering toward hers. "No punishment will befall you if you decide to slip away from the ball for an hour or two." He brushed his cool lips against her cheek. "I will follow you. My own apartments are not far from here."

Brigitta closed her eyes tightly, her skin burning from the general's contact. *Oh, Lisa, I am sorry!* she thought to herself. *I should slap this man for his forwardness, but—but I cannot! He is a general and I am only a servant!* She knew Lisa would be crushed if she knew Erik had made such an advance. The princess loved this man with all her heart, and it was obvious Erik Bjord took Thora-Lisa's undying love lightly.

Deciding her allegiance lay with Thora-Lisa, Brigitta pushed against the man's chest. But his lips did not move from her skin, until the sound of metal scraping metal could be heard. Brigitta knew the origin of such a sound.

She looked up to see Devon Courtenay, costumed in swashbuckling attire complete with white ostrich-plumed hat, knee-length, white satin-lined cloak, black breeches, and a short-waisted open doublet with a plain white shirt beneath. He looked for all the world like a French musketeer. A black mask was affixed firmly across his face, shielding his eyes and nose, and his dark hair was secured at the nape of his neck. Even though he hid his face behind a mask, Brigitta would have known him anywhere. He had a bold, devil-may-care air about him that could not be denied.

Flinging his cape back over his shoulders and brandishing his sword, he appeared formidable and ready for a fight.

Erik whirled instinctively toward the sound, holding his small dagger ready and his other hand on his own sheathed sword. "What is this?" he demanded, an oddly excited note in his voice. Though newly from the battling field, he obviously still thirsted for spilled blood. "Are you offering me a challenge?"

"I am," Devon answered. He motioned to Brigitta and she quickly obeyed, stepping out of Erik's reach. She ran up the passage toward Thora-Lisa's room.

But once she rounded the bend in the hall, she

stopped, and—pressing her body against the jagged stone—listened to the men. They spoke not a word. She heard Erik draw his sword and then the clank of metal striking metal rang in the air, and the *whoosh* of nimble, booted feet moving over the stone floor came to her ears.

"Up to your old tricks again, are you, Erik?" Devon asked, his words punctuated by the clash of swords.

"And who are you to ask?" Erik demanded.

Devon did not respond to that inquiry. Instead, he taunted, "I thought perhaps by now you would have given up pursuing innocent maids."

Erik gave a breathless laugh. "Worried for the young girl's virtue, are you? Could it be you want the young thing for yourself, masked man? Do not fear, I am known for generosity."

Brigitta peeked around the corner and watched as Devon expertly sliced the air near Erik's blond head. The general merely laughed, stepping to the side, but his lazily hooded eyes held a spark of respect for his opponent. The two circled each other, both experimentally thrusting and parrying with their weapons, neither intent on drawing blood just yet. They toyed with each other, gauging strengths and weaknesses.

"There is something familiar about you, masked man," Erik said finally, his breathing becoming labored as their swordplay became more vigorous. "Do I know you?"

"I am a man you have never known."

"But you know of me."

"Who has not heard of the great General Bjord? Your campaigns are popular, your victories much applauded. Let us see how the brave general fares without his army behind him to save his neck."

With that, Devon advanced on Erik, causing his opponent to back against the wall. He brought the tip of his sword to Erik's right arm and cleanly sliced the man's sleeve. Erik's sardonic half-smile instantly vanished. Devon allowed him a moment to whirl away from the wall.

"Your passion for drink is still great, Erik. It might soon prove to be the death of you," Devon commented as the two again began circling each other.

Erik's gaze was murderous now, his mind obviously trying to affix a name to the hauntingly familiar voice of his adversary. "I should know who you are, shouldn't I, masked man? Will you undo the strings of your mask, or shall I slice them from your head?"

"You may try, Erik. But you have yet to best me with your swordsmanship." Devon did not give his opponent a chance to dwell on the mystery a moment longer. With a lunge, he once again advanced on Erik, swinging his sword toward Erik's midsection. Just as the tip of it would have passed through the man's body, Devon parried swiftly and knocked Erik's weapon to the floor. The sword clattered upon the stone and spun away with the force of the blow.

To Brigitta's surprise, Erik began to laugh, a deep sound that grew more intense as the moments passed. Devon stood silently before the man, and Brigitta could see how tense he was. What private vendetta could he have with Erik?

"It has been years since anyone of Vardighet has

dared challenge me with a sword," Erik said finally, sobering as he bent to retrieve his weapon. As he resheathed it, he said, "You are a brave man. My army could use such skill and bravery. Tonight, at the celebration, we will talk of such things, eh?"

Devon did not answer.

"A soldier's rewards are many," Erik continued, clearly trying to tempt Devon. "Even Lisa's little companion would not be too much for you to request from me should you agree to march with my troops." He gave Devon a comradely slap on the back. "Think of it, my friend. You and I would be formidable upon the battlefield." With that, the blond campaigner turned and walked down the hall, away from Brigitta.

She watched him leave, her body trembling from his words. He would *give* her to Devon Courtenay for marching in battle with him?

"You may come from your hiding spot, Brigitta," Devon said, slipping his sword into the scabbard at his side and removing his mask. "Erik is gone."

Quickly, she stepped into his line of vision. "What madness seized you to draw a sword on the general?" she asked, stunned. "You could have killed him!"

Devon appeared unaffected. "I could have, yes." His black gaze brushed hers casually, then glanced away to make sure no signs of the struggle remained. "You don't truly believe a man like Erik Bjord would have released you after just one kiss, do you?"

Brigitta was no longer concerned for her own safety. "But Lisa—what will she say when she hears you challenged the man she will marry? Why, she'll be upset again and—"

"Who will tell her?" he cut in fiercely. "Not I. And certainly not Erik. Will you, Brigitta? Will you tell Lisa how her beloved touched his lips to your cheek and suggested you meet him in his rooms?" Devon's voice was accusing and his face was tight with tension.

"I—no, certainly not."

"Good. See that you don't. And take another bit of advice from me, Brigitta. Stay away from Erik Bjord. The man is dangerous—not to be trusted."

Suddenly, in a flash of a second, Darlana's words rang in Brigitta's head: *Beware the dark man, he is not to be trusted.* Uneasy with such memories, she snapped at Devon, "And am I to trust you?"

He gave her a bitter smile, shaking his head. "No—but I am not the one who offered your body to another man." He let his black eyes travel down the length of her near-naked body and smiled. "Just think, Brigitta, if I have the urge to join Erik's troops, *you* will be my reward."

Brigitta shivered while her cheeks flamed. "A pox on you!" she snapped, then spun away, heading back to the safety of Thora-Lisa's chambers as Devon's laughter rang in her ears.

Once Brigitta retrieved the key to Lisa's spare room and fetched Lisa's slippers, the two women began to prepare themselves for the costume ball. Lisa was radiant, and Brigitta said not a word about the incident in the hall.

Costumed as a woman of the nobility, Brigitta

wore a golden gown of imported Holland velvet
brocaded in a deeper gold. Thora-Lisa had designed
the dress and oversaw its creation. The neckline left
Brigitta's shoulders bare, and the sleeves were full
and slashed showing frothy lace and ending just
above her wrists at the place where her gloves began. The skirt, although tight near the waist, belled
out over numerous underskirts and flowed gracefully to the floor in an abundance of shimmering
gold velvet. Brigitta had never seen such an exquisite gown and she felt magical when she put it on.
Around her neck she wore a topaz and diamond
necklace Thora-Lisa had given her, and beneath it,
affixed to the neckline of the dress, was a matching
topaz pendant encircled by a row of cut diamonds.
Her fair hair, coiled into slim, golden ringlets,
brushed the tips of her shoulders and seemed to
glimmer in the soft candlelight.

"Oh, Brigitta, how lovely you look!" Thora-Lisa
breathed as she watched her friend twirl in a slow
circle for inspection. "Everyone will be green with
envy when you enter the room. Even I am envious
of you!"

Brigitta smiled shyly at the compliment. She'd
never dreamed of wearing such magnificent things.
"Thank you, Lisa. But you—you look more beautiful than ever!"

Thora-Lisa did indeed look lovely. Dressed in an
ocean-blue silk gown with underskirts varying in
shades of light blue to almost silver, Thora-Lisa's
clothing appeared far lovelier than anything she'd
ever worn before. The sleeves of the gown were
medium length and slashed, showing brocade un-
dersleeves of a deeper shade of blue. A gauzy veil

of a very light cornflower blue was affixed to a simple headcovering of the same material, and it covered all but her eyes. This night the princess's eyes seemed not so pale since the color of her gown heightened their natural color. They sparkled with excitement, too. Small, stiff curls of her favorite peeped from beneath the headcovering in a little tendrillike fringe, and the delicate color complemented her eyes.

"I *feel* beautiful, Brigitta," Thora-Lisa said in a soft, whispery voice. "This night I feel lovelier than I ever have . . . I feel like the princess I am! And you know, my friend, it is because of you that I feel such loveliness."

"Me?" Brigitta asked, surprised. She handed Thora-Lisa the strand of pearls the princess had chosen to wear, and gently argued, "I have nothing to do with it. The reason is because you are getting well and . . ." she paused only a second, then said, "because your Erik has returned home to you."

Thora-Lisa's eyes smiled.

Brigitta would not destroy Lisa's happiness with tales of how lecherous Erik had been in the passage. Perhaps he had only been very drunk. He was newly home from the battlefield, also, she decided. War could do strange things to a man, Brigitta knew. Her own grandfather had gone quite mad during his later years of life, and Brigitta's grandmother claimed the man's insanity had been brought on by all the gruesome things he saw in battle.

Thora-Lisa clasped the strand of pearls around

her neck and paused, looking at her friend. "I believe you are the reason I am so happy, Brigitta. Your friendship, the time you spend with me—all of what you do makes me feel better about myself. Since Devon Courtenay left Sweden, you were the first to give me such true friendship. I value that friendship, Brigitta, more than anything."

Brigitta felt her throat constrict with emotion as she listened to Thora-Lisa. She felt a great responsibility for the princess's happiness, and even more than this, she felt a love for the young woman; a sisterly love that caused her to hurt when Thora-Lisa hurt and to smile and feel good when the princess was happy.

"I too value our friendship, Lisa," Brigitta replied softly.

As they left Lisa's chambers, Brigitta wished she could see Thora-Lisa healthy and forever happy as she was this moment. But as Brigitta watched her princess walk toward the hall, she knew her wish might not be granted. The pallor of Thora-Lisa's skin showed through the powder that had been so meticulously applied. The princess's frail, thin body with its protruding bones was clearly visible even beneath the heavy silk. Indeed, the heaviness of the material almost emphasized Lisa's flat chest and thin neck. But if one looked *closely*, as Brigitta could, one could see the beauty in Thora-Lisa this night. Her eyes did shine and her voice was light and lilting—more musical than ever before. Her step was graceful, her movements artfully and gra-

ciously executed. Yes, Brigitta decided as the two
descended the main stairs, her princess did indeed
look grand this evening.

Brigitta could hear the merriment of the celebration that had started hours ago. Raucous laughter,
the sounds of cups clanking, a dog barking, and a
woman's laughter floated up to surround her. The
smells of fresh baked rye bread, ham, liver pie,
sausage, and rare-smoked reindeer wafted around
her, and Brigitta felt her pulse quicken.

They passed through a yawning archway lit with
the fire of flaming torches along the walls and then
the huge, thick wooden double doors before them
were pulled open by Thora-Lisa's own guard to
reveal a vast room filled with richly costumed people. A hush fell over the crowd as Thora-Lisa entered, and Brigitta knew it was due to the fact that
Thora-Lisa was not one to frequent such celebrations. Hers was a fragile health and all the people
of Vardighet knew this. Her presence at such functions was a rarity.

Brigitta felt pride well within her as she watched
Thora-Lisa accept the curtsies and bows given her.
*This is your moment, my Princess. Show these people
how elegant you truly are. Put all their ugly rumors to
rest!*

Erik materialized from the crowd, dressed as he
had been earlier when Brigitta had encountered
him in the hall. He wore no mask. He bowed low
over Lisa's extended hand, and then, with a smile,
brought her hand to his lips and placed a chaste
kiss upon it. Lisa's eyes glowed with happiness.

As he led Thora-Lisa into the thick of the crowd,

Erik glanced briefly at Brigitta, making her shiver inwardly.

"I'd say the general has taken an interest in you, sweet Brigitta. Were I you, I'd keep out of his sight and out of his reach," whispered a low voice.

Brigitta whirled to find Devon Courtenay beside her, magnificently handsome in his swashbuckler's attire. His ebony eyes, beneath his mask, seemed to fill with flame when he gazed at her.

"I can take care of myself, Devon Courtenay—" she began.

"Hush," he interrupted, leaning closer. "To you and all others of Vardighet, I will be known as Count Anthony Bourdelot—lately of France." Taking hold of her elbow, he led her near the center of the room, away from the throng. "Keep my secret, Brigitta, or I will bend a few ears with what I have learned about you."

Brigitta ignored his threat. She was too enthralled by the scene that spread before her. She had never imagined such luxury! Long wooden tables laden with food and drink lined the tapestry-covered walls, and costumed men and women helped themselves to the elaborate feast while others danced to the melodies the musicians played on wind and string instruments. Devon led Brigitta into the group of dancing couples, his feet easily picking up the tune as he moved across the floor with her. It soon became clear that her dancing skills did not equal his. Noting her faltering steps, Devon slowed their pace, allowing her time to accustom herself to his smooth lead. "I do not recall saying I wanted to dance with you, D—

Count Bourdelot. My duties are with the princess this night, not in pleasuring myself."

He gave her a roguish grin and swung her effortlessly into the dance. "So, dancing with me pleasures you, does it, sweet Brigitta?" Even through her gloved hand she could feel his warmth, and it was impossible to ignore how easily their bodies slipped into the same rhythm.

"Certainly not!" she quickly replied. "I only meant—"

"No matter," he interrupted, guiding her expertly around the floor. "It is my intent to let Erik know I have laid claim to you—nothing more. As for serving Lisa this night, I, better than anyone, know she would want you to enjoy yourself."

"No man lays claim to me," she retorted, stung by his possessive manner. "Not Erik, and certainly not you!" She made a motion to step away from him, but Devon would not release her. He pulled her closer, and danced smoothly to the outer rim of the throng.

"Not so fast. Erik is watching. You don't want him to believe you've found fault with me, do you? Erik would like nothing more than to do me one better now that I've bested him with a sword. What better way to humiliate me than to conquer a young girl who slipped from my grasp?"

Brigitta glanced toward the blond general. Though he held Lisa's elbow possessively, his gaze was on her and Devon. Reluctantly, Brigitta continued dancing with Devon. She had to concentrate suddenly, for the steps became intricate.

"Why do you dislike Erik Bjord?" she asked Devon as they came together once more. "What has he done to you in the past? And why is Lisa so upset by your presence at Vardighet?"

"It is a long story," he answered curtly. "One I do not relish retelling."

"But just look at Lisa," Brigitta coaxed. "She has never looked lovelier! Erik obviously makes her happy—how can you think of destroying her dreams for the future?"

The muscle along his jawline tightened. "There are things you do not know, Brigitta, things even Lisa does not understand." Cryptically, he added, "Love can be a powerful motive for a person but it can also make that same person blind. The princess sees only what she wants to see in Erik; it has been this way since we were children."

Frustrated by his unwillingness to reveal more, Brigitta said, "Perhaps you are the one with the distorted view of things. Could it be all the success and honors Erik has achieved cause you to be jealous of the man? Could it be a childish rivalry between you two has festered within you all these years and now you have come to wreak havoc on Erik?"

Devon stiffened, and Brigitta knew she had struck some chord within him. Pressing her advantage, she asked, "Are you jealous of the man, Devon? Does it bother you that the princess chose Erik and not you to be the man of her dreams? Perhaps what was once a childhood friendship with a young girl has become . . . something more, and now you wish *you* were a great general betrothed to the princess of Vardighet."

Devon ceased moving about the floor, and his cold gaze was inscrutable. "Leave it alone, Brigitta.

Such an innocent one as you could never fathom what lies between Erik and myself."

"No, Devon Courtenay," Brigitta snapped. "You are wrong. I believe I am beginning to put the mystery of you together. Let this be a warning to you: Do not attempt to come between Lisa and Erik. She has chosen him to be her husband, and I will do everything in my power to ensure Lisa's happiness. I will not let you destroy what little happiness she now has."

"Then prepare yourself for battle, sweet Brigitta," he said coldly. "For I've come to Vardighet to see that Lisa and Erik never wed."

With that, he strode away from her, leaving Brigitta alone amidst the moving crowd. She watched him go, and a feeling of dark premonition washed over her.

Chapter Six

A POX ON Devon Courtenay, Brigitta thought to herself as she watched him brush by several dancing couples and head toward the far side of the crowded room. Anger bubbled up inside of her while she tried to think of some way to foil his plans. Perhaps Brigitta could persuade Thora-Lisa to move up the day of her wedding to Erik Bjord. Surely Lisa would not object, for even now the young princess had fears she would not live to see her wedding day.

"I see your gallant swashbuckler has chosen to desert you, Brigitta. Could it be the two of you have had a lover's quarrel?"

Brigitta turned to see Erik standing beside her. The man's blue eyes were bloodshot and his lids were only half-opened. He held a tall tankard, crudely fashioned of silver and filled with ale, in one hand. After taking a draining drink, he wiped the sleeve of his wrinkled shirt across his mouth, then grinned at her. "I'm beginning to believe our masked friend is not as sharp of wit as I had thought. I cannot fathom why he would leave a woman as beautiful as you unattended."

Brigitta dropped into a quick curtsy, cursing her luck. Erik Bjord was obviously drunk. Straightening, she attempted to keep her disgust from showing on her features. "The masked man and I are not friends. I—I barely know him."

"Come now, Brigitta. I watched the two of you as you danced. You were quite engrossed with the other's company. Tell me the man's name."

Brigitta fought the urge to divulge Devon's true identity. Doing so would probably result in an instant duel between the two men. "Anthony Bourdelot," she murmured, turning her face ever so slightly away from him and trying to find Lisa's friendly countenance among the crowd of bodies.

"What?" he asked, touching her cheek with his left hand, causing Brigitta to look at him.

"The man's name—he told me his name is Anthony Bourdelot. I hear he is lately from France."

Erik let his bleary gaze linger on her upturned face for long moments, moments that felt an eternity for Brigitta. *Where is Lisa, and what must she be thinking?* Brigitta wondered nervously. Instinctively, she knew she must get away from Erik, even Devon had warned her to stay clear of him.

"Forgive me, General Bjord," she said softly, afraid of causing his ire. "I—I must see to the princess."

Erik appeared not to have heard her, for he began to gently stroke her cheek with rough fingers. His eyes were slits now. "Lisa is fine. She has no need of you."

"But I am here to serve her and—"

"She requested I dance with you, Brigitta. In fact, she nearly commanded it. Why is that, I wonder?" He took a step closer, wrapping his right arm around her slim waist, his tankard still in hand.

Brigitta stiffened. "I—I have no idea," she murmured, panic seizing her.

"Perhaps she knows how hungry I am for female companionship. Perhaps she is offering your services to me this night." He pulled her body roughly against his own muscled frame. "Is that the reason you were summoned to Vardighet? To occupy me until my wedding day?"

Sweet Lord! Brigitta thought to herself. Erik must be more inebriated than she'd imagined. Lisa surely did not expect her to pleasure Erik! But then why had Thora-Lisa asked Erik to dance with her? Brigitta's mind reeled with half a dozen unanswered questions.

She laughed nervously, trying to make light of

the situation. "I do not think the princess intended anything more than for you to grant a lonely servant a dance."

"Hmmm. I suspect Lisa's reasons are far more involved than that." He tilted his head to one side, rubbing his forefinger along her cheekbone up to her temple. "You resemble Lisa in many ways," he muttered, the smell of potent ale wafting across her cheek. "The way you walk . . . even your speech reminds me of the princess." His fingers dipped low on her face again as he brushed them across her lips. "If only I could peek beneath Lisa's veils, I would know if you also resemble her in appearance." He smiled then—a smile that did not reach his eyes. "I am making you uneasy, am I not?" Chuckling, he dropped his arms to his sides and released her. "Scurry to shelter behind the princess's skirts, then, Brigitta. Frightened young virgins do not interest me tonight."

Brigitta did not stay another moment. With a quick motion she hoped would pass as a curtsy, she lifted her skirts and brushed by him. The sound of his drunken laughter caused the fine hairs at the nape of her neck to stand on end. Brigitta wished the man were a commoner so she could tell him exactly what she thought of him! Goodness, how could Thora-Lisa endure him? The man was unbearable.

She found Thora-Lisa speaking with a group of women who were garbed in various costumes. One woman had chosen to be a shepherdess, another obviously a French aristocrat, and the third was so richly attired she could have been the Queen of Sweden, although Brigitta knew better.

As soon as Lisa saw Brigitta approaching, the princess nodded regally to the women and then excused herself.

"Brigitta, are you enjoying yourself?" the princess inquired as she latched one hand on Brigitta's elbow and guided her away from the women who stood listening.

Brigitta nodded once. "I've never seen so much food and merriment," she said truthfully. "And you, Lisa. Are you enjoying yourself?" Brigitta wanted to ask the princess if she'd truly requested Erik to demand a dance with her, but Brigitta held her tongue.

"This celebration is much like all the others," Lisa answered. "I rarely enjoy myself at such functions."

"But I thought you were looking forward to this costume ball!"

Thora-Lisa nodded to a few passing people, then lowering her voice, she continued, "It is not the festive time I had envisioned."

"It is Devon's presence, isn't it? Please do not let yourself become ill over that man again, Lisa!"

"Hush," Thora-Lisa commanded sharply. "Do not speak his name outside of my apartments." On a softer note, she added, "It is not he who upsets me. It . . . it is Erik."

Of course Erik had upset Lisa. Erik was a barbarian and Lisa was gentle and kind and loving. "What has Erik done?" Brigitta asked.

Thora-Lisa's eyes grew sad and pensive. "He has done nothing, Brigitta. That is the problem. He—he ignores me. Whenever we are together, Erik immerses himself in his drink. It is as though

I am too ugly to endure and he must escape me in some way . . ." The princess's voice faded away then as the young woman stared out into the sea of moving bodies in the middle of the room.

Brigitta knew not what to say. Personally, she thought Erik not fit to share quarters with a hound, but Brigitta knew Lisa was in love with the general.

Love. What an odd affection, Brigitta thought. Love had obviously blinded Thora-Lisa to Erik's worst faults. Did love alter all people's views, or was Lisa only affected due to her disfigurement? Brigitta had no idea.

Even as Brigitta and Lisa stood engrossed in their own thoughts, the crowd of dancers broke apart so that the troupe of court jesters could move out onto the floor. Dressed in garish costumes that emphasized their lack of size, the midgets appeared grossly tiny as they tumbled about in hopes of entertaining. Brigitta immediately sensed Thora-Lisa's unease.

"Are you all right, Lisa?" Brigitta asked.

The princess had tears in her eyes. "He knows I hate this," she whispered fiercely. "Erik knows I cannot endure the sight of these people!"

The crowd around them broke into a burst of laughter as one of the jesters, who had crawled atop another, fell to the hard stone floor. Thora-Lisa immediately turned away, and after a moment of obviously composing herself, she made a hasty exit. Brigitta followed her, but not after catching sight of the satisfied smile on Erik Bjord's face across the room. The man was no doubt pleased with himself that he had succeeded in upsetting Lisa.

Brigitta nearly had to run to keep up with the

princess. "Lisa, wait!" she called as she took the steps leading to the upper apartments two at a time. "Please don't run away from me."

Thora-Lisa reached the doors to her room. "I wish to be alone, Brigitta."

"I don't want to leave you alone. You need someone to talk to, Lisa."

"There is nothing to talk about. I—it is silly of me to be bothered by odd-looking people. I must learn to overcome my unease around them, that is all."

"It is not silly of you! It was unfeeling of Erik to order the jesters when he knew very well how you would react. No one can blame you for being upset."

Thora-Lisa did not reply, and her frail hands shook as she lifted the latch to the door. Over her shoulder, she said, "I wish to be alone now, Brigitta. I'll see you in the morning." The tone of her voice brooked no argument.

"Yes, of course," Brigitta whispered. "Good night." But the door had already swung shut.

Brigitta stared at the portal for long moments, wondering how life had become so complicated in such a short period of time. Deciding there was nothing more she could do for Lisa this night, she headed toward her own room, suddenly realizing how weary she felt. The events of the day had been many. Quickening her pace, she rounded the slight bend in the flame-lit passage. She wanted nothing more than to crawl into bed and sleep until daybreak.

Her heartbeat fluttered with fear when she eyed

the door of her chambers. It was opened and pale
yellow light spilled out into the passage. Someone
was inside her room. Could it be Erik, she wondered? Had he known Lisa would flee to her chambers at sight of the midgets, with no intention of
returning to the celebration?

Brigitta stood motionless, wondering what to do.
From inside her chamber, she could hear the sound
of wood creaking. Her wardrobe was being
opened. A man's muttered oath could be heard
and then one by one she heard her footwear being
tossed to the floor.

Silently, Brigitta stepped up to the door and
peered into the room. Devon Courtenay, his back
toward her, was squatting before her wardrobe,
tossing her belongings over his shoulder as he
rummaged through the contents.

"What do you think you're doing?" Brigitta cried
angrily, rushing inside the room. "Stop before I
call the guard!"

Devon's back straightened at the sound of her
voice, but he did not turn toward her. Instead, he
continued with his rummaging. "I've heard that
threat fly from your pretty lips before, Brigitta.
Remember? Even then, it was an empty warning."
He tossed a silk-covered clog over his shoulder and
Brigitta caught it. Aiming carefully, she threw the
shoe at his back. It hit him with a thump.

Devon cursed her soundly.

"How dare you come into my room and search
through my belongings! What do you think you'll
find, hmm? I have nothing of great value," she
said, marching to his side and grabbing the matching clog he was about to toss out of his way.

Devon glanced up at her, obviously annoyed she had chosen to return to her room. "What I'm looking for does not belong to you. In fact, my reasons for being here do not concern you at all, so indulge me for a moment and forget I'm here." Abandoning the wardrobe, he stood and walked to the windows that were covered with carved panels. He ran his hands along the panels, gently guiding his fingers over the decorated wood. He no longer wore his waist-length cape, or even his mask. Brigitta noted how tightly his black doublet fit him, noted, too, how broad his shoulders were. The sight stirred some deep, untapped emotions within her. His dark hair appeared blue-black in the light of the small fire within the hearth and the single candle Devon must have lit upon entering her chamber. His hair was arrow-straight and shone in the dim light. The full sleeves of his white shirt fluttered as he moved along the windows and reached to touch a place in the panels here, then there.

Angry that the sight of him was distracting her, she demanded, "Whatever are you searching for?"

Devon ceased his search, wondering what had possessed him to come rioting through Brigitta's room as though he had a right to do so. Even though his mother had once lived in this chamber, he knew it was doubtful any of her belongings might still be here. In a frustrated gesture, he ran one hand through his dark hair. "Forgive me," he began, bringing his gaze to hers, "I've no right at all to be here, I know, but you must understand that lately I've not given much thought to the feelings of others. I apologize if I've upset you in any way."

Brigitta blinked, surprised by his sudden change of attitude and a little disturbed by the abrupt metamorphosis. Not quite able to let her anger seep away, she said, "I will forgive only if you tell me what it is you're looking for. Surely it is no possession of mine you seek."

He smiled at her choice of words. If only she knew what just her nearness did to him, and how he wished he had met her under other circumstances. . . . "No," he answered, forcing a lightness into his tone that he did not feel at all, "what I am looking for is nothing that belongs to you."

"What then? Perhaps I can help."

Her guileless response was heartwarming. He had met few people in his travels who were willing to extend any kindness to him, and his early years at Vardighet had been totally void of generosity, save the friendship of Thora-Lisa and her mother. Devon studied her for a moment, debating whether he could trust her. The fact she had kept his identity hidden this long was proof enough that he could, although he suspected Brigitta kept his secret only because of her allegiance to her princess. Perhaps that sense of obligation could keep those beautiful lips sealed with a few more of his secrets. He decided, in that instant, that she very well might be able to help him. And if she couldn't and the need to silence her in some way became necessary, he could see to that with relative ease.

"Very well," he replied, his dark gaze holding hers intently, "I will tell you of the reasons I have come to Vardighet. But first, you must promise me something."

"And that is?"

"That you will utter a word of this to no one."

Brigitta hesitated. "That I cannot promise, for if your purposes are nefarious, I—"

"They are not, I assure you. Justice is my motive, nothing more."

"And when you speak of justice, is it the universal definition of the word, or is it, perhaps, your own distorted translation?"

He smiled, oddly pleased with her interrogation. A woman of such bold resolve and one who had, he remembered fondly, stood her ground with him when he'd held a blade to her throat, was indeed a rare gem. Those things coupled with her stout devotion to the princess were traits Devon greatly admired. Here, standing before him, was at last a woman who would be had only on her own terms. His smile deepened, for above all things, Devon Courtenay loved a challenge. "Justice is justice, sweet Brigitta," he replied. "Do I have your promise or not?"

Brigitta wanted to question him further, but her curiosity was too great. Against her better judgment, she said, "So be it, you have my word. Now tell me, what is it you seek at Vardighet?"

"First you must close the door. I want no other ears to overhear our conversation."

With his request came the vivid memory of the last time she'd been with him behind a closed door. Well, she decided with a lift of her chin, if it was a kiss this scoundrel sought from her, he'd not find her so obliging. With determination, she moved to obey his command, and when the deed was done, she stepped back to the center of the room, waiting.

"Please," he said, "take a seat. My story is a long one."

Reluctantly, she sat down on the edge of her bed while he dragged the small stool toward the wardrobe with one booted foot, then sank down upon it, leaning his back against the cedar closet.

"I don't know what all Lisa has told you about me, so I'll begin, as all stories do, at the beginning. I was born at Vardighet to a woman named Augusta who was then a lady-in-waiting to Thora-Lisa's mother. My coming into this world was a joyous event only unto my mother; the rest of Vardighet's inhabitants despised me even before I drew my first breath. You see, all believed me to be the illegitimate son of an English pirate, Michael Courtenay, who sailed for the then King James of England. To say Michael Courtenay was an unwelcomed guest at Vardighet would be a gross understatement. He was, in short, a man who spoke his mind, the world be damned, and his outspokenness gained him more than a few enemies." He paused a moment, trying to envision the father he'd never known but had been told about by his mother.

Not until he was twenty-five did he learn where his father lived. Devon and Augusta had run out of gold years before, and their search for Devon's father had had to end when Devon was forced to find a small apartment for his mother in Dover. She had become frail and ill from all their travels, and so Devon had taken whatever odd jobs were available to support his heartbroken mother. For ten long years he worked and saved his money only to set off on small jaunts in search of Michael, always coming home with no news to brighten his mother's life. And then, finally, Devon had learned of Michael's whereabouts. Michael had lived in the English countryside in a grand home he'd called Courtenay. But by the time Devon learned this news, Michael had been murdered, leaving Devon to return to his mother with the gruesome tale.

Even now, thinking of the hardships his mother had endured alone still caused Devon great pain. That he himself had also shared those lean, harsh years did not bother him as much as knowing how crushed his mother had been when she'd been forced to flee Sweden in shame. Had Devon the power, he would have given his life to spare his mother such grief and heartache.

"And were you," Brigitta asked, breaking into his thoughts, "an illegitimate child?"

Devon glanced up, not realizing he'd stopped speaking. "Ah, do you mean am I a *bastard?*" he replied, hating even the feel of the word as it rolled off his tongue. "If I am to believe my mother, then no, I am not. My mother told me that she and my father were secretly wed before my birth. It seems a man of God had taken pity on them and performed the ceremony, but he did so against the wishes of his people. There were no witnesses to the marriage save the three of them and so when Michael sailed back to England to fulfill his duties to his king, my mother went into seclusion until my birth. She told no one of her secret vows and the only proof she carried of the ceremony was a document signed by the minister, and of course a ring my father had given to her."

"So why did anyone not believe her? Did she not produce this document for all to see so that you would not be labeled . . . so people would not believe you were illegitimate and she a fallen woman?"

Devon lifted a brow at how delicately she avoided the word "bastard." Her reaction was both balm and bitter medicine, and caused the age-old knife in his belly to twist a little deeper. "Augusta is a proud woman, and if people could not believe her with her word, then she would have nothing further to do with them. It was enough for her to know the truth."

"I see. And where is this document now? Is that what you have come to Vardighet to retrieve?"

"Precisely. There is a provision in my father's will that states whoever carries his signet ring shall be the sole heir to Courtenay, his estate in England. It is the document along with my father's ring that have been the burnished goals of my life—my menace and my savior. Both were stolen from my mother the night we fled from Vardighet."

"But who would steal them and for what purpose?"

He shook his dark head, a small, tight laugh escaping him. "I don't know. I suppose childhood jealousies can be deep-rooted, to grow and fester with age, but as I sit here now I cannot recall anything I might have done to bring such horrors upon my mother and myself. I was only a lad of twelve at the time so I can't imagine how my presence could have been a threat to anyone, especially since the inhabitants of Vardighet ignored me."

Brigitta heard his words, and the underlying pain accompanying them. But although the tone of his voice hinted at his inner anguish, his face remained stony, impassive. Had she not been listening so intently, she might have even overlooked the small telltale note that told her how vivid his memories were.

He had mentioned childhood jealousies. The words nagged at her memory, causing her mind to conjure up the scene with Erik in the flame-lit passage. "It was Erik Bjord who took these things from your mother, wasn't it, Devon?"

He gave her a silent nod, not trusting himself to speak. Even now he wanted to bolt from the room and spear the heartless Bjord with the tip of his blade. Brigitta's words, so soft and poignant, were nearly too much to bear. Gazing at her now, his dark eyes taking in her slender form as she perched on the edge of the narrow bed, he had to quell the rising emotions within him. Her heart-shaped face, radiant in the single light of the candle, with its smooth, unblemished glow and blue eyes as soft as summer skies, were enough to take his breath away. And yet, amid the picture of beauty, was also a touch of pity. This last caused him to sit up on the stool and lean toward her.

"Yes," he breathed, "it was Erik Bjord who beat my mother until she begged for mercy. He would have raped her, too, had I not been there. He took my father's ring, and the document—all that was dear to my mother; and before he was through, he had stripped away even her spirit." He caught the look of horror that washed over her delicate features, followed by a deepening of the pity. But Devon did not want her pity. "But alas," he added in a husky whisper, "I did not tell you this story because I seek compassion from you. I only want you to understand the dark forces which compel my actions. Had I known a moment ago that my story would cause such sadness in your eyes, I would have kept the sordid details to myself."

"No, I am glad you told me." She reached out to lightly touch one hand to his shirtsleeve. Beneath her cool fingertips she could feel his warmth and the contact stunned her. She drew her hand away, as if she'd suffered a burn, while her lashes fluttered down in embarrassment. "Forgive me, I . . . I didn't mean to—"

"To touch me? There is nothing to forgive. You felt compassion and wanted to comfort me, there is nothing wrong with that. However, I don't need an angel of mercy, no matter how beautiful, to soothe my troubled soul," he finished angrily.

Brigitta's blue gaze, suddenly fiery, met his inky black one. "You mock me when all I had meant to do was simply—"

"Take pity on me," he interrupted. "If you think I am a man who needs a sorrowful maiden taking his hand to salve his wounds, I've misled you. But if you so desire to touch me again for purposes other than condolence, I will gladly accept such laurels. . . ."

His meaning was clear and Brigitta felt the heat of a blush suffuse her cheeks. "And if you think I could ever be so wanton, then it is you who have been misled!" She made a motion to stand and head for the door panel, but her movements were not as quick as his.

Before she had a chance to stop him, he took her gently by the shoulders and pulled her body to just a hair's breadth from his own. His eyes, as dark and lonely as a winter's forest, caught her gaze, holding it with fierce intensity. That he was among enemies at Vardighet, his life in peril as it had been for years, were both reasons that could have given a lesser man license for horrid deeds done in vengeance. But thus far, Devon Courtenay had held himself in tight rein. Gazing up at him now, Brigitta wondered if his dam of reserve would soon burst, and fear pricked along her spine at the thought. "Please," she whispered, "do not hurt me."

His eyes narrowed, but his hold remained gentle. "Do you think I am the type of man who would hurt you? Is it my flagrant lack of chivalry thus far which brings such terror to your face . . . or is it my past and the blight it places on my soul? I would know now so in the future I can take care never to see you shy away from me as you are now."

"You have every right to be bitter and—and uncaring."

"Is that how you view me? It is my deepest regret then that I have painted such a portrait of myself. Shall we start anew, Brigitta, and forget the first moment when I came upon you in Lisa's chamber, and all the heretofore moments when I've been less than considerate? Let me introduce myself, I am Devon Courtenay, and I am from now unto the end of time at your service."

As he spoke, he tilted his head and slowly lowered his mouth to hers. He paused, their lips nearly touching, and waited to see if she would deny him a kiss. She did not.

Brigitta, mesmerized by his words and the slow descent of his smooth mouth, stood transfixed, unable to move. Her breath caught in her throat as her heart thumped wildly in her chest and her senses soared with the nearness of him. That he intended to kiss her was apparent; that she wanted him to do so amazing. Her lashes fluttered down over her eyes as, quiescent, she let his mouth cover her parted lips.

Gently, tenderly, his lips brushed atop hers, teasing their sensitive corners and then the pouty bow of her lower lip, and all the while Brigitta felt a dangerous languor pour through her body like warm honey. Sweet yet beguiling, gentle yet firm, his touch seemed to hold the secrets of the universe. She ached to reach for such mysteries, suddenly confident that he and he alone could lay them before her. Slowly she melted against his lean frame, reaching up to shyly place her hands on his broad shoulders.

For Devon, the combination of her warm curves and her slightly opened mouth were invitations he could not resist. But resist he must, for to continue his gentle assault would be to take her into territory as yet unknown to her. Brigitta Lind was an innocent. For him to introduce her to such delights would be unfair. To dally with Brigitta's tender heart was something Devon would never do, despite his history of clandestine affairs with women willing to part with their favors for a price.

With these thoughts invading his mind, he

ended the sweet kiss just as gently as he'd begun it. Softly, he brushed his lips atop hers, then slowly drew away.

Brigitta, her face tilted upward, sensed the swing of his mood. Lifting her lashes, she asked, "Why do you stop?" Although she knew she should not, she had enjoyed the kiss. Had she done something to displease him? she wondered. Suddenly, the answer to that question mattered very much to her.

Devon smiled, catching her chin between his thumb and forefinger. "I must leave you now, Brigitta. My duties call me away."

Confused, and not a bit stunned at her response to him, she said, "Wait. Can . . . can you not k— kiss me again before you leave?"

His smile deepened. "Sweet Brigitta, if I kiss you again, I won't *be* leaving." With that, he stepped away from her and left the chamber with a swirl of his cloak he'd lifted from the edge of the bed.

Brigitta watched him leave, the blood singing in her head as she touched her fingertips to lips still burning from his touch.

Chapter Seven

AFTER BRIGITTA LEFT Thora-Lisa at the door following the banquet, Thora-Lisa leaned back against the cool door panel and clutched her thin waist, trembling uncontrollably. It was starting again—the horrible nausea, the cramps within her stomach, and the sickening dizziness that accompanied them. She clamped her eyes shut, willing herself not to cry any more tears of self-pity.

"Oh, Erik," she whispered longingly. How she wished he were here with her. How wonderful it would feel to be taken in a passionate embrace by the handsome warrior, to experience the gentle touch of his hands as he soothed her pains. . . .

Once again, as she had so many times in her young life, she fervently wished she could cast off the shackles of royalty and go to Erik—not as his princess or even as his betrothed, but as a woman in love. What would be his reaction should she approach him with whispered words of how much she desired him? Would he sweep her frail body into his arms, forgetting her illnesses and even the fact they were not yet properly wed? Or would he roughly turn her away?

Thora-Lisa had seen the hungry light in Erik's eyes as he'd gazed down upon the lovely Brigitta this evening. She'd been painfully aware of Erik's keen interest in the young woman, and even though Lisa wanted Erik to be intrigued with Brigitta, the picture of the two of them dancing had disturbed the princess. Why couldn't Erik gaze at *her* with such intensity? Why did he not reach out and request a dance with her?

But of course, Lisa knew the answer: Erik was sickened by the sight of her. Perhaps he even believed the ugly rumors about her that were passed from ear to ear within Vardighet. Had Devon been correct when he'd said Erik only wanted to wed her for her wealth?

Bitter tears pushed past her sparse lashes, splashing atop the ugly veils covering her face. Long moments slipped past, moments in which she thought of all the times she'd been tempted to slip through the secret passage that led, if one took the proper route, to Erik's private chambers. What would be Erik's reaction if she should steal into his sleeping quarters, her arms outstretched, and invite him to love her as she so desperately needed to be loved by him?

With eyes closed, she let her fancies take flight. . . .

"Erik," she heard herself whisper.

He stood across the chamber before a blazing hearth, his back to her. At the sound of her voice, he turned, surprise lighting his coarse features. "Lisa?" he said thickly.

"Yes, it is I."

"But how—"

"Hush. Do not say another word," she whispered, her voice husky, deep. Slowly, she stepped into the warmth of the bed chamber, closing the secret panel behind her. Her footsteps across the stone floor were muffled by the pounding of her own heart. She heard nothing save his even breathing and the echoing of her heart that pounded with just the sight of him. How glorious he looked standing there attired only in his breeches and loose-flowing shirt. His blond hair was the color of wheat gilded by a hot summer sun and fell about his broad shoulders in thick waves. She wanted to caress those tresses, to feel their silken texture as they slipped passed her fingertips. "I want you, Erik," she heard herself boldly say. "How I want you. . . ."

To her pleasure, a low growl escaped him as he stepped forward, meeting her at the center of the room. Gently, reverently, as though she might only be an apparition and might, should he move too quickly, disappear as silently as she'd come, he lifted one large hand up to brush one tendril of shimmering blonde hair from her brow. "And I want you, Lisa," he whispered in reply. "I had thought, since you are a princess, you did not desire the things a man and a woman can share." His hooded blue eyes devoured the sight of her. His powerful chest lifted and fell as he took in and expelled a deep breath. "Had I known, I would have come to you. I would not have kept my distance."

She closed her eyes as his fingers brushed by her temple, her senses reeling. "So that is the reason," she said, relief flooding through her tortured body that had so long been denied his touch. "I had thought you stayed away because you—you could not stand the sight of me."

"Oh, Lisa, my dear, Lisa, nothing could be further from the truth."

She lifted her lashes, her eyes misting with unshed tears. His fingertips, roughened by the wooden handles of numerous battle-axes, caressed her burning skin. She leaned her veiled cheek against his palm, reveling in the sensation of his warm skin that came to her through layers of material. "Then you *do* desire me."

"Of course. Why else would I want to marry you? My Lisa, so beautiful." He leaned forward, his blue gaze locked with hers as he lowered his head to place a kiss to her forehead. His fingers fumbled with the clasps of her headdress, disengaging the jeweled clips.

And suddenly, for the first time in her life, Thora-Lisa was willing to allow another person to gaze upon her uncovered face. He had called her beautiful . . . he had called her *his.*

The material fluttered away. She felt his warm breath upon her naked cheeks. Her nostrils filled with the heady scent of him. The feeling was wondrous, enchanting.

Slowly, he brought both hands up to her face, pressing gently. "Why do you cover such beauty?" he asked throatily. His thumbs rubbed her cheeks, his fingertips skimming her hairline.

Thora-Lisa's world spun, expanding as, like a great tide of emotions kept dammed until this moment, feelings burst from their captive well and flowed through her body. Suddenly she was alive, a sparkling candle burning brightly, chasing away a hundred years of oppressive darkness. Like one newly born, she perceived feelings she'd heretofore been barred from experiencing. With just Erik's touch, she was propelled upward into a whole other world. It was a dazzling realm, breathless in its heights, rapturous in its warmth.

Finally having found contentment, she sighed deeply.

"Oh, Erik," she whispered, her lips nearly touching his, "I knew this is how it would be . . ."

But, with a kiss, he quieted any other words she might utter. Never had she dared to even touch her own lips, so ugly were they with their odd formation. But now, her beloved intended to touch them. Where others had smooth upper lips, Thora-Lisa's top lip was marred by a disgusting inverted U.

Thinking of her deformity, she tried to pull away, but Erik would not let her go.

"No," he whispered, shaking his head once, slowly. "I love you just the way you are."

His mouth covered hers then. His lips were warm and full, brushing gently atop that odd cleft that had barred her from a normal life. But he seemed not to notice her deformity. For once in her life, the shape of her mouth did not matter.

Her knees felt weak as he wrapped strong arms about her, pulling her close against his lean body. She moaned, in relief, in ecstasy. Why had she waited so long? Why? His kiss deepened, warming her, thrilling her. And she responded to him, casting off all the cloying inhibitions that had built up over the years only to leave her as lonely as a leper. Overwhelmed with joy, she clung to him, returning his fervent kiss. *Erik, Erik,* her mind chanted. *How I love you!*

* * *

Thora-Lisa snapped her eyes open, the image of her and Erik bursting apart like a piece of crystal dropped to the floor.

Oh, there was so little time! she thought desperately. If she was ever to share such a moment with Erik, she must act quickly. Even now she could feel the strength seeping from her body. She could not waste another precious moment spent on fantasies.

As a bird flying free of a dark cave, she scurried across her chamber toward the wooden screen that hid the secret door. Quickly, before she could change her mind, she swung the panel open and stepped into the cool passageway that led to snaking catwalks throughout the castle. As a young child, she used to walk these very passages that would take her to various chambers of the castle where she could then peek in on others. Such exploits had been her only ventures into the "normal" day-to-day lives of others. But now, these same passages would lead her to Erik. . . .

Leaving her rooms behind, the darkness of the passage swallowing her in its tight grip, she hurried along. She didn't mind the darkness though, for it had been her closest companion since she was a youngster. With her hands and memory as her only guides, she made her way past familiar bends and turns. Cool, refreshing air wafted about, fluttering the ends of the veils covering her face. *Soon*, she thought, *soon she would be with Erik* . . .

The last turn behind her, she groped along the stone wall for the panel of wood that led to Erik's private chambers. Beyond the door was hung a huge tapestry which covered the secret entrance.

Thora-Lisa doubted that Erik even knew of the hidden passages snaking through Vardighet. Whereas she had been born and raised within these walls, Erik had come to Vardighet with his father when he'd been only a lad of seven. Erik's father had been a bold warrior who'd won favor with her own father, now deceased, and it was Erik's chambers where her father had once resided.

She pressed the palms of her hands against the coarse wood, pushing gently. The panel gave way, easing inward. She pushed until the door was opened only a fraction, afraid to venture any further just yet. Fearing someone might have heard the dull squeak of the ancient hinges, she paused a moment, listening.

The sounds of voices floated to her, along with a warm waft of air that was filled with the scent of the hearth fire and lightly tinged with the strong smell of ale.

"We've much to celebrate this night," a man was saying. It was Erik's voice she heard, roughened by drink. Her heartbeat accelerated. "My men were brave upon the battlefield, unmatched in skill. The Danes and their sniveling leader Jorgen are no foil for us."

"*Ja*," someone agreed. She recognized the voice of Erik's manservant.

A moment passed when nothing but the crackle of flames in the hearth could be heard. And then there came the familiar sound of a solid thud. Although the door panel and the hanging tapestry beyond shielded her view, Thora-Lisa could envision Erik draining a silver tankard and placing the thing heavily upon a table.

Immediately there came the sloshing of liquid as the unseen tankard was refilled.

"You are a loyal servant, Arvid," she heard Erik say to the servant. "Once the princess and I are wed you will be properly rewarded for such obedient service. What do you desire, man? Tell me and it is yours."

"You are too kind, General. I am more than satisfied with serving you. I need nothing more."

Erik's laughter filled the air. "Come now," he coaxed. "Surely there is something you desire. Gold, lands? A title, perhaps? Where there are no titles, I will soon have the power to create them. Believe me, my friend, once I am married to Thora-Lisa there will be nothing out of my grasp. She is wealthy beyond belief. Tell me, what do you desire? In just the span of moments, you could become as wealthy as a noble. Think of it! Should you not take advantage of the situation? You should make the most of this—as I plan to do. Taking a sickly, ugly creature to wife is not appealing—but the greatness of her title is what attracts me. Do not insult me by not even considering my offer."

With Erik's cruel words, Thora-Lisa froze. *Sickly, ugly creature . . .* How could he say such things? At once, she felt nauseated again. Her palms grew sticky as her head swam. Ugly. He had termed her ugly! *Oh, Erik, my love, not you, too!*

Fearing she might regurgitate at his door, she spun quickly away, leaving the door ajar, and running as fast as she could through the passage. The air felt suddenly icy whereas only moments before it had felt refreshingly cool. Now, though, that same air burned her flushed skin as she ran. She stumbled on the uneven stones, falling to her knees. He palms scraped atop the cold stone as she fought to break the fall. Breathless, she righted herself, snatching at the cloying, despicable veils she sucked into her mouth as she tried to breathe evenly.

Erik hated her, it was true! He'd never loved her, only her title and wealth! She pushed forward, needing to be far away from the man she loved more than her own life.

Sobbing, choking on her own tears, she finally made her way back to her apartments. Once inside, she fell to her bed, clutching one pillow to her chest as she curled her body into a tight ball, crying brokenly.

"I hate you, Erik," she sobbed aloud. "I hate you for your cruelty."

But even as her own voice echoed around her, she knew she could never hate Erik Bjord. It was herself she despised—her deformity, her maladies. Not Erik, never, ever Erik.

And so, in the darkness of her chamber, with only the dull flames of the fire dancing upon unfeeling walls, she cried bitter tears, wishing she could be beautiful and vibrant, wishing, as she always had, that she'd been born whole. . . . Wishing, always wishing.

Chapter Eight

Three days had passed since the feast held in honor
of Erik and not once since that evening had the
handsome warrior graced Princess Thora-Lisa with
a visit. Indeed, the man had not even sent word to
his wife-to-be and Brigitta suspected that he had
no intention of contacting the princess. Because
she loved Thora-Lisa, this vexed Brigitta greatly,
and as she stood in the large kitchen overseeing
the preparation of the princess's breakfast, she was
hard put not to seek out the callous Erik and vent
her full rage on the barbaric man.

She had not seen Devon since the feast either,
but she suspected he had been in to see Lisa on
more than one occasion. Brigitta did not like their
private visits. Lisa would invariably be upset after-
ward, and since the ball, Lisa's health had been
failing. Lisa had made Brigitta promise not to speak
with Erik about Lisa's illnesses. In fact, she had
made Brigitta promise not to utter a word. If Thora-
Lisa had not looked so terribly frightened at just
the mere thought of Brigitta speaking to the warrior, Brigitta would have gone directly to Erik the
morning after the feast. But Brigitta had given her
word to the princess and so now she found herself
holding her anger in check and forcing herself to be
silent when she really wanted to yell to the entire
castle of Thora-Lisa's needs. Yell to the cruel people, especially the head cook, who continued to
whisper behind their hands of the ugliness of their
princess and gossip about the reasons a handsome

man like Erik would be interested in such a sickly creature. Even now, the cook was entertaining her staff with tales of the princess's looks.

"A sickly color Princess Thora-Lisa was," the woman said, her gray-haired head dipping nearer toward the large kettle she stood over. "Marta said she had to be helped to her rooms, and since that night her food goes uneaten. Some say she is a witch, poisoned by evil from the day of her birth. Isn't it so, Brigitta?" the older woman asked as she stirred the contents of the kettle.

Usually Brigitta ignored the head cook but this morning she had no patience for Anna's meanness. "Lisa is no witch! And not all you say is true, Anna. The princess did not need assistance to her rooms that night. And as to her coloring that evening, I think she looked beautiful."

Anna nodded her head, her fine-lined lips pursing, *"Ja,* you are loyal to the princess. We all know this to be true."

"Loyal, yes," Brigitta replied. "But I am also truthful. Your only correct observation is that the princess hardly touches her food and that is why I am here this morning. I want to see only her favorite foods on her tray."

Anna dropped the crude wooden spoon into the kettle, letting its long, curved handle hang over the iron edge as she wiped her hands on her embroidered apron, then turned sharply toward Brigitta. "What is put on the princess's tray is what I am ordered to put on the tray. You," the woman said, her words becoming more drawn out and precise, "do not give orders to me!"

Brigitta, in her worry for Lisa's health and her

anger at everyone's insensitive behavior toward the princess, was in no mood to tolerate the cook's bullying. And so, with a cool gaze and an even colder voice, she replied, "Anna, to you my words are orders and no more will I tolerate the greasy foods that you have been preparing for the princess. This morning I should like a light breakfast served to her and if you have nothing for drink other than beer or wine, then the princess shall have plain water. If you do not see to these things immediately, you shall be dealt with."

Anna's mouth dropped open but she quickly shut it. Clearly she realized she could not go against Brigitta's requests. As she once again took up the task of stirring the contents of the kettle beside her, she said, "Believe me, Brigitta, I will see you pay for your assuming ways. You come to Vardighet from some distant land and though you are unlearned and of peasant folk, you attain some title. Well, enjoy it for the time you have it, for soon I will find a flaw with you and the last word shall be mine."

Brigitta straightened a bit, her heart beating rapidly. Glancing around the room, she could see all eyes were upon them and she did not want to give fuel to set their tongues wagging. Slowly, she replied, "See my requests are carried out." With that, she turned and left the room, feeling many pairs of eyes on her.

People could be so cruel, Brigitta thought to herself as she hurried toward Lisa's private chambers. The princess wanted only acceptance from the inhabitants of Vardighet, wanted only to be treated as a whole person.

Not bothering to knock upon Thora-Lisa's door, Brigitta entered into the dark chamber and was momentarily taken aback by the rush of oppressive, warm air that met her. No tapers were lit and the drapes were drawn tightly against the brightness of the sun. Only the golden glow of a burning fire lit the room, causing elongated shadows to dance eerily upon the walls. Lisa lay motionless in her huge bed, the furs tucked tight about her slim body. Brigitta frowned. Lisa had not changed her nightdress in three days and the princess still wore the veils she had worn to the feast. Enough was enough, Brigitta decided. She would not allow Lisa to hide in these chambers and let the world pass her by! With a determined step, she moved toward the windows and pulled open the heavy drapes. Glorious sunshine streamed in, filling the darksome corners of the room and chasing away the shadows.

Thora-Lisa groaned. "Close the drapes," she whispered from the bed. "I cannot stand the bright light."

Brigitta ignored the desolate tone of her princess's voice. She was determined to see Lisa out of her depressed state. "And I cannot stand to see you abed all day. Get up, Lisa! The winter birds are singing and the air is calm. Why, I even hear some ladies of the court are planning a day out-of-doors. Why don't you join them?" She reached for Lisa's brush and comb. "Here, I'll do your hair. You can wear your ermine cape—"

"Enough," Lisa interrupted. "I don't want to join any outing and I certainly don't want to spend the day with women who would resent my presence." She rolled over in bed, turning her back to Brigitta.

Brigitta hesitated for only a moment before she tossed the brush and comb back onto the stand and then moved toward Lisa. Trying very hard to be gentle but firm, she said, "You are their princess, Lisa. They would be honored if you accompanied them." The small bundle in the bed didn't move, so Brigitta tried another tactic. "All right then, why don't you and I take a walk today? Just the two of us. We could ride toward the cliffs and look out at the sea. It is a breathtaking sight with all the pack ice sparkling in the sunlight. As a child I used to love to sit near the shore. The wind that blows across the Baltic is so clean and fresh." A smile touched her lips as she remembered the carefree days of her youth. "Let us go, Lisa! It would do you such good to get away from Vardighet for a day."

Thora-Lisa said nothing for long moments and Brigitta wondered if the princess had even heard her. "You don't understand," Thora-Lisa finally said.

"What don't I understand?" Brigitta asked. "Look at you, Lisa. You are miserable! You hide in your chambers and let the circumstances of your life rule you. I—I think you are feeling sorry for yourself," she continued in a rush. She hadn't meant to say the words, but now that they were out there was no snatching them back. In truth, she knew Thora-Lisa was ill, but by urging her princess to get out of bed, she'd hoped to put the spark of life back into Lisa's eyes. Biting her bottom lip between her teeth, she waited breathlessly for

Lisa's reaction, and she felt her heart constrict when she saw Thora-Lisa's slim shoulders start to shake. "I—I'm sorry," she began. "I should not have said—"

"No," Lisa replied in a small voice. "You are right. I am feeling sorry for myself. But you see, Brigitta, I—I am running out of time. My life is ending and I have so much I want to do—so very, very much." Her voice broke with a sob as she rolled toward Brigitta and huge tears filled her pale-blue eyes. "I'm frightened, Brigitta. I'm not ready to die but I know that soon I will. . . ."

A terrible realization struck Brigitta. Thora-Lisa was not just suffering from black moods and disappointment. The princess looked pale and fragile, and her words, so honest, pierced Brigitta's heart. "Oh, Lisa," Brigitta said through her own tears, "don't say such things." She leaned over and gave her friend a tight hug. "Please, Lisa, do not dwell on such dark thoughts."

"But I feel I am forever in the dark, Brigitta. I cannot leave these hated rooms, cannot meet with other people. I am forever tormented—forever a disgrace to my people . . . to Erik."

Brigitta clasped her tighter. "Hush," she soothed. "Hush and be still. You are a beautiful princess who is to marry a great warrior. I have seen your beauty and you are more lovely than any person I have ever met."

"You just speak these words to soothe me."

"No, that isn't so. I mean what I say, Lisa. You *are* lovely. And you can get well again if you only try."

Lisa hesitantly moved out of Brigitta's embrace

and wiped the tears from her eyes with a shaky hand. "Do you think so?" she asked quietly, her pale-blue eyes looking like a child's.

Brigitta smiled. "Yes. I do."

"And you truly think I can get well—well enough to make a good wife for Erik?"

Brigitta nodded. "You had the will to get well when you learned of Erik's homecoming. Find that feeling again, Lisa. Flee this darksome prison. Do not let others decide your fate."

Thora-Lisa slowly nodded, an odd light glistening in her eyes at mention of Erik.

Brigitta felt a thrill of anticipation course through her own body. Perhaps all *would* be well. "Shall I get you a change of clothes?" Brigitta asked, helping Lisa to sit up in bed.

"Yes, my prettiest. And be sure it is blue—for Erik once told me how beautiful I look in blue," she said dreamily.

Brigitta's eyes narrowed with Lisa's mention of Erik. Why must Lisa always say his name as if he and he alone made the sun rise and set? At the moment, there was a fanciful light shining in Thora-Lisa's eyes. The sight disturbed Brigitta—as though Thora-Lisa's thoughts were far away. Shrugging away the dark feeling of premonition that swept over her, Brigitta grabbed the perfect day dress, then returned to the bed to help Lisa stand.

Thora-Lisa threw back the heavy covers and furs and carefully stretched out her slim arms, letting Brigitta take hold of them as she maneuvered herself to the edge of the bed and timidly set her feet to the cold floor. Slowly, carefully, she put her weight onto her feet and legs and with Brigitta's help tried to stand.

Feeling Thora-Lisa's weakness, Brigitta held tightly onto her princess, afraid to let go.

"I am fine, Brigitta," Lisa whispered determinedly as she motioned for Brigitta to release her and let her stand on her own.

Reluctantly, Brigitta did as Thora-Lisa requested. For awkward seconds, the princess wavered precariously in the air, her frail body going side to side as a wispy willow would. Brigitta instinctively held out her hands, but Lisa brushed them away, insisting she needed no help. Lisa took only one step and then she crumbled to the hard floor in a heap of frail body and thin nightdress.

Brigitta immediately was on her knees beside Lisa trying to pull her up and place her back in bed but Thora-Lisa only slapped away Brigitta's helping hands.

"Don't!" Lisa cried. "I want no help! I want only Darlana's medicine. Get it for me!"

"Lisa, just try one more time—"

"No! I will never be well. Only Darlana has the power to cure me. I want her here at Vardighet with me! Bring her to me, Brigitta. Now!" Thora-Lisa covered her veiled face with her thin trembling hands and her whole body shook as she sobbed hysterically.

Brigitta wrapped her arms around the princess, pulling her close and saying nothing, knowing Lisa's aches could not be soothed with mere words. She held her tight, stroking Lisa's thinning hair as a mother would caress a sick child, and wished she could give some of her own strength to her princess. "You know I would do anything for you, Lisa," Brigitta whispered. "I will go."

"Go where?" came the masculine voice from the far side of the room just beyond Lisa's bed. Devon walked into a ray of sunshine that was alive with dancing dust particles, his black eyes filled with concern as he stared down at Lisa. "What has happened? Lisa, are you all right?"

"No," Brigitta answered for the princess. "And don't you ever knock before you come into a chamber?" She didn't release her hold on Lisa, her arms creating a shield against Devon's presence. Unmindful of her own fluttering emotions caused by Devon's arrival, Brigitta's concerns were mostly for Thora-Lisa and her comfort. "Go away, please. The princess is ill and you upset her."

Devon ignored her request. Dressed in deep-blue velvet breeches and matching doublet, he appeared to be the French fop he wanted all of Vardighet to believe him to be. A low-crowned black hat with peacock plumes adorning the band sat atop his unbound ebony hair, and a love lock—a few strands of braided hair tied with a slim, red ribbon—dangled near his right ear. "What has happened? Lisa, talk to me!" He strode toward them and gently took Lisa from Brigitta's arms. Thora-Lisa, weakened from her hysterics, sagged like a limp rag doll in his hold and laid her head on his shoulder.

"Darlana . . ." she whispered.

Devon glanced questioningly at Brigitta, who squared her shoulders as she forced herself not to remember the feel of his arms about her or the touch of his lips upon hers. That she should think of such things while Thora-Lisa was so ill was, in her mind, unforgivable. She didn't care to admit how much Devon Courtenay affected her.

"Thora-Lisa has taken ill," Brigitta explained. "She wants me to bring Darlana to her."

Devon glanced back at Lisa and his gaze softened immediately. "Very well, Lisa. We will bring Darlana to you. Here, you must rest now." Tenderly, he laid her upon the bed and drew the robes around her body. Brigitta watched as his large hands lovingly brushed a tendril of hair from Lisa's forehead and then as he bent he placed a chaste kiss upon the same spot. "Where is Marta? I will summon her before we leave."

"No," Lisa breathed. "No time. Go now. I will be fine on my own. Just . . . please . . . hurry." The lids closed over her eyes and she turned her head away, her breathing shallow.

A gasp escaped Brigitta's lips as she moved toward the bed, but Devon held her back.

"There's no time," he said softly. "We must get to Darlana."

Brigitta shrugged out of his hold, not trusting her emotions should she feel his tender touch again. "She needs a physician," she insisted, keeping her voice low. "Are we to indulge her with this fantasy that Darlana can cure her?"

"Not here," he replied. Then, to her discomfort, he took her by the wrist and led her toward the secret passage he had used to enter into the chamber. "We will be back," he called gently to Lisa. "You rest and think of getting well."

Lisa gave no response.

Once on the stairs that led to the princess's pri-

vate gardens, Brigitta came to a standstill. "I won't
go," she said. "One of us should summon Lisa's
physician. It is madness for both of us to leave
Vardighet."

Devon turned on the stairwell and found himself
having to forcibly quell the urge to gather Brigitta
in a sheltering embrace. She looked so young and
vulnerable standing there, torn between staying by
Lisa's side and leaving to fetch Darlana. But letting
Brigitta worry at Lisa's bedside would do neither
woman any good.

"You must know how Lisa feels about physicians," he explained. "We both promised to bring
Darlana to her, and we will." His hand closed
tightly around her wrist. "Come, Brigitta, there is
nothing you can do here." When he saw her hesitate once more, he added, "You are coming with
me whether you like it or not. Darlana has some
perverse aversion to the male of the species. I need
you to enter the cottage and convince her to return
with us."

"I don't like it," Brigitta replied. "I think one of
us should stay with Lisa. We should not have left
her alone."

"I don't like it either. But we haven't much
choice, have we? We are the only people Lisa can
trust."

At that, Brigitta shut her mouth and hurried
down the stairs after him. She *had* promised to
bring Darlana back to Vardighet, and even though
it was against her better judgment, she would do
exactly that.

"How will we bring Darlana back with us?" she
asked as Devon moved the stone door open wide

enough so they could squeeze through. She saw only Devon's mount tethered in the exact spot he'd been when she'd first come this way.

Devon moved quickly toward the horse, saddling the animal in a matter of moments. "Lisa has bestowed many gifts upon Darlana for the making of the potions. Darlana has a horse as well as a cart. I think the crazy old woman buries half of what Lisa gives to her. Here," he said as he easily hauled himself up onto the saddle. "Give me your hand."

Brigitta did as he said and in a moment they were off at a mad pace. Once again she was forced back against Devon's lean, hard body as the horse galloped toward Darlana's *byalag*. And once again she had to wonder if Lisa would be alive when they returned to Vardighet.

The sun moved across the sky. Its dazzling light was unending, reflecting in the tiny icicles that hung like icing from tree branches, and playfully sparkling and winking on the mantle of snow upon the ground. Even though the horse traveled at a great speed, the air was not as cold as it had been on their previous trip and Brigitta could smell the sweet freshness of nature. She breathed deeply, wishing Thora-Lisa could smell it too.

Once at Darlana's cottage Devon was the first to dismount. The feel of his hands upon her waist as he helped her from the saddle was warm and intimate, but her worry for Lisa's health kept her mind on the task at hand.

"I won't be long," she told him. "I'll help Darlana gather only what she needs to help Lisa." She started toward the portal of the cottage and was surprised to see Devon fall in step beside her. "What are you doing? I thought Darlana did not trust men. I think you should stay here."

"I have a few questions I want answered and I've the feeling Darlana can answer them for me. Whether she likes it or not, I'm going in."

"But—"

"Let's go, Brigitta. As usual, I haven't the time or inclination to argue with you." He closed one hand tightly over her elbow and pulled her along the tiny path in the deep snow. The brim of his hat left his face in shadow and the darkness of his skin and hair was emphasized even more by the stark whiteness of the day. Brigitta decided to let him do as he pleased. She wanted only to return to Vardighet as quickly as possible.

After three sharp raps upon the cottage door there was still no answer from within. "I wonder if she is even here," Brigitta said.

"She's in there. She's hiding because she knows I am with you. Open the door, Darlana, or I will break it in!" Devon said loudly.

"Go away. Darlana does not want to see you," came the raspy reply from beyond the door.

Impatient, Devon pulled Brigitta away from the door, then smashed the portal in with one booted foot. The latch broke away from the splintered wood and hung uselessly, rattling, as the door swung inward and slammed against the box framing running along the inside of the cottage. Darlana screamed then and Brigitta watched, stunned, as the old woman scrambled across the room to crouch behind the battered chair she had sat upon while telling Brigitta of her vision.

"Go away!" she screeched, hiding her face from them.

Brigitta gave Devon a scathing look. "Devon! You've nearly frightened her to death. We'll be lucky to calm her down, let alone get her to Vardighet." Without waiting for an answer from him, she walked over to Darlana and knelt beside the old woman. "Darlana, listen to me," she said soothingly. "We need you to return to Vardighet with us. The princess is very ill. She wants you to come and stay with us until she is well again. We must hurry, Darlana, Lisa needs your medicines."

Darlana shook her head, not looking up. "No," she mumbled. "Tell him to leave. His presence here is an omen. He—he must leave. *Now.*"

Brigitta glanced up at Devon who stood silhouetted in the open doorway. He shook his head once. "I'm not going anywhere. Get up, Darlana. You know who I am. As a young boy, I used to come here often. You remember, I know you do. You used to tell Lisa and me tales of ogres who inhabited the forests. Your stories would frighten me but Lisa loved to come visit you so I would swallow my fears and accompany her," he said. "It is you who must swallow your fears now, Darlana. I mean you no harm."

"Your presence here bodes ill, Devon Courtenay," she said in an odd voice as she snapped her head up and stared him straight in the eye. "I knew you would return . . . I saw you coming.

Bastards are restless, and you, Devon, will not soon find peace."

Brigitta's brows rose with Darlana's words and she turned to see Devon's reaction. He stood motionless, his face covered by darkness, the sunlight haloing his body.

"I've not come to hear the voice of your visions, Darlana, and you'd best be careful whom you call a bastard."

Darlana seemed not to hear his words nor the threatening tone of his voice. "I told your mother years ago not to let the seed within her grow. I even gave her the potions she needed to bleed it out of her, but she wouldn't listen to me. No, she had to show the world she'd lain with a man she had never wed. I knew when I pulled you out of her body that your coming would cause trouble— trouble that is now only beginning." Her voice rising with each word, Darlana pulled her hunched body to a standing position, her twisted hands clutching the chair in front of her for support.

Brigitta reached out a hand to help steady the woman, but Darlana brushed her hand away. Brigitta gave Devon a beseeching look. "Perhaps you should wait outside," she suggested, still reeling from Darlana's words.

"The hell I will," he tersely replied. "Gather your medicines together, old woman. Lisa needs you— and on the way to Vardighet you can tell me all you know about my mother and her . . . *lover*."

The last word was a sneer. Not knowing what to do to ease the situation, Brigitta watched helplessly as he began randomly yanking vessels off the shelf nearest to him. He snatched a mangy cat fur lying atop the box frame and set the vessels on it, securing the ends and making a bundle. "Devon," she said. "Calm yourself. Darlana will come with us willingly. Won't you?" She turned toward the old woman, but what she saw took the breath from her lungs in a rush. Darlana, the bones of her hunched back now higher than her head as she leaned forward against the chair, was rocking back and forth, her entire body twitching oddly. From her cracked lips came a sound like that of a dying animal. She was having another of her "visions," and her voice, when she spoke, was low and forceful. Brigitta took a step away.

"You are the son of darkness, Devon Courtenay," the old woman began. "Beneath a red sea lies the circle of your eternity, but the key to your freedom is in the realm of a cruel lord. Alone you do not have the power to defeat that lord. Leave, Devon! Leave Vardighet now, for your coming will be the passing of another . . ." Her breathing came fast then, as though she was under great physical strain and as she began to shake violently, Brigitta moved to grab hold of her.

"Devon!" Brigitta yelled. "What is wrong with her?"

The old woman threw her head back then, her watery eyes opened wide. "No!" she wailed. "No! Not Lisa!" With crazed eyes she turned on Brigitta and grabbed her with surprising force. "You must leave!" she screeched. "Now, Brigitta. Go, go before it is too late!"

"Wh—what are you talking about, Darlana? What is wrong with you? Let go of me, you're frightening me." Brigitta cast a nervous glance toward Devon as she tried unsuccessfully to pry Darlana's bony grip from her arms. The old woman was possessed with a terrifying grip and the more hysterical she became, the tighter she held Brigitta.

"The princess," she screamed. "She—she is dying, today! Oh, Brigitta, hurry. Her pain is great!"

Brigitta let go of Darlana as if the old woman were a demon. *Thora-Lisa dying?* How could Darlana say such a thing? "You're mad," Brigitta yelled, a horrible fear engulfing her. "The princess cannot be dying!"

Darlana sank to the floor, her sobs uncontrollably loud. "She is, Brigitta who will not be Brigitta for long. Lisa needs you!"

Tears stung Brigitta's eyes as confusion and fright whirled about her in a sickening dance. Lisa could not die! Darlana spoke riddles!

But even as she spun away from the old woman and headed for the door, she saw a fleeting glimpse of Thora-Lisa as she had looked that morning. Gentle Lisa falling to the floor in a heap, unable even to pull herself up. . . . "Oh, God," Brigitta cried. "Don't let Lisa die!"

It was Devon who wrapped his arms around her, guided her out of the cottage and toward the horse. "Do you think it's true?" she asked him, her tears constricting her throat and burning her eyes. "Do you think Lisa is dying?"

Devon lifted her up onto the saddle, then climbed up beside her. "I don't know," he said softly into her ear, his voice grim. "But Darlana is no help to us now. We'll return to Lisa and do what we can for her." With a quick word to his mount they headed westward, the setting sun shining in their eyes. Brigitta closed her eyes against the bright ball of light, and when Devon pulled her body close to his, she went willingly into his embrace. Her falling tears froze on her cheeks and she hardly noticed as Devon wrapped his own cloak around her.

Chapter Nine

ONCE BACK AT Vardighet, Brigitta jumped down off the mount unaided, and ran to the secret entrance and thrust open the stone passage, squeezing her body through the narrow opening. Devon was right behind her, leaving his lathered mount until he could see for himself how Thora-Lisa fared.

"She can't be dying," Brigitta said to herself, willing her words to be true. "Darlana's words were just the ravings of a woman gone mad," she continued, taking the steps two at a time. She wondered why she felt the urge to voice her thoughts. Was she trying to convince herself Lisa would be all right? Tears stung her eyes and blurred her vision as she scurried along, and if not for Devon's hand on her arm, she would have tumbled to the cold stone beneath them.

Devon hadn't said a word since the tall towers of the castle had come into view and his stoic silence did nothing to calm Brigitta's fears. It was as though he believed Darlana, as though he did not expect to find Thora-Lisa lying upon her bed as they had left her hours ago. Finally at the top of the stairs, he stepped in front of Brigitta and pushed open the secret door leading to the princess's chambers. With a powerful gait he crossed the space to Lisa's bed, Brigitta right beside him.

"Lisa? Lisa, can you hear me?" he asked, leaning over the still form. An eerie hush filled the cool, stale air and the fire in the hearth had burned down to only red-hot embers. Thora-Lisa's breathing was shallow, her closed eyelids a pasty white.

Brigitta noted the tray of food on the stand beside the bed. The breakfast she had ordered for Lisa. The food was cold, untouched. "I don't think anyone has checked on her since breakfast," Brigitta whispered, reaching out to lift Thora-Lisa's hand from its position upon the bed. It was pale and sickeningly frail. Brigitta wondered why she hadn't noticed before how thin her princess was. *Had* she noticed? She couldn't remember. She couldn't remember anything now that the fear of death was stealing up her spine.

"Brigitta . . . is that you?"

Brigitta's heart fluttered with hope. "Yes, Lisa. I am here. Can . . . can I get you something?"

Lisa's eyelids opened slowly, the blue of her eyes now only a faint eggshell blue. "Darlana would not come with you, would she?" she asked, each word slow and painfully drawn out. "I knew she would not come. This is the day she warned me about so very long ago. She—she said on the day of my death she would not be near me . . . she said I am to die without her."

Brigitta cast a worried glance to Devon, hoping

he would be able to find the right words to stop
Lisa from saying such things. But he merely stood
silently, his black eyes inscrutable as he stared
down at Lisa. "Do something," Brigitta hissed.
"Summon Lisa's physician, for God's sake!"

"No!" Lisa cried weakly from her bed, her eyes
searching for Devon. "I—I want no physician near
me. You, my oldest and dearest friend, know what
I wish for this day."

Devon nodded, dropping to his knees and tenderly touching Lisa's forehead with one hand.
"Yes, Lisa, I know what you want and I will carry
out your wishes, do not fear . . . I love you, Lisa,"
he whispered. "You are the sister I never had. I'll
remember you always."

Brigitta listened in fear to the exchange between
them. How could they be speaking as though Lisa
were going to die? There should be a physician
here, someone who could do something to help
the princess! "Stop this!" she said. "Lisa, you're
not going to die. I—I won't let you!" She dropped
Lisa's hand and whirled toward Devon. "We have
to help her," she pleaded, suddenly frightened by
what was unfolding before her. It was as though
this very scene had been ordained eons ago, as if
the smell of death were seeping in from every corner and there was nothing she could do to alter the
course. Brigitta turned large eyes toward her princess and her own tears came, hot and gagging. She
loved Thora-Lisa. She didn't want her to die! Brigitta had lost only her grandfather and that had
been when she was just a young girl. For Brigitta,
death was something cold and foreign, something
unknown but knowing. . . .

"Oh, Lisa," she whispered. "Let me bring a physician to you—or a bishop. *Someone*."

Thora-Lisa shook her head once, a painful thing to do. "No. I need only the two of you, my truest friends. I would have liked Erik to be here, but . . ." She closed her eyes again, taking in a shallow breath. "I have a last request of you, Brigitta, something you must do."

Brigitta choked back a sob, biting hard on her lower lip as tears fell freely down her cheeks. "You know I will do anything for you."

Thora-Lisa's eyes closed slowly. "Thank you. I have prayed you would do this for me."

Brigitta leaned forward, so intense was Thora-Lisa's raspy voice. "What is it, Lisa? What can I do to help you?"

"You—you can, if I should pass away before my wedding day, a—assume my role and marry Erik Bjord."

Brigitta sat back, at first confused, then totally horrified by the request. *Could she have heard correctly?* She felt her heart fall to the pit of her stomach. "What?" she breathed incredulously. "You want me to pretend that I am *you?* Lisa, you must be—" She stopped her words. She was about to say the princess must be delirious. Yes, that was it. The princess had a fever, and had no idea of what she was saying. Gently, she coaxed, "You do not know what you are saying."

Thora-Lisa ignored Brigitta's words, continuing. "I will not live much longer. My body grows weaker." Suddenly Lisa's eyes opened, searing Brigitta with their intensity. "Brigitta, you *must* do this for me. You must don my hiding veils and go to the altar with Erik!"

Brigitta was stunned by the princess's words and manner. Surely Lisa must be burning with a fever. "Lisa, I think you should rest now. Do not strain yourself. I—I will order a broth for you to eat and then you can go back to sleep," Brigitta said nervously.

"Brigitta, listen to me!" Thora-Lisa exclaimed, trying unsuccessfully to raise herself to a sitting position. She fell limply back upon the bed, breathing hard but still managing to grasp Brigitta's hand in her own bony one. "I want you to promise me. Promise me by all that you hold sacred! You will take my place should I pass away before my wedding day. Swear it! Only then will I go to my death peacefully. If you do this, I will rest knowing the loved ones I leave behind will finally be proud of me."

"Proud?" Brigitta asked pleadingly, a paralyzing fear stealing up her spine at the mention of death. "Lisa, you are frightening me with such talk."

"Hear me! I have been a disappointment to my family since the day I was born. The people of our lands have branded me a witch and my poor parents had to live with the hideous sight of me. I know the court of Sweden wishes I would never have come into this world. They secretly hope I will never become sovereign; it would never do to have an ugly, sickly queen. And Erik—oh, Brigitta! He longs to have a beautiful wife, one who can bear him healthy children. I—I have disappointed *so* many, Brigitta." Her crushing grip on Brigitta's hand finally eased, and she closed her eyes, a stream of bitter tears escaping her lashes.

Brigitta squeezed Thora-Lisa's frail hand, holding tightly onto it as she cried, too. "Please do not cry, Lisa. You are not hideous—you—you are beautiful and I love you like a sister."

"If you love me, promise to do what I ask. When I die, assume my role and be the lovely, healthy princess Vardighet deserves!"

Brigitta knew not what to say. Turning desperate eyes to Devon, hoping he would do or say something to stop Lisa from uttering such madness, she was shocked to find him with his head bent and his eyes closed. He seemed not to have heard Lisa's request. Indeed, he appeared to be steeling himself for Lisa's death! Brigitta turned back to Lisa, shaking her head. "Please, Lisa, don't—"

"Tell me you will, Brigitta! Say the words . . . I—I must hear you promise me!"

It was a death-chased voice that pleaded with Brigitta, and she didn't know how to answer. Didn't Lisa remember that nearly all of the court had seen her as companion to the princess? And surely Erik would not be fooled! "Lisa, stop this nonsense," she said, forcing a tremulous smile to her lips. "You—you are not going to die. Why, just this morning we were talking of taking an outing—"

"Enough," Lisa cut in. She closed her eyes for a moment, then focused them on Devon, who, kneeling silently beside her, had lifted his head. His eyes glistened with unshed tears. "You know what to do in the event of my death. You—" She swallowed heavily. "Promise me you'll do—do as I've requested."

"I will," Devon told her, his voice even, strong.

"Good-bye, Devon."

Lisa spoke the words so softly Brigitta barely heard them. Oh, Lord, Brigitta thought. Lisa was dying! Even now the cold hands of death were clutching at Thora-Lisa's weakened body and pulling her away from the only world Brigitta knew. "No," she sobbed. "Oh, Lisa, do not die!"

"Tell me you will take my place, Brigitta. Tell me . . ." Lisa's strength was fading fast, her words tumbling pathetically from her lips. Her voice began to trail off into regions unknown by humans and even Devon leaned nearer to her, his hand soothing as he stroked her temple.

Brigitta pressed a hand to her own mouth and forced herself not to cry, to be brave. "I'll do it," she sobbed, unable, even though she tried, to not lose control in front of Lisa. "You know I will do whatever you ask, my Princess." As she said the words, she watched Thora-Lisa close her lids over eyes weary of the world, watched as her closest friend took in her last breath of air . . . and Brigitta knew that never again would she hear Thora-Lisa's beautiful voice. Lisa was dead.

Brigitta dissolved into tears, falling helplessly against the bed. Clutching Lisa's hand to her own breast, a hand as white as the snow outside, she cried uncontrollably, feeling a piece of her heart fall away.

Ages passed, horrid moments filled with intense, gut-wrenching grief, but Brigitta was unaware of the lapse of time. She knew only that her princess was gone, and life would never again be the same.

"It is done, Brigitta," Devon said quietly as he pried Lisa's lifeless hand from hers. "She's gone."

Brigitta jerked her head up, fire in her eyes. "Get away from me!" she spat. "How dare you be so—so unemotional! Lisa is dead!" she screamed. "I knew I should not have left her side this morning. I should have stayed here, sent for her physician. Oh God, I—I should have done something for her!" Crazed with grief, Brigitta lashed out at Devon, pushing him away. And when he closed strong arms around her and pulled her body toward his, she pounded her fists against his chest, fighting the comforting embrace he wrapped around her.

"Hush," he soothed, holding her tight, enduring the force of her fists. "There was nothing any of us could have done, Brigitta. Be comforted to know Lisa will never again experience a day of human pain and suffering. She is at peace now, and that is all she ever wished for." His hand was warm as he stroked her hair, and he whispered a string of calming words against her ear, words that made no sense but helped ease her pain.

Brigitta ceased to fight the embrace. She felt drained, as though she had lived a hundred harsh years all in one day. Wiping the wetness from her cheeks, she pressed her face against the soft velvet of Devon's doublet and leaned toward him, drawing from his strength. He was like a sturdy tree in a violent tempest; the only thing in her life that had not gone totally mad. "We—we must alert the people of Vardighet," she whispered, finally gaining some control of her emotions. "A—a man of the church should be here."

Devon said nothing, only holding her for a moment longer before he grasped her by the shoulders and pulled her away from him. "Are you all right now?" he asked. His face might have been etched in stone. No emotion played in the depths of his black eyes.

"Yes, but—"

"Good. We've a great deal to get done this night. Wrap Lisa's body with some furs from her bed."

"What?" she breathed, shocked as she watched Devon cross the room and pull a crude litter from behind Lisa's huge wardrobe. "What are you doing?" Good Lord, Devon didn't intend for them to put Lisa's body upon that thing?

He hauled the wooden litter toward the bed, letting it clatter upon the floor. "We're going to give Lisa the burial she requested," he answered. "Are you going to help me or not?"

Brigitta was horrified. "Certainly not!" she said, feeling new tears burn her eyes. What kind of odd burial could Thora-Lisa have requested? Knowing how Lisa had dreaded having others fawn over her or even look upon her, Brigitta was afraid of the answer. "What kind of burial?" she asked lowly, not moving to do Devon's bidding.

Devon was distracted and he ran a hand along the back of his neck as though the events of the day had worn on him. If he could spare Brigitta this moment, he would, and even now he was tempted to let her stay at Vardighet and not have to witness Thora-Lisa's burial. But he and Lisa had discussed many things over the past two days: the specifics of her burial one of them. The princess had requested that both Devon and Brigitta take her body to the cliffs. She'd wanted them to be together to help each other through the difficult task. "Lisa knew two days ago her time had come for leaving this world and she told me exactly what she wanted me to do with . . . with her body. We will ride toward the cliffs and when we get there we'll toss her body over the edge." He noted the horrified expression upon her face. "Please, Brigitta, do not fight me on this. Thora-Lisa wanted to be buried in this fashion . . . she also wanted the two of us to do the deed. I like it even less than you but it is what Thora-Lisa wanted. I made a promise to her— and I will keep that promise."

Without another word, he lifted Lisa from her deathbed and gently placed her on the litter, covering her body with thick furs, and after dropping a kiss to her cool forehead, he drew them over her still, closed eyes. He glanced up at Brigitta. "Lift the other end," he instructed as though they would simply be carrying a load of dry goods and not bearing the body of a princess. "We'll exit through the secret passage and once outside you'll wait for me until I've secured a cart, then we'll ride toward the sea."

This wasn't real, Brigitta thought. Thora-Lisa wasn't actually dead, she and Devon weren't really going to toss the princess's body over some desolate cliff!

"I—I can't," she whispered, shaking her head and stepping away from the litter. "L—Lisa was a princess—she deserves a decent burial! Why all this secrecy? Erik must be told, a man of the church should be here to say prayers! I don't understand!" She was becoming hysterical again but she couldn't stop herself. "Why would Lisa want to be tossed down into the frozen sea?" She wrung her hands together nervously, hating the stillness of the room, the terrible emptiness she felt in her heart.

Although Devon mostly agreed with Brigitta's words, it was his burden to see Lisa's request carried through, and even though he had lost his dearest friend, he could not give in to his grief. He had to be strong for Brigitta's sake. Abandoning the litter, he moved to Brigitta's side in one fluid movement.

"Do you truly need to ask me why Lisa would want her body thrown over a cliff? Why she would not want the people of Vardighet to gather around her lifeless form and stare until they had had their fill?" he gently asked, stroking her hair. "Think on it, Brigitta. All her life Lisa was ridiculed and looked upon as a deformed madwoman. Besides myself and you she had no true friends at Vardighet. She has made her own peace with the Lord and now that she has entered into another world she has no use for a body that was nothing but a prison to her. I, for one, will not deny Lisa the burial she planned."

Brigitta turned her face away from Devon's. She didn't want to see his disapproval, for the truth of his words rang in her ear. Slowly, with numb limbs, Brigitta moved toward the litter and lifted one end, her stomach whirling with sick revulsion.

The following events were a blur to Brigitta as they managed to maneuver their light burden down the narrow, secret passage. She still wasn't certain the whole day wasn't a terrible nightmare as they placed Lisa's lifeless body into the back of an old cart and started away from the castle.

Night fell swiftly but the reflection of the bright moon and stars chased away the darkness and lit the world with a bluish light. Eerie. A hushed universe filled only with the sounds of the horse pulling the cart through ankle-deep snow. No solemn ceremonies, no great procession or hordes of mourners. Nothing to mark the day of Thora-Lisa's passing. Nothing. Just another night that would soon give way to another day. Life continued.

But for Brigitta, life could never be the same. It was as if another person stood beside Devon near the edge of the cliff. It wasn't Brigitta smelling the wintry air blowing in off the Baltic, feeling it whip her long hair about her neck, not she who could hear the powerful movement of water beneath the pack ice. All thought and reason had fled from her mind and she now only moved at Devon's instructions. She couldn't afford to think her actions through, for if she did she would run from this hellish night and never look back. Tears freezing on her lashes, Brigitta lifted her end of the litter, saying a prayer for forgiveness—and for Lisa's soul.

In a moment the deed was done—too fast for an action that could never be undone. Over the side of the cliff Thora-Lisa's body tumbled, the dark furs unfolding and showing a brief streak of white as it toppled toward the ice-encrusted rocks below.

Brigitta choked back a sob, watching with eyes she could not turn away, watching as Thora-Lisa's body hit the hard stone below and landed sickeningly limp upon it. Bile rose within Brigitta and she turned and spit it out along with everything else she'd eaten that day, retching as if she could purge her system of the day's cruel events.

But as she righted herself and wiped her mouth, she knew she could not. Still the wind blew, still the turbulent emotions inside of her raged. She glanced over at Devon and saw that he fared no better than she. Brigitta wanted to tell him to go ahead and cry, to scream at the unfairness of it all. But no. Devon Courtenay would never give in to his grief. He would hold all of his emotions inside and deal with Thora-Lisa's death in his own way.

Devon stood still, his face turned toward the sea, his eyes trained on the horizon, like some fierce gladiator, his legs braced wide, and his nostrils flaring as he breathed in great gusts of air. His black hair blew wildly about him and his eyes were narrowed and stormy. Brigitta found herself wanting to reach out to him, because they had each lost someone they dearly loved . . . because tonight there was only herself and Devon in the world.

He turned toward her then, staring for long seconds before Brigitta found the courage to take a step nearer to him. He, more than she, needed comfort this night and yet it was Brigitta who had dissolved into tears and nearly refused to give Lisa the burial she'd requested.

"Devon?" she whispered, taking another step. "I . . . I'm so sorry. I wish there was something I could say to you, some way in which I could lend comfort." She lifted one arm toward him, the Baltic breeze blowing the folds of her cloak behind her and lifting the hood away from her long, unbound hair. She didn't feel the biting chill of the wind, didn't notice the new rush of tears springing from her eyes. She saw only Devon standing at the edge of the cliff, his black gaze filled with pain and unbearable loneliness.

She touched his sleeve, hesitantly at first, half afraid he would shrug away from her. When he didn't move, she grew bolder, drawn to him by an unseen thread of friendship gained and lost.

Devon watched her slow approach. There were tears clinging to her lashes and rolling down her smooth cheeks. She was like a lachrymose angel drifting toward him, a vision of comfort in a world that had suddenly gone mad. In her summer-blue eyes he could see his own desolation mirrored and it pained him greatly that she should have to suffer so.

"Lisa loved you," he said hoarsely, accepting the gentle soothing of her hand on his arm. "She told me how happy your friendship made her. I am only sorry she did not summon you to Vardighet sooner. You were the brightness of her last gray days, sweet Brigitta, and for that I will be eternally grateful to you."

It was the balm of his words that broke her tenuous control. With a cry of anguish, she flung herself against his chest, her face in her hands as she sobbed uncontrollably. That she had so recently blamed Devon for Lisa's illness she now found unforgivable . . . and unbearable. Besides herself, Devon had been Lisa's truest, dearest friend; his actions of this night proved beyond a doubt he would do anything for the princess. It was Erik

Bjord who had stripped away Thora-Lisa's desperate hold on life. Erik and Erik alone had held the magic that could have cured the princess.

Devon gathered her slight body into a hard embrace, squeezing her tightly as though he could force out all the pain and grief of the past hours. Murmuring hoarse words of comfort, he held her close, smoothing her fair hair, his own heart overflowing with sorrow.

On the cliff's edge, high above their princess's battered body, they clung to each other, each seeking a sturdy mooring amid the turbulent march of a harsh life. And within each other's arms they found such a haven.

Much later, as they rode over the snow-packed ground back toward Vardighet, a swollen moon lighting their way with its bluish tint upon the mantle of white, Brigitta pondered the events of the day. She wondered if Devon's thirst for revenge against Erik Bjord would be even more keen within his breast with the princess's passing.

"What are your plans for the future now that Thora-Lisa is . . . is gone?" she asked.

Devon sat beside her, the reins held loosely in his gloved hands, the wide brim of his hat pulled low on his forehead. "They remain the same. The course of my actions has not been altered."

"No? But I had thought once Lisa married Erik she might have been of some assistance in helping you achieve your goal."

"You mean in helping me see Bjord brought low? Hardly. Lisa was against my being here, you know that. She would have done everything in her power to see Erik and I never crossed each other's path."

"What I meant to say was, I thought perhaps Lisa might have been able to locate the document you seek along with your father's ring. Surely she would have helped you secure these things so you would be able to return to your father's homeland and lay claim to your rightful heritage."

"Yes, I suppose you are right. She might have risked her own position and searched Erik's private apartments. But now, that route has been sealed by the permanence of death, never to re-open itself unto me. I must find another way."

"And that is?"

"The only thing I can do: unmask myself to Erik and face him man to man as I should have done when I first arrived at Vardighet."

His words, so solemnly spoken, struck terror in her breast. Although she herself had witnessed Devon's expertise with a sword, Erik Bjord was a renowned warrior with the awesome strength of the entire guard to stand behind him. How could Devon expect to survive such a confrontation?

"No! You cannot!" The words were torn from her lips even before she had time to consider the weight of them.

Devon heard the urgency in her voice, saw the fear in her beautifully upturned face, and he cursed again the winds of fate that had brought him to the place of his birth under such circumstances.

"I have no other choice, *kära* Brigitta. Please, do not torture yourself with worry of my safety. My childhood feud with Erik has been the bane of my life, and I knew, even as a lad of twelve fleeing under the cover of darkness, my day of reckoning with Bjord would come."

"But surely there must be some other way—"

"At the moment, I can think of none."

Brigitta sat back on the hard wood, her body being jostled as the wheels of the cart dropped into a rut created by frozen ice, then bounded out again. Devon steadied her with one arm, and even when the rut was behind them, he did not remove his hold. By slow degrees, Brigitta leaned against him, welcoming the support his solid form offered. She was bone-weary, the prospect of returning to Vardighet and informing the inhabitants of their princess's death looming before her like an ugly specter.

She would not think of such things now, she decided, nor would she think of Devon's dangerous confrontation with Erik. For there must be something she could do, once her head was clear, to aid Devon, some course of action she could take that would endanger neither his life, nor hers. Resting her head against his shoulder, she closed her eyes wondering how, in the span of only hours, she had lost a dear friend and yet, somehow, gained a deep-rooted allegiance to the mercurial Devon Courtenay.

The closeness she felt to this man, the feeling of safety she found in his arms, were results merely of her grief and fatigue brought about by the events of the day, she told herself. And her wish to see him unharmed by Erik Bjord merely a sentiment encouraged by her sense of obligation to Thora-Lisa. Surely it was imbecilic for her to think these feelings meant anything more.

As these thoughts swirled through her head, fresh tears sprang into her eyes, burning her throat, and when Devon gave her a gentle squeeze and more tears pushed past her lashes, Brigitta didn't know whether she cried for Lisa . . . or for herself.

Chapter Ten

THE FIRE IN the hearth raged, spitting and hissing as the yellowish flames danced ever higher, licking away at the kindling Brigitta threw into the center of the enclosed inferno. She was restless, her movements jerky as she stepped away from the intense heat and hugged her arms around her waist. In another hour the sun would rise and it would be her duty to inform Marta and all the others of Thora-Lisa's death. There were bound to be endless questions; questions to which Brigitta would have no answers. People would demand to know where Lisa's body now rested, would want to know why Brigitta had not summoned anyone to help the princess. How could she explain? How could she tell anyone she and Devon had tossed Lisa over a cliff and left her royal body to the ravages of nature? Also, there was the vow she made to Lisa that she would assume her role as princess. Brigitta had made a promise to her dying princess—and yet, how could she possibly do such a thing?

The latch to Brigitta's chamber lifted then and Brigitta nervously glanced up to see Devon enter. He appeared haggard, his long, unbound hair windblown and falling carelessly over his broad, velvet-clad shoulders. His eyes, so dark and brooding, reminded her of the first time she'd seen him in Thora-Lisa's chambers brandishing a sword. All the ghosts of his past had crowded in upon him this night, and Brigitta regretted the loss of the carefree soul she'd seen momentary glimpses of over the past few weeks.

She moved toward him, drawing him to the center of the room where the warmth of the fire could touch him. "Where have you been? You've been gone for hours. I—I thought perhaps you—"

"Went to seek Erik? No, although I was tempted. Fear not, Brigitta, I will not tarnish the bright memory of Thora-Lisa by slaughtering the man she loved only hours after her death." He lifted his hand to her and it was then Brigitta noticed the wrapped bundle he held. "Here," he said. "I bring you sustenance. Had I a feast of ambrosia to lay before you, I would. Alas, all I can offer is cold meat and boiled potatoes, meager portions at that."

"You ventured, unmasked, into the kitchens? But what if someone saw you?"

"What if they did? My identity will soon be known by all of Vardighet. With the rising of the sun, I shall request a private audience with Erik Bjord regardless of his approval to such a meeting."

"But if someone saw and recognized you, then Erik might not wait until morning before he alerts the entire castle to your presence!"

"Sweet Brigitta, your concern is touching, but not reassuring. I'm capable of handling Erik on my own—you need not trouble yourself with worries for my safety."

"And can you also hold off dozens of Erik's loyal men who will stand behind him? I think not. Tell me, Devon, *did anyone see you?*"

"Only one of the cooks. Anna, I think, is her name. She never cared for me as a child, and I'm sorry to say she cares less for the man I've become."

Brigitta felt the horror within her etch itself on her features. Anna, the same she had reprimanded only yesterday. "Then you must hide yourself, Devon. Anna is a spiteful old woman. If she knows you are at Vardighet, she will run to Erik with the news!"

"Let her," he replied. "It will save me the trouble of summoning him myself." He took the wrapped bundle from her and made a motion toward the narrow bed. "Come now," he instructed. "Sit down and eat. The past twenty-four hours have been taxing for you and I do not want to see you fall ill from lack of nourishment. Eat the victuals or my journey to the kitchens will have been in vain."

Brigitta did as he asked, her mind whirling with fear for Devon's life. If Anna knew Devon had come to her chambers, then the old woman would have found the perfect avenue of repaying Brigitta for the harsh words they'd exchanged.

She took only a few bites of the overcooked, tasteless meat before she dropped it back on the cloth. "I—I'm sorry. I'm just not hungry."

She heard his sigh and the jangle of his spurs as he crossed the space toward her. The bed ropes sagged with his weight as he sat down beside her. Gently, he took her chin between his thumb and forefinger, tipping her face up to his.

"Had I the power to turn back the hands of time and erase all the pain of the past, I would. Sweet Lord," he breathed, his handsome features contorting, "for involving you in my coil, I should be tortured upon the rack. I should not have told you of my purpose at Vardighet, for then you would now only have to deal with the loss of Thora-Lisa, and not carry the extra burden you do. Fear not for my safety, Brigitta. My fate was sealed long ago. You must understand that I will not rest until Erik and I have faced each other as equals."

"But you are not equals! He is a general with vast armies at his command. As long as you are at Vardighet, he will always have the upper hand, don't you see?"

"Your reasoning is correct, but you do not know Erik as I do. I bested him too many times as a lad; he will want to prove his male prowess and will forego the advantage his position gives him. He will meet me on equal ground, I am certain, just as I am certain I will be the victor." Although his words were forceful, a flicker of softness came and went in his eyes as he leaned forward to place a chaste kiss upon the tip of her nose. "Come now, enough of these lamentations," he whispered. "Our souls are heavy with the loss of

our princess, let us not find other woes to heap
upon our weary minds. Eat the food, Brigitta,
and then rest."

"I don't want to eat, and I am not tired. I . . . I
am worried for you, Devon—"

He stopped the flow of words with a gentle
finger placed upon her lips. "Hush. We'll speak no
more of Erik, vengeance, or the past . . ." Slowly,
he moved his lips to the spot his finger had just
touched, brushing his mouth atop hers in a silencing gesture. Brigitta quivered, her mouth opening
infinitesimally, and with her response his kiss
deepened, becoming passionate.

Suddenly, Brigitta was unaware of time and
space, unmindful of the dangerous outcome
should she give into the swiftly rising ardor within
her. His mouth bruised hers, slanting, burning as
he tasted deeply of the sweetness she offered, and
yet, although frightened, Brigitta could not turn
away. Fueled by utter despair and the growing fear
that she might lose Devon on the morrow, she
clung to him, sliding her hands up his broad shoulders and grasping the corded muscles there. A cry
of anguish broke in her throat, bubbling up only to
be drowned by intense kisses that bonded them
together for eternity.

Devon heard her soft murmur and sensed the
melting of her body within his embrace. He should
stop, he knew, should cease his gentle assault and
leave now while he still had command of his
senses. But he craved the taste of her. She was an
innocent, he reminded himself. But her kisses were
tantalizing in their sweetness. "Ah *kära* Brigitta,"

he breathed against her mouth. "Just utter the command and I will leave you in peace. . . ."

"No," she murmured. "Don't leave me, not now—not ever."

Her hold tightened on his neck, pulling him closer still, and all his resolve melted away on a hot tide of passion that started in his groin and burned its way up through his body.

"This is madness," he tried to reason. "You know I cannot stay within the walls of Vardighet, cannot offer you the riches you deserve."

"I have no use for riches, for I have found more enticing enchantments within your arms."

That she should be the one begging him to stay was unbelievable. Surely the roles should be reversed. But, she rationalized in a fleeting moment of sanity, Devon Courtenay, she was learning, was a man driven by self-inflicted responsibilities, a man whose boundaries of right and wrong were clearly defined.

"Stay," she murmured huskily as she kissed one sensitive corner of his smooth lips. "Stay and teach me the ways of love. Life is fleeting; precious moments as this given only sparingly. If nothing else, Lisa's death has proven this to me. Come, let us hold fast to the moment and if you must leave Sweden, then give to me a few hours on which I can draw strength."

"And if our coming together leaves you to grow heavy with a child in your womb, what then?"

She had no answer but soon realized none was necessary, for her invitation had finally scaled the wall that held him from her. With a swiftness that jolted her senses, Devon gathered her to him, plundering her mouth with hot, searing kisses that left her tingling. As one they eased back on the narrow bed, touching, seeking, finding fulfillment only they could give to each other.

With patient, practiced hands, he undid the enclosures of her garments, parting the material by slow degrees to reveal her petal-soft skin. In a matter of moments, she was unclothed, lying beside him, quivering with passion. She felt no shame in her nudity, felt nothing beyond the burgeoning of her own newly awakened desires. It was as if she'd been waiting for this man her entire life, as if this shared moment had been ordained eons ago.

Devon, his eyes soft as a velvety summer night, gazed down at her. She was exquisite, every curve and indentation of her womanly body perfect and unmarred. She was beauty taken to great heights . . . and for this moment, she was his. The incandescent light of the raging fire spread across her form, catching in its glow the sparkle of golden hair between her thighs and the fine, blonde hairs barely visible upon her legs. She nestled trustingly against him in the crook of his arm, her fingers undoing the enclosures of his doublet and her long, fair hair fanned out like a swatch of silk atop the counterpane beneath them. He aided her in divesting himself of his doublet and then his shirt and, naked to the waist, he paused a moment to pull her roughly against his chest, reveling in the feel of her breasts pressing into him.

Brigitta gasped at the contact of warm skin to warm skin. Her fingers slipped along the planes of his muscled back, blazing a trail to his sides and then up his rippled stomach and sifting through the silky hairs that covered his pectorals. Pressing her face to the base of his neck, she breathed deep of his scent, her breath coming out ragged and heated. She was burning inside, fires raging in places she'd not known she possessed feeling, and she yearned for release. She wanted, more than anything, to be a part of Devon, for Devon to be a part of her.

"Please . . ." she whispered, rubbing herself against him.

Devon smiled then lowered his mouth to hers, parting her lips with a long, deep kiss that shook her to the very core. His fingers brushed across her abdomen, hovering for a fraction of a second above the triangle of hair at the apex of her thighs until, with gentle but firm pressure, he closed his hand atop her.

Brigitta moaned in sweet agony, her hips straining upward of their own accord. Her heartbeat strummed wildly in her ears and she was moist in anticipation for him. Surely her reactions were wanton, immoral. . . .

But her fears were soon drowned in a flood of intense pleasure as Devon's hand moved upon her, parting, stroking, coaxing her into a maddening realm of boundless pleasure. She stiffened, then relaxed as his fingers probed deeper and his gentle rhythm grew rough, intoxicating her senses. The feelings were wondrous, exquisite, but still, something was lacking. There was an ache within her that could be assuaged only by him, with him.

Brigitta clasped his face between both hands, her blue, blue gaze intense, as she whispered, "I want you Devon. I want to be a part of you."

He let forth a low growl with her words, his mouth swooping down to capture her pouty, lower lip between his teeth. "And I want you, sweet Brigitta—how I want you . . ."

The crash of splintering wood muffled his words. In one fluid movement of trained muscle, Devon pushed himself upright, springing to his feet and shielding Brigitta's naked body from the sea of intruders who barged into the chamber. Six men of the castle guard, faces impassive, and armed to the teeth, filed into the small room, their sights trained on Devon.

Undaunted, Devon stood his ground. "Cover yourself," he ordered curtly to Brigitta over his shoulder.

She did as he commanded, scrambling up the bed to gather the covers over her while she did her best to dress beneath the meager shelter. It was a difficult task, and when she attempted to shove her arms into the sleeves of her gown, the counterpane nearly fell away from her body. Hastily, she ducked totally beneath the covers and jammed the material over her head and arms all the while straining to hear what was going on.

"What is the meaning of this?" she heard Devon demand. There came, in answer, the jangle of spurred boots atop the stone as another man entered the chamber. Even before she thrust the covers from her way, she knew Erik Bjord had learned of Devon's presence at Vardighet.

"There he is! Didn't I tell you you'd find him here, General?"

It was an old woman's voice, familiar and unwelcome, Brigitta heard. She snatched away the covers and glanced up to see the tall, imposing figure of Erik. Anna, the cook, stood directly behind him.

"So, we meet again," Erik drawled in his native tongue, his lazily-hooded eyes resting on Devon. "The last time I entered this chamber you were a mere lad of twelve, sniveling at your mother's feet. Once again I find you pawing at a woman's skirts. You'll forgive me, won't you, for intruding?"

"Is it forgiveness you seek, Erik, or something more?"

"You of all people should know the answer to that."

Devon, his molded, bared torso gleaming bronze in the firelight, held his ground. "You know why I am here, Bjord. Call off your guard and we will deal with the matter, just you and I."

"But why should I when I can easily let my loyal men do the deed for me?"

With merely a nod from Erik, the guards moved in on Devon. Seeing their intent, Brigitta screamed, lunging off the bed in an attempt to shield Devon from harm, but she was no sooner on her feet than one of the guards grabbed her by the arm and yanked her back, roughly pushing her against the cedar wardrobe. She hit it with a thud, the air escaping her lungs with a *whoosh* as she slithered helplessly to the floor.

Devon fared no better than she. Even though

one guard suffered a split lip and swollen eye and another nursed a broken jaw, Devon had been subdued, mercilessly beaten by four of the guards and was now being dragged away.

"No!" Brigitta screamed, rising to her feet.

Erik turned toward her, an odd mix of revulsion and wanting in his eyes. "No? You, a lowly servant of the princess, dare to tell the general no?" He laughed then, a sick sound. "Save your theatrics, Brigitta Lind, for you will need them when I return to you from the tower. It matters naught to me you are Lisa's companion; this day I shall punish you for your lust for Devon Courtenay. But not before I've had a sampling of your sweetness. Surely, giving yourself to a general should reap more rewards than to a bastard?"

With those words ringing in her ears, Erik Bjord left her.

Numbly, Brigitta sank down into a heap upon the hard, cold floor, her body trembling uncontrollably. She had to do something to aid Devon! But what could she do? Erik had been right in labeling her a lowly servant. There was no one in Vardighet to whom she could turn, no one who had the power or even any reason to help her. Thora-Lisa had been her only claim to worthiness here, the only voice in her life that held any weight—but Thora-Lisa was gone, taken away in death.

With such thoughts, Brigitta's head snapped up. Lisa was dead, but save Devon and herself, no one else at Vardighet knew of the princess's passing.

A plan began to form in her mind, and with it echoed Thora-Lisa's dying words: *Take my place as princess.*

No! She couldn't possibly, she thought vehemently.

But what else could she do? *Was* there another way to aid Devon? Until the day of Lisa's marriage to Erik, Lisa's word would be rule at Vardighet. There would be no one to deny any of her requests, and of course, it would be well known to all that, as children, Devon and Thora-Lisa had been close companions. It would not be such an odd request if Thora-Lisa were to demand that Devon Courtenay be set free.

In the end, Brigitta realized that she had no choice. If she was to save Devon's life, then she must don Thora-Lisa's hiding veils and use the princess's powers to release him from Erik's wrath.

For Devon, Brigitta would do anything.

Chapter Eleven

THERE WERE FOUR towers in all at Vardighet: one tower containing Erik's cabinet and Thora-Lisa's apartments along with her drawing room, Brigitta's small chamber, and two extra chambers used as storage; the second tower was a theater tower used mainly by Erik and his comrades; and the last two towers in the south range served as ordinary defense towers, completing the hexagonal shape of Vardighet.

Brigitta, hastily dressed in one of Thora-Lisa's

royal gowns, now rushed toward the extreme southern tower, for it was here, far from the residential quarters, Erik closeted any wrongdoers, torturing them slowly, delighting in their cries of anguish. Brigitta had heard many stories of how Erik Bjord, brave warrior that he was, enjoyed dragging hapless souls back to Vardighet where he could strap them to the wheel and watch their eyes pop out of their sockets. Then, of course, Brigitta had only listened to the gossip with half an ear, not truly believing the general could be so cruel.

Now, as she scurried along the dimly lit passages, she wished fervently that she'd listened more closely to the stories. How could she find Devon when she had only a vague idea of where she was going? Rounding a sharp bend, she came to an abrupt halt, drawing in a sharp breath beneath Lisa's hiding veils. There, before her, was a massive oak door with one guard posted as sentry. The ultimate test of her life loomed before her. Would the guard believe she was the princess, or would he call her bluff and strap her to the wheel beside Devon. In the end it would not matter. If Devon were to die, her own life would be empty and incomplete.

Squaring her shoulders, she stepped forward into the light the meager torch offered. "You there," she called out in imperious tones.

The guard, who had not heard her approach and was even now leaning lazily against the door with eyes closed, snapped to attention. His mouth dropped open at the sight of Brigitta in the princess's garb before he bowed in a deep genuflection, murmuring, somewhat dazedly, "Your Highness . . ."

Brigitta allowed herself a moment of gathering her wits. To have someone bow before her, a peasant girl, was unsettling. She sought Thora-Lisa's soft but commanding tones.

"Arise and tell me if you've a prisoner by the name of Devon Courtenay."

"Yes, Your Highness, I do but—"

"Very well. I bid you bring him before me."

"Release him? Pardon me, gracious Princess, but it is my duty to keep the prisoner locked in the tower until—"

"By whose order?" she demanded, interrupting him. To her memory, Thora-Lisa had never used such a harsh voice. But it could not be helped; she could not waste moments portraying a sickly princess who would have no doubt employed gentler tactics to seek Devon's release.

"General Bjord's orders, of course."

"*I* am the princess of Vardighet and to you my word is law. If you do not wish to feel the full weight of my vengeance, you will obey my command. Release Devon Courtenay. Now."

The guard was already fumbling with a heavy ring of keys, inserting one in the lock and opening the panel. Within moments, he stepped back into Brigitta's line of vision, Devon at his side.

Brigitta experienced a moment of extreme relief. Devon was not dead—yet. He stood before her, gloriously alive, bare-chested, his long dark hair falling carelessly atop his broad shoulders. There was a nasty bruise even now deepening to a

bluish-black along his jawline and he sported a
fierce cut above his right eye, but other than these
injuries he appeared well enough.

At the sight of her clothed in Lisa's veils and
finery, his black eyes widened then narrowed. She
stopped, with an imperious nod of her head, any
words he might utter.

"You will follow me," she commanded, then
with a dismissive glance toward the guard, she
turned and led the way through the narrow passages.

Their footfalls echoed in the eerily lit space,
bouncing from stone to stone with such intensity
Brigitta thought surely the entire castle would hear
their escape. They had traveled no more than five
minutes' time before Devon, hurrying behind Brigitta, grabbed her gently by the shoulders, halting
her progress. Swiftly, he whirled her around, his
arms dropping to catch her at the waist.

"Sweet Christ," he breathed. "I thought I was
seeing a ghost—you look so much like her. You
take great risk in donning Lisa's veils."

"Not so great as the risk you take in discussing
the adventure here, in this passage," she replied
distractedly. "Come, Devon, we've no time to
waste. Dawn is only moments away and with the
rising of the sun, Erik will no doubt be coming to
visit his prisoner—"

Devon silenced her frantic rush of words with
the touch of his hand at the base of her throat.
Gently, his thumb smoothed over the delicate skin,
pausing for a moment, atop the spot where her
pulse beat erratically. Then, with tender care, he
lifted her veils, pulling the material away to plant a

possessive, burning kiss atop her pliant mouth. "Thank you," he murmured against her lips. "Thank you . . ."

Even though every nerve in her was alive with the danger of their situation, Brigitta allowed herself the brief pleasure of such contact. As an antidote to her distress, it was incomparable.

His lips, so full and soft, bruised hers with fevered insistence, and his tongue, as it darted out to entwine with her own, ignited baser instincts within her. Her hands, trapped between them as she'd attempted to deny them such closeness, pressed against his hard, muscled chest. She was acutely aware of the soft, springy hairs beneath the pads of her fingertips, aware also of the hammering of his heart. Flashes of their too-brief interlude within her chamber danced before her eyes, and she felt once again the heady anticipation for his touch that she had experienced not so long ago.

"No," she said, half to herself, half to him. "We mustn't tarry. Your—your life is in danger."

"And yours, Brigitta, if you would only stop to consider your own welfare. I thank you from the bottom of my heart for donning Lisa's attire, but if you are found out, your life will not be spared."

"Then why do we stand here discussing such things? We must flee at once!"

Devon emitted a low laugh against the shell of her ear. "You need ask why I had to stop and take you into my arms? We have unfinished business, you and I. Damn Erik Bjord for once again snatching something dear from me."

They did indeed have unfinished business, Brigitta thought, the note of promise in his voice thrilling her. Fueled by her own selfish desire to be alone with him in safer territory, and by the imminent danger, she pushed him gently away, smoothing her veils back in place.

Devon took her lead, satisfied, for the moment, to leave amorous pursuits for another time. "Come," he said. "I know of a lesser known route to Lisa's chambers." He took her hand and the two of them started off.

Brigitta soon became confused as to the direction they took, for Devon directed her this way then that. Surprisingly, they met no one, not even on the stairs leading to the princess's apartments, and once behind the closed door panel in Lisa's rooms, Brigitta began to worry that Devon's rescue had been absurdly easy. Standing in the middle of Lisa's chamber, Brigitta wrapped her arms about her waist as she tried desperately to calm her nerves. Not twenty-four hours ago, she had been in this room and watched her dear friend pass away. The chamber was cold and empty without the gentle presence of the princess to warm it.

If Devon was concerned either with Lisa's absence or of his own danger, he made no outward show of it. Immediately, he knelt to lay a fire in the cold hearth, using the poker until a small flame took hold.

"What are you doing?" Brigitta asked, casting off her sadness and letting her mourning be overtaken with concern for Devon's safety. Later, when there was time for peace, she would mourn her princess's passing. "We should leave at once through the secret passage. Surely you do not intend to stay here?"

"Where else would you have me stay?"

She heard the dangerous tone of his voice and knew then that he had never planned to leave Vardighet—not without accomplishing his mission.

"I did not rescue you from the tower so you could be impaled upon Erik's blade! I won't let you do this, Devon; it is much too dangerous for you to stay within these walls."

"I will leave," he replied, his back toward her as he crouched before the fire, "only when I have what rightfully belongs to my family."

"And Erik will subdue you the same way he did this morning. He has only to snap his fingers and his guards will surround you. You are a skilled fighter but your skill is no match for twenty armed men!"

The poker clattered to the hard floor, echoing in the chamber as Devon came to a stand. "I am well aware of the facts, Brigitta. That is why I plan to create a diversion of sorts. I may yet reap the spoils if the aid I seek is granted."

Suddenly wary, she asked, "What aid? What are you talking about?"

He smiled then, shaking his head as he strolled toward her, a dangerous glint in his ebony eyes. "No . . . no longer will I involve you in my troubles. It is best if you do not know, for if you are knowledgeable of my secrets then you become a clear target for Erik. Ignorance, they say, can be bliss and in your case it will offer you a mantle of protection." Coming to a standstill before her, he reached up to undo the heavy veils and head-covering she wore. Her hair, piled atop her head, spilled down around her shoulders in a shimmering rain and Devon ran his fingers through the silky tresses as he whispered, "Let us not waste precious time with questions that must ever be denied answers." Her hair entwined in his fingers, he tightened his hold and pulled her face to his. "Let us continue where we left off when we were so rudely interrupted. . . ."

Slowly, he lowered his mouth to hers, slanting his lips over hers in a hot, provocative kiss that melted any resistance she might have offered. Over and over, his mouth played atop hers, teasing the sensitive corners, bruising the pouty bow until, maddened by passion, his tongue darted out and entwined with her own.

Brigitta suddenly became bereft of will, a mindless creature whose only thoughts were of surrendering to the overwhelming fires of desire just his nearness kindled within her. There was no time for such dalliance, but her senses, once ignited, could not be denied. She was not a wanton, and yet, even without the vows of marriage, she wanted desperately to share with Devon the wondrous delights of love. With a slight whimper, she succumbed to the heady power of his seductions, reaching up to wrap her arms about his neck.

He lifted her in his arms then, intent on carrying her to the huge, fur-covered bed, but once at its side could not lay her down.

"No," he murmured. "Not here." With one hand he ripped the top fur from its surface and then turned back toward the hearth, tossing the fur to the floor and placing Brigitta gently down upon it.

Devon gazed deeply into her eyes, his own soft as a velvety night. "I'll be gentle," he whispered. "The first time brings but a moment of pain." And with that vow, he reached to help her out of her clothing.

For Brigitta, the moments before dawn passed by in a haze of wondrous delights. Devon was as tender as he promised, bringing her to the peak of ecstasy again and again even before he entered her. With hands and lips skillful in the act of lovemaking, he explored every curve and dip of her heated body, stroking her to great heights of pleasure.

And Brigitta did her own exploring as her passions were awakened. Her hands moved over strong, corded muscle that was hidden by smooth skin. His chest was well-defined and covered with a matting of dark hair. She ran her fingers through the surprisingly soft hairs, following, with one long fingernail, the narrowing line which led to his nether regions. At his low growl of pleasure, she smiled. His broad chest led to tapered haunches, which led to thighs thick with muscle, and once to his thighs, Brigitta boldly caressed them. She had never imagined a man could be so beautiful. She could hear his breathing, could smell the masculine musk of his body, and decided he was all the world she needed or wanted. Her body was beginning to sing a siren's song as his skillful hands played sensually over her, touching and teasing, bringing to her never before felt sensations. Brigitta had never imagined such exquisite pleasure.

With a low growl, Devon moved his lean body

atop of hers, his member hard as he lowered himself, and Brigitta moved toward him, opening like a flower to the morning sun. The once-warm fires within her were now beginning to rage, and she craved a release from the sweet torment he created. In a moment, he was inside of her and after a brief burning pain there was a budding of pleasant sensations that, with each wonderful thrust, built into wild, strumming ones that carried Brigitta away. She was soon soaring on a rushing wind that was Devon's breath in her ear, and every nerve in her was alive—tingling and wavering. Each touch of his lips pulled her higher, every thrust of his hips thrilled her. He was all she could want, he with his hard male body and skillful ways of pleasing her. Brigitta clung tightly to him, scaling a height she had never been before and when she shuddered and at last cried out her ecstasy, she felt him move one last, glorious time within her, then he, too, shuddered and was still.

A sweet eternity passed before Devon moved. Gently, he rolled to one side, bringing her against his body and stroking her with warm fingers, the afterglow of their love touching them both.

Brigitta sighed delightedly as a wave of intense feeling washed over her. She was Devon's woman now. And, she realized with a sort of dazed wonderment, she loved him. For good or bad Brigitta had just given herself to him forever. . . .

"To my regret, I must leave you now."

Brigitta, her head resting on his broad shoulder as she nestled against his hard form, pushed herself up, eyes wide. "What?" she breathed. "Leave me? No! You—you cannot . . . not now!"

He silenced her with a kiss, then explained, "You misunderstand me. I do not intend to leave you here at Vardighet where Erik can give vent to his rage and punish you for assuming Lisa's role. I only mean I must go now and see to adequate transportation for you. I have a man to meet in the South and I must ride hard and fast to make the crucial engagement. You could not endure such a strenuous trip, so I will secure you a horse and cart along with a driver who will escort you to one of the small *byalags* along the coast. You will wait for me there until I can come to you."

Something in his voice alarmed her. If she allowed him to leave, *would he truly return to her?*

"But who are you going to meet?" she asked, fearful of staying at Vardighet alone. But if she were to carry out Thora-Lisa's request of assuming the role of princess—as she must—then she would have to do so alone.

"Hush," he said, placing a finger to her lips. "You must trust me. Quickly now. We've tarried too long already." He stood and pulled her up beside him. "Pack yourself some warm clothes— take Lisa's if you must. I don't think you should return to your own chamber, it is too risky. When you've gathered some things together, leave through the secret passage. The cart and driver will be waiting for you." He turned away as he spoke, gathering his clothes and hastily donning them.

Brigitta bent to retrieve her own scattered garments, her mind awhirl. She couldn't leave, and yet, how could she stay at Vardighet without Devon? Her hands trembled as she dressed. Life could be so cruel. She had only found Devon and had been awakened to the beauty of love, and now he was leaving her—just as Lisa had left her. Tears in her eyes, she whispered, "You—you do intend to come back for me. You . . . you will not forget me?" Surely, they could, somehow, find a way to be together.

"Ah, Brigitta, my sweetness, my light, how can you doubt me?" He pulled her to him in a tight embrace, holding her so securely, as if he could brand the feel of her body to his memory. "I must go now."

He kissed her one last time, and then he was gone.

Brigitta stood motionless for a full minute. She was alone, utterly alone. Her vow to Thora-Lisa clamped about her like a gripping trap. "Godspeed, Devon," she whispered brokenly.

Feebly, she began gathering a few of Lisa's gowns, knowing in her heart that she couldn't actually leave without fulfilling Lisa's request. There was a loud knock upon the door panel. All her motions ceased as she stood holding her breath, praying whoever it was would go away. Seconds passed. The knocking grew louder, bolder. Frightened beyond belief, wrapped bundle in hand, Brigitta raced toward the secret passage.

She made it as far as Thora-Lisa's bed.

The portal swung wide, banging against hard stone as Erik Bjord strode angrily into the chamber.

"Thora-Lisa!" he boomed. "What madness possessed you to free the bastard Devon Courtenay from my tower?"

Brigitta halted in her steps. The bundle fell from her nerveless fingers, hitting the floor with barely a sound. Before Erik could see the evidence of her flight, she kicked the bundle behind the bed. Thora-Lisa's veils lay atop the rumpled furs, out of reach.

Her mind wheeled with fright, her thoughts skidding in all directions before she gained enough composure to think clearly. She would be killed, she knew, for her deception.

Without turning, she spoke. "You come unannounced and without my leave. I demand that you leave this chamber at once."

To her astonishment, Erik Bjord only gave a harsh laugh in answer. "You know better than to disobey me, Lisa. Your head must still be filled with the same sickness that urged you from your bed to free your childhood friend. I will have an answer to my question, and I will have it now."

So this was the fashion in which the warrior had treated the gentle princess. The reality angered Brigitta and she forgot her own perilous position. "How dare you enter my chambers unannounced! It is barely dawn and I've not yet affixed my veils. You will leave me and let me finish my dressing."

"I go nowhere until I have the answers I seek. I will indulge you only so far as turning my back. There," he said. "My back is turned. Hurry and cover yourself lest I grow impatient."

Brigitta bowed her head and chanced a peek at him over her shoulder. His back was indeed turned

to her, and he was alone. It was not possible for
her to dart through the passage while he wasn't
looking, for he would hear the door open and
would then follow her. Brigitta knew not how far
Devon had gotten and she would do nothing to
put his life in further jeopardy. And also, she knew
she could not leave Vardighet without fulfilling
Lisa's last request. Without further hesitation, she
snatched up the veils and headcovering, whipping
them over her face and head and securing them.
That done, she turned to face the general's wrath,
her only strength in the knowledge that, as long as
Erik and Lisa had not wed, Lisa's word was supreme. There was nothing Erik Bjord could do to
the princess.

"You may face me now, Erik," she replied,
amazed at the tone of her own voice. It was as if
Thora-Lisa were speaking the words and not Brigitta Lind. The weeks spent as Lisa's companion
had reaped Brigitta more than a deep friendship;
they brought her now intimate knowledge of the
princess and her thoughts, words, and actions.
She lifted her chin defiantly and gazed at the general with cold eyes. "You, of all people, should
know why I released Devon Courtenay," she began, knowing she must not let this man think he
had frightened her. "As children he was my closest
ally, his mother a faithful servant to my mother. It
is abhorrent to think you would lock him away in
the tower. Did you believe I would stand idly by
and let you do what you would with him?"

Erik, dressed in coarse buff-colored breeches,
brown shirt, and jerkin, raised a bushy blond brow
at her imperious tones. Then he smiled, obviously

amused with her show of hauteur. "Truth be known, I did not take pause to consider your reactions. You surprise me, Lisa. I had thought you to be sick and confined to these chambers, when in reality you are quite capable of rising with the sun and venturing about. Tell me, who informed you of Courtenay's imprisonment?"

She was growing weary of their conversation. She did not dare take a step near him for he might see past her disguise, nor was she certain she could continue in the vein she was, for her knowledge of Lisa and Erik's past was meager at best. She had to end this conversation.

"It matters not."

"I've no doubt it was your trustworthy companion, Brigitta Lind, who came rushing to your bedside with the news. Did she also tell you I found her in Courtenay's arms, naked? Your servant is a fallen woman, Lisa, and I'll not suffer her presence within these walls. She is unfit to serve you."

Brigitta was thankful for the veils that covered her suddenly hot face. To have Erik Bjord say such things about her moments with Devon was too much to bear. "Brigitta Lind is *my* servant. You, Erik, have no say in the matter. Besides," she added, seeing the dangerous glint in his blue eyes, "she—she is gone. She . . . she fled after telling me of Devon's plight. I—I believe she was afraid of your wrath."

This seemed to please Erik. "And what of Devon Courtenay? Did he flee also, or have you tucked him away in some safe haven?"

"Devon is . . . is gone. We parted ways once I released him from the tower."

"Gone?" he repeated harshly. Anger contorted his features Brigitta had found so handsome not long ago. He swore beneath his breath, turning to slam the portal shut and then pace the confines of Lisa's chamber. "You should not have interfered!" he bellowed. "Devon Courtenay is a threat to all the inhabitants of Vardighet! He is a worm who has burrowed its way into our core! You've done a foolish thing, Lisa. Courtenay has been at Vardighet for some weeks now, he has walked our passages pretending to be some French fop, using his disguise to gain secrets of our defense! He has befriended a number of my men, cajoling them until they shared with him the secrets of my battle plans. The man knows far too much about our military strategies and I'm certain he will carry this knowledge to the Danes. I've no doubt he is even now on his way to Jorgen in the South, ready to whisper my defense strategies in the man's ear."

"Jorgen?" Brigitta whispered, caught up in Erik's words. *I've a man to meet in the South, one who will help aid in my quest to see Erik Bjord brought low. . . .* Devon's words echoed in her mind. Could it be possible that Devon had truly meant to share Erik's strategies with a Dane? The thought was abhorrent. All her life, Brigitta had been raised to hate and fear the Danes. They had killed many of her people and were the constant scourge of her beautiful homeland. If a villager was not touched directly by a Dane's hand, then he was stripped of his provision and coins that were used to aid Sweden's vast armies sent to fight the Danes. That Devon could stoop to such a hateful measure was beyond belief.

"No," she whispered. "Devon would not lend assistance to Jorgen. Vardighet was his birthplace, he would not aid in our downfall!"

Erik seemed not to hear her as he sank into the chair before the hearth. Moodily, he stared at the licking flames, the firelight dancing and catching in the blue orbs of his eyes and shimmering against the blond tresses of his long hair.

"I must send word to my troops at once," he said, half to himself. "But even if the weather is mild, the journey will be a long one. Courtenay will no doubt have reached Jorgen long before my men can be alerted—we will suffer heavy losses, I will have to send in reinforcements. . . ." He continued muttering to himself, thinking through his strategies as he gazed into the hearth.

And Brigitta, feeling sick at the news, sank down onto Lisa's bed, her right hand reaching up to cover her veiled mouth.

Erik remained in the chamber for nearly an hour as he mulled over his course of action. The stressful minutes ticked by for Brigitta. She didn't dare speak, and in truth, she hadn't the power to form any words or decide how she was to get away from Erik. She could only think of Devon riding hard toward the South, toward the Danish general, Jorgen. *How could he?* she asked herself over and over. It would not be Erik who would suffer. It would be her own people whose blood would be shed, and perhaps even her own village would be raided by the Danes.

Finally, Erik rose to leave, his face grim. "You have done us all a terrible injustice this day, Lisa. As princess, you should safeguard your people, but you have, by releasing Devon Courtenay, brought about our demise. You should pray for forgiveness."

Brigitta had no words of anger to fling at him. Instead, she was filled with deep revulsion at Devon . . . and herself. When the door panel was closed she bent to gather up her wrapped bundle of clothes, needing to hear from Devon's own lips that he had no intention of consorting with Jorgen. Then she quickly exited through the secret passage, tears blurring her vision.

Later, she wondered why she'd even shed tears, for there was no cart and driver waiting for her as Devon had promised; there were only the tracks in the snow where he had fled from Vardighet. . . .

Brigitta, not knowing what else to do, turned and reentered the passage, making her way slowly back to Lisa's rooms. She had just arrived when Marta entered, chattering away with castle gossip. Brigitta was too numb to worry if the older woman could see through her disguise. She no longer cared. That Marta seemed to believe Brigitta was Thora-Lisa was only a slight balm to Brigitta's broken heart.

"Will you be wanting your morning meal now, Princess?" the lady-in-waiting asked.

Brigitta looked up from her sad thoughts. *Princess*, Marta had said. The word sounded odd, but yet, not so odd. Again, Brigitta was reminded of Thora-Lisa's final demand for her to take Lisa's place.

Without another thought, Brigitta replied, "Yes, I think I will eat now. Have a tray brought up to my apartments."

BOOK II

❧❧

The Princess

Chapter Twelve

Nervousness had now become her constant companion, and though the sun dappled the world outside her window and her every wish was instantly granted, Brigitta felt she might near break from the strain of having to walk in the shoes of Thora-Lisa. She was not certain she could take another day of answering to the name she knew belonged to a person dead, a person who should rightfully be mourned! Her nightmares were many in the large bed she alone knew had been Thora-Lisa's deathbed, and the waking hours were even more torturous.

The clothes she wore, the same she had silently altered in the privacy of her rooms, seemed to echo the very name of the silent, gentle being who had worn them briefly before her. It was with great difficulty that she donned the ice-blue satin with its fur-lined interior and listened to the constant drone of Marta's talk of how beautiful Erik would think she was.

"You are much more vibrant," Marta said as she twisted Brigitta's hair and wound it in a comely cascade of curls at the nape of her neck. "Your eyes look more blue."

Indeed, thought Brigitta. *My eyes should look more blue—everything about me should look more something or less something!* Her guilt weighed heavy on her mind and she wondered for the thousandth time why she had ever taken Thora-Lisa's place. The idea was ludicrous! But she had made a promise to Lisa, and even more important, her position as princess made her privy to news of Erik's comings and goings. So far, no word had been had about Devon or whether or not Erik's men had hunted him down. As far as Brigitta knew, he was safely away from Vardighet—and had not, as word had it, gone to the Danish general, Jorgen. Brigitta was glad of this, for she did want to believe Devon capable of such an act. But he sent no word to her, and had never sent for her.

She had considered slipping away under the cover of darkness in hopes of finding Devon, but she'd decided against such a measure. Devon had wanted only two things from Vardighet: his father's ring and the document proving his parents had married before his birth.

"Your hair," Marta observed, cutting into Brigitta's thoughts, "it is gaining its old luster and becoming thick again."

Brigitta closed her eyes briefly. "Yes," she

agreed. What else was she to say? "I feel much better."

But in fact Brigitta felt much worse than she ever had. Her only friend was gone from Vardighet, taken from her in death, and the only man she loved had left her. Her future seemed fraught with pitfalls, and every day she was reminded by her conscience that she was living a lie. Could she, she wondered, escape without much fuss to her parents' home? Would they take her in, be able to protect her? Would Devon return for her?

"General Bjord awaits," Marta announced as she stepped back and admired the curls she had created with comb and brush.

Brigitta sighed beneath the veil she was now sentenced to wear. She could scarcely breathe beneath its heavy texture and she had a new respect for Thora-Lisa, one of many within the wake of the young woman's death. Brigitta rose from her chair, forgetting to act the invalid as she patted her curls and said a quick dismissal to Marta. "Very well," she said. "I shall descend on my own."

"But I could not—"

"No," replied Brigitta a bit too harshly. She meant no hurt feelings for Marta, but her head was buffeted with a raging headache and she dreaded the moments she must be near Erik. What if he recognized her? Would she be flogged? "I shall descend alone," she said on a kinder note and was glad when Marta bowed away. She was finally left alone in the large chamber. More candles were lit than Thora-Lisa had probably ever seen lit in her entire life, and although Brigitta knew Thora-Lisa would not have commanded it, the windows had been opened to allow a substantial amount of air into the clustered rooms. Fresh air—fresh *something* was what Brigitta needed!

The ice-blue satin clung to her heaving bosom and the precious gems at her throat hung too heavily. Surely among the crowd of many someone would notice that her breasts were uncommonly large, that she was a shade of an inch taller, her hips more rounded, her hair longer, thicker, blonder than what they were used to seeing on the frame of Thora-Lisa?

She shivered, forcing herself to go along with the charade, forcing herself to move when she didn't want to move. The stairs, one after the other, brought her closer to the person she dreaded meeting. Erik's voice, loud among the many others and sounding slightly slurred, carried to her through dimly lit passages. As she entered the great hall, Brigitta heard the hush of disbelief. She wondered if she played the part of Thora-Lisa that badly or that well. As Erik stood and came toward her, she still hadn't decided. He said nothing as he held out his arm, thick with muscle, and Brigitta laid a trembling hand upon it, trying hard to keep her head high, to not despise the man who could have, in her mind, saved Thora-Lisa from death.

"You look lovely this night, Lisa," Erik said lowly as they walked together toward their appointed chairs. People curtsied and bowed as they passed them, but Brigitta did not acknowledge them. This hall was filled with people who had never bothered to show Thora-Lisa any spark of warmth or friendship. They had tolerated her presence only because Lisa had been a princess. To the devil with them all, Brigitta decided. Especially Erik!

"Marta has sent word you are feeling much better these days," Erik continued once they were seated. Servants moved quietly around them, placing dishes in front of Erik but leaving her place bare, as was Lisa's custom. Lisa had more often than not eaten alone.

"Could it be," Erik asked, piercing a piece of tender reindeer with his knife and shoving the food in his mouth, "that by our wedding day you will be totally recovered?" His eyes were bloodshot, the lids heavy over the blue orbs, and his gaze was like that of a lazy predator.

By the time *their* wedding day arrived, Brigitta planned to be far away.

"Perhaps," Brigitta murmured, uncomfortable with how often he looked at her. Could he detect a difference in his bride-to-be? Brigitta fidgeted.

The room was full of odors and sputtering candlelight, and higher up, near the rafters, were a score of flying birds. She felt a slight air brush by her, but it was not enough to chase away the other smells and she thought she would suffocate beneath the pretty veil draped pleasingly across her fine features. How could Thora-Lisa have endured it, she wondered?

The evening went by in a blur. The entertainment came and went and many of the men became drunk, some of the women following suit. Abruptly, Brigitta stood, not caring if Erik noticed her absence or not. He was much too preoccupied with his gathering of followers circled around him listening to his drunken tales of battle. With a quick step, she left the great hall and headed toward her own chamber. No one tried to stop her or even bade her a good night. It was no wonder Thora-Lisa had been so desperately lonely.

Her room was pleasantly warm due to the great fire in the hearth. "Shall I help you prepare for bed?" Marta asked, coming inside the chamber behind Brigitta.

Brigitta shook her head, uncomfortable in Marta's presence. Surely Marta would soon discover that Brigitta was not Thora-Lisa! "No. I won't be needing you this evening. You may be excused," she said and noted the look of surprise in Marta's face. Marta obviously wanted to be in Lisa's favor once again now that Brigitta was supposedly gone from Vardighet. With a confused look, Marta left Brigitta alone.

Only four days ago Lisa's body had been discovered at the bottom of the seaside cliff but it had been so badly disfigured from hitting the hard rocks that no one had been able to identify the person. Many of the people at Vardighet believed the body was Brigitta Lind's since news had spread that the princess's newest companion had run away. Brigitta decided the course of events had been exactly what Thora-Lisa must have planned. Lisa had *wanted* her body to be smashed upon the rocks so that no mortal would ever be able to see the face she had always hidden beneath the veils. But what Lisa must have never considered was Brigitta's family and their reaction to Brigitta's "death."

Brigitta knew she could not send word to her

family that she was actually alive and living the life of a princess. So she had done the only thing she could do. She had sent to them large amounts of coin, letting them believe the gifts were from Thora-Lisa because of their daughter's loyal service. It was a balm, although small, for Brigitta to know her family would be well taken care of. She forced herself to think of the good things the money would bring—but even that thought was not enough. All Brigitta could see was her mother's tearstained face and her father's impassive, but clearly grief-stricken one. No amount of coin could blot out their hurt and this troubled Brigitta. She wanted nothing more than to go home to them. But she could not. She would play out the charade for as long as it took her to aid Devon in his quest, for then perhaps he would return to her.

The weeks passed, blending into time suspended by guilt, by promise, and Brigitta's worry for Devon increased with each passing day. What had happened to him? Why didn't he return? She spent her hours restlessly, pacing her apartments and barely touching the food brought to her. She couldn't leave Vardighet in search of Devon, but then, she could not stay within the castle walls either. It seemed she was bound by her loyalty, for she had told Devon she would help him but she had also made a vow to Thora-Lisa.

To Brigitta's horror, Erik began calling on her frequently, and only twenty-four hours ago he had announced that the day of their marriage had been moved to a closer date. He was soon to be taking his men on another march and he wanted to make Lisa his wife before he left for battle! Brigitta fervently prayed Devon would return before then. Perhaps, even if he did not love her, he would surely be willing to snatch Erik's bride-to-be from the altar. For even if he did not want to marry her, he would at least help her escape.

But Devon did not return and Brigitta was kept from fleeing by a number of servants who were in and out of her apartments hurriedly preparing for the wedding. Life became madness, a sick nightmare that wore on and on.

Her wedding day dawned bright and bitterly cold, and although all the guests had been snugly planted into their rooms days ago, Brigitta was up and worrying furiously. She half-expected Devon to miraculously appear and spirit her to safety. Just as she was about to run to the secret passage and scurry to an uncertain freedom, Marta and two other women entered the chambers and began to dress Brigitta in her wedding wear—the very clothes, the very act she dreaded more than the plague! Too soon she was bound and tucked into a vision of white silk and satin with her usual veils covering her face, and her hair gathered in a simple but elegant curls. She nearly choked on the image she saw in the looking glass before her. Her eyes were cold, blue as the frozen Baltic was beneath its layer of ice, and she knew, as she gazed at her reflection, that she could not, *would* not go through with the ceremony!

But no avenue of escape presented itself and so, with a sinking feeling in her heart—as a trout must feel when finally snared on a fisherman's line—she left her rooms, and the great tide of events swept her along.

Richly attired and surrounded by a bevy of servants, Brigitta let herself be helped into her carriage that would transport her to the cathedral, to the altar where she would be expected to say her vows and then be forever bound to Erik Bjord.

Despite the chill in the air, Brigitta felt overly warm and it took a great amount of effort to keep herself from pushing away the many hands that reached out seemingly all at once to help her to her seat, to fix her lap robes, or to brush a bit of snow from the hem of her *merveilleux* satin dress. She breathed a small sigh of relief when the carriage door was shut and she was finally left to her own thoughts. Snow was falling in large, white flakes and the sky overhead was dove gray. Brigitta closed her eyes, leaning her head back against the cushion of her seat. She took a deep breath, trying to steady her nerves, but it was useless. There was no potion in the world that could calm her now.

She could hear excited voices from outside the carriage as people prepared for the great procession that was to march into the town of Vardighet. A horse snorted. Trumpeters tested their instruments. Then, with a jolt, her carriage began to move. And so it began . . .

Trumpeters marched at the head of the procession of pages, equerries, and noblemen. They were followed by sixteen Swiss halberdiers, a litter, and further trumpeters, then came the coach of Erik with thirty footmen marching around the vehicle. Body guards and fourteen coaches drawn by six horses each followed.

It was a grand procession that reached Vardighet Cathedral, and all around the narrow streets peo-

ple came to watch. Their coarse clothing looked
drab alongside the brilliant costumes of the para-
ders, and Brigitta could see an underlying hostility
in many of the faces they passed, but mostly the
villagers smiled and looked in awe at the finery
passing them.

The spires of the cathedral seemed to reach up
forever and the tips of them were barely visible
through the snow, which now fell in greater
amounts. Brigitta ignored the wind that hit her as
she stepped from the confines of the carriage,
and with an elegance that came naturally to her,
she swept by the multitudinous crowds and into
the cathedral. It was a while before she would
have to proceed down the long aisle to her intended and in that time she was ushered to a
small anteroom where she was fussed over for
yet another time. By the time her hair had been
rearranged, her skirts brushed, and the gems at
her throat straightened, Brigitta had very nearly
worked herself into a trancelike state performing
all the necessary movements, but without
thought, without conscience.

Thora-Lisa should have been laid to rest in this cathe-
dral, she thought to herself. There should have
been a great mourning over Lisa's passing, but
there had been nothing. Again, Brigitta remembered the horrid sight of Lisa's lifeless body upon
the ice-covered rocks—and then, as if being
touched by Lisa's own hand, she remembered why
Lisa had requested such a thing be done with her
body. Lisa had wanted to pave the way to this very
day! All of Lisa's last days of life had been given to
the planning of this very moment. Thora-Lisa had

wanted Brigitta to don this wedding finery, to walk out of the cathedral doors wed to Erik Bjord.

And Brigitta had vowed to the dying princess that she would marry Erik.

I owe this to Lisa, Brigitta thought to herself. *I must marry Erik!* As she left the anteroom and took her place in front of the large doors behind which she knew Erik waited, she knew she had to keep her promise to Thora-Lisa.

The great doors were opened to reveal the expansive room before her, and as trumpets blared a regal sound, Brigitta whispered, "I do this for you, my dearest friend. I hope you are watching, Lisa, wherever you are."

Brigitta took a slow step forward, her decision made, and the congregation turned to view her. She kept her eyes forward, trying hard to maintain the graceful serenity she knew Thora-Lisa would have had.

Erik stood at the altar, looking tall and extremely handsome in his finest military attire. Yes, Brigitta decided as she took the last steps toward him, Erik would wear military garb on his wedding day. He was a great warrior who was feared by all. As she took her place beside him she wondered what he would do if he ever learned she was not Thora-Lisa.

With the words of the bishop echoing around her, she tried to make herself believe it was Devon standing beside her, that Devon was the man she was marrying and not the barbarian Erik.

Minutes slid into longer minutes as the service wore on and prayers were said. Brigitta, not really listening, watched the flame of one candle on the altar. It waved in the slight wind, sputtering only

once. Someone behind her coughed. Erik stood
beside her, his back straight, his gaze fixed ahead,
his blue eyes rarely blinking. She could hear the
rustle of her own skirts as she kneeled for yet another prayer and then stood to recite words from
the bishop. The ceremony wore on.

Had Erik really just taken her left hand in his,
had he really slipped a band around her finger?
She heard herself say words she did not mean—
could never mean! Till death? Such a very, very
long time. Oh, Devon, how she wished it was his
ring she wore! But Devon was a traitor—to her and
their country. The bishop said more words, more
prayers. Her mind was reeling now, her heart beating at a rapid rate as the full realization of what
she'd just done hit her. *She was now married to Erik
Bjord, who believed her to be a princess! Or was she
married to him? After all, everyone believed Thora-Lisa
had wedded Erik, not Brigitta Lind!*

With frightened eyes, she looked toward Erik.
The service was ending now and slowly Erik
turned toward her, a smile on his full lips, a gleam
in his eyes. He looked proud, certain of his position. Suddenly, reality forced its way through to
Brigitta's brain and it hit her like a cold slap to the
face. Tonight was to be their wedding night—and
Erik would expect to share the nuptial bed with
her. . . .

Chapter Thirteen

TWELVE TENSION-FILLED hours had passed since she'd recited her marriage vows, hours in which Brigitta had played the blushing, nervous bride. And now, as she sat alone in her chamber dreading the arrival of Erik, she wondered how she had endured the ordeal. The events of the day were already hazy in her mind and the faces in the crowd forgotten. Her steely determination of the morning had dissolved into a heavy weariness and Brigitta was terrified by thoughts of the coming night.

The room was softly lit by the fire in the hearth and the dancing flames emitted a warmth Brigitta was finding more and more uncomfortable as she sat in the overstuffed chair waiting for Erik. Marta, having helped her mistress out of her wedding finery and into a lacy nightdress, had left nearly an hour ago, and still Erik had not come. Brigitta brought her knees up and tucked her feet under her body as she moved to a more comfortable position in the chair. Perhaps Erik wasn't coming. Perhaps warriors did not exercise their marital rights, especially when married to a princess. But no, Brigitta thought, remembering how amorous Erik had been when she'd met him in the passage that long ago evening. Erik Bjord would take his rights as a husband no matter who he married.

Suddenly, she heard the latch of her door being lifted, and her blood froze in her veins as Erik stepped into the chamber, a gush of cold air swirling in behind him. Brigitta shivered.

"Erik," she said, letting her feet slide to the floor as she sat up straight.

Fully dressed, mug in hand, Erik shut the door behind him, swaying slightly, his long blond hair falling in careless disorder over his shoulders, his ocean-blue eyes hooded. Brigitta felt a nameless fear course through her. "I hope you're not overly tired from waiting," he said in a thick voice as he lifted his mug to his lips.

Brigitta watched him take a long swig of the brew. Thora-Lisa had been convinced Erik drank to excess only because she thought he could not stand the sight of her. But Brigitta had decided Erik was a weak person and was slave to the brew he so often guzzled. Her eyes narrowed. "No, Erik, I no longer tire easily."

He leaned back against the closed door, smiling as he moved his free hand behind him for a quick second, then brought it once again into Brigitta's view. "Good! Until a few short weeks ago, I wondered if you would even make it to our wedding day. You've outdone yourself, Thora-Lisa." His words were slow, slightly slurred. He was drunk. "In truth, ours must surely be the longest betrothal ever. Any other man might not have waited so long and patiently as I did."

Oh, but Lisa's wealth—a wealth that is now yours— will certainly be reward enough for your unfailing patience! Brigitta thought bitterly. Trying very hard to keep the edge out of her voice, she said, "My—my illnesses have kept us apart as man and wife."

"But no longer. I've seen a miraculous change in you over the past few weeks, Lisa. And I must confess that suddenly you are on my mind of late.

Never once during our betrothal did I think overly much of you—thoughts of you did not interest me. But now . . . now you are forever in my thoughts, bewitching me."

Brigitta did not like this turn in the conversation. Erik's mind was obviously numbed with drink and his tongue was becoming more loose by the moment. She pushed herself to a standing position and took a deep, steadying breath. "Would you care to sit by the fire?" she asked. Perhaps he would pass out in the chair and she would thus be saved from an ugly scene.

Erik shook his head, a blond wave dipping lower on his forehead as he did so. He took another swig, this time emptying the heavy mug, then he wiped his wet mouth with one sleeve and flung the vessel onto the chair, his eyes never leaving Brigitta. "Sitting is not what I've in mind. Come here, Lisa. Come to your husband."

Brigitta hesitated, forcing herself not to flee as she longed to do. Running away from him now would only create more of a problem for her. She had to somehow avoid sharing a bed with him this night—and every night.

"I—I know that lately I have appeared to be regaining my strength, Erik, b—but today's events have greatly taxed me. I—I am tired and wish—"

Erik's boom of laughter stopped Brigitta from continuing. "Tired?" he roared. "Not until I am through with you can you say you are tired. Cease your chatter, woman, and do as your husband commands!"

Brigitta blinked in angry surprise. Is this what he had had in mind for Lisa all this time? To order her

about like some chattel? Well, Brigitta was not
Thora-Lisa and she would be damned if she'd let
Erik intimidate her! To the devil with the laws of
marriage. No man—whether or not he believed
himself wed to her—would order *her* about!

"I said I am tired, Erik. We've a whole lifetime
ahead of us. Do not push me. My health is frail."

"Frail?" he repeated, his blond brows rising in-
quisitively. "No, Lisa, I think you are just frightened." He fixed his bleary gaze on her. "There is
something about you. Something different." He
paused for a moment, studying her. Brigitta swallowed heavily. "What is it you hide beneath those
veils? Is that why you are like a frightened kitten
this night? Do you fear the sight I will see when I
lift your veils?"

Brigitta's heart thumped wildly in her chest. Not
only had Erik planned to deflower Thora-Lisa this
night, but also to unveil her! She was suddenly
glad Lisa had been spared the grief of her wedding
night. "Not even you will gaze upon my uncovered face, Erik." Her voice was surprisingly calm,
but the threat her words contained was obvious.

Erik merely lounged against the door like a
golden giant. He was a powerfully built man, one
who had come into his high ranking by his own
strength and bravery. Not only had he managed a
flawless military career for himself, but he'd also
snared a wealthy princess for his wife. The only
reason he had not taken Thora-Lisa to the altar
before this day was because he'd been too im-
mersed in battles and the intricacies of mercantile
trade to be bothered with the burden of a sickly
wife. After all, being betrothed to Lisa reaped

nearly the same benefits as being married to her. Erik Bjord was no man's fool and even though he overimbibed on a regular basis, he still kept his wits about him enough to gain all that he desired. And this night he desired Brigitta.

"I begin to grow weary of your games, Lisa," he drawled. "My patience has been put to its limit. If I find you not to my liking in bed, I'll simply leave you to yourself and seek out others to pleasure me. Our marriage can be simple—or it can be complex, you decide."

"You pig," Brigitta breathed, for she could not help but remember how highly the gentle Thora-Lisa had thought of this man.

Erik's smile broadened. "Now I know you are not the Thora-Lisa I always thought you to be."

He moved away from the door, toward her, and Brigitta stepped instinctively away. Could he possibly know she wasn't Thora-Lisa? Her own fear latched its icy grip onto her spine and Brigitta backed away until she came in contact with the bed. She was a fool to have thought she would not be caught in such a dangerous deception!

"Tell me, Lisa," he continued as Brigitta stared at him in confusion. "Have you entertained young men in these very chambers while you've let the court believe you are an invalid? Are you afraid that I will find not a virginal bride but one well practiced in the arts of pleasing a man?" He stood only two steps away from her now, and his bleary blue eyes were filled with an odd light. His drunken mind was enjoying their cat-a-mouse game. "Of late, I've been watching you, Lisa. Something about you draws my attention. I know not what."

He laughed. "Surely 'tis not your face, for you cover your countenance as a nun would hide her body. But I'm finding it difficult to believe your face could be so hideous that you must hide it beneath these ugly veils. You move with too much grace and I see no other scars to mar your bright beauty."

He reached a hand toward Brigitta, but she pulled away. "Believe me, Erik, what I hide you would never want to see."

His hooded eyes were hungry. "Let me be the judge of that. Now come to me, Lisa."

Fear overtook her. "I—I wish to be alone," she stammered, frantically trying to think of some way to get Erik out of her rooms. With her eye on the door, she took a quick step around him and then lunged toward the portal. But once there, the door resisted her, and no matter how hard she tried, it would not budge. With panic clouding her brain, she pulled hard on the latch, straining with all her might and still the barrier did not give. She whirled toward Erik, who stood across from her, a pleased expression on his face.

" 'Tis locked, Lisa," he told her in a husky voice. "You've no place to run. Come, do not displease your new husband."

Brigitta could think of nothing but her hatred for him. He was vile and disgusting . . . and she was terrified of him. "No!" she breathed, panic making her voice quiver. "I demand you unlock this door. I do not want you in my chamber!"

"But you haven't any choice, Lisa. You are my wife now and I've a great need for you." His "need" was apparent. "Come. I want to gaze upon your naked beauty—your *uncovered* face."

Brigitta attempted to calm herself, but her panic-numbed brain made rational thought impossible. Shaking her head slowly, the silk veils fluttering gently with the gesture, she said, "Please don't, Erik. I do not want you to see my face. The—the sight will only disappoint you."

"I think not."

"It will only anger you."

" 'Tis probably only a skin blemish. You are mine now, Lisa, and I'm taking my right as your husband. This night I will see all of you." Slowly, he began to remove his shirt. "Come, Lisa. Come help me undress and I will do the same for you."

Brigitta's back was to the door, pressed tightly against it as if she could sink into oblivion within the cold wood and thus be out of Erik's reach. But such was not to be her luck. She watched with wary eyes as Erik crossed the room in slow strides, dropping pieces of clothing from his powerful body. Thick muscles along his chest rippled with each flex of his brawny arms, the fine blond hairs that covered it and trailed down beneath his washboard-like stomach catching the firelight with every sensual movement. Like a proud Roman gladiator advancing on his prey, he moved toward her, his feral eyes indicating his excitement.

Here was a man who had killed upon the battlefield, who, even as a young man, had had no regard for the rights of others. He had viciously beaten Devon's mother and then, years later, had still felt the hatred enough to murder Devon's father. For Brigitta believed all of what Devon had told her about Erik Bjord. There was no doubt in her mind that Erik had been involved in the murder of Michael Courtenay.

"Don't come any closer," she warned, her own heartbeat thundering in her ears. "I am a princess! My word is law here!"

"Your word is nothing to me. As your husband I command all you do. Now shut your mouth and be an obedient wife." Reaching out, he took her wrists in large hands and guided her arms around his neck, not releasing his hold as he pressed his hot body against hers. "Relax," he murmured, smiling and moving his hips in a circular motion. He could barely stand so intoxicated was he, and the weight he leaned into her was great. "I love taming you, Lisa. You excite me," he whispered, bending his head and placing a kiss to her veil-covered cheek.

Of course a warrior would love the chase of the hunt! She had been an idiot to fight him; her reluctance only whetted his appetite. She knew she must avoid him by other means, only by wits would she escape his clutches—but Brigitta was beyond rational thought. "You drunken fool," she hissed, then yanked her arms from his tight hold. She slapped her open palms to his chest and pushed with all her might as she wiggled from her spot by the door and quickly darted behind the chair near the hearth.

She had only a moment to catch her breath before Erik lunged toward her, knocking the chair over with a crash and toppling to the floor on top of it. Brigitta side-stepped his advance and fled to the opposite side of the room, once again by the portal and jiggling it wildly. As she tugged without gain on the latch, Erik's hand came around her waist and he swung her away from the door tossing her to the hard floor, then stifling her screams as he fell on top of her.

Pinning her by the shoulders, he breathed, "Right where I want you, Lisa." Groping for her breasts beneath the thin nightdress, he roughly fondled them. "No scars here," he murmured. "Nothing but smooth, soft skin." His roughened hands skimmed over nipples that hardened at his touch. His lips tilted up at the corners, pleased with her bodily reaction. He was sickeningly close, his face only inches from her veil-covered one, and Brigitta could smell the ale on his breath. She nearly gagged.

"Get . . . off . . . of . . . me," she hissed as she freed one hand and grabbed a handful of his long hair. Savagely, she yanked, and when he flinched and tried to undo her hold, Brigitta brought her knee up and slammed it between his legs.

Erik yelled in pain and clutched his groin, his eyes slits as he watched her roll away, then quickly scramble to her feet. "You bitch!"

"Give me the key to the door," she demanded, her chest heaving from exertion, "or I promise you, the next time I kick you, you'll not put your filthy seed into any woman!"

To her horror, he laughed. "Do not prize yourself," he said succinctly, "on your aim; you didn't hit your mark on the head." He rose first to his knees, then, with the help of the chair he'd knocked over, he pushed himself to his feet, swaying with drunkenness as he stood. "Enough of your games! I haven't the strength to tame you any longer."

"You mean you fear you may pass out at any moment," she shot back. "No, Erik, you'll not have me this night—nor any night!"

"Think what you want."

He came toward her with the quickness of an arrow in flight and in a moment had her in a crushing embrace, one that she could not wiggle out of.

"To bed with you, Lisa, for that is where you were made to be."

Brigitta kicked her legs and clawed at his arms but his hold was tight as he dragged her to the huge four-poster bed and without ceremony tossed her upon the furs. Brigitta immediately sat up.

Erik merely growled, shoving her back down. "Now I shall see what it is you hide so well from me," he slurred, and although his movements were forceful they were not as quick as they had been.

Brigitta realized that all his exertion had helped to speed the alcohol through his body and now his drunkenness was beginning to overtake him. If she could just keep him from ripping her veils away for a little longer he might succumb totally to his drunken stupor.

Hoping to gain the advantage from his drunken state, she found new strength, and every time his hand reached up to pull at her veils, hers pushed him away while she kicked her legs and wiggled her body like a wild horse that would not be ridden. It was a long struggle and Brigitta was surprised by Erik's strength. He would surely be a foe to contend with when he wasn't filled with drink, for even in his present state he was strong as an ox!

"Enough of your defiance!" he growled as he placed his lips upon her neck, kissing her, and

Brigitta squirmed violently beneath him, tears filling her eyes. She hated him! Everything about him was vile.

"No! Stop!" she screamed.

He grabbed her by the shoulder then, lifting his head to look fiercely into her eyes, shaking her hard and making her head snap back and forth. "I'll have you when I want you! Do you hear me? I'll force you into submission if that is what it takes."

"I hate you, Erik! You make me sick!"

He scowled at her. "I should have you punished for your disobedience!"

She recovered quickly from the shock of his actions, not wanting to give him the pleasure of seeing he had affected her. "What do you think I am? Your property? I am a princess!" she spat, not wanting to let the tears that were dangerously close splash over her lashes.

He laughed, swaying even in their inclined position. With a quick jerk, he pulled her up to a sitting position while he tried to stand above her at the side of the bed. He was so drunk he could hardly stand alone, and if not for his hold on her shoulders, Brigitta was certain he would have toppled face first on the bed. But somehow he managed to bring his head up, then leaned toward her.

" 'Tis time to unveil now . . ." he whispered drunkenly as his right hand left her shoulder, then, with a vicious yank, he ripped the silken veils from her face.

A gasp burst from her trembling lips even as she tried to turn her face from him and her hair, loosened from its pins in their struggles, fell to cover her features. But Erik yanked that silky curtain from his way, then with his other hand cupped her chin and forced her face toward him. Brigitta kept her eyes downcast, waiting for the inevitable blow he would give when he saw her face.

But no blow was forthcoming. Nothing but an eerie silence filled the room as long moments passed.

Hesitantly, Brigitta lifted her lashes, fearful for her life. But when she looked into Erik's stupored face she saw no rage, saw no emotion at all.

He said one word: "Brigitta?"

Chapter Fourteen

BRIGITTA TREMBLED with fear as she brought her hands across her bosom and boldly met Erik's bleary gaze. Why did he just stand there? Why didn't he bellow with rage, call the guard—do *something?* The tall giant swayed back and forth, his blue, blood-shot eyes never leaving her face.

"Erik, I can explain," she began, hating the silence he was seemingly glad to let hang between them. "Thora-Lisa was—" she faltered, wondering just exactly how she should phrase her words, for her future hinged on what Erik made of those words. "She wanted me, no *begged* me—" Her words stopped in her throat when the warrior, towering dizzily above her, spoke.

Again, he said only, "Brigitta." He shook his

head, blinking his eyes once, then twice and still he stared at her as if not believing what he saw.

Brigitta would have continued her explanation but Erik's hands reached out to her, though not in anger, but for support. His drunken state had finally overtaken him and no longer could he stand on his own two feet. Brigitta tried to hold up his weight, but he was much too heavy for her and in a moment he fell atop her, crushing her slight form beneath his large one as he fell onto the bed, muttering·incoherent words.

"Oh, sweet Lord," Brigitta whispered as the tears she'd been fighting to gain control over finally pushed past her lashes. Now that Erik knew her identity what would he do? Surely he would think she had killed Thora-Lisa in order to take her place as princess! Not daring to move for fear of rousing Erik, Brigitta attempted to calm her nerves so she might rationally form her next step of action. But her mind was awhirl with all that had taken place. Her body trembled uncontrollably as she tried to breathe beneath Erik's crushing weight.

The minutes ticked slowly by and with them Brigitta's fear-caused paralysis lessened until, when Erik began snoring loudly, Brigitta was enough in command of her senses that she could wiggle out from beneath his heavy form. The hem of her nightdress caught beneath Erik's knees and Brigitta gently yanked it free, ripping the frail fabric. She scurried toward the exit.

"The door," she whispered aloud to herself. She'd forgotten Erik had locked the portal. Now she had to find the key. Looking around the chamber, she wondered where Erik put it. No doubt on his person so he would be sure she would not be able to find the thing.

She bent down and began picking up the garments Erik had shed one by one. When she had rummaged through each pocket with no luck, she retraced her steps back to Erik who was lying immobile on the bed. His loud snores now filled the room and Brigitta was almost certain he would sleep for a few hours. As stealthful as a thief in the night, she ran her hand along his leg and found the key tucked into his right boothose. Clutching it, she raced toward the portal and unlocked it. Freedom was nearly hers. She needed to gather some clothes from her old chamber and then she would slip out of the castle and be gone. Swinging the portal open, she started to step into the passage. But her breath caught in her throat as she ran straight into Marta's bulky form.

"Marta!" she blurted, and too late remembered she'd not put her veil back over her face. Brigitta turned away, intent on going back in the chamber, but Marta's grip on her arm stopped her flight. "Marta—please, do not stop me!" she said, turning to face the older woman. "You—you don't understand . . . I—"

Marta shook her gray-haired head. She wore a white nightcap, and her long braid of hair was draped over one white shoulder and swayed with her movements. Holding her candle closer to Brigitta's face, she commanded, "Come."

"Where? Where do you want me to go?" Brigitta whispered, trying to shake off Marta's tight grip. But Marta only pursed her weathered mouth and commanded again.

"Come with me, *Brigitta*."

Brigitta fought down her nausea and reluctantly followed Marta along the narrow passage. The shadows their bodies cast played on the damp stone walls like evil phantoms about a fire, and a cold gust of air swirled around them, chilling Brigitta to the bone. Surprisingly, Marta led Brigitta to the very room Brigitta had slept in when she'd first come to Vardighet. When they were both inside, Marta shut the door and set her candle and holder atop the small stand near the bed. Brigitta shivered from the cold—and her fear—and waited for Marta to speak.

"I went to the princess's chambers tonight because I heard you scream. Are you all right?" Marta asked.

"Well enough," Brigitta answered slowly, confused by Marta's actions. Why had the woman brought her here? And why wasn't she more surprised at learning Brigitta was not Thora-Lisa?

"How long have you known, Marta? How long have you known I am not Lisa?"

"Since the beginning," the older woman answered frankly, ignoring the widening of Brigitta's eyes. "I was merely waiting to see what you would do with all of Lisa's wealth and power. I wanted to be certain you had assumed the role of the princess for the right reasons."

"And?"

"And I see that you have. You see, Lisa mentioned her plan to me years ago. She was just a young girl then and I thought it only a dream of hers to have the inhabitants of Vardighet enjoy the presence of a healthy, beautiful princess. But when she summoned you from afar and I saw your beauty and likeness to her, I realized she truly intended to go through with finding another to walk in her shoes." Marta paused a moment, folding her hands and staring sightlessly at them. Brigitta could see the older woman was desperately trying to keep her emotions in check. "I—I loved Lisa as a daughter, Brigitta, and I would have gladly given my life for hers. . . ." She swallowed heavily, quickly brushing away her tears as she glanced up at Brigitta. "Lisa didn't always consider the consequences of her actions and I fear you have greatly jeopardized yourself by complying with her wishes. I feel partly responsible for the predicament you are in so . . . so I will help you in any way I can."

Brigitta breathed a deep sigh of relief. "Thank you, Marta. Bless you. But I'm afraid I don't know what I'm going to do. I only know I cannot stay at Vardighet. I must flee. Tonight!"

"You did not kill the general, did you?" Marta asked in alarm.

"No! Of course not!" *Although he deserves to die*, Brigitta thought to herself.

"Praise the Lord," Marta exclaimed, then scurried toward the wardrobe that was once Brigitta's. "Here, make a bundle of some of your warmest clothes. I will do what I can to find you some transportation."

Brigitta cringed. She had not thought about the fact she might have to ride a horse alone. "A horse and cart?" she asked hopefully.

"No, 'twould be faster for you to flee on horseback. I am familiar with the workers at the stables. They will help me, I am certain."

Brigitta was quickly pulling out the clothes she

had worn as Thora-Lisa's companion, her mind racing. "I'll need provisions. Can you manage that, too?" Devon! He was her only hope. Brigitta had to somehow reach Devon. He had mentioned England to her, something about his mother living in Dover. "I'll need gold to buy myself passage on some sailing vessel," she added. "I hate to ask, Marta, but I'm no longer safe even in Sweden. Who would believe Thora-Lisa died a natural death and had asked me to take her place?"

Marta nodded in agreement as she helped Brigitta into a fur-lined dress. "*Ja*, you are right, but I have no gold of my own. I—I will try to get you some jewels, if I can."

Fully dressed now, Brigitta drew on the beautiful ermine cloak Thora-Lisa had given her. It was much too extravagant for travel and would draw the attention of passersby, but it was all Brigitta had. She fastened the inner cords of the garment. "*Varmt tack*, Marta. I'll never forget all you're doing for me. If you can, have the horse saddled and left in the princess's gardens. I shouldn't have any trouble getting there myself," she said. That was, if Erik was still passed out from drink.

"Godspeed, Brigitta. I wish you well," Marta said and then she slipped quietly out of the chamber, leaving her candle and holder for Brigitta.

In a matter of minutes, Brigitta had her most practical clothing wrapped in a medium-sized bundle, and after pinching out the candle, she headed for the princess's chambers. To her relief, Erik's loud snores greeted her once she entered the warm room. Brigitta quietly passed him. "Good riddance, Erik," she whispered just before she stepped into the secret passage. "I hope you wake with the worst headache of your life!"

Huge snowflakes, twirling lazily to earth, clung to Brigitta's garments and eyelashes, absorbing the sounds of the peaceful morning as Brigitta rode sidesaddle atop the mammoth mount Marta had secured for her. The beast was as gentle as it was big, and he and Brigitta had come to a mutual understanding in their hours of travel. She had at first been frightened of the animal when a small lad had brought him to her in the princess's gardens, but necessity had spurred her atop him and Brigitta soon learned riding a horse was far easier than she had ever anticipated. She recalled how Devon had commanded his horse with soft words and she did the same, pleased to find the animal responded well to her guidance. She talked endlessly to him, of her family, of Devon, and the horse nickered softly now and then, flicking his ears as if in answer.

Vardighet was far behind, two days' ride to be exact, and the Baltic lay to Brigitta's left, its vastness hidden by a curtain of falling snow. Brigitta had stopped to rest only when she absolutely needed to and then she didn't dare tarry overly long. During their rests she would strip the coverings from her feet and hands and rub them vigorously until she felt the numbness leave them. She had found a small amount of oats for the horse in one of the saddlebags, and she shared her small store of water with the beast.

A few hours ago they had come upon a well-worn path in the snow and Brigitta could now see a small cluster of cottages spread over a hillside up ahead. She estimated they could reach the village by midafternoon, so her fears of freezing to death or pushing her mount too hard were not great. Surely, someone in the village would offer her shelter and she could then ask how and where to obtain passage upon some sailing vessel.

But when Brigitta and her mount finally reached the small *byalag* the snow was falling harder. The wind off the Baltic swirled the white stuff into small funnels that whipped across the drifts and created a white-out so that Brigitta could barely see her own gloved hand in front of her face. Her lips were numb and the air she sucked into her lungs turned deathly cold. If she didn't soon find shelter, she knew she would die in the harsh climate. Slipping off the saddle and crooning softly to the horse, Brigitta bent her head and plunged forward toward a dim light in the distance. Coming upon a tiny cottage, she left her horse as close to the building as possible, then banged on the door, silently praying the people inside would offer her shelter for the night.

"Please," Brigitta shouted. "Please open the door!" Dear Lord, it was cold. She wrapped her arms about her waist, shivering as she watched the door open slowly. A tiny, old woman stood on the threshold, a threadbare shawl wrapped tightly around her frail shoulders. "Hello!" Brigitta cried. "I—I mean no harm. I seek only shelter for the night. Do you have room for myself and my beast?"

"Och, child! What are you doing out on a day like today?" The old woman stepped to one side, waving Brigitta inside. "Hurry, child, before I catch my own death standing here!"

Brigitta stepped into the warm one-room cottage,

teeth chattering. "Th—thank you," she sputtered as she pushed her hood back from her head and shook the snow from her hair. A low fire burned in the center of the room, its orangish glow falling gently on the cottage walls and earth floor. An old man reclined on a pallet near the fire, whittling a piece of wood. He did not look up at Brigitta.

"You say you have a horse, child?" the woman asked.

"Yes. Is there a place I can keep him for the night?"

"*Ja*, there is a barn a short distance from our home. You'll have to stay with your beast out there, for we've not enough room for you here. A young boy from the village stays with my husband and me at night. Here, get yourself warmed by the fire. I've some extra linen you can use. There is hay in the barn, too." She motioned Brigitta toward the fire, then turned away to get the promised linen. She was a sparrow of a woman, Brigitta thought. Small in frame and fine-boned. Her gray hair was coiled into a knot at the back of her head, and beneath her shawl protruded the bones of her back hunched from years of hard work.

Brigitta undid the cords of her cloak and opened it to let the warmth of the fire penetrate to her chilled body. As the snow melted and dripped tiny beads of water onto the dirt floor, she felt the numbness leave her lips and fingers. Her toes were another matter though and she worried she might have been exposed to the weather too long.

"What is your name, child?" the woman asked as she handed the linen to her.

"Brigitta," she responded automatically, then

wished she would have thought to give a different name. Surely Erik would have his men scour the countryside looking for her. She wanted no harm to befall this couple because of her.

"I am Svea and that is my husband John. John!" she said then, nearly shouting. "We have a guest for the night! A young girl by the name of Brigitta!" Svea took Brigitta by the sleeve and led her to the old man's side, repeating what she'd just said. Finally, the old man looked up. His face was a mass of wrinkles and his dark gray hair was sparse and thin. A light quilt covered his lower body and a baggy, plain linen shirt fell against his shoulders and chest that had long ago lost their strong form. His hands and head shook as he whittled the wood and he only smiled weakly at Brigitta, then turned his attention back to his work.

Brigitta knew not what to say. There was obviously something terribly wrong with the man.

"His hearing and mind left him long ago," Svea supplied as if reading Brigitta's mind. "He's a good husband, and he was a good provider in his day. I thank the Lord I still have him with me."

Brigitta nodded, feeling tears threaten her eyes. "Is there something I can do for you, some chores you have not the time or strength to get to this day?"

"No. The people of the *byalag* take care of me and my husband. They have large hearts, they do. Not a day goes by that someone isn't bringing the evening meal or a stack of wood. They help me so I have the time to care for John, and when one of the families has a sick member, I return their kindness by caring for the sick. No," she continued as she moved to a rickety chair in the corner of the room and took up needle and thread, "you just make yourself comfortable in the barn and not worry about us. I'll have the young lad bring some warm food to you once it arrives. Run along now, I have no need to know why such a young woman as yourself dressed in such rich attire would be alone and in need of shelter."

Brigitta stood there by the old man, who shook violently yet still had patience enough, or loss of mind, to whittle continuously, and watched as Svea rocked back and forth on the chair, running needle and thread through a piece of plain material. Not another word was spoken and Brigitta thought again of the danger she might be putting this couple in.

"*Varmt tack*," she murmured and then walked quietly to the door, shutting it quickly behind her so the wind and snow didn't swirl inside. "Come," she said to the horse as she picked up the reins and went in search of the barn. What she found was a dilapidated building that offered little shelter against the elements. True to Svea's words there was fresh hay though and no other animals. Obviously John and Svea were too old to be able to care for livestock. Stripping her mount of its heavy saddle, Brigitta watered and fed him, then made a comfortable spot for herself. The wind howled and whistled outside the structure but Brigitta was surprisingly warm and comfortable. A small lad later brought her a warm meal. He stayed long enough to explain to Brigitta that if she desired to buy passage upon a vessel she needed to travel farther south. He then warned her about Danish raids along Sweden's coast. Not once did he pose personal questions and he stayed only long enough to answer her inquiries and to see if she had all she might need. Although kind to her, these villagers knew enough to realize Brigitta was in some sort of trouble. The mount she had taken from Vardighet was indeed a prize bit of horseflesh and her own clothing was far too grand for any peasant. It was after the lad left that Brigitta realized the blunt reality of her situation. She was truly alone. With that sad thought in her head she curled up in the hay and fell asleep, visions of Devon dancing in her mind.

Brigitta rolled over, thinking the commotion was in her dreams, but some instinct within forced her to open her eyes. She opened them to hell. One after the other, screams pierced the oddly lit night, causing Brigitta to scramble to her feet and quickly run out of the barn. The sound of powder blasting in the frigid air filled her ears and she gasped as she took in the scene around her. The snow had ceased falling from the sky and now wherever she looked she could see huge, half-armored men carrying torches and weapons, bludgeoning people and setting fire to every cottage. Erik. People were running in all directions and animals, loosed and frenzied, skittered first here then there trying to escape the bedlam, but only creating more. Oh Lord, she thought, could Erik do this to his own people? Brigitta caught sight of a woman running away from a burning building, her skirts flying behind her as she held her crying baby close and tried to outrun the man pursuing her. The man reached out a long arm and grabbed the woman by the hair, yanking her back and pulling her and the babe to the ground. A scream tore from the woman's throat as the man pried the baby from her arms and left it wailing on the ground beside him. He drew a knife and slashed her skirts from her thrashing body only to undo his breeches and fall upon her, raping her as people ran by too engrossed in saving their own selves to help the woman.

Brigitta couldn't help the cry that came from her own lips, and her anger boiled to the surface as the scene unfolded before her. Could this be the work of Erik's soldiers? Could they be searching this village for her and destroying all in their path? Surely they would not be so destructive! And then, like a horrible nightmare come to life, she realized what was happening. The Danes from the South were once again attacking her homeland.

"No!" she screamed, running to the fallen woman who was trapped beneath the disgusting man. Brigitta saw the knife lying beside the screaming baby and she quickly grabbed it, then with all her strength plunged the thing into the man's back. The action caused the man to stop his assault and arch his back in pain, but Brigitta did not wait to see if one plunge of the knife would kill him. She pulled the weapon back out and then thrust it deep between his shoulder blades one more time. Horrified, she watched as he fell forward dead.

"Oh, God," she sobbed, trembling, but she didn't have time to waste reflecting on what she'd just done. Kneeling in the deep snow now turning crimson with blood, she heaved the man's heavy body from the screaming woman. "Hush," Brigitta tried to soothe, but the woman only lay on the ground, curling up and sobbing. Brigitta raised her head and looked around her. People, innocent peo-

ple, were being clubbed and beaten, raped and
then slashed with knives or hatchets or both.
Surely Swedish soldiers would not do such things
to their own people! She had to get away! She
scooped the tiny baby up in her arms, and yelled to
the mother, "Get up, do you hear me? You must
get up!" With her free hand she grabbed the woman's arm and pulled her to her feet, shaking her.
"Here," she said, putting the baby into the woman's arms, "you've got to get away. Get hold of
yourself so you can save your babe's life!"

At mention of the baby the woman seemed to
snap out of her hysterics, for she nodded her head,
cradling the infant close to her body. Brigitta
pointed in the direction away from the village and
prodded the woman to run, then she turned back
and headed for Svea's cottage. She had to get her
mount and ride out of here!

When she turned, she saw Svea's cottage was in
flames and Svea was in the doorway. John, one
arm slung around his wife's shoulders, was
slumped against her, his whole body violently con-
vulsing. Brigitta had to help them, but first she
knew she should let her horse from the barn before
it was engulfed in flames. As she turned her attention to the barn, she saw she was too late. Already
flames were spewing out of the roof and Brigitta
watched in horror as her horse flew out of the
doors, his hooves barely touching the ground. In a
second he was gone into the eerily lit night, running to safety. Brigitta ran to help Svea.

"My God! My God!" the old woman screamed,
her watery eyes wide as she gaped at the scene
around them while she struggled to help her hus-

band down the steps. The heat was so intense from the burning building that Brigitta had to wipe the sweat from her eyes as she took John's other arm and put it around her shoulders, helping Svea take him down the stairs and away from the flames and murderers about.

"They're going to kill us," Svea screamed, hobbling as fast as her arthritic legs would take her. It wasn't fast enough. "My God, we'll all be killed! Lord have mercy!"

"No, we will get away," Brigitta said, trying to reassure the woman. "We will! Hurry now. Do not let your fear blind you, Svea." Brigitta wished she could pick them both up and carry them, for even in their haste they were too slow, and who knew how long it would be before one of the raiders took notice of them? "We'll get away, Svea, we'll—" Her words were cut off, caught in Brigitta's throat when she felt the force of something hit John. The heavy blow pushed both her and Svea forward and it was all Brigitta could do to keep from dropping John. He felt suddenly lifeless, his shaking had ceased and no longer did he help ease the burden he made by moving his feet. *Please, no,* Brigitta thought as she turned and looked to his back. She saw only the shine of metal, then could look no more. A warrior's axe had embedded itself in the old man's back. Svea screamed and fell to her knees, dropping her husband's arm and leaving Brigitta to ease the lifeless John to the ground alone.

"They've killed him!" Svea screamed over and over, crawling atop the snow-covered ground to cradle her husband's head on her lap. "Dear John, my dear John. No!" she sobbed, tears coursing down her weathered face as she rocked back and forth. "Do not leave me, John!"

Brigitta felt her own tears form but she wiped them away. She had to be strong and keep her wits about her. She had to get Svea and herself out of the village! She tried to pull Svea from John's body but the woman wouldn't move, she just sat there stroking her husband's ashen cheeks.

"Svea, come, we must flee! H—he is gone, I'm sorry." Even as she said the words she heard the war howl. Looking up, she saw a huge man with long flowing brown hair and tiny feral eyes lunging toward her. Frenzied by the excitement of the attack, the man flew through the air and knocked Brigitta down upon the cold ground. She hit the earth with a thud, and even though the wind was pushed from her lungs, Brigitta knew only one thing: kill or be killed. She felt the knife handle within her palm, her fingers closing tightly around it, and without hesitation she shoved the blade deep into the man's side, feeling the flesh give and the warm blood flow out onto her hand. Drawing the knife out, she shoved the man's heavy body away from her, leaving him face down in the snow.

"Svea!" she screamed, scrambling to her feet and seeing the sticky, red blood covering her cape and hands. "Svea!"

But there was no answer to her cry, nothing but the painful screams of human suffering, the sputtering hiss of flames as they licked away at the many cottages, and Brigitta's own wail of fright as she stared down at Svea's decapitated body. Poor, helpless Svea. Brigitta's only balm was in knowing Svea and her husband were now in a realm untouched by human pain and limitations. Quickly, Brigitta turned and ran from the sight.

Horrible. This whole night had been horrible. She staggered, nearly tripping over her own feet as she began to run away from the death and destruction behind. She didn't get far, for a meaty hand clamped onto her shoulder and spun her around. She raised her knife, but the man only sneered and knocked her hand away, grabbing for the knife with his free hand.

"I saw you murder my comrade," he growled in her own language, but his words were heavy with a Danish accent. Brigitta cringed. She tried to shake out of his hold but her captor was quicker, and in no time he had his hands around her waist and lifted her from the ground.

"You will pay for what you've done," he hissed.

Brigitta kicked and thrashed wildly in his tight hold, but to no avail. The commotion around her died away. Every building had been set afire, every man killed, every woman raped and then either taken hostage with the children or else killed along with the men. Brigitta felt her fear mount and she tried not to focus on the dismembered bodies that littered the bloodied snow around her as the man pulled her body closer to his. His breath stank of decay and his body was greasy, sweaty, and filthy.

"Reassemble, men! We leave immediately," a voice boomed from nearby.

The man who held her turned toward that voice and Brigitta looked up to see a tall man walk out of the flame-filled night. The breastplate of his half-armor was covered with blood, as were his hands and bearded face; his wheat-colored hair fell free to his shoulders and his amber-colored eyes bored holes in Brigitta as he sized her up. He sported two pistols: one on each side of him, plus a sword and club. Brigitta put her head down, kicking and thrashing anew, for she knew the warrior who strode toward them would almost certainly order her death.

"Be still!" her captor commanded. "Let the general get a look at you. He decides whether you live or die!"

Brigitta ignored the man's words as she opened her mouth and brought her teeth down upon his one arm. She nearly gagged but she bit him as hard as she could.

"Aagh!" the man yelled even as he yanked her shimmering blonde hair viciously.

That action brought her head up sharp, and as her head was forced back against her captor's shoulder, she stared wild-eyed into the face of the warrior before her.

"What have we here?" he drawled easily in faultless Swedish. His voice was coarse and guttural.

Brigitta suppressed a shiver of fear, and to show her hatred, spit at the ground before him.

"You shouldn't have done that," he said and then took the club that hung from his waist belt and smashed it against the side of her head.

Brigitta felt the blow, heard something crack as pinpoints of light blurred her vision. The man holding her released his grip, letting her crumble to the ground. Blood spilled into Brigitta's mouth and the whole side of her head was numb. She couldn't speak but still she tried to push herself up with her hands. She was almost to her knees when the man in the half-armor brought his booted foot up and caught her in the ribs, kicking her hard. She fell back to the snow-covered ground, the wind knocked out of her.

"I will not tolerate such disrespect!" he bellowed loudly. Brigitta could barely hear him. "No man lives who has spit at my feet—and you, a mere woman!" His foot made contact with her body once again.

The pain was intense and her lungs couldn't get enough air. She couldn't hear properly, her head buzzing with a loud piercing ring and when he kicked her again the new pain was covered by old pain. Brigitta gasped for breath, trying to crawl away, her fingers digging into icy snow that melted away from her and still the man kicked her—her ribs, her stomach, her head. Finally, she ceased crawling and let herself sink into the oblivion that pulled her down. Oblivion, sweet, sweet oblivion . . .

Chapter Fifteen

SHE WAS STRUGGLING toward the surface, her lungs taking in more of the oppressive, heated air as her body, bruised and aching, fought to kick away the confining layers that held her down. So long, it seemed, too long to be held down, held under. She was weak, so very weak, and yet she had to find the strength to flee this imprisoning darkness where the only sensations she felt were pain and sticky heat.

Slowly, Brigitta's eyelids fluttered open and the swirling darkness that had for so long filled her mind broke apart and dissipated, leaving only a hazy fog behind. She felt the fire within her own body and so kicked away the furs that covered her, the hasty movements sending new waves of pain rocketing through her battered body. Unable to help herself, Brigitta cried out in agony.

Immediately, the surrounding curtains of the huge bed were pulled apart on one side and a middle-aged woman peered intently down at Brigitta. Words of another language spilled from the woman's lips, making no sense to Brigitta, who in fear crawled to the other side of the bed.

Grimacing with pain, Brigitta demanded, "Who are you? Wh—where am I?"

The woman shook her brown-haired head, her hands going out to Brigitta, then clasping together in frustration. She said something Brigitta didn't understand, then turned and took a cup from a small table beside the bed, thrusting it toward Brigitta.

Brigitta looked at the vessel, wondering whether she should take it. "What is it?" she asked, feeling suddenly very dizzy. She put her hand to the side of her head, instantly drawing it back in frightened horror when she felt the puffiness of the right side of her face. What had happened to her? Gingerly, she touched her cheek, then moved her fingertips slowly toward her temple. There was a cloth wound around her head and she felt something dry and crusty. Blood. Memory returned to her then. She remembered the attack on the small village, remembered the fires, the killings . . . the man with the half-armor. She leaned back against the elaborately scrolled headboard of the bed, taking in a deep breath, and wondered how disfigured her face would be once it healed.

The woman beside the bed said something, then added, "Water. Water." She said the word in Swedish, causing Brigitta to turn and look to her.

Slowly, Brigitta extended her hand, seeing the bruises and scratches along her own arm as she did so, and she took the cup and brought it to her cut lips. The cool water went down easily and Brigitta wanted to drink it all, but the woman would not let her. She quickly took the vessel from Brigitta's shaking hands after Brigitta had only a few long swallows.

At that moment, the doors of the spacious chamber were opened and the man who had viciously attacked Brigitta entered the room muttering something to the woman, who then quickly exited. Brigitta self-consciously pulled the material of the nightdress she wore closer to her body as she felt her heart race with fear.

"I am glad you are finally awake," the man said as he pulled a straight-backed chair to the side of the bed and sank his bulky frame onto it. "I was beginning to wonder if perhaps I was too harsh with you."

Brigitta said not a word, too frightened to speak, but her eyes threw daggers at the man who so casually sat near her.

He smiled at her show of hatred. This day he

wore no armor, only a plain linen shirt beneath a light-colored jerkin. His trousers were of a deep brown shade and the boots he wore were highly polished. His wheat-colored hair was long and shaggy, as were his mustache and beard, and the lightness of his amber eyes caused him to look like a tawny lion.

"Have you a name, my beauty?" he asked disgustingly, leaning back in his chair and letting the lids of his eyes shutter half closed. "No?" he asked after giving her a moment to answer. "I thought not. My name is Jorgen, and this," he said with a sweep of his hand, "is my home. And, for the time being, it will also be your home."

The words had their desired effect. "Never," Brigitta breathed, her voice trembling with rage and fright.

"Ah, so a tongue still remains within that pretty head of yours! You have no say in the matter, my beauty. I am now your master, your lord."

"I'll not stay. You can not keep me here!" Brigitta said, her ice-blue eyes challenging the cruel stranger.

He gave her an ugly smile as his eyes held hers for long minutes, and then he stood, pushing back the chair. "You speak strong words, but I've no fear. You'll not get far in your condition." He turned and walked to the door. Just before exiting, he said, "Rest and let your body heal. A dead woman will do me no good." He turned away from her, and then added, "I will be away for some time to come. When I return, we will discuss your position here." With that he was gone, closing the great doors quietly behind him.

Brigitta stared at the closed portal, feeling suddenly very weary, and although she tried her best to hang on to her anger, it slowly slipped away and was replaced by a great tiredness that could be denied no longer. "Tomorrow," she whispered to herself as she lay on her side. "Tomorrow I shall flee." Thoughts of freedom and Devon swam in her mind for only a second, then she was fast asleep.

The days passed slowly by with Brigitta forcing herself to eat the meals brought to her, and when she was alone, she would walk circles in the chamber trying to regain her strength. The swelling in her face soon went away, the bandages were removed, and now there were only traces of the ugly bruises. Remarkably, the only scar she carried was a crescent-moon-shaped one just above her temple where her hair easily covered it.

Winter had given way to spring and the landscape outside her window had blossomed beneath the warm sunshine. The tiny stream that cut through the vivid green countryside was swollen now with water from the melted snow, and on the farther side of the stream was a small flax field. The flowers suspended on slender stalks blew gently in the slight breeze, and birds chirruped as they soared through the air. The sky overhead was intensely blue with only a few sailing clouds. The radiance of the spring day was great, and it seemed to Brigitta that wherever she looked out the window the sun freshened and awakened nature. It had been a long winter for her—with Lisa's passing, Devon's betrayal, and her imprisonment—the longest of her life, and she vowed that with the advent of spring she would somehow find a way to extricate herself from the situation she was in.

She turned away from the window determined to get herself freed. She constantly wondered what had become of Devon. Why hadn't he returned to Vardighet as he had promised? She remembered he had mentioned visiting Jorgen, but there was no sign of him here. And now after months of contemplation she no longer believed he would be so cruel as to give Jorgen Erik's battle plans, for then all of Sweden would be at risk. Had he instead traveled to see his mother in Dover? Brigitta had no choice but to go to Dover herself and find out. Surely, once she made it to Dover, finding Devon's mother would be an easy task.

Her eyes searched the room for the hundredth time looking for some instrument to help aid her in her escape. But the room had been stripped of loose objects. All that adorned the chamber now were a few tapestries of hunting scenes, a straight-backed chair, the bed, and a bedside table. There wasn't even a poker for the hearth! Before leaving Brigitta in the care of his servants while he led his troops northward once again, Jorgen had certainly read Brigitta's mind correctly. She heard a key turn in the outer lock and in an instant was lying on the bed, playing perfectly the role of an invalid.

Jorgen entered the chamber, his long legs carrying him across the room in only a few strides. He stood beside the bed with a look of amusement in his dark orange-yellow eyes. In his hand he held a familiar-looking bundle.

"Is the lady well enough to leave her bed this

day?" he asked, gazing down at her. "You appear to be in the same state as when I left you last."

Brigitta feigned sickness, as she always did when anyone was near her. "No," she replied, staring blankly at the canopy above her. "I am not well." She wanted him to think her a sickly creature, too ill to be bothered.

"'Tis a pity," he said. "I thought you might enjoy a change of clothing and scenery. The night-dress you wear does nothing to enhance your beauty."

Brigitta felt her heart skip a beat. Something was wrong. By the tone of his voice, Jorgen had more on his mind than of her getting a change of scenery. She chanced a look at the huge man.

"Does this look familiar?" he asked, then held up the bundle in his meaty hands. With a quick shake, he let the bundle unwrap and out of it floated a rain of *merveilleux* silk and then one of sea-green satin. A pair of slippers along with a small black pouch fell to the floor as the dresses, still held in Jorgen's hands, fluttered prettily in the air before Brigitta's eyes. "Well?" he demanded. "Are these garments yours?" The sapphires along the sleeves of the silk dress sparkled magically, brilliantly, in the sunlight that streamed through her window.

Brigitta stared at the gowns she had so quickly bundled and shoved into her saddle on that long ago night she'd fled Vardighet. How did Jorgen get them? Had he had them all these weeks? She'd thought her meager belongings had burned with everything else in Svea's barn!

"Answer me!"

"Y—yes, they are mine."

Jorgen threw the wrinkled dresses across the bed, then quickly snatched up the black pouch from the floor. Brigitta had never seen the pouch before, but as he began withdrawing jewels from the bag, she realized Marta must have secured the pouch in her saddle. One by one, he pulled out a pearl necklace, then matching earbobs, a golden bracelet, and a shiny, ruby ring.

"How came you by such wealth?" he demanded.

Brigitta could only stare at the gems. There was a fortune there—a fortune that could help transport her to Devon!

"Are you a thief?" he pressed.

"No!" The answer was torn from her lips before she had a chance to think. She had spoken too quickly, now how could she explain where the precious pieces had come from?

"Then where did you get them?"

Brigitta sat up and lifted her chin, defying the man before her. She would not answer him. It was none of his affair—*she* was none of his affair!

Ignoring her silence, Jorgen tossed all the jewels to the same spot the dresses occupied on the bed. "I've something else I think is yours." He extended his arm but Brigitta ignored him. "Come," he ordered, then when she did not obey, he grabbed her roughly by the arm and pulled her toward the window.

"Let me go!" she screamed as she struggled to be free of his vicious hold.

His grip only tightened as he thrust her body in front of him and forced her to look out the window. Instead of the empty landscape she had so recently viewed, there was now a horse chomping leisurely on the green grass—the same horse she had fled upon from Vardighet! Brigitta couldn't help the gasp that came from her throat. She'd thought the beast had gotten away.

"I thought the animal was yours," he said from behind her, his beefy arm coming around her shoulders to pull her body against his bulky frame. "I have many spies who travel great distances to bring me news of the enemy. You, being a Swede woman, are an enemy. One spy has just returned with interesting news. It concerns a man I have a deep hatred for."

Brigitta felt her spine tingle with fear. She tried to move away from his grasp but he would not let her go.

"It seems a precious bird has flown from its cage. A great reward is being offered for return of that bird."

He knew! Jorgen knew! Brigitta closed her eyes, dreading her future.

"Should I take you back to Erik, Lisa?" He tightened his hold, as though he wished to squeeze the blood from her. It was as though he wanted to punish Brigitta because of his hatred for Erik.

Brigitta trembled with fear. "Unhand me!" she demanded in a cold voice. "I am a princess and my husband is a great general, leader of vast armies. When he learns I am being held captive here he will come for me." She meant to frighten him, to impress upon him her station, but Jorgen was a fearless man.

"Ah, Lisa, do not threaten me. *You* ran from Erik," he hissed. "It must have been a horrible marriage indeed to make you flee your own homeland. Or, perhaps there is some other reason you fled. . . ." He let his words trail off.

Brigitta kept her silence. She didn't want to encourage Jorgen to seek out Erik. Her dilemma was how to escape Jorgen before he sent word to Erik. She heard Jorgen's slight chuckle as he released his tight grip. Angrily, she shrugged from his hold and stepped away from the window, away from Jorgen.

He was content for the moment to allow her some space. With a calmness that bothered her, he moved to lean against the wall, his tawny gaze looking out the window down upon the green lawns. After long moments of heavy silence, he spoke. "I will tell you now, Thora-Lisa, that you will never again see your husband alive. Erik Bjord has been a menace to my people and my family. He is the murderer of my brother and it has been my thirst for revenge on Bjord that has brought me to my high military status." His feral eyes narrowed as he turned his large, bearded face toward her. "It is not for the glory of Denmark that I pillage Sweden's coast, but for the satisfaction of seeing Erik Bjord's attempts at broadening his own realm thwarted." His voice lowered, turning raspy. "Your presence here is a godsend. *You will be the bait which lures Erik to my home.* As I watched Erik murder my brother upon a cold battlefield, he will watch as I take the life of his precious wife."

Brigitta stiffened, a gasp escaping her lips. "You—you are mistaken," she whispered, "if you think Erik will come for me. He—he does not love me, that is why I fled Vardighet."

"You lie!" he thundered. "Erik *will* come for you,

not out of love, I am certain, but because he is a man who desires supremacy. You are his wife, the princess of his people—these are what matter, not love and surely not honor."

"But to—to kill me? I have done you no harm!"

"You are a Swede, that is enough."

Along with the fear gripping her body, Brigitta felt a wave of pure hatred wash through her. This beast of a man across from her had murdered innocent people, had burned countless villages, and had slaughtered precious livestock. Although Erik Bjord thought only of himself, his gains were also the gains of her people. Not only would Erik lose his life if Jorgen's plan succeeded, but so, too, would many, if not all, of Erik's loyal soldiers who would march with him to Jorgen's home. Because of Brigitta, more of Sweden's men would die.

She felt sick with guilt and anger. "You are a heartless, vile man," she whispered.

Jorgen laughed, as though her choice of words suited him. "Yes," he agreed. "And soon I will be the man to impale the mighty Erik Bjord upon my sword." He pushed off from his place near the window, striding toward the door with heavy steps. "Rest now, Thora-Lisa. I want you well enough to be able to scream loud and long . . . for your screams will be the last thing Erik Bjord ever hears."

With those words, he left the chamber, the smell of his sweating body lingering behind.

It seemed that after her encounter with Jorgen her status in his household was raised. The guard at her door was only posted at night and during the day Brigitta was free to walk the great house.

She took advantage of the "privilege" and seared to her memory every portal leading outside, every corner darkness claimed, every window at ground level. Jorgen's guards surrounded his home, all prepared for Erik Bjord's arrival.

Each night she was forced to dine with Jorgen, and now, a week after their talk, another meal hour drew near. Brigitta was more nervous than she'd ever been. He had requested, no, ordered she wear her *merveilleux* silk gown, the same he had tossed onto her bed along with the jewels. Brigitta knew the reason. He was trying to taunt her, attempting to remind her, through the dress, of Vardighet and of Erik. He had succeeded.

In vexation, she jammed her delicate slippers onto her feet, then left her chamber, heading for the dayroom she knew Jorgen would be in. She was about to knock upon the huge door when she heard voices drift to her from inside the room. Pausing, Brigitta turned one ear to the door and strained to hear. Jorgen's ugly voice was quite clear to her, but the other voice, a man's, was muffled, as though the person stood across the room from the door. Holding her breath so she could hear better, Brigitta leaned closer, then felt all of her nerves tingle as the stranger's low voice became clearer. *Devon! It was Devon's voice she heard!*

Putting one hand to her mouth so she didn't cry out with joy, Brigitta forced herself to remain calm. Although Devon and Jorgen were conversing in the Danish language, she could catch bits and pieces of what they were speaking of. Devon mentioned Erik's name several times and it didn't take Brigitta long to figure out Devon was revealing

Erik's battle plans to Jorgen. Was Devon actually helping a Dane who had slaughtered peaceful Swedish villages? It would not be Erik who would be killed in these battles but Swedish men who were fighting for their country—Brigitta's people. She felt her stomach turn with revulsion. *It was all true!* Devon had planned all along to come to Jorgen with news of Erik's strategies! *How could he?* her mind screamed. By revealing Swedish war tactics to the Danes, Devon was jeopardizing hundreds of men and the safety of all of Sweden! Erik and his armies had, in the past, protected her own dear family from the very horrors Brigitta had seen the night in Svea's village. Even though her hatred of Erik Bjord ran deep, she did not wish to see the man beaten in this way.

"Oh, Devon," she whispered. "How could you?"

Hearing the voices come closer to the door, Brigitta quickly scurried out of the way and around a bend in the passage. Pressing her body against the cool stone of the wall, she listened and waited. It was a long while before the two men were finished with their secret conversation and Brigitta thought she would go mad with the waiting. She *had* to speak with Devon. Even though he had left her alone at Vardighet and even though he was now uniting with the hated Danes, she needed to see him face to face. She needed to hear from his own lips that he wanted nothing more to do with her.

She heard the men bid farewell to each other. The sound of solitary footsteps rang in the passage. Closer, they were coming closer. It had to be Devon.

As soon as the man rounded the bend, Brigitta reached out and grabbed hold of his arm, silencing him with just a look as she pulled him down the corridor and into an empty sitting room. Latching the door behind her, she looked up into Devon's startled face.

"Brigitta?" he breathed. For a moment, he stood transfixed, his black gaze devouring her. "Brigitta, wh—what are you doing here? I thought—"

"What did you think?" she demanded too quickly. Her hushed voice was filled with pain, and she cursed herself for suddenly feeling so weak. If Devon didn't love her, if their stolen moments together had meant nothing to him, then she was being a fool for even standing here with him. The silence between them suddenly grew uncomfortable.

Devon reached out, slowly, his fingers brushing her fine-boned jawline. Although his touch was gentle, the look in his eyes was anything but tender. "I thought you were still at Vardighet," he replied.

His touch was that of gold, shimmering, yet not with beauty but warmth. Brigitta felt her knees grow weak. Suddenly, she forgot the conversation she'd just overheard. All thoughts of Devon's traitorous acts fled from her mind, and she could remember nothing but the feel of his hands upon her naked skin. Oh, sweet heaven, how she loved him. She didn't care that he had left her at Vardighet, did not care that he was now in Jorgen's home for nefarious purposes. The only thing that mattered was that she was with him once again.

Throwing caution to the winds of fate, she

moved toward him and wrapped her arms about his strong shoulders. "Oh, Devon!" she breathed, not being able to help the trembling of her limbs. "Oh, God, I've missed you. I'm so glad to see you!" She rained kisses upon his clean-shaven cheek, then his jawline, then buried her head against his shoulder as she clutched him tight. His long hair, unbound, was clean and soft . . . and felt glorious against her face. "Devon! Where have you been? I—I waited and waited for you to return to Vardighet. What kept you from me? I was so frightened—for you and for me! I—I didn't know what to do. Erik—he—he knows about me, that I am not Thora-Lisa. I—oh, please just hold me. Don't ever let me go." Her tears were choking her now, causing Devon's hair to stick to her face, but she didn't care. He was here with her. That was all that mattered.

But even though Devon's arms were around her, his hold was not tight. It was as though he had been shocked into silence by her presence.

"I can explain," Brigitta began, knowing they could be discovered at any moment. "I fled Vardighet when Erik learned my true identity and, well, it is such a long story! Jorgen and his men attacked the village where I was staying and he—he abducted me and brought me here." Glancing up, her heart in her eyes, she was taken aback by the impassiveness of Devon's countenance. His mouth was set in that grim line she remembered oh too well and his black gaze was emotionless. "Devon? Wh—what is the matter? Say something! Please don't look at me like that. I—I feared I'd never see you again—and here you are! Aren't you happy to see me?" She reached out a hand to gently brush across the tense muscles of his jawline. "Devon?"

His arms came up and he caught her hand in both of his, his hold not at all gentle. In a harsh whisper, he demanded, "Why did you marry him, Brigitta?"

"What? Things happened so quickly. I was all alone. You know why I married Erik. I—I *had* to go through with the ceremony! You know that, Devon. I had no choice."

"No choice? Or do you mean you were beginning to enjoy playing Lisa? Perhaps even Erik's prowess was beginning to entice you. Is that how it was, Brigitta? Did Erik's lusty pursuit of you finally change your views of the man?"

"How can you say such things?" she breathed, trying to break free from his grasp. "You know better than anyone how much I despise Erik. You were the one who left me all alone!"

"It was none of my doing, Brigitta, that moved you to the altar with that barbarian."

Damn him! She wanted to slap him, but then she wanted him to take her in his arms and give her the comfort she so badly needed. There was so much they needed to talk about.

"Devon, you must understand that after the time we—you and I spent together, I had no intentions of going through with the marriage. But you left and then events just started to sweep me along and before I realized what was happening, the ceremony had begun and I—"

"Enough," he said, pulling her close to him as though he wanted to believe and forgive her. But

Brigitta could see the doubt clouding his eyes. Devon's hatred for Erik Bjord ran deep, and now the fact Brigitta had married the man was a bitter reality for Devon. She should have known he would react this way!

As these thoughts swirled pell-mell through her mind, another more horrible thought joined them. Surely Devon could not think she had shared Erik's bed! One look at Devon told her that was exactly what he thought! Oh, there was so much to explain to him . . . and so little time. Later, she vowed. When she was safely out of Jorgen's home and Devon had time to cool down, she would explain all to him. For now, though, they had to find a way to get her freed.

"Devon, listen to me. We can discuss all this later. Right now you have to help me escape from Jorgen. He—he intends to use me as bait for the trap he's set for Erik!"

Devon gave a harsh laugh as he released her and then stepped away. The last rays of a setting sun, peeking through dark clouds, spilled into the sitting room and bathed all with a soft, yellowish glow. From beyond the huge windows of the chamber, sounds of life outside the great building floated to them as Devon stood staring at Brigitta. "Do tell how you came to be here, Brigitta, looking so radiant in your jewels and rich attire. Being a captive of the general must agree with you, for you look even more beautiful than when I last saw you." He motioned to the elegant furnishings surrounding them. "Is this how Jorgen houses all of his prisoners? Indeed, I could think of worse fates."

"Devon, stop it! You don't understand and I haven't the time to explain. We must leave here at once. Jorgen tells me Erik is looking for me and that there has been a reward posted for my return. Jorgen has no intention of returning me to Erik. I think he hates Erik as much as you do."

"I'm well aware of Jorgen's feelings toward Erik Bjord. But I've no idea of his feelings toward you. Tell me, Brigitta, what are you to Jorgen? Why has he housed you in such splendor? And please do not tell me you are a prisoner here. It is very unlike the Danish general to be kind to any Swedish prisoners, whether or not he believes them to be a princess."

"Devon, please! You are making assumptions that are not true—could never be true! I've thought of no one but you these past months, I—" She stopped herself from saying more. It was apparent Devon was not hearing a word she said. He stared at her with piercing eyes that looked much like the horizon outside with its gathering storm. And right now was not the time for them to be at each other's throats. He could be angry all he wanted when they were safely out of Jorgen's reach. Certainly she had a few questions for him, but now was not the time.

She said, "You can pass judgment on me later, Devon, but now you must help me flee from Jorgen. He—he has requested me to dine with him tonight . . . and once he has Erik in his clutches, he will murder me!"

Devon took in a sharp breath, his features turning hard. "I'll help you escape. Be ready to leave. Tonight."

Finally! Brigitta's heart lifted with joy. "But there is a guard posted at my door during the night. Can you get by him?"

"Do not worry," he assured her. "I'll take care of him. Here," he continued, pressing a packet from his pocket into her hand. "Pour this into Jorgen's drink."

"What is it?"

"Trust me. After he ingests this, Jorgen will not awaken until well into tomorrow. As children, both Thora-Lisa and I visited Darlana, and I learned many things from the old woman."

Brigitta took the packet, hoping that perhaps she and Devon might be together again after all. Quickly, she gave directions to the room she was kept in.

Nodding, Devon said, "You must be ready to flee at any moment. I don't know when I'll be able to reach you."

"Yes, of course. Be—be careful, Devon," she said and then turned toward the door. After checking the hall, she quickly stole out of the sitting room and headed toward Jorgen. The packet Devon had handed her was tucked securely in the neckline of her dress and was now tickling her skin as she walked.

After a knock on the door, Brigitta entered the large room. Before her, laid out on a long mahogany table, was a veritable feast. A variety of steaming meats and vegetables, fresh-baked breads and pastries were all set in the middle of the table, their aromas mingling and floating to Brigitta. Candles shoved into elaborate holders held sputtering flames on their tips, and the wax was even now dripping down the sides of the tapered sticks. Silver goblets held a deep-colored wine in them and Brigitta's immediate thought was how to dump the contents of the hidden packet into Jorgen's goblet. She knew the task would not be easy.

"Ah, the vision of a Swedish princess," Jorgen said, his words laced with contempt. His bulky frame came out of the shadows of the room to Brigitta's side. He led her by the elbow to her chair and assisted her to her seat.

Brigitta wanted to shrug off his assistance, but she knew better than to arouse his anger. She was too close to getting away.

A servant, silent and precise in every movement, served them, then quickly left the room. Brigitta was nervous and it took great control not to let her hands shake as she sipped the wine and began to pick at her meal. Although her stomach was empty, she knew she would not be able to eat. Jorgen consumed his meal in a barbaric manner, attacking the portions on his plate and drinking heavily of the wine. Brigitta watched from the corner of her eyes. So close. His goblet was so close to her, yet he watched her every movement.

"You are nervous this night," Jorgen commented as he tore a chunk of bread from the nearest loaf. He dipped the piece into the puddle of gravy on his plate, then popped it in his mouth. "And well you should be," he said around the food in his mouth.

Brigitta took another sip of wine, hoping it would soften her raw nerves. "I'm of the opinion you like

the thought of my being frightened of you. I think
you take great delight in knowing you have the
upper hand."

He laughed. "Perhaps you are right, fair Lisa,
perhaps you are right." He leaned back in his chair,
swiping a drop of gravy from his chin. "I should
tell you I've sent word to Erik you are here."

Brigitta's back stiffened.

"I thought the information would disturb you."
Once again, he ran a hand along his beard, his
orange-yellow eyes holding hers intently. "Soon,
both you and your husband will meet your death."

Brigitta tore her gaze from Jorgen and focused
her eyes on the sputtering candle flame before her,
forcing herself to remain calm. But her mind
whirled. How was she to get the packet from her
dress and pour the contents into his goblet? There
seemed to be no easy answer to that question.
There was an urgent knock upon the door then
and Brigitta nearly jumped from her skin at the
sound of it. The look on Jorgen's face was murderous.

"Yes?" he bellowed from his seat. "What do you
want?"

The door was thrust open and a harried-looking
man entered, his clothes wrinkled and dirty, and
his features pinched with weariness. To Brigitta, it
appeared as though the intruder had traveled a
great distance to speak with Jorgen. In a moment,
Jorgen was off his chair and striding to the door.
Obviously this man was an intrusion Jorgen didn't
mind. The two men stepped outside the chamber
and Jorgen pulled the door shut behind them.

In a second Brigitta was in action. With a quick

hand, she withdrew the packet, carefully opening it with trembling fingers and then dumping the powder into Jorgen's wine. She shoved the empty packet back into her dress and then added more wine to Jorgen's goblet, then stirred the mixture with a nearby knife. She'd no sooner leaned back in her chair than the door was thrust open and Jorgen reentered, a look of extreme pleasure on his coarse features.

"Well, my dear Lisa," he announced, returning to his chair and taking his goblet in hand. "Your faithful husband has taken the bait. He is on his way here."

Brigitta watched as Jorgen put the goblet to his lips and drank deeply of its contents. Her heart was pounding double time and she had to clench her hands into fists to keep her nervousness from overtaking her. She wanted him to drink all of the liquid, but he did not.

He set the vessel down, then grinned at her. "It seems the great warrior is anxious to get his errant little wife back home."

Brigitta gave him a level look as she put her own goblet to her lips, hoping he would follow suit and drink more of his own. How much need he drink before the potion took effect? she wondered. How long did it take before he would succumb to its power? She had no idea.

"Do not look so distraught, Lisa. Erik will die slowly—but you, I will be merciful."

Brigitta felt her body shudder. She hated Erik, true, but to think he would soon meet his death was unsettling. Jorgen was a cold-blooded man and she wondered if he had always been so cold.

Why had Devon confided in the Dane? She watched as Jorgen put the goblet to his lips again and this time downed all of the liquid.

A moment later, it seemed as if he had forgotten Brigitta's presence. He bellowed for the guard and gave orders for the man to take Brigitta back to her chamber. "I will join you there shortly," he told her. "But first I've things to do in preparing for Erik's arrival." Roughly, he deposited her into the hands of the stone-faced guard.

Brigitta said not a word as she shrugged from the guard's hold and walked regally out of the day-room and proceeded to her own chamber. Once there, after hearing the key turn in the outer lock, she sank down onto the huge bed and began her wait.

Who would reach her first? Devon or Jorgen? Perhaps neither. Perhaps it would be Erik!

BOOK III

The Mistress

Chapter Sixteen

THE MINUTES SLID into an hour, which slid into another hour and still there was no knock upon her door. Brigitta paced the chamber for the hundredth time, her knuckles white from clenching her hands into fists. Her head throbbed unmercifully and she could feel the tension knot her neck muscles into tight cords. Outside Jorgen's home, nature raged just as violently as her nerves did. Stormy clouds, blown in across an angry, churning sea, swept over the land and brought with them lashing rain and fierce winds. Brigitta nearly trembled from the sound of the storm, but instead forced herself to bear it, for if Devon finally came to her they'd have to ride out in the storm. How much longer could she be expected to wait? Where was Devon? What had happened to him?

Impatient and sick with fear and worry, she flung herself back onto the great canopied bed and clutched her meager bundle of clothing to her cloaked form as a loud boom of thunder echoed within the walls and seemingly shook the vast structure to its core. A sudden spring thunderstorm, nothing more, she scolded herself: nature's raging. It would soon pass. Lightning flickered, a ghostly, bluish-white light that burst into the room with savage intensity, its flash dramatized by an accompanying clap of thunder that sent Brigitta's skin crawling. Another streak and then nothing but the sound of rain against the window and the lonely *whirrr* of wind whipping about outside. She shivered, her eyes trained on the latch of the door across the room.

Slowly, the thing was lifted from the other side. Her heart skittered, faltered, then beat a pounding, unnatural rhythm. She stood, ready to do what, she knew not, only that she must move if she was to survive. Staticlike lightning showed fitfully in the chamber, blinding snaps of light that evaporated into total darkness just as quickly as they appeared. Movement looked odd in such light, eerie, too quick but yet in slow motion.

She saw his face in a fulgurant blaze. Even the whiteness could not penetrate those dark pools that were his eyes. He moved toward her quickly, stifling her scream with one hand clamped tightly over her mouth.

"Do not," he warned in a hiss, "scream."

Terrified, and wide-eyed, she nodded. Beyond his shoulder she could see the lifeless body of the guard outside the portal, his head twisted grotesquely.

Devon pulled her face toward his own so that

she was forced to look at him and not the dead man in the passage. Brigitta wished desperately there was some spark of tenderness in his harsh gaze, but there was not. There was nothing but the raging tempest she had seen in them when she had first met him. The demon behind those black orbs that had always been there, so frighteningly close to the surface, was now once again in full rein of Devon's actions. It had been Devon's intense hatred of Erik Bjord that had brought Brigitta and Devon together, and it was now that same hatred that had brought her to him this night. Even as he led her silently from the chamber and down the corridor to a crudely built set of back stairs, Brigitta knew he was taking her not away from Jorgen but keeping her with him so as to be nearer to Erik Bjord.

It was as if the queer flickering lightning was making her world clear to her. There was a part of Devon that *wanted* Brigitta to be wed to Erik, to have inside knowledge of his comings and goings, of Erik's deepest secrets. And yet, Brigitta knew just as surely, there was also a part of Devon that wanted her to be far away from the cruel Erik, never to be near him or to let him touch her. It was a push-pull sort of war going on within Devon. Brigitta could feel it pulsating like a living thing. Devon had made love to her once, tenderly, thoroughly, showing her the one side no other could touch in him. And yet . . . now that she was married to Erik, the outcome of Devon's lifelong quest hinged somehow on this night.

And it was here that Brigitta finally became confused as to the lay of Devon's plans. For what good

could she be to Devon now that Erik knew she was
not Thora-Lisa? She could never return to Vardighet, nor could she ever hope to lure Erik into a false
sense of security and thus in some way aid Devon.
Her mind was clouded with these thoughts as she
stumbled after Devon down the dark stairs. They
emerged through a small doorway that led to another passage that finally took them outside to a
world gone mad with the raging elements. Cold
rain flattened against her cloak as she scurried beside Devon into the inky blackness that was split
apart by glaring flashes of lightning. Thunder
clapped, then boomed and rolled over the land,
then fell away into night only to repeat itself. Lightning, thunder, lightning, thunder, again and again
. . . The storm was in full force all around them.

Devon led her to the stables and then told her to
be still and wait for him. She did as he said, frightened Jorgen would, at any minute, spring upon
them with all of his men and do the same terrible
deeds they had done that long ago night in Svea's
village. She shuddered at the thought but stood
rooted to her spot, her eyes ever watchful for human movement. The rain was coming down harder
now, and if not for the great cloak she wore, she
would have been soaked to the skin. Wind-pushed
drops of water hit and stung her face, but still she
kept her body into the wind, for that was the direction of Jorgen's main house. At any moment she
expected to see a group of Danes come rushing
toward her, murder in their eyes.

She pulled her hood closer about her face as she
stifled the urge to call out for Devon to hurry.
Perhaps Devon had encountered someone. Surely

Jorgen wouldn't leave his stables unattended, especially when he expected Erik soon. For that matter, the whole outskirts of his lands were no doubt well protected by loyal Danes. Her fear mounted just as the stable door was thrust open and Devon emerged with two horses.

Brigitta stepped to him and grabbed his sleeve. "Did anyone see?" she whispered above the wind.

"Mount up," he ordered tersely, shrugging out of her hold and motioning an arm toward the black beast to his right.

Brigitta did as he said and a quick look of surprise passed her features, for the mount Devon had brought her was none other than the royal horse she'd taken with her from Vardighet. If there was one horse that could lead her to safety, she being a very inexperienced rider, it would be this horse. Without further hesitation she let Devon help her onto the saddle. Quickly she was shooting into the thick darkness, one with the horse that suddenly felt so familiar to her. Rain stung her face like so many straight pins pushed to prick her skin. She had to squint her eyes to mere slits, and she leaned her body way forward, her hands tight to the reins as she urged her horse forward following the crazy path Devon created. She wondered if he knew his direction, if *anyone* could know their direction in this fathomless night. She felt as if she were charging straight into a wall of black and would at any time meet with a solid object, and ultimately her death.

"Do you know where we're headed?" she asked breathlessly as she pulled up beside Devon.

He too was leaning forward, his black cape flow-

ing behind him like great wings. His hair was plas-
tered to his scalp, for he'd lost his fancy hat long
ago, and his brows were furrowed tight over intense dark eyes. "I know enough," was his quick
reply.

"But Jorgen expects Erik at any time! Surely his
home is well guarded!"

"Yes, there are men on the borders ahead."

"Then how shall we get by?"

They raced under grabbing branches of a budding beech tree and Brigitta felt the sting of a
scratch to her cheek. She swatted angrily at the
next, slapping twigs as she maneuvered her horse
through a dangerous maze of forest that was suddenly upon them.

"We haven't a chance of getting *by* any of Jorgen's men, Brigitta."

"Then what—" she began to question, but there
was no time for words. She must simply trust Devon. He was a man accustomed to danger, a man
who had traversed continents to return to a home
that had never really been a home to him at all.

The rain began to come down in greater torrents
and the earth beneath their horses' hooves was
soggy and made for a slick track. She thought
surely she would tumble from her saddle.

"Slow up!"

Brigitta heard the command, though barely, and
as one they reined their animals in. Brigitta's
mount was near to bursting, so caught up was he
in their mad dash, and it took all of her strength
and newly acquired skill to keep him under control. Her beast pranced nervously as Devon spoke.

"Up ahead. There should be four men," he said in a low voice.

Brigitta could barely see his face in the dark night, though she did catch the gleam in his eyes. It was a fierce kind of light that shone through, one filled with determination.

"Do you think you can make it past?" he was asking, his strong arms keeping tight rein on his eager beast. The steed beneath him pranced as did her own. Tension cracked the air.

"I—I think so," Brigitta blurted, suddenly unnerved by their situation. A long moment of silence passed between them but was soon broken with a flash of lightning that was instantly followed by a loud clap of thunder. She added, "If I must, then I will."

Devon nodded and in a moment they were off—two shadows in a shadowless night.

Brigitta felt her steed move easily beneath her, felt his great muscles strain with each stride forward and she leaned toward his neck, her thighs brushing him lightly now and then. Beside her Devon rode and the two of them cleared the forest that had held them so tightly and emerged into an open field. As luck would have it a great streak of lightning filled the night sky, illuminating all with a bluish-white light, and it was then Brigitta saw the guard posts ahead. In an instant she discerned not four but five shapes spread across a distance, each with a flintlock gun in hand. The guards' backs were toward Brigitta and Devon, for the Danes expected the intrusion to come from outside Jorgen's home, not from within.

She turned wide eyes to Devon. "How?" she asked. "How are we to get by them?"

"We'll have to jump the gate. You can do it, can't you?"

Jump the gate? Good Lord! Despite their wild ride, she was still a novice on horseback . . . and now she had to jump an obstacle with bloodthirsty Danes all around?

"Brigitta, we can't go back. Ahead is our only route of escape. Just follow my lead and trust your mount." His voice was comforting but Brigitta knew well enough that the terror she was feeling did indeed touch him.

"Yes, yes of course," she answered, drawing courage from him.

"Good girl. Now stay low. Give them no target to mark, and no matter what, *keep going!*"

She nodded, but Devon was already in motion. This was it. No time to turn around, no time to change her mind. She couldn't think about the thunder that clapped louder than gunfire or of the rain that clung to her clothes and gathered to pull her skirts and cloak downward, making her a heavier load for her beast. Spurring her horse into a gallop, she refused to let her mind dwell on the danger. She could think of one thing only: forward, no matter what.

Their horses' hooves sounded distressingly loud now on the muddied earth as they neared the guards, and when Brigitta heard the first shout, she felt her heart trip.

"Ho, you there! Halt! Halt, I say!"

"Now, Brigitta! Now!" Devon yelled.

The guards hesitated in their attack, for they'd

not expected the assault to come from behind. It was then Brigitta pressed her legs closer to her beast. *Jump, sweetheart, jump!* her mind chanted as fire was let loose from several flintlocks. The sound of powder bursting, some sputtering into the wet night, filled her ears just as her steed pushed off the ground and straddled the low gate. Eyes squeezed tight, her entire body taut with fear, Brigitta felt her stomach whirl with the sensation of being airborne and then was jolted forcefully to the side when the horse landed solidly on the ground. She fought to keep her body upright in the saddle and her movements confused her mount, for he slowed up, jerking his head back. She soothed him with a pat to the neck, a few quick words, and soon he was sprinting forward again into the pitch black night. But there was no sign of Devon. She'd lost sight of him when she'd shut her eyes and now her horse, while once comfortable speeding behind Devon's mount, faltered.

She started to pull back on the reins, but just as she did the sound of gunfire whizzed past her ear. A long branch splintered and fell from a tree beside her. Brigitta didn't give second thought. She dug her heels in and urged her beast forward on the unfamiliar terrain. The earth below flew by as did low-hanging branches of a new wood that had sprung up. She wondered crazily where she was headed. Had Devon been shot? Fear clutched at the base of her spine, its icy grip shooting sickeningly up her back. Devon had told her to keep going, no matter what. But how could she without him?

She heard the pounding and sloshing of hoof-beats behind her. Surely the Danes could not have mounted their own horses this fast? In no time the threatening sound was upon her and she panicked, veering to the right and nearly crashing into Devon as she did so.

"Faith!" he cried. "You'll see me dead yet!"

"Devon!"

"Of course it's me. No, don't slow up. Keep going. You're doing fine, Brigitta. I've never seen a more beautiful jump than the one you just executed!"

Despite the danger, she felt herself smile. "Damn you, I'm lucky I didn't break my neck!" She heard his laugh and her heart lifted. Perhaps they'd left the Danes far behind.

But not so. The guards were now on mounts of their own—and in pursuit.

"Ride fast or Jorgen's men will have us for their midnight meal."

Brigitta needed no other incentive. "Lead the way!" she called, letting him pass on the twisting path then following him.

They flew over rugged, wet ground and the wood around them thickened and presented itself with tangled vines and branches that slapped wet and piercing in the night as she and Devon blazed a wild path through it. They dashed through a small stream, then up and over a bank that was covered with wet leaves and hidden roots. Brigitta worried her mount would trip on a root or, worse yet, step into a hole. But their speed left little time for worry as they veered left for a ways, then right and crossed yet another stream that was wider with more rocks jutting above rushing black water.

The constant sound of pursuing hoofbeats

spurred them on through the black night and Brigitta tried to keep her mind on staying seated on the saddle, keeping low, and keeping her horse at a fast pace. Her hands and face began to bleed where stinging thorns and branches had sliced the skin, and she felt blisters form on her hands from holding so tight to the reins. And still the Danes were close behind. Too close.

"Devon!" she shouted against the elements. "They're gaining!"

Devon turned in his saddle, his face a mask of steely determination as he slowed his horse only a fraction and motioned for Brigitta to pass him.

"But I know not where we're going!" she shouted, thinking he had a safe haven in mind and was heading for it.

"Wherever," came his sharp reply. "Just go!"

Brigitta's mount whizzed by his as she squinted into the driving rain and pressed her legs closer to the horse's body. Their pace was maddening, much too fast for the treacherous terrain. Just as she thought one of their mounts would break a leg, she heard another *crack* of gunfire behind them, and then the horrid shriek of a horse. She turned her head just in time to see Devon and his horse crumble to the ground in a tumble of flailing limbs.

"Devon!" she yelled, yanking hard on her own reins. In a moment she was off her horse and reaching to help him away from the thrashing animal that had only moments ago been a healthy stallion racing in the wind. Now the beast lay on the ground, its right front leg at an odd angle. The rugged terrain and the guards' gunfire had finally taken their toll.

"Are you all right?" she asked, catching hold of Devon's sleeve. "Are you hurt?"

"I'm fine. God's teeth, I hate to lose this beast!" He stood indecisive for a moment, the seconds punctuated by pounding hoofbeats in the distance. Finally, he reached into the great folds of his cloak and pulled out a wheel-lock pistol, put it to the straining horse's head, then fired. The sound was final, loud, and as it burst forth so did all life from the injured horse. The stallion lay still on the sodden earth.

Brigitta closed her eyes tightly, forcing back the tears. Senseless. Every day since she'd been abducted by Jorgen had been senseless. There were yells in the distance that brought Brigitta abruptly back to the present. She mounted, turned the horse in the right direction and then waited until Devon swung up onto the saddle behind her. He took the reins in his hands and spurred the animal forward.

Surely they could not outpace the Danes on just one horse, especially in a maze of wooded land that was unfamiliar to the beast. Trembling with fear, she clutched at the horse's mane and dully realized the eye of the storm was passing overhead. The stinging pelts of rain had lessened to only a shower of fat drops and the booming thunder was now rolling away far to their right. More shots rang in their ears and Brigitta knew that now with the passing of the storm the Danes would have a better chance of having more fires than misfires.

"Hold on," Devon whispered into her ear, his body pressed hard against hers as they both leaned low over the horse's neck. "We may be able to lose them yet. Up ahead there is—'' The crack of a flintlock sounded from behind and Devon slumped in the saddle, his sentence unfinished.

"Devon? What is it?'' But she knew the answer to her question even before the words passed her lips. Visions of the night she and Svea had carted John's body away from the burning cottage filled her mind. Devon's weight was now heavy against her back. Oh, Lord, was he dead? "Devon, speak to me!'' she urged as she grabbed the reins from his nerveless fingers. "Should I stop, Devon? Tell me. I don't know what to do!'' Terrified, waiting for him to answer, she kept the horse at a fast pace. She thrust one arm out behind her and steadied his heavy weight on the saddle and was relieved when she felt him move to help her. Assured that he wasn't dead, she wrapped his arms about her waist, and with one hand on the reins and the other clutching tightly to both of his, she kicked her mount to an even more maddening pace. Not knowing where they were headed, she veered the horse sharply to the right, down a slick knoll and into a thicket. Their pace slowed as the horse picked his way through a tangle of whipcordlike branches, and Brigitta wondered if she'd made a grave error. But then she heard the thunder of hoofbeats passing behind them headed in the opposite direction and she let herself grab hold of the hope she'd outfoxed the bloodthirsty Danes. "I think we lost them, Devon. They're headed away from us. I—I don't know where I'm going though. Can you hear me, Devon?''

He didn't answer so she doggedly kept the horse plodding forward. She didn't dare stop to check on

Devon's wound. She rode for nearly an hour, and not until they came upon a small clearing nestled within the thicket did she bring her mount to a stop. "We'll rest here," she told Devon. "I think we'll be safe for a little while at least." Supporting Devon's body with one arm, she carefully slid from the saddle, then tried to ease him down beside her. But he was much too heavy and before she knew what was happening he slumped against her and she fell to the ground pinned beneath him. "Devon? Oh, Devon, are you all right?" She attempted to crawl out from under him, but as she grabbed hold of his arm she felt the hot flow of some sticky substance. She felt terror seize her, for he was motionless, and covered with blood.

Chapter Seventeen

AFTER CAREFUL INSPECTION, Brigitta found his wound to be no deeper than just a skimming of the flesh. With material ripped from her underskirt, she staunched the flow of blood and then made a crude sling so that his left arm would not be jolted by any sudden movement. With much maneuvering she soon had Devon lying on the ground and covered with her cloak. It was not until the hour before dawn that he awoke.

"Brigitta?"

She had huddled against a tree after rubbing

down her mount and her muscles had grown stiff from her position. "Yes, I am here," she answered, moving quickly to his side.

"Where are we?"

"I—I don't know," she answered, shivering as she took in the gray mist that covered the world around them.

"The Danes—"

"We lost them. I haven't seen nor heard them for some time now. But we must move on, and quickly. Can you walk?"

He tried to sit up but the weight he put on his one arm was too much to bear. He leaned back on his right arm. "Yes," he ground out. "But not yet."

"Oh, Devon," she whispered, hesitantly reaching out one hand to gently brush her fingers across his now-sweating brow. "Are you in much pain? I—I don't know what to do for you."

He managed to give her one of his reassuring smiles. "I'll be fine. Do not worry about me. God's teeth, but one of those Danes had good aim!"

"No, I think not," she said with no humor. "If so, you would have most likely been shot through the heart." Just saying the words aloud made her tremble. She sat back on her knees, wrapping her arms about her waist as though it were the nip in the air that had caused her to shiver.

Devon was not fooled. Straightening his body, he motioned for her to sit beside him, and when she'd complied, he wrapped his right arm about her shoulders. "I'm fine," he repeated softly in an attempt to reassure her. "And the two of us will make it safely out of Jorgen's reach."

"How can you be so certain?" she asked. "We've

only one mount and . . . and you've been shot."

He shrugged, doing his utmost to make light of the situation. "I've suffered worse," he confided. "I've also gotten myself out of stickier webs."

"But where will we go? I—I'm not even certain which direction we should take."

She felt the touch of his forefinger beneath her chin. With delicate pressure, he lifted her face to his. "*I* know a way," he told her. "Please, trust me, sweetling, and believe me when I tell you I will never let any man harm you ever again."

She felt unshed tears burn her eyes. How long she'd waited to be with Devon once again. And now he was here with her, beside her, offering his protection. "Why did you leave me alone at Vardighet?" she asked. "Why, when you said you'd send a cart and driver for me, did you just leave? I—I was so afraid and—and hurt when I stepped out of Thora-Lisa's secret entrance to find no one there. I—"

"What?" he interrupted, his tone incredulous. "Brigitta, I paid a man to meet you in the gardens! I swear I did!"

Her eyes grew wide. "But there was no one there, Devon. I—I thought you'd changed your mind, or worse, had never meant the words you'd spoken." Her lashes dropped to conceal the pained expression in her gaze.

But Devon forced her to look at him. "Brigitta, my sweet, sweet Brigitta, I swear to you I paid a man, in gold, to whisk you away from the castle. He was to take you to a small village where I would meet you later. When I got to the village, you were nowhere to be found. God's teeth! It is I who thought *you'd* changed your mind!"

Her voice just a whisper, she asked, "You mean to say you—you never intended to leave me alone with Erik?"

"After what we'd shared? Of course not!"

Elation with his words coursed through her, but close on its heels was a deep, deep sorrow. Oh, sweet heaven, she thought. She'd married Erik thinking Devon wanted nothing more to do with her. Out of deference to Thora-Lisa's wishes, Brigitta had married a man she did not love, could never love! What must Devon think of her now? The world spun sickeningly around her and she suddenly felt nauseous.

"Oh my," she groaned. "What have I done, Devon?" In shame, she bowed her head. Her tears came then, hot and gagging. "I'm sorry," she whispered brokenly. "I never meant to hurt you. I—I did not want to wed Erik, you—you must know that. Oh, Devon! I thought of no one but you . . . you were the man I was plighting my troth to, not Erik. Never Erik!" Speech became too difficult past the lump in her throat then, so she fell mute, her quiet sobs punctuating the stillness of the predawn.

Devon said nothing for a full minute. Her crying tore at his heart, but he had to carefully consider his next words. The rage he'd felt when he'd first learned she'd become Erik Bjord's wife had been nearly too much to bear. Had it been any other man besides Erik he could possibly have been able to understand. But Brigitta knew how deep his hatred of Erik ran. She knew how cruelly that barbarian had treated him, his mother, and Thora-Lisa. How could she have allowed herself to be united to him in holy matrimony?

"Did you allow him to take you to his bed?" he demanded tautly.

Brigitta stiffened, snapping her head up. "No!"

"I find that difficult to believe."

Brigitta wanted to slap him, but she could not. His intense pain caused by her "betrayal" was evident in his black gaze. She hated the sight of it. She wanted only to soothe him, to reassure him that he had been the only man to know her intimately. "It's true," she whispered, her face wet with tears. "He—he attempted to do so, but I fought him and . . . and then, with Marta's aid, I fled Vardighet."

He made no response, only stared deeply into her eyes.

"You—you believe me, don't you?" Her heart tripped with fear when he didn't answer. "Devon?" she pressed. "You *do* believe me . . . please, tell me you believe me."

Of course he believed. How could he not? She was the treasure of his heart. Somehow, over the past few months, Brigitta Lind had become his world. He, Devon Courtenay, a man with no country and labeled a bastard from the day of his birth, had at last found someone with whom he could confide in and love with all his heart. Finally, he nodded. "Yes," he answered softly. "I believe you." Without another word he pulled her close against him, squeezing her tightly. "I believe you, sweet Brigitta."

Trembling uncontrollably, she allowed herself to relax within the shelter of his right arm, breathing deeply of the cool morning air and the pleasant musky scent that was Devon's own. She never wanted to be anywhere but here in his embrace. All of the horrible moments since he'd left her alone at Vardighet receded in her mind, tumbling rapidly to be locked tight into some small part of her brain where she intended to keep them. Never again did she want to remember the horror and fear she'd experienced while in the princess's chamber with Erik.

Into her ear came the sound of Devon's voice, thick and husky. "Let us forget the past few months, sweetling," he murmured. "They are behind us now, to be forgotten and not remembered. It is my deepest regret that I was not at Vardighet to aid you in your time of need. Forgive me, my love . . . forgive me."

Her cheek flush to his chest, she whispered, "There is nothing for me to forgive. It is I who should be repentant. Not only have I wronged myself in marrying Erik, but so too have I harmed you. I am sorry."

Before she had a chance to continue, Devon gently cupped her chin in his hand and drew her face upward. His eyes, so black and filled now with a mixture of tenderness, regret, and love, gazed down at her. "No more apologies," he breathed. "It matters not to me that all of Vardighet believes you are the wife of Erik Bjord. You unselfishly went to the altar as Thora-Lisa, and I am certain, wherever our princess is, she is grateful to you and can now rest in peace, knowing her last wish has been fulfilled. Her people could all be proud of her that day. As for me, Brigitta, you were mine from the moment I took you in my arms and made love to you before the hearth. I care not that Erik believes you are his by right and by law. Here now, I ask you to come with me so we may live together as man and wife, to build a future as bright and shimmering as your fair hair." He let his fingers slip into her long, unbound tresses, fingering the silky swath. "Here now, Brigitta Lind, I plight my troth to you for all time."

Brigitta, although momentarily speechless with his request, was suffused with a warm, golden glow. *To live with him as man and wife . . .* The words tumbled over in her mind, swirling in an enchanting circle.

"I know that I have no home, or even a name, to offer you," he continued, "but these past months without you near me, have been the worst of my life. And even though my life's quest to claim all that is rightfully mine by birth is nowhere near its end, I realize I do not wish to travel the road alone. I want you with me, Brigitta. I want yours to be the face I see each night before I drift into slumber, I want yours to be the body that warms me through a long winter's night. I want you beside me to greet each new day, I want to know that, no matter how dark and cruel life may seem at times, I will have you, always . . ."

Her eyes bright and glistening with new tears, Brigitta reached up to clasp his right hand in both of hers. She gently touched her lips to the pulse point of his wrist. "Yes," she whispered, her voice catching. "I will go with you, Devon. To your homeland, back to Sweden—even to hell. I will go wherever you are bound. The vows I made to Erik Bjord I made in the name of Thora-Lisa; they mean nothing to me. It is you who holds my heart. I care not if you haven't a home or a name to offer, for all of Lisa's royal wealth held no joy without you by my side. Without you, I am only half a being.''

She heard Devon's small sigh of relief at her words, and her heart swelled with happiness. Slowly, his black gaze devouring her, Devon leaned his face to hers, lightly pressing his mouth atop the soft swell of her lips. Brigitta tilted her face back, greeting his tender kiss.

His mouth was soft and warm, tasting slightly salty due to the tears Brigitta had cried, and when his tongue gently invaded her mouth, twirling with her own, Brigitta felt a familiar languorous longing spread through her. She wished they were some place other than the damp thicket, wished she and Devon had hours to reacquaint themselves and share the intimacy of lovemaking he had so recently taught her. Carefully, certain not to disturb his wounded side, she smoothed her hands across his muscled back, reveling in the feel of masculine, corded tendons. Through the material of his clothing she could sense the steady beating of his heart, the even, deep breaths he took in. Her explorations continued until she touched upon a stray splattering of blood. Immediately, she disengaged herself, moving away.

''Devon?''

''I'm fine,'' he whispered, smiling as he caressed her cheek with his right hand. ''Your presence washes away all pain.'' The heady look in his eyes thrilled her. But despite her own desires, she knew they must be on their way.

"Your wound needs tending by skilled hands . . . and Jorgen's men will soon resume their search."

Reluctantly, he agreed. "Yes, we've tarried too long as it is. But you must realize how your beauty blinds me to reason. I wish I had something to give you, sweet Brigitta, some lovely piece of jewelry you could wear to remind you of my declaration made this day. Our troth has been plighted, but I've nothing with which to symbolize it."

She knew he was speaking of the ring his own father had given his mother the day they'd been wed. She knew it cost him much to be leaving Vardighet without the signet ring he sought. In hopes of soothing him, she said earnestly, "I have no need of material things, Devon. Your words are more than enough."

"Even so . . ."

The note in his voice saddened her. Suddenly, a thought occurred. "Wait," she said, remembering the bag of jewels Marta had given her before leaving Sweden. "Perhaps I do have something." She moved quickly toward the horse and saddle, removing the heavy pouch from one of the bags. Seated once again, she opened the pouch, spilling the precious gems it held to the wet ground. "Marta gave me these so that I might purchase passage to—to England."

"England?" he asked, somewhat surprised.

"Yes, you see, after you'd left Vardighet I was determined to find you. I—I thought perhaps you'd gone to be with your mother and I remembered you'd once mentioned she was living in Dover."

He tilted her chin with strong fingers, ignoring the pile of wealth before them. "You mean to say you were willing to travel across continents, alone, to find me?" he asked.

She nodded, whispering, "I would cross all the oceans, and more, just to be with you."

He smiled, laughing happily then as love, respect, and deep admiration filled his black gaze. "You are indeed a rare woman, Brigitta Lind."

She returned his smile, basking in the warmth of his gaze. One by one, she lifted the precious gems spread out before them on the grass. Looking at them, she realized she didn't recognize any of the jewels as she had anticipated. Puzzled, she lifted a sapphire brooch that was encrusted with sparkling diamonds. "I had thought Marta would bring me some of Lisa's jewels, but I've never seen these before," she told Devon. "Granted, there is probably a great deal of Lisa's treasures that I have never viewed, but how would Marta have secured them?"

Devon, who had so recently had eyes only for Brigitta, tore his gaze from her and looked at the jewels. A mask fell over his face as his eyes peered at only one object—a shiny gold ring adorned with a fat, blood-red ruby. Silently, he reached for the ring, his fingers trembling. Holding it in the palm of his hand, he studied the ring for long moments, staring sightlessly at the elaborate markings on each side of the ruby. Two fierce-looking lions, both standing on hind quarters, were etched into the smooth gold, each appearing to hold up one side of the stone.

Brigitta watched in stark wonder. "Devon," she breathed, "is this—is this your father's ring, the ring you've been searching for?"

He nodded, his fingers closing tightly over the cool gold as he closed his eyes.

Brigitta said nothing, half afraid to intrude upon the moment with any words. Finally, after years of searching and endless hours of pain and grief, Devon had found a link to his long-lost father. At last, he held in his hand the key that would open up the, until now, untouchable gate to his father's estate. With this ring, Devon could now rightfully claim his inheritance. The reason none of these jewels were familiar was because they had not belonged to Thora-Lisa but to Erik Bjord! Of course, Brigitta realized in amazement, when Marta had scurried away to get Brigitta a pouch of gems, the old woman had known Erik was in a drunken stupor in the princess's rooms and so she had gone to Erik's chambers, taking Erik's treasures! Brigitta wondered if Marta had known exactly what she was doing when she chose to tuck the signet ring in the pouch.

Devon slowly opened his eyes, reaching for Brigitta's left hand. His ebony eyes moist, he lifted her slender fingers, slipping the heavy ring onto her ring finger. "As my father gave this ring to the only woman he would ever love, so too do I, Brigitta. The circle of this ring is representative of my love for you—forever and never ending."

The gold upon her finger was warmed by his

body heat, sending precious waves of intense heat through her. Brigitta stared down at the exquisite piece, watching in fascination as the meager light of dawn twinkled in the ruby's pool of red. She pressed her fingers tightly together so that the heavy, oversized ring did not twirl downward with the great weight of the stone. "It is beautiful," she breathed, deeply touched that he should bestow something of such value on her.

"Not nearly as beautiful as the woman who wears it."

"But I—I cannot accept this, Devon. This ring is your only proof of your paternity. What if I lost it in our travels, what if—"

"Hush," he insisted. "I want you to have it."

"But you must show this to those who are holding your father's estate from you," she continued, gazing up at him with wide eyes.

"And so I shall, with you beside me. I shall merely wag your hand beneath the lawyers' noses." He laughed then, deliriously pleased with their find.

Brigitta joined his laughter, knowing she would remember this day for the rest of her life and feast on the happiness they'd shared whenever her soul was heavy.

"Come, Brigitta," he said, standing without help, the pain of his wound temporarily forgotten. "We're bound for England, you and I, to lay claim to that which is rightfully mine. Soon we will be at Courtenay Castle and I will make you my bride. Brigitta Lind and Devon Courtenay will become one, and no one, ever, need know of the lives we lived while in Sweden."

She came to stand beside him, her left hand, adorned with Devon's ring, feeling light and heavy all at the same time. She allowed him to take both of her hands in his, let him rain her knuckles and their ring with warm kisses.

"Yes," she breathed. "To England to build our new life, together."

On one mount, they headed north, toward Copenhagen. *Köbenhavn*, in Danish, Devon explained, meant "merchant's haven." Copenhagen was the gateway to the Baltic Sea and soon Devon and Brigitta would be there. But first, they traveled through the small town of Köge, stopping at a farm just outside of the town. The Andraesen family, comprised of Harald Andraesen, his wife Erika, and their four children, lived on the small farm. The buildings, built in a hollow square and comprising four wings, all stood with their backs against the prevailing winds that constantly swept the unprotected land. All Brigitta would remember of their overnight stay with the Andraesens was her fear of being recognized—and the pigs. There were dozens upon dozens of pigs. Being Danish bred they were characterized by their long ears and tails and their loud squeals as they ran about in packs within the courtyard. Like sheep who followed each other, the pigs darted here and there, bumping clumsily into one another. And the stench! With the smell, Brigitta was sharply reminded of her childhood in the small *byalag* where the animals lived in close proximity to the people. Having lived for the past months as a princess, she had quite forgotten such a lifestyle.

Devon's wound was mended by his friends and,

to Brigitta's relief, no questions were asked. Obviously, the Andraesen family had learned it was better not to know of Devon's journeys. They were kind to Brigitta even though they must have realized she was from the north and a Swede.

Leaving Köge behind them, Brigitta and Devon traveled north toward the port city, passing by undulating fields of wheat, rye, grass, and green fodder. The weather of Denmark was a changeable thing, Brigitta soon learned; wont to be sunny one minute, then with rains and low-hanging clouds the next. And always there was a breeze to blow Brigitta's fair hair from her face. Riding upon one saddle with Devon was a memory Brigitta would always cherish. It was during these moments when Brigitta felt the closeness of their bodies and souls, felt the isolation with which the beautiful land of Denmark encompassed. Devon whiled away the time twirling a strand of her bright hair between his fingers or gently massaging the weary muscles of her back as he coaxed her to tell him stories of her childhood. Brigitta thoroughly enjoyed talking to her captive audience.

At last they reached the port city. Copenhagen was a city of towers. Everywhere Brigitta's eye wandered she was greeted with towering spires, all shooting straight up, sometimes being capped by seemingly lanuginous clouds. Greenish, copper-colored roofs and turrets rose on all sides, creating an uneven skyline above the flat-fronted buildings whose windows were filled to capacity with merchandise and price tickets. They traveled slowly along narrow lanes that were teeming with people of all nationalities.

"This is the entrance to the Baltic," Devon told her as they made their way down the *Vimmelskaft*, Copenhagen's busy main thoroughfare.

"Yes," Brigitta replied, "I heard Erik mention the importance of the Baltic states."

"Indeed," Devon responded darkly. "Erik's thoughts have always been on the Baltic states. He's a shrewd man and he realizes Europe's dependence on the Baltic states for their sea power. Without the Baltic states, Europe would not have the timber needed for suitable masts, nor the tar and pitch which are preservatives for the structure of ships and their canvas. Neither would she have the hemp and flax needed for sails. The English are dependent upon the Dutch for the essentials of naval construction, and Erik's greatest desire is to prey upon that weakness. In fact, all of Erik's energies are being channeled into gaining supremacy of the Baltic for Sweden. Before my father was murdered, he was working to see the Baltic free of dominance. As a seafaring man, my father knew what a powerful part the Baltic states played in Europe's naval strength."

"And that is why you think Erik played some part in your father's murder?" she asked, remembering the conversation they'd had long ago, just after Lisa's death.

He nodded. "I'm almost certain of it."

"But how could he? If Erik was in Sweden and your father was murdered in England—"

"I didn't say Erik did the deed himself, but I do know he was involved somehow. Also, you must know that Erik traveled abroad as often as possible since he was involved in mercantile trade with the wealthy burgers in Göteborg and Stockholm. It was only before I left for Sweden that I learned Erik had been in Dover the week my father was murdered. Since my mother's condition had worsened, I decided the time was right to travel to Sweden in search of the ring you now wear and also the marriage documents my mother claims exist."

"Oh, Devon, how tragic for you to have to leave your mother at such a time."

His hold on Brigitta tightened. "Yes, it was a difficult decision, but once you meet my mother, you'll realize why I decided to go. You see, she's a woman of incredible strength. She's vowed she will not let go of life until she proves to her friends that she did indeed actually marry Michael Courtenay those many years ago. No one ever really believed her claim. I am certain she will not let death take her until she sees the ring upon your finger. Only then will she go willingly. In my heart I know she is still alive, and she will remain alive until I come home to her with the proof she's been waiting for."

Brigitta fell silent then, realizing for the first time what a mixture of blessings the ring she grasped in her hand held for Devon. With the signet ring, Devon could claim his inheritance, and his mother would finally be able to prove to all that Michael Courtenay had indeed married her and given her this precious symbol—for to no one but his bride would Michael have given this ring, for it had been given to him by King James himself, a token of appreciation and meant to be given only to Michael's wife and first-born son. And yet, once Devon's mother had seen the ring, Devon knew she might very well let go of her clinging hold to life. . . . Once again, Brigitta came to realize what sacrifices Devon Courtenay would make for those he loved: Devon had given Lisa the unadorned burial she'd requested; and then he had forgiven Brigitta her betrayal of walking to the altar to wed Erik Bjord in the name of Thora-Lisa.

What a noble man she had fallen in love with. Brigitta only hoped she could honor him as totally as he honored her and those he held most dear.

The hustle and bustle of people thickened as they neared the wharves that were choked with an international tangle of masts and sails. Wares were being loaded and unloaded simultaneously as peddlers shouted of a variety of goods to be had, many yelling in varied languages. There were silks and pearls from the Orient, a range of materials from Italy, and Turkey carpets from the Near East. There were even beaver hats from a place called the New World. Brigitta was fascinated by the name, and Devon indulged her, buying one of the hats.

"The New World," she repeated, awestruck. "Just the name holds a note of promise, don't you think, Devon?"

He laughed at her innocent wonder of a new place as he agreed, then led her to yet another stall where he bought her a swath of Italian silk, as blue as her eyes. "When we reach England," he told her, "I shall hire someone to create a gown out of that silk. Whatever you desire, Brigitta, shall be yours."

Brigitta fingered the watery silk, her eyes bright with dreams. "And I shall be married in the dress," she answered. "Within Courtenay Castle."

Her words caused Devon's heart to swell, for he could think of nothing finer than being united in matrimony to Brigitta in the home his father had built.

Together, they ambled from stall to stall, and Devon, anticipating a wonderful celebration upon landing on English soil, bought her everything she fancied. Delicate china, fine teakwood screens, linen for their tables, silver candlesticks, elaborate fans for Brigitta to carry, yards of varied material for her gowns and underskirts—he bought it all. And then, their shopping complete, they ducked into one of the many inns situated near the docks, where they dined on a scrumptious feast of fish herring and eel, drowned in melted butter, along with fresh vegetables and dark bread and heady wine. Satiated, they climbed up a narrow flight of stairs to a cozy room that was warmed by a small fire in the hearth and that housed an inviting, huge, feathery bed. Bathing together in a too-small foot bath, they then climbed into bed, exhausted and replete, going easily into each other's arms for a dreamy two hours of lovemaking. Brigitta had never been so happy in her life. Even though Devon's wound was far from healed, he was a skillful and attentive lover. He brought Brigitta to delicious heights of sensual pleasure only to let her float back down to earth and then repeat the escalating journey.

Feeling daring and provocative, safe in the knowledge that soon she would become his wife, Brigitta returned his favors, moving over his lean, male body to press her soft curves upon him and fulfill his every need.

As dusk melded into a deep, star-filled night, they were insatiable. Although tired by their journeys, sleep was the last comfort they sought. It was as though their lovemaking gave them each an inhumanlike energy. The longer they made love, the more they wanted to tumble and touch, caress and explore. For Brigitta, the night could not be long enough.

At mid-morning, they walked across the plank onto the waiting ship that would transport them far away from their birthplace, far away from Jorgen and Erik. Soon the strong winds of the North Sea swept them along, cleansing their souls. The promise of a bright future sang in the sails above that flapped as loud as thunder. Even though this was Brigitta's first sea voyage, and many of the sailors spoke English, she was not afraid. With Devon beside her she would have gladly traveled to the ends of the earth.

Soon she was beginning to speak the English language, practicing at night in their tiny cabin. Devon delighted in the lilt of her voice, chuckling at how she pronounced many of the syllables. Brigitta was determined to perfect her speech, for she wanted more than anything to be able to meld into the life of upper English society where Devon rightfully belonged.

As their ship entered the choppy English Channel and the craggy, white cliffs of Dover came into view, Brigitta was certain she was ready to meet Devon's mother. She was also certain she carried his child within her womb.

BOOK IV

❧

The Beloved

Chapter Eighteen

WHILE THE GOODS they'd purchased in Copenhagen were being unloaded from the ship along with their mount, Devon and Brigitta made their way through the congested lanes of Dover. To one side of them tall-masted merchantmen choked the harbor, scraping sides in the busy waters as wares from all over the world were being either loaded or unloaded from the holds. To their left rose stately storied buildings housing inns, homes, and shops. Now and then one could spot a huge bird's nest perched atop one of the many wind-tortured chimneys shooting skyward. Stork's nests, Devon told Brigitta. There was another type of bird that caught Brigitta's eye, a huge white bird with a long dark beak, gliding gracefully through the air above their heads. The "petrel," it was named, and Devon explained to Brigitta, in a hushed voice, that the bird only came inland to mate. Brigitta found that

odd characteristic fascinating, and they both
laughed at her interest in such a habit.

Walking beside her, with her hand securely
tucked into the crook of his left arm, Devon realized with a start that he had never been happier in
his life. Finally, he was going home to the estate
his father had built, home with the woman he
loved and would soon marry. She was his beloved,
this bright beauty who had known both poverty
and extreme wealth. In her gorgeous, summer-blue
eyes, he could see his future. It was as golden as
her fair tresses. At last, fate had been kind to him.

"What are you thinking?" Brigitta asked him in
that soft, breathless voice of hers that could catch
at his heartstrings.

Devon gazed down at her, his dark eyes twin-
kling. "I am thinking of you and how lovely you
are. Courtenay Castle will be a grand home with
you at the helm, my love."

"Courtenay Castle." She repeated the word, liking the feel of it as it rolled off her tongue. "I
cannot wait to be there."

And she couldn't. But first, she knew, she must
meet Devon's mother. Brigitta worried the woman
might not care for her, or worse yet, feel Brigitta
was beneath Devon. After all, she'd been born a
peasant's daughter. Brigitta knew how much Devon loved and respected his mother, and Brigitta
wanted very much to make a good impression on
the woman who had given Devon life.

Brigitta soon learned all her worries were for
naught. Augusta Courtenay, once a lady-in-
waiting to Thora-Lisa's own mother, banished all
Brigitta's fears the moment they met. In a warm

gesture Brigitta would find to be characteristic of Augusta, the older woman gathered Brigitta in a warm hug, welcoming her to the small Courtenay family.

Dressed in a laced night rail, her gray hair pulled away from her lined face into a severe bun, she appeared frail, but her voice was rich, lilting. Augusta had been in her late twenties when she'd met the dashing, seafaring Michael Courtenay, and she had been close to thirty when she'd given birth to her only child. Now, nearing sixty, the woman looked worn and tired. Her skin was as fine as ivory parchment, touched here and there by the lines only a life well lived can bring. Sitting up in bed amid a swirl of brightly colored quilts, she appeared as small as a sparrow. But her eyes, watery blue in color, were filled with wisdom and a rare quick intelligence. Although her body might be failing her, it was apparent her mind was still sharp.

"So you are the fair maiden who has stolen my son's heart," Augusta said in Brigitta's native tongue. "I received a letter only yesterday from him posted weeks ago. In it, he described you." She turned her face toward Devon. "She is even more beautiful than you described," she told her son. "You have done well."

Devon, seated on the side of his mother's bed, holding her tiny, gnarled hand in both of his, smiled. "I am glad you approve, Mother. We plan to be wed as soon as possible."

"At Courtenay Castle?" she asked, a hopeful tone in her voice. At Devon's nod, she continued. "Your father would be proud. He built his home

for you; everything he did, he did for you, son."
She leaned back against the pillows, closing her
eyes, her thoughts skimming back in time.

Brigitta, standing silently nearby, wondered if
perhaps she should step into the adjoining room
and leave the two of them alone. She had been
touched to hear Devon had written to his mother,
telling about his love for her. Looking over at Devon, she noted the tears shimmering in his black
eyes. She realized now that there *had* been a part of
him that worried he might find his mother gone
when he returned to Dover. When he gazed up at
her, she nodded toward the door, silently asking
him if he'd like her to leave.

Devon shook his head. He reached one hand out
to her. Brigitta moved closer to the bed, instinctively slipping the signet ring off of her finger.
During their travels she'd wrapped a piece of twine
about the band so that she wouldn't lose the precious treasure.

"Augusta," Brigitta said softly. "There's something we have for you." Gently, she placed the
ring in the older woman's palm.

For a moment, Augusta said nothing. She merely
closed her twisted fingers atop the signet ring and
held it tightly, her eyes still closed. "Oh," she
breathed on a sigh. "I feared I would never hold
this again. . . ." She opened her eyes, tears spilling over her sparse lashes. "You've made me very
happy," she said. "The both of you. But this ring is
now yours, Brigitta. Even if I could wear it, which
I cannot since my hands have become so twisted
with age, it belongs to the woman who will be
mistress of Courtenay Castle. This was given to

Michael by King James himself for Michael's loyal service to the crown and it is to be passed down from generation to generation. Take this, Brigitta, and give it to your son so that he may then pass it on to his." She held the ring out for Brigitta, her hands trembling as she watched Brigitta slip the ring back on her own finger. Her watery gaze settled on her son. "So, you shall finally be going home to claim your birthright . . . it hardly seems possible."

"I know," Devon said quietly. "We've been waiting so long for this moment."

"Your brother's not going to like it, not one bit," she added. "There'll be a nasty scene, but I don't want you to back down, Devon, do you hear?"

"I won't, Mother. You have my word. I should think we can come to some kind of understanding. There's no reason why we all can't live under the same roof together."

"No reason?" Augusta echoed, her voice rising a note. Eyes flashing, she said, "Courtenay Castle is yours, Devon. The entire estate belongs to you and only you! You are the true heir, not Roger. He will just have to accept the fact. You have every right to boot him out baggage and all."

Brigitta listened to the exchange in astonishment. "You have a brother?" she asked.

"A half brother," Augusta explained. Her brows knitted together for a moment, as anger quickly darted across her features, then disappeared just as quickly. She waved one hand in the air, as though to dismiss the subject. "Michael had a . . . dalliance with a chambermaid before he met me. Years later, this young man showed up on Mi-

chael's doorstep, claiming to be his son. Of course
no one knows for certain who Roger's true father
is, but Michael, forever the gallant, took the young
man in. But knowing we had created a child, Michael added a provision to his will that states whoever carries Michael's ring should be sole heir to
Courtenay."

"Roger has been seeing to the estate since my
father's death," Devon added.

"And does he know of your claim?" Brigitta
asked.

"Of course he does," Augusta cut in. "But he
has refused to allow either Devon or myself to live
at Courtenay and has even gone so far as to employ a number of lawyers whose sole purpose is to
work at ensuring Roger's security. Roger would
rather die than see Devon claim his birthright. The
ring you wear is the only proof that can legally
bring Devon complete control of Courtenay Castle.
Roger will of course be irate when he sees the three
of us riding up to his doorstep." The older woman
smiled to herself, suddenly full of spirit. "Yes,"
she said softly. "I've waited long for this day. And
if it is the last thing I do, I *will* see my son in his
proper place."

Brigitta feared it might very well indeed be the
last thing Augusta Courtenay did.

Devon came to his feet then, leaning over to
place a kiss to his mother's cheek. "Enough talk of
Roger," he said. "We've tired you with our visit.
You rest now, Mother. We've a long trip ahead and
I don't want to tax you further."

"Nonsense," she muttered, but even before Brigitta and Devon had reached the door, Augusta

had settled back on her pillows and was beginning to drift off to sleep, a ghost of a smile playing across her lips.

Augusta's tiring-woman, Elise, was in the adjoining room seated on a small settee, a bit of needlepoint in her hands. She was nearly as old as Augusta but not nearly as frail in health. Born and raised in Kent, the gray-haired woman had been widowed early in life, was childless, and had never remarried. She had been living with Augusta ever since the day Devon and his mother had landed on English soil. For Devon, Elise had become something very much like a doting aunt. She fussed over him as though he were her own son.

Elise immediately stood when Devon and Brigitta entered the room. "How is she?" the woman asked, moving to pour Brigitta and Devon a cup of tea from the tray on a small table near her seat.

"She's resting now," Devon replied, taking one of the cups Elise held out. "I was afraid our return home along with the news we bring would excite her overly much."

"Oh, no," Elise responded. "Do not worry about that, Devon. Your mother's been waiting for you to return. She knew you'd bring proof of your paternity with you, too. Now don't you be worrying about her health. Her heart is weak, yes, but she's not too weak to see you properly in the home that is yours by birth. She's waited twenty-eight years for this day and she'll not be denied a moment of it."

"Do you think she's fit to make the trip north?" Devon asked.

"I'm certain of it," Elise replied. "It's what she's

been anticipating since the day you left for Sweden. Will you be staying here until we depart?"

Devon shook his head. "No. I've arranged for rooms for Brigitta and myself at the Haycock. I want Mother to get her rest, and if we stayed I'm afraid she would feel as though she must see to our needs herself."

"Aye, you're right about that," Elise agreed. "Well then, you two hurry on and get yourselves a warm meal. I'll take care of things here."

Devon reached for Brigitta's cloak that was draped across one of the straight-backed chairs nearest the front portal. He placed the garment about her shoulders while Brigitta tied the inner cords together. "We'll be here in the morning, Elise. I'll hire someone to help you pack. I want to be on the North Road by the end of the week."

Elise smiled, opening the door for them. "Your mother will be glad. She had me pack her necessities two days ago. She's got a sixth sense, I always said." Giving both Devon and Brigitta a quick hug, the old woman sent them on their way.

Outside the day had turned gray and thundery. Dark clouds were rolling in from the Channel along with a wind that was quickly turning into a gust. Scurrying along beside Devon as they headed for the Haycock Inn, Brigitta felt the first huge raindrops begin to fall.

"We're going to get soaked," she said on a laugh, pulling up the hood of her cloak.

"How right you are! You don't mind, do you?"

"Have I any choice?" she asked. The rain came down in buckets then, showering them with huge fat drops. Together, they began to run, both of them laughing like carefree children as they finally reached the Haycock. Because of the downpour, the common room was filled with patrons, many swarming near the huge hearth with its merry fire where they could dry their clothes and get warm.

Hugging her waist, Brigitta stood beside Devon just inside the door. Her own long hair had stayed dry beneath the hood of her cloak, but Devon's was drenched and clung tightly to his scalp, bring into sharp focus his classic features.

Shrugging the water off him, he turned to Brigitta, watching intently as she slipped her sodden hood from her head and brushed a few damp tendrils of shimmering hair from her face with one slim hand. He'd never seen her look lovelier. There were droplets of rain clinging to her dusky lashes, and her eyes, alight with mischief, sparkled brilliantly. It was a magic moment for Devon, one he would never forget.

Brigitta glanced up noticing his intense gaze. "What is it?" she asked. Her question was followed by a swift, dazzling smile.

Devon felt his heart thud. Leaning his face close to hers, he murmured, "I am just thinking how gorgeous you are . . . and how I cannot wait to take you upstairs to our room."

"*Our* room?" she teased. "I thought you told Elise you secured two rooms for us."

"To hell with what I told Elise," he said huskily. "Come, Brigitta, I want you all to myself. This petrel has come inland for the night."

She laughed, adoring the passion and love she now saw in his eyes. Together, they headed up the narrow flight of stairs that led to the second floor and to their room. Once in the chamber lit only by a single taper and a drowsy fire that filled the hearth, they fell into each other's arms. As the heavy rains beat a fidgety rhythm on the rooftops above, Devon and Brigitta came together to create their own special storm.

They moved slowly at first, entwining their arms about each other as their lips met in a tender, provocative union. His mouth was firm above her own, toying gently with the delicate contour of her lips. Brigitta felt her knees go weak and her body becoming warmed by a languorous heat. Even through layers of material, she could feel the steady thump of Devon's heart and the heat of his body. Her breast tingled, anticipation causing the nipples to tauten. Their mouths melded, slipping sensuously together. Over and over, he wooed her with the gentle caress of his mouth on hers, his tongue slowly rolling over her own. Brigitta was soon swept away, and time and space became superseded by their mutual desires.

Slowly, still kissing her, Devon untied the inner cords of Brigitta's cloak, lifting the heavy folds of material from her shoulders and then letting the wet garment slide to the floor beneath them. With skillful hands, he loosened the hooks of her bodice and chemise, gently pushing the material away from her warm skin. Soon, Brigitta stood naked amid a pile of skirts and petticoats, her pale skin glistening in the firelight. And still he was kissing her, his large hands exploring her body in gentle strokes.

"You're gorgeous," he murmured, bending his

dark head to plant fiery kisses along the long column of her neck. "So beautiful . . ."

Brigitta let her head fall back, exposing her throat. Her long hair fell behind her in a shimmering swath, brushing the top of her buttocks in wispy tendrils. Devon ran one hand through those long tresses, wrapping them about his wrist as he brought his hand up to cup around her neck. Slowly, he drew her lips to his once more, but not before he took a long moment to gaze into her face.

Lord, but she was a beauty, he thought. Even now, he could feel the fire in his loins. He wanted nothing more than to have every part of her. He wanted to lose himself inside of her, to leave a part of himself there. Never before had he felt so intensely for any woman. Certainly he had had his share of them, but never had he had the desire to make any of them *his* woman. For years, he had traveled the world alone, facing uncountable dangers, never needing anyone. The quest to gain his birthright had filled his every waking thought. But then Brigitta Lind had entered his life. From the first moment he'd seen her in Lisa's chambers, he had been struck by her bright beauty and her reckless nature. The memory made him smile. There she'd stood, royal pearls adorning her neck and her hands deep in the princess's jewels! How bold she'd been . . . and was still. From that moment on, Brigitta had enslaved him. And now, she was to be his wife. Now, she was his lover, his beloved. . . .

Brigitta gazed into Devon's black eyes, her heart beating a loud rhythm in her ears. There was no place else she'd rather be, she knew. There was no other being with whom she wanted to share her life. She watched from beneath dusky lashes as Devon moved his mouth close to her parted lips. Gently, he tasted her mouth, nipping her slightly. An audible sigh escaped her. Soon she would be Devon's wife, the mistress of Courtenay Castle. And soon, she would give birth to their child.

She met his deep kiss with one of her own, eyes still open and shining with the love she felt for him. Devon's gaze mirrored that love. Trembling with excitement, Brigitta slipped her hands down the front of his shirt, undoing the buttons of his garment as she went. Their shared kiss turned deeper still as she pushed open the fine lawn of his shirt, running her palms atop his muscled chest. Her senses were swimming now. She felt adrift upon warm, caressing waters. Beneath the tips of her fingers she could feel the hard sinews of his body, the smooth texture of his skin.

Eager to lie beside her and cover her body with soft kisses, Devon pulled slowly away, taking her hands in his. She smiled up at him, loving his rakish appearance. His long black hair, drying into feathery wisps on the ends, was swept back from his face, showing to advantage his smooth, classic features. The firelight danced upon one side of his face, illuminating the broadness of his cheekbone and the sensuous curve of his mouth. His shirt, opened at the waist and untucked from his breeches, fluttered romantically as he motioned toward the bed. But before Brigitta had a chance to take a step, Devon surprised her by lifting her lithe

body in his arms. Giggling, she wrapped her arms
about his neck.

He stood still for a moment, holding her firmly
against him, one arm beneath her knees, the other
snaking around her back so that he could touch the
underside of one breast with his fingers. She was
as light as air, he thought. He could carry her
weight forever . . . and he realized that he wanted
to. For Brigitta, he would do anything, anything at
all. He wanted her burdens to be his. He would
care for her, cherish her, and, most of all, love her.
From this day forward, Brigitta Lind would want
for nothing. He would see to it all her wishes came
true, and while he was alive, he would make certain no harm ever befell her again.

Making this silent pledge, Devon carried his precious bundle to the bed, laying her upon the coverlet
as though she were as fragile as china. Gazing lovingly down at her, he removed his garments, letting
them drop where they would, his eyes devouring
Brigitta as she lay upon the bed waiting for him. Her
skin was like carved ivory, pale in the firelight. Not
a blemish marred the perfection. Her young breasts
were lush, fuller than he remembered, pink-tipped,
her legs long and shapely. In the firelight, he could
see the glimmering blondeness of her most secret
place. She looked, at the moment, like a rich oil
painting come to life. Firelight danced on her beautiful body, creating shadows here and there where
her limbs curved, glimmering in the thick tresses of
her long hair. And her eyes, as blue as the summery
sky in her heart-shaped face, captivated him, beckoning him to her.

Devon moved onto the bed, loving the way she lifted her arms to welcome into a warm embrace. He hovered above her, holding his own weight with muscled arms placed on either side of her shoulders. Poised above her, his black locks brushing her collarbone, he gazed down at the only woman he would ever love. Her cheeks were flushed, her lips parted and moist.

Brigitta's blood sang through her veins. Between them, she could feel the hardness of his male member as it pressed urgently against her. She ran her palms across his back, then down toward his lean haunches as she pulled him to her, her own body caught up in a maelstrom of raging desire. Brigitta thought she would go mad with wanting if he did not soon take her. She moved enticingly beneath him, teasing him, pressing herself upward.

Devon smiled, catching her face in both of his hands. She wanted to end the sweet torture as much as he. Only too willing to comply, he covered her mouth in a deep, searing kiss as he pushed himself into her with slow, earth-shattering sureness.

Brigitta's breath left her in a rush. Relief and pure pleasure washed over her in tingling waves as he moved and rocked her. Opening to him like flower petals to a life-giving sun, she was momentarily transported to another world where only she and Devon existed and there was nothing but the sensations he provoked in her and the sweet enchantment of their shared love. There was no purpose beyond this joining, nothing that mattered but the touch of his lips and the searing, liquid heat that flowed through her body. Time stood still as together they scaled heights heretofore unknown to both of them. He thrust into her again and again as over and over she tumbled joyously in a realm only spirits can inhabit, falling and soaring all at once. He filled her, penetrating deeper than he ever had, and Brigitta held him close, never wanting to release him.

"Ah, Brigitta," he whispered into the shell of her ear just as she was scaling the highest peak. "How I love you. . . ."

His breath became the rushing wind on which she soared as suddenly, violently, her passions exploded in an intense conflagration of fiery heat and wondrous sensations. The moment held, ecstasy gripping them, binding them forever, until, slowly, they twirled back to a hazy reality that could never again be quite the same as it had been only moments before. Exalted, satiated, they stroked each other, snuggling close, whispering heartfelt endearments. Together they had found the secret of the universe, the only thing in life worth fighting and dying for. Together, they had entered love's blood-red heart and had become one.

Chapter Nineteen

BRIGITTA AWOKE WITH a start, her lashes fluttering quickly open. For a moment, she could not remember where she was. Without the rolling pitch of a ship's deck beneath her, she felt oddly confused.

Devon watched as she stirred awake. "I am here," he whispered huskily, seeing her confusion and kissing it away with a tender peck to the tip of her nose. Sleepy-eyed, her golden hair fanned atop the pillows in tumbled disarray, she looked more beautiful than he'd ever seen her. He'd awakened only a few moments before and had, much to his delight, spent the past few minutes gazing down at the woman who had come to mean the world to him. The coverlet had slipped to reveal one dusky-tipped breast, enticing him enough so that he reached out to caress its fullness. He marveled at how she'd grown into a woman since last winter when he'd first met her. They'd shared much since then, and now, having had the chance to truly look at her, he realized, with an awed wonder, that soon they would share even more. Her secret was there for him to read in her eyes, and in the lushness of her young body. Even though he was not totally certain, Devon felt the presence of another being even now growing within his woman. "When?" he asked, his voice rich with emotion. "When will our babe be born?"

"How did you know?" she questioned, feeling suddenly shy yet so very happy. "Even I was not certain until a few days ago. My moon cycles have never been regular."

"The signs are here," he whispered, brushing first her eyelids and then the tips of her breasts with his lips. "And here." His left hand moved beneath the coverlet, seeking the flat expanse of her abdomen. "He'll be a healthy babe," he said. "Healthy and strong. Already your body is changing to accommodate him."

"Him?" she queried, smiling. "How do you know we'll be blessed with a boy? Perhaps I'll deliver a girl child."

"Then *she* will be strong and healthy . . . and just as beautiful as her mother. Whatever you deliver, be it a girl or boy, I will be happy, Brigitta, for I love you and it is from our love this child has been conceived." Sliding deeper beneath the covers, he wrapped both arms about her, giving Brigitta a gentle squeeze. "Do you know how happy you've made me?" he asked. "All of my life I have been searching for something, never knowing just exactly what that something was. For many years I believed the elusive thing I sought was my birthright—but now I know differently. It is you, Brigitta, you are the one I've been waiting for, have been searching for. Your love and the family we will soon raise—these are the things I've been wanting. Even if I were to learn today that I could not legally have my father's name or his vast estates, I would not be unhappy, for I would have you and our babe."

Brigitta felt a quick rush of tears gathering in her eyes. "Oh, Devon," she murmured, her voice catching. "What a beautiful thing to say. I would be happy with you anywhere, anywhere at all! I care not for riches or titles. I want only you, and our children."

"And you have me, my love . . . body and soul."

To prove his point, he pressed her gently down upon the bed, moving his body over hers, and once again he took her to dizzying heights that left them both breathless and giddy. In the small chamber, lit only by the dying embers of a fire that had gone unattended for hours, they gave to each other the richest gifts of all.

By the end of the week, Augusta and Elise were packed and ready for the trip north to Courtenay Castle. Comfortably ensconced in their own private post chaise, both women traveled with numerous lap robes and braziers to keep the chill of the rainy days from their bones. Augusta, although somewhat pale and fragile-looking upon the day of Brigitta and Devon's arrival in Dover, had undergone a subtle metamorphosis. Knowing she would soon be in her husband's home, she appeared several years younger and very capable of handling the stress of a long journey. Devon knew very well this moment was the crowning glory of his mother's life. She'd waited years for this trip, had planned every detail in her mind's eye over and over. At long last, she would be in the home she'd deserved to inhabit. She would not let go of her tenuous hold on life until she saw with her own eyes that Devon and his bride-to-be were at Courtenay Castle.

Their small cluster of carriages lumbered along

the muddied roads of England at a snail's pace. Devon made certain there were numerous stops at the many inns they passed. Even though he was anxious to be home, he would not hurry, for although his mother constantly assured him she was feeling fine, Devon was not fooled. He knew Augusta was making this journey on the sheer power of her will.

By the fifth day of their travels, they reached the outskirts of his father's lands—*his* lands, Devon reminded himself. The early afternoon was overcast with low-hanging gray clouds and a chill wind that swept across the beech-lined roadway. Devon had chosen to ride Brigitta's mount the last few miles, leaving Brigitta alone inside the warm confines of the post chaise. He rode ahead of the carriages, his body erect in the royal saddle that had come with them from Sweden, and as he viewed the lands that had once belonged to his father, he felt an overpowering sense of awe fill him. He'd known he'd be affected by the sight and that was the reason he'd chosen to ride ahead of the others, alone.

He brought the black steed beneath him to a halt, surveying the sight before him. Just ahead, above the thick line of gray-barked trees, the great chimney stacks of Courtenay were visible, their dull-colored stone looking stark against the stormy sky.

Home. Finally, after years of being denied his birthright, he was coming home. He urged the beast to move forward, slowly, his eye taking in every detail of the land surrounding him. A wet spring was giving way to summer and wild roses were bursting into rich blooms and dotting the woodland floor with vibrant yellows, deep reds, and pristine whites. Rhododendron, its leafy green bushes poked up here and there, hung heavy with purple blooms, and white and pink blossoms as well. Beyond him, to Devon's right, stood a silent doe and her twin fawns, their spots looking huge and silky soft in the gray day. They sprinted away when they heard the rattle of carriage wheels rolling atop the earth.

Devon kept his leisurely pace. He would not deny himself the pleasure of viewing these lands as his own for the first time. The children he and Brigitta created would romp across this countryside—as he should have done. There would be picnics in the woods, he decided. One every late spring to mark the anniversary of their homecoming. There would be balls and countless gatherings of friends whom they would soon meet. And celebrations as well. Christmases would be gay and bright with mistletoe dug up fresh from the earth and brought in to surround every hearth and hang from the chandeliers. Musicians would be hired to play in the drawing rooms bedecked with holiday ribbons. There would be sleigh rides across the snow-covered landscape, bells tinkling in the crisp air. And there would be a huge Christmas goose stuffed with chestnuts and oysters which Devon would carve for Brigitta. There would be plum cakes and chestnut cookies thickly iced for their children. And presents! Yes, he thought, dozens of presents for their little ones. He would read his children countless stories as they sat near the hearth, their beautiful faces flushed with excitement of the twelve days of Christmas and all the merrymaking that heralded the special time. With Brigitta beside him and their children surrounding him, life would be grand within the walls of Courtenay. Devon vowed he would give to his children the life he'd been denied.

The tree-lined road led directly to a grand archway, the gates of which were flung open. No one stood guard, nor was there anyone to welcome them. Devon had expected as much. He'd sent a messenger days ago ahead of their party to inform his half brother of their arrival. He'd also sent a messenger on to London whose sole duty it was to inform Roger's lawyers of Devon's arrival in England. Soon, the lawyers, all five of them, would be at Courtenay, demanding to see the signet ring which would grant Devon the lands of Courtenay. There would be numerous questions, he knew, as well as defiance from Roger. Devon did not expect Roger to relinquish his title without a fight, but Devon had not come to Courtenay to do battle with his half brother. He wanted only to live in peace. His goal was not to usurp Roger, but to join him in the running of the estate. It did not matter to Devon that all of this was rightfully his. He was willing to share the wealth. In fact, he looked forward to meeting this half brother of his. He'd always wondered what it would be like to have a brother or sister. It was Devon's dream to live at peace with his half brother, sharing the burdens side by side. He only hoped Roger would see things this way.

Devon led their small procession beneath the cold archway and into a rectangular courtyard surrounded on three sides by a high, windtortured wall. Before them, rising up in magnificent splendor and meeting the protective courtyard wall on each side with two projecting wings, was Courtenay with its twin, lead-glazed bay windows. The eye-catching windows, positioned at each end of the two-hundred-and-twenty-foot structure, were set between stately columns, their rough and uneven texture causing the greenish-colored glass to sparkle even in the gray light of day. A parapet surrounded the upper front, hiding from total view a balcony projecting from the second story, beyond which could be seen numerous windows and a door leading inward here and there.

As Devon brought his mount to a halt and swung down off the saddle, he thought he caught a glimpse of a shadowy figure moving behind one of the upper floor windows. The figure stood still for a moment, then stepped out of view. Devon turned away knowing that it wouldn't be long now until he met his half brother.

Brigitta, seated alone in the post chaise she and Devon had shared until only a few short miles ago, strained to peer out of the window. Her first view of Courtenay and its surrounding lands enchanted her. A light mist veiled the deepening green of the property and the red brick walls of the structure built during Elizabeth Tudor's reign. It was a dominant, picturesque mansion with two huge towers and ancient fountains set in the courtyard, water splashing softly. This was to be *their* home. Her body tingled with an excitement she was hard-pressed to contain. Even before the carriage had

rumbled to a stop, the huge oaken door of Courtenay swung open and a bevy of servants flowed
out, all eager to assist the new arrivals. The carriage door popped open, and Brigitta, expecting to
see Devon standing there ready to help her descend, was surprised to find a short, portly gentleman with white hair and a dour face extending his
arm. She allowed him to help her to the ground,
gazing past him to find Devon among the small
group of servants who were beginning to unload
their trunks.

Devon stood apart from the others, looking
splendidly regal in his black embroidered doublet,
frilled, full white shirt beneath, and black knee
breeches. His wide-topped boots gleamed from a
recent polishing at the last inn they'd stayed at,
and his long ebony locks flowed to his shoulders
beneath a low-crowned hat adorned with long
black and purple plumes. His dark gaze was fixed
on the doorway where another man stood. Brigitta
turned to see what held his attention.

A tall man, dressed resplendently in a blue waistcoat embroidered and fringed with silver atop
breeches of black velvet, white stockings, and black
buckle shoes, stood imperiously on the threshold
of the mansion. His stance was stiff, as though he
were bracing himself, and as Devon stepped forward, moving toward him, the man made no motion of greeting. Brigitta watched the tense scene
unfold. There was no doubt in her mind that the
man Devon approached was none other than Roger
Courtenay. The likeness between the two men was
striking. Roger, like Devon, was dark complected,
and his hair, fashionably long, was just as deep in

color as Devon's. And his face! From a distance, Brigitta thought the men were identical: Roger possessed the same perfectly chiseled features, the same expressive dark brows over brooding eyes, and those broad, flat cheekbones. Brigitta watched in fascination as Devon stepped up to his half brother, and then after a moment's pause, swept his hat from his head in a grand gesture and gave him a deep bow. Brigitta wished she were standing beside Devon so that she might hear what words would be exchanged. Picking up her skirts, she left the manservant behind and moved quickly toward the main entrance of Courtenay.

Devon felt his half brother's presence even before he saw him. As the servants of Courtenay scurried to the carriages, Devon turned his gaze toward the oaken doors of the mansion. There, standing beneath the bold archway, was Roger Courtenay, his handsome face set in grim lines. There came no gesture of greeting from the man, no warm smile, nor even a flash of acknowledgment within the black depths of his eyes. He said nothing, did nothing.

So, Devon thought, there is to be no warm homecoming. I am to be viewed as a threat in the home that is mine by right. So be it then. With a calmness he did not feel, he strode boldly up the few stone steps to where his half brother stood. He allowed their gazes, so very alike, to clash for only a moment before he swept the low-crowned hat from his head and honored his brother with a deep bow, a gesture he hoped would alert his half brother to the fact he would honor Roger's position in their father's home. Straightening, he saw a flicker of anger pass through Roger's black gaze, but then the emotion vanished and Roger appeared to be pleased with Devon's arrival.

"Hello, Roger," Devon said, extending his right hand in greeting.

Roger Courtenay eyed with disdain that gauntleted hand. A long moment slid by, punctuated only with the clatter of grooms seeing to the luggage atop the carriages. Finally, he took Devon's hand, shook it with perfunctory style, and then eased back, once again assuming his watchful stance.

"Hello, Devon," he replied. His voice was deep, gravelly. His lips, much thinner than Devon's, barely moved when he spoke, and his dark, bushy brows came together over his brooding black eyes. He said nothing more, determined to hold an upperhand in this confrontation. Clearly, any bridges that would be spanned between them would have to be crossed by Devon alone.

Undaunted, Devon gave his half brother a smile. He would ignore the icy greeting, he decided. This was his home and he had every right to be at Courtenay. "I trust you received my message?"

Roger nodded curtly. "I did."

"Then you understand my reasons for being here?"

"I understand fully. You've come to reap what you believe is yours. Though I must warn you now, *brother*, that I've no intention of relinquishing my title to you," he said in a low voice. "I care not a whit of the proof you claim to have. You have overstepped all boundaries by barging in upon me

and my household with your mother and wife-
to-be." He motioned with a tilt of his leonine head
toward the carriages behind Devon where the
women were now disembarking. "It will only cause
your mother undue pain to be tossed out of this
home, and as for the woman you've brought with
you, she will no doubt be crushed to learn she will
never be the mistress of Courtenay. You should
have come alone. Better still, you should have gone
directly to London with your *proof*. In so doing,
you could have spared us all a scandalous scene."

Devon maintained an unaffected air. He hadn't
expected a warm welcome, and now that he had
met Roger face to face, he was surprised the man
had even ordered his servants outside to assist in
the unloading. Obviously, Roger was not certain
Devon's proof of his heritage could be so easily
disclaimed. The man knew better than to bar Devon and his family totally from Courtenay, yet he
wasn't about to let Devon inside without a warning.

"There'll be no scandalous scene," Devon assured the older man, his own voice quiet and
strong. "Unless, of course, you choose to create
one. I have come to Courtenay in peace, not to
usurp you." From behind him, he heard the light
tapping of Brigitta's pattens atop the stone. Not
wanting to upset her, he quickly sought to direct
the conversation toward safer territory. "We will
discuss my coming here at a later time, Roger. You
will soon learn how unfounded your fears are."

"Fears?" Roger repeated, his upper lip twitching
unbecomingly. "I have no fear of you or your presence. Indeed, I could even prohibit you from en-

tering my home. You are here only by my sufferance."

Brigitta was coming closer, and Devon did not wish to upset her in any way. He wanted this homecoming to be special for her, to not be tainted by Roger's vindictiveness. In a low voice, he said to his half brother, "It would bode you ill to turn me away now. You know not what proof I bring with me. Also, it would be very bad form to turn out guests on a day such as this. Besides, if the lawyers decide in my favor—which they will—then you would do well to welcome us with open arms."

The threat hit home. Roger's position at Courtenay was precarious at best. It always had been. He'd known of Devon Courtenay years ago, knew that even though he, Roger, was the eldest son of the now deceased Michael Courtenay, Devon was most probably the legitimate son. In this case, being the first-born son mattered not. In the eyes of English law, legitimacy carried more weight than order of birth.

"Very well." Roger relented. "We will discuss our business later." He turned his gaze away from Devon and noticed keenly for the first time the woman who now moved to stand by Devon's side. Ever impressed by feminine beauty, Roger Courtenay sucked in a sharp breath of damp air at sight of the glorious creature. Dressed in amber velvet, her stunning, golden locks coiled into an artful arrangement beneath her fur-trimmed hood, she looked a vision of innocence and beauty. Her eyes were bluer than any he'd ever beheld and the skin of her heart-shaped face, so fair and delicate, looked not to be of English descent. Of course,

Roger realized when he heard her speak a gentle greeting to him, she was from Sweden, for was not that where Devon had been headed the last time Roger had heard? Roger had made it his business to know where Devon Courtenay and his elderly mother were at all times. So, his younger half brother had found himself a Swedish maiden to bed. Shafts of heated jealousy coursed through Roger. It goaded him greatly that Devon should not only come to Courtenay with proof of his ownership but also with such a dazzling beauty on his arm!

Brigitta moved silently up the stone steps, her pulses racing. She was so awestruck at the likeness between Devon and his older half brother that she missed seeing the sparks between the two men. Although Roger was slightly taller than Devon, and his features were much sharper, he held that unmistakable quality of supreme male dominance. And Roger's eyes—she had seen that unemotional, frightening gaze once before in Devon, when she had first encountered him in Thora-Lisa's chambers. She nearly shivered at the sight, and wondered how two men, related by blood but raised within different worlds, could carry the same wariness of the world in their eyes. Perhaps being raised without a male figure did that to a man, she mused. Perhaps being labeled a bastard by their peers had forced each man to look inward and to rely on only one person: himself.

Tucking her gloved hand into the warm crook of Devon's arm, Brigitta gave Roger a delicate smile. Devon stroked her hand with a gentle, reassuring pat.

"Roger," he said, "this is my betrothed, Brigitta Lind. Brigitta, my half brother, Roger Courtenay."

Roger swathed his voice in a warm, rich tone. "Welcome, Brigitta," he said. "Welcome to . . . my home." He bestowed upon her a handsome grin, one that caused his younger half brother to tighten his hold on his young wife-to-be. Roger was amused. He loved a challenge and here now before him were two exquisite prizes to reach and fight for; one was complete ownership of Courtenay, and the other was his half brother's woman.

Roger's emphasis of the word "my" did not go unnoticed by Brigitta. But in her innocence she hoped the inflection was made only out of habit and not for any other reason. She felt Devon stiffen beside her at sight of Roger's private smile of greeting. Feeling lost, Brigitta wondered at the relationship between the brothers. She had not truly considered what all would be involved in gaining Courtenay from Roger. By Roger's imperious stance and the coldness in the depths of his black gaze, she realized the feat might well be a dangerous one.

The awkward moment was not helped by the arrival of Augusta and Elise. Augusta, remarkably agile, had stepped quickly out of the carriage to view her husband's home with tear-filled eyes. Her aged face shone with happiness as she moved beside Devon.

"Is it not beautiful?" she asked him. "Your father would be so proud to see you here now, Devon." She turned to the tall man in blue velvet. "You must be Roger," she said. "I am Augusta Courtenay, Michael's widow, and this is my tiring-woman, Elise. I can see with my own eyes that you've done a splendid job with the upkeep of the lands. Now, let us see if your skill has also been used on the interior."

Roger lifted one dark brow at Augusta's boldness. "Of course," he replied. "I'll have one of the servants show you to your chamber."

"My chamber and every other one as well," came Augusta's sharp reply. "I've waited years to be in Courtenay and I'll not be denied a thorough tour."

"Mother," Devon cut in smoothly. "Would you care to rest first? We've traveled far this day. I don't want you to overexert yourself."

"Pah!" Augusta spat. "I'm fine. I want only to view the home that is now yours."

Roger's back straightened with her words. "May I remind you all that Courtenay and its lands have been mine for three years now? You are my guests and are here only at my sufferance."

Augusta snorted. "We are here because this is our home, young man." She waved one gloved hand in the air, dismissing for the moment the touchy subject. "All details shall be discussed later, of course. At the moment, though, all I am interested in is seeing this grand home my late husband toiled so hard to maintain."

Devon thought Roger would attempt to toss them all out on their ears, and he was ready to spring to his mother's defense. But Roger relented, and in an about-face of mood, swept his left arm toward the great hall.

"As you wish," Roger replied. "I shall personally escort you through every chamber, and on the morrow, weather permitting, I shall walk you across the grounds."

For the next hour, as numerous servants scurried to prepare a meal and rooms for the guests, Roger walked the small group through every wing of Courtenay. Having been erected in Tudor times, the building had been occupied by a wealthy squire until the reign of King James, at which time a favored noble of the new king had taken residence. Upon the noble's death, the lands had reverted back to the crown and were then bestowed upon Michael Courtenay for his loyalty to the king. The first floor contained the great hall where meals were taken and where various forms of celebration were held. The room was large and lofty, sectioned off from the other rooms used by the family with elaborate screens of wood ornamented with rich fretwork and pilasters. High windows set on one side of the chamber illuminated the lower reaches but left the detailed roof timbers in gloom. At one end of the room, upon a raised step, was the high table lighted by a bay window through which could be viewed the surrounding grounds of Courtenay. To the left of the great hall lay the pantry, the buttery, and the passages to the huge kitchens which housed two fireplaces. A summer and winter parlor were positioned conveniently close to the kitchens.

The upper floors housed the great chamber, numerous bedrooms, day rooms, and a long gallery. These could be reached by either of several staircases that rivaled the panels of the great hall with their elaborately carved banisters and newel posts on which perched heraldic animals of great proportions and intricate details.

Brigitta was fascinated by the handsome decoration of the rooms. Although she had lived briefly amidst the splendor and riches of Vardighet, she had thought such wealth to be enjoyed only by the nobility. But everywhere her eye wandered within the rooms of Courtenay, she saw riches that rivaled even the royal chambers of Vardighet. Where the walls were not paneled with intricate woodwork, there hung tapestries affixed to great hooks showing in splendid detail hunting scenes or breathtaking vistas of lands she'd never before viewed. Each room had its own fireplace topped with striking chimney-pieces, needlework chairs, Turkey carpets covering the wood floors, numerous stools, and even window cushions where one could sit and gaze out at the tended lawns of Courtenay.

By the end of their tour, Brigitta was left speechless. Even Augusta, who had previously been so full of spunk, had fallen silent by the time she was led to her own chambers for the night. As Devon escorted Brigitta through the narrow passage that led to the bedroom she would occupy, he wrapped a strong arm about her waist, glad for a moment alone with her.

"Courtenay is beautiful," she said. "You must be very proud of your father's home."

Devon nodded, pushing open the oaken door leading to the bedchamber. A warm fire, fueled with wood and smaller billets, burned in the hearth, casting a soft glow about the room with its huge four-posted tester bed of down, court-cupboard, sitting chairs, and wardrobe. "Yes," he said quietly. He stood near the door, watching Brigitta with appreciative eyes as she moved about the room, searching through her trunks for a suitable dress to wear for the evening meal. "I am proud of Courtenay. But you must remember it has been Roger's supervision that has kept the house and grounds in superb condition. I fear he will not relinquish his title, no matter of what the courts say."

Brigitta whirled toward him, holding tightly to a gown of shimmering gold silk Devon had purchased for her in Dover. "But the proof you have is valid . . . and Courtenay belongs to *you*."

He leaned back against the paneled wall, a dark frown creasing his handsome brow. "Yes, but does Courtenay not also belong to Roger in some way? He's maintained the place for three years, and he is just as much my father's son as am I. I've lived too long under the title of bastard, Brigitta. I know what it is to feel the brunt of society, to be stripped of all that is rightfully mine."

"So you do not wish to take away Roger's title. Are you saying then that you would be content to share this home with your half brother?" she asked quietly.

"Yes, if I thought it could be so, I would be willing to try."

She abandoned the gown, leaving it to lie across the linen of the bed. Moving on silent feet, she crossed the Turkey carpet until she stood before Devon. Gently, she took his hands in hers. "But you do not believe Roger will accept such an offer, do you?"

Devon shook his head. "No, I do not. He sees me as a threat, and I cannot blame him. Were I in his shoes, I would have the same opinion."

"But you're not a threat, Devon. You're a good, caring man. Your mutual love of Courtenay should be a bond between you, not a sword with which to harm the other. In time, Roger will realize this."

"Ah, Brigitta," he sighed, lacing his fingers with hers. "You've such wisdom for one so young." Tenderly, he dropped a kiss to the tip of her prettily upturned nose. "Let us hope you are correct, for I want nothing more than to live in this home with you and raise our family here."

"And I want that too, Devon," she whispered.

As he drew her into a tight embrace, Devon wondered if, finally, their dreams would come true. If Roger had his way though, he knew they would not.

Chapter Twenty

FOR BRIGITTA, the days at Courtenay whisked by on swift wings. To her relief, Roger was a consummate host as he presided over the evening meal on the day of their arrival. No mention of the estate was made other than Devon making polite inquiries as to how Roger went about business. Roger's answers, although not as detailed as Devon would have liked, came quietly and with good grace. It seemed to Brigitta that the two brothers might indeed be able to work together overseeing the lands. Augusta's health, though, soon took all of Brigitta's thoughts away from the subject of ownership of Courtenay. The older woman made an appearance at the high table only twice: once for the first meal on the day of their arrival, and then again the next morning. After that, she was confined to her chambers where Elise and one of the three kitchen maids sought to make her comfortable. The damp journey from Dover to Courtenay had taken its toll on the aging woman. She developed a cough that left her weak and pale, and she complained daily of pains within her chest. Brigitta feared the woman would not live to see another week. A physician was summoned from the nearby village, and after a lengthy examination, he emerged from Augusta's chambers to inform both Devon and Brigitta there was nothing to be done but see to the woman's comfort. Devon took the news hard. He had known his mother was dying, but still, to be confronted with her impending death was a terrible blow for him. Brigitta consoled him as best she knew how, and when, in the middle of the night, he stole into her chamber to crawl into the high tester bed beside her, she welcomed him with open arms. They spent each night together, entwined in each other's arms, whispering soft words that would carry them through the day until they could again be alone together. But Brigitta always awoke alone, for Devon rose before the sun to sneak back to his own chambers where he would dress for a long day of acquainting himself with the running of Courtenay—much to his brother's disapproval.

On the morning of the fifth day at Courtenay, Brigitta awoke early and dressed in a simple day-gown of bright yellow, the bodice of which was low-necked and fastened down to her waist with gay ribbons. Her long locks were fashioned into ringlets that she allowed to fall over her shoulders in a gentle caress. The collar of the neckline, which slipped down to reveal her shoulders, was a loose ruffle of lace which she draped like a scarf about her shoulders, fastening it together with a pearl brooch. The froth of lace hid from view the ruby signet ring Devon had given her. On his request, she had taken the ring from her finger and attached it to a long gold chain she now wore about her neck.

As she stepped into the passage leading to her rooms, she ran straight into the solid form of Roger Courtenay.

"Roger!" she exclaimed, her right hand flying involuntarily to her breastbone. "You startled me!"

The tall man blocking her way gave her a lazy grin. "Forgive me," he drawled in a dulcet tone. "That was not my intent at all. I was merely looking for my brother." Dressed handsomely in expensive-looking honey-tan velvet, with his long wavy black hair recently brushed and hanging loose against his shoulders, he appeared ready to greet guests in the great hall instead of heading out to survey his lands as was his usual custom in the early morning hours. Procuring a tiny and bejeweled snuffbox from within his waist coat, he took a pinch of the tobacco and then, with his dark eyes scanning over Brigitta and then beyond her to the rumpled linen of the bed, he smiled. "But I can see my brother is not here, is he?"

Brigitta collected her wits. She did not like the glint that hovered just beneath the surface of his black eyes. She didn't like it at all. "No, Devon is not here. Why should he be? Did you . . . search for him in his own chambers?"

Roger's smile deepened. "Of course. But he was nowhere to be found. Indeed, it appeared as though his bed had not been slept in the whole night through. But then again, perhaps my brother is accustomed to tidying his own rooms before he leaves in the morning."

His insinuation was not lost on Brigitta, but she was determined not to be ruffled. "May I ask why you are looking for Devon? Is something wrong?"

"Wrong?" He considered for a moment, then said, "Perhaps. Augusta has been asking for him. It appears she has taken a turn for the worse."

Brigitta was instantly alert. "I must go to her then!"

"Yes, of course you must . . . but first, Brigitta, let me tell you also that I've received word the lawyers from London will be arriving in a few short hours. Devon will doubtless want to meet with them. I only hope Augusta's condition will not keep him from the gathering. These men, as important as their posts are, cannot be kept overly long. They must needs return to the city as soon as possible."

"Surely they can stay a day or two!"

Roger gave an indifferent shrug of his shoulders.

"They may or they may not. Quite frankly, Brigitta, I believe nothing will come from this meeting. I have no intention of sharing the estate with Devon, nor do I intend to let him usurp me of my position."

His words were not spoken with malice, but rather, with a sad, almost pensive note. Brigitta did not quite know how to reply. Seeing him now with his face crestfallen at the thought of losing Courtenay to a half brother he barely knew, Brigitta felt sorry for him. Carefully, she said, "But Devon is the legal heir. It would appear as though you have no choice in the matter."

With her words, his nostrils flared suddenly with anger. "Oh, but you are wrong," he breathed. "I will do everything in my power to keep Courtenay. I am the one who has toiled these three years past. If not for me, Courtenay and its lands would be nothing but an overgrown patch, its buildings covered with cobwebs and dust. *I* am the one who has maintained and kept the estate—no mean feat in these turbulent times. I will never let this land be passed to another! I care not of the proof Devon claims to have." He shook his head sadly. "Such proof probably does not even exist! He is no doubt wasting precious time and money in his request that the Courtenay lawyers travel here from London only so these men can hear his aging mother tell of how my father married her, begat her with child, and then left her."

"But it is the truth," Brigitta insisted.

"Whose truth? Devon's? Augusta's? They want all that I have and the two of them will go to any length to get it. They're fools if they believe Augusta's wretched story will influence the courts. Words alone are not proof enough."

Angered that he should talk so heartlessly about the man she loved and his mother, Brigitta did what she'd been told not to do, she revealed the ruby signet ring. With a jerk, she whisked off the delicate shawl she'd wrapped about her neck and had secured with a pearl brooch. Affixed to her neck on a slim gold chain was Devon's ring, its blood-red ruby sparkling dully in the meager light of the passageway.

"Devon has more than words to lay claim to the Courtenay wealth," she proudly declared. "He has *this*—Michael Courtenay's signet ring, given to him by King James himself and intended only for Michael's first-born son! Tell me now you disbelieve Devon's claim, Roger! You've read your father's will. You know he had intended for Augusta's child to have this ring and that all of Courtenay is to be bestowed upon that child. *Devon is the rightful heir of Courtenay.*"

For a moment, Roger went deathly still, his ebony eyes fixed on the shiny band of gold and its blood-red precious stone. A mask of pure dread drew down to cover his harsh features. "Where did you get this?" he asked in a whisper. He reached out to lift the heavy ring, his warm fingers brushing the skin her low neckline left bare.

Brigitta stood perfectly still, fear stirring within her. Perhaps she should not have revealed Devon's proof. What if Roger, with this new knowledge, could undermine Devon's plan?

"Where?" Roger repeated, his voice oddly hushed. "Where did you get this?"

"From—from Devon. He . . . it is my betrothal ring."

"But where did Devon get this ring? If he has had this in his possession, why did he not lay claim to his inheritance sooner?"

Her head was swimming. The fear she was feeling was unfounded, she told herself. Surely, there was nothing Roger could do to Devon now! "He—he didn't have the ring until recently. You see, this ring has been in Sweden, at Vardighet where Devon was born."

"Vardighet? How? I do not understand." He shook his head again, reaching up with his left hand to impatiently brush his fingers through his hair. Still, his right hand held tightly to the ring. A muscle twitched near his jawline, his black eyes glazed over. Suddenly, his fist closed tight over the ring and he pulled it toward him, wrapping the chain once about his wrist.

Fearing he meant to rip the chain and ring from her neck, Brigitta took a step back, her hands flying up to pull the precious ring from his grip. "Roger!" she exclaimed.

At the sharp sound of her voice, something snapped within Roger. Immediately, he dropped his hand. It fell to his side like a bird in flight brought down by a hunter's gun. "I—forgive me," he whispered brokenly. "I don't know what came over me. It is just—I hadn't realized what proof Devon carried. Now that I have seen this ring, I know Courtenay truly belongs to him. I cannot tell you how much this saddens me. Courtenay is my life . . . I do not know what I'll do now, where I'll go . . ." He brought his gaze up to meet hers, and

Brigitta was astonished to find tears threatening to spill over his black lashes.

How foolish of her not to realize the depth of Roger's love for Courtenay! The agony he must be suffering wondering what will become of him. She was ashamed of herself for thinking only of Devon and Augusta. Roger, too, had suffered greatly, being labeled a bastard from the day of his birth. And yet, whereas Devon had drawn strength in knowing that he had every right to the Courtenay name, Roger had not had that slim ray of hope to cling to. For Roger, there had been no hope, for he truly was a bastard and he had known from the beginning that there was, somewhere in the world, the true and rightful heir to Courtenay.

"Roger," she began hesitantly, hating the way he turned away from her now. "You must realize that Devon has no intention of turning you out. He—he has told me his wish is for the two of you to oversee Courtenay together. He does not want to take anything away from you. He wants all of us to live here together . . . to be a family."

Roger peered down at her, uncertainty written in his dark eyes. When Brigitta and Devon had first arrived at Courtenay, Roger hated them on sight, but over the past few days, he had come to know the pair. Now, he only hated what they represented— the loss of Courtenay. His gaze slipped to the ring once again, lingering there until Brigitta drew the scarflike lace together once again.

"You are too kind," he whispered, bringing his gaze up to meet hers. "You should go to Augusta now. She needs you."

Brigitta nodded. "Yes," she said, somewhat reluctant to leave her lover's half brother who now appeared so forlorn. "Everything will be fine, Roger," she added. Why she wanted to comfort and reassure him, she knew not. Only a few minutes ago, he had spoken harsh words about the man she loved, and yet now, there was such pain in his eyes that it tore at her heart. "You will see. Devon is a good and fair man. He will not send you away."

Roger merely nodded, stepping to the side of the passage so that Brigitta could pass by him. As she moved toward Augusta's chambers, she felt the intensity of Roger's stare following her. She could not help but feel a small bit of sympathy for the man who was about to lose the home he had thought to be his own.

Augusta's room was dark and frightfully quiet. The minute Brigitta stepped inside the chamber she was sharply reminded of the day Thora-Lisa had passed away. There came again that same portentous tingle of fear at the base of her spine, her stomach whirled, and as she walked to the side of the huge tester bed with its flowing white canopy, Brigitta felt as though she were walking through another dimension. The world did not feel as it had only moments ago. The threat of death hung heavy in the room. Suddenly, she felt sick and weak. She did not want Devon to have to say good-bye to yet another loved one.

Augusta was alone in the room. Elise, who had been by the woman's side all through the night, had discreetly stepped out when Brigitta entered. A small, drowsy fire burned in the hearth, barely able to chase away the damp, and there was only a single taper flickering its meager light atop its golden holder.

"Augusta?" Brigitta called softly.

The sparrowlike form upon the bed moved slightly. "Ah, Brigitta, you came. I knew you would. Elise wanted to summon you earlier but I told her not to. I—I knew you would come as soon as you were awake. You're such a sweet child, Brigitta, a very good match for my son. Very good indeed." Her voice was weak, whispery, and she coughed horribly between breaths.

"Shall I put another log on the fire?" Brigitta asked.

"No. Leave it. I am warm enough. Please, sit down. I want to speak with you. We've matters to discuss, you and I."

Brigitta did as she was instructed, pulling one of the elaborately embroidered chairs to Augusta's bedside. When she was seated, Augusta looked at her with loving eyes. The dim light of the room flickered softly upon the older woman's features, softening the deep lines brought on by a hard life, and causing her watery-blue eyes to sparkle within the pale oval of her face.

"Elise tells me the lawyers shall be here soon," Augusta began.

"Yes. I—I have heard."

"The road ahead for Devon will be a difficult one. I do not believe Roger will give over his title easily. But nothing and no one must stand in the way of Devon becoming the sole heir of Courtenay! I am counting on you to help Devon, Brigitta. You have intelligence and spirit, and Devon will need your support."

"Of course," Brigitta responded quickly. "I—I will stand by Devon no matter what. I . . . I love him."

Augusta smiled weakly. "Yes," she said. "I know you do. But Devon—he has been lonely much of his life. I have loved him with all my heart and given him all I can, but always he has yearned for a family and a home. This dream of his will be his weakness in dealing with Roger. I fear Devon will let Roger have whatever he wants . . . including Courtenay. You must not let Devon give in to Roger's demands. I knew from the moment I saw Roger that he is evil. I do not trust him, Brigitta . . . I don't want him living under the same roof as my son and his bride."

Brigitta didn't know how to answer. She had seen the pain in Roger's eyes when he'd seen the signet ring, had watched as he turned away and tried to hide the tears that threatened to overwhelm him. Roger, evil? Brigitta found it hard to believe, for in her eyes Roger was merely a man facing the loss of his home and lands. Perhaps Augusta disliked the man only because his existence was proof that Michael Courtenay had loved and bedded a woman before he'd met Augusta. Could it not be a goad to the woman to know her husband had sired not one, but two sons, by two different women?

"Augusta," Brigitta began, "I—I don't know what to say. Are you asking me to—to suggest to Devon that he disown his half brother? Is that what you want?"

"That is exactly what I want!" Augusta replied, her eyes flashing, and for a moment, she appeared years younger, full of spirit and fire. Augusta must have surely been a formidable opponent in the prime of her years. Even now, beneath the frail ivory of her skin, there shimmered a beauty that could not be diminished by the mere passing of years. Hers was a regal bearing learned at the feet of Princess Thora-Lisa's mother and brought forth by Augusta's knowledge of her own strengths. Her deep-flowing love for Michael Courtenay had carried her to the twilight of her years, and now, physically weak, her intense love for her son had carried her here to Courtenay where she had longed to be.

"Promise me," Augusta said, clutching a lacy, scented handkerchief in one frail hand, "that you will never leave my son's side. You must never, ever let your guard down, for Roger will be lurking in the shadows, always seeking a flaw in the both of you. Roger will stop at nothing to have Courtenay. *Nothing.*"

Such words cost Augusta much. A paroxysm of violent coughing overcame her then. Leaning forward, she clutched her chest, her slim body wracked with dry coughs.

"Augusta!" Brigitta exclaimed, coming to her feet. She reached for the vessel of water placed near Augusta's bed by the ever-efficient Elise and pressed the small cup into Augusta's shaking hand. "Are you all right? Shall I send for the physician?"

Augusta shook her head, taking a tiny sip of water. "No," she breathed. "There is nothing anyone can do for me now. I—I am fine. Please . . . I wish to see my son. Send for Devon." Wearily, she leaned back against the mound of feather pillows behind her. "You will remember what I've asked you?"

"Yes, of course, but—"

"Good. I shall rest in peace knowing you will be here for my son. Take care of him, Brigitta."

"Augusta—"

"No, don't say anything. Just go now and send Devon to me. Don't alarm him. Just—just tell him I'd like to talk. Yes, that's it . . . I want to talk with him. We used to talk a great deal, did you know that? Always, he would ask endless questions about his father. And I would answer him. I loved to talk about Michael. . . ." She sighed, a sound of peace and contentment.

Brigitta moved silently toward the door, frightened by Augusta's abrupt change of mood. As she stepped out into the passage, she heard Augusta whisper, "Soon, Michael. Soon I will be with you once again."

Brigitta hurried away, passing quickly through the narrow passage that led to the front staircase. Bounding up the steps was Devon, his face grim.

"My mother—have you seen her?" he asked, coming to a stop beside Brigitta. He appeared to have just come in from the out-of-doors. His ebony hair was wind-tossed, flowing over his shoulders like a dark cloud, and his wide-topped boots and snug fitting breeches were dirtied with mud. He looked at her with troubled black eyes, his hands reaching out to catch her arms.

"Yes, I've seen Augusta. She—she is asking for you." He said nothing for a full minute. "You should hurry, Devon, I—I fear she will . . ." She couldn't say the words.

"I understand," he whispered, and a steely resignation fell across his features. He straightened, took in a deep breath, and then turned away to hurry up the few steps.

Brigitta watched him go, her heart aching. She wanted to go with him, to offer her support, but he hadn't asked her. Not knowing what to do, feeling sad and out of sorts, she headed aimlessly down the stairs, but realized she didn't want to encounter anyone, especially not Roger. She turned and moved back up the stairs, seeking the solace of her own chambers. She would wait there, alone, until Devon came to her. No matter of her own desires to be near the man she loved and help him through his darkest hour, she would not interrupt. Sitting down on one of the elaborately embroidered chairs, she began what felt to her to be the longest wait of her life.

Devon found his mother sitting up in bed, her frail body resting against a mound of pillows Elise had lovingly plumped and arranged for her. Augusta's eyes were closed, her hands folded in front of her. At the sounds of Devon's entry, she looked up, her face spreading into a gentle, quivering smile.

"Devon . . . my son. Come, sit beside me."

"Hello, Mother. Brigitta said you asked for me. Tell me, is there anything I can get for you? Some medicine perhaps? The physician said you may have as much as you require."

Augusta shook her head, smiling up at her handsome son. "No. 'Tis only sleeping drafts he left, you know, and I don't want to sleep away my last few moments with you." She reached one thin hand up to him, sighing as he took it in both of his. "Do not look so sad," she said. "We all must leave this world at one point. I don't regret that my time has come. I—I am just so very happy that I shall die here, at Courtenay."

Devon nodded, unable to speak past the tightness in his throat. He wanted to assure her that her time had not come, but he knew better. Giving false hope was something Devon Courtenay had never done. Sitting down on the bed beside her, he forced himself to be strong and face his mother's death.

There was an odd light in her eyes, an expectancy almost, as though she was looking forward to a state of peace unknown by any mortal. He realized he'd never seen her so serene, so beautiful and dear as she looked now. He admired her bravery.

"I'm so very proud of you, Devon," she whispered, her voice sounding weak and far away. "You have faced great obstacles in your life and have met them head on. You are very much like your father, you know. Michael . . . he was such a strong and brave man. He would be pleased to know you've finally returned to Courtenay, for this is where you belong, where you've always belonged."

She'd closed her eyes again, and Devon could feel the energy seeping from her small frame even as he clutched her hand in his. "You needn't talk,

Mother," he said quietly. "We—we can just sit here, silently. Save your strength."

She seemed not to have heard him, lost as she was in her own thoughts. "Michael never loved that other woman, you know," she began. "He—he told me so, said he'd wished he'd never married her. I believed him, of course, for I was the one he loved . . . only me."

Devon froze, his breath catching in his chest. "What?" he asked, thinking he hadn't heard correctly. "What woman, Mother? Who are you talking about?"

Augusta shook her head, sighing, her eyes still closed. "He was drunk the night that woman took him to her bed. In the morning she claimed he'd ruined her, screeching how her family would be shamed. He—he felt honor-bound to do the right thing by marrying her. She was just a tavern wench, used by many men, a woman seeking a wedding band so she could force her brat upon the first man who'd take her. Roger isn't Michael's son. He couldn't be! Michael loved me and he wanted *our* child to inherit Courtenay, not that— that woman's brat! Courtenay is *your* birthright, not Roger's!"

Devon's world spun sickeningly with the impact of Augusta's words. He couldn't believe what he was hearing.

Augusta, unaware of Devon's shock, continued. "Michael gave *me* his signet ring, not that wench. . . . I knew then that he truly loved me. We—we said our vows, alone, outside the walls of Vardighet. It did not matter to me there was no man of the cloth to wed us . . . I didn't care if Michael was already legally married to another. In his heart, *I* was his only wife. No matter what happens, Devon, you must remember that *you* are the rightful heir to Courtenay—*you* have the ring."

"What are you saying, Mother?" Devon asked, though dreading to hear the truth. "I thought you and father had been wed in Sweden. I—I thought a minister in Darlana's village performed the ceremony—"

"Dreams," she whispered, her voice weak. "All the stories I told you were dreams. Michael couldn't marry me because he was already wed— wed to a woman he despised. But it doesn't matter, does it? Because you have the ring that entitles you to these lands. Michael made the provision in his will, knowing I might have borne him a child." Her eyes opened suddenly, bright, feverish. "He loved *us*, Devon, not Roger and his mother. *Us!* Michael knew I would give you the ring; he knew that, someday, you would find your way to Courtenay and reap what is rightfully yours."

Devon was stunned. It was true, then. He was a bastard. The label he'd hated, had forever fought against, was in reality what he'd always been! Anger filled him. All the rage he'd felt since he was a child and could understand the tauntings his peers at Vardighet had hurled at him came back to wash over him once again. But this time, there was no dream for Devon to cling to, no illusions. There was only reality. He was a bastard, the illegitimate son of Michael Courtenay. Roger was the true and rightful owner of Courtenay. It was Devon who did not belong here. It was Devon, not Roger, who could not even lay claim to the name of Courtenay.

Sick and angry, he abruptly stood, pacing the spacious chamber. "Why?" he asked. "Why did you not tell me this years ago? Why did you let me pursue a name and inheritance that does not even belong to me? Sweet Lord! I've spent my life chasing after something that is not even mine! Why, Mother? Why?"

"Because I love you," Augusta replied weakly, her voice filled with pain. "Because Courtenay is yours, son. It belongs to you! Michael loved me, he did! He wanted us to be a family. His ring proves this! Why else would he have bequeathed all of his riches to the child who carried his ring?"

Devon whirled around, his face grim, his eyes filled with unspeakable pain. "That ring means nothing to me, do you hear? This place means nothing to me! I don't deserve it, I never did! Courtenay is Roger's, for he is the legal heir!"

"No, Devon, don't say such things. Please," Augusta cried, her whole body shaking now. "Oh, son, do not be angry with me. Everything I've done, all the lies I've told, have been for you. Only you. You—you can't imagine how painful it was to hear the people of Vardighet label you a . . . a bastard. You were conceived in love, a love that has defied time and space. Even when Michael was miles away from Sweden, he remembered us. He left you his home and lands. He—"

"He didn't marry you," Devon cut in, his anger unbearable. "He was married to another woman when he took you to bed—a woman who was already raising his first-born son!"

"No! Michael didn't love Roger or Roger's

mother. He loved us! He wanted to be with us, Devon!" She leaned forward then, her hands going to her chest, clutching her heavy night rail. "Oh, oh, Devon . . ."

The desperate plea in her voice sent a tremor of alarm through him. "Mother!" he said, rushing back to her side. "What is it, Mother? What's wrong?" He swore at himself. He shouldn't have upset her, shouldn't have said such things. "Mother!"

But Augusta couldn't hear him. Her eyes grew horribly wide as she clutched at her chest, gasping for air. Small, animallike sounds of pain came past her lips in breathless grunts. Devon drew her frail body toward him, holding her close, smoothing her wiry hair back from her face. Panic and dread filled him.

"You must relax, Mother. Try—try to rest, do you hear? I—I'm sorry I've upset you. Please, forget what I said. I—I don't blame you for letting me believe I wasn't illegitimate. I don't. Please, just relax. You must calm yourself." He yelled out for Elise, his voice rising to a shout that could surely be heard throughout the entire house.

But there was nothing anyone could do. Even as he held her, tried to soothe her, Augusta drew her last breath. Her sparrowlike body went limp in Devon's strong arms, all color draining from her weathered face as her white-haired head fell gently against Devon's chest.

"No," he whispered, clutching her tightly, his tears blinding him. "No . . ." She was light as a feather in his trembling arms, the last warmth of her body reaching him through layers of clothing.

So frail, so precious. And she was gone. Elise whimpered softly as she stood beside Devon, touching his shoulder with one hand. Silently, Devon eased his mother's body back onto the bed, tenderly folding her arms about her chest and bringing the linen sheets around her. He kissed her cheek one last time. Then he straightened himself, brushing away the first tears he'd ever shed in his adult life and quietly left the room.

Brigitta paced her chambers, waiting. Her stomach whirled and her palms grew moist. Twice she had to hold herself back from scurrying to Augusta's chambers to be with Devon. He would come to her when he needed her, she reminded herself. She made the bed, folded her night rail she'd tossed to a nearby chair earlier, all the while her mind swimming with unconnected thoughts. The minutes ticked slowly by. An eerie silence seemed to fill the four walls surrounding her. She couldn't stand any more, she thought. She should be with Devon, she should—

She whirled at the sound of the door being pushed open. Devon stood there, his face grim, tight, his eyes haunted, and Brigitta knew. He said nothing as he stepped into the room and closed the door quietly behind him. Brigitta went to him, wrapping her arms about him, holding him tighter than she ever had before.

He clung to her, burying her face into the thick swath of her hair. "You are all I have left," he whispered huskily, his voice sounding strained. "You and our babe."

"Oh, love," she said, her voice breaking. "I'm sorry."

He let out a deep, long sigh as he tangled his fingers in the long strands of her hair. "Immediately following the funeral," he said, his voice sounding odd, "we shall be wed."

"Yes, of—of course," she whispered, not understanding why he should talk of a wedding even before his mother was laid to rest. "Whatever you want, Devon."

"I just want to hold you, Brigitta, and never, ever let you go." His embrace tightened, and the two of them stood alone in the middle of the warm chamber, time standing still as it always did whenever they were together. For a precious few moments, the harshness of the world was far away.

Chapter Twenty-one

NOT EVEN AN HOUR had passed before a number of carriages could be heard drawing up before the impressive structure of Courtenay: Roger's legal counselors, all five of them, had arrived. Within Courtenay, the servants were in a flurry of motion. There was a funeral to be planned, Augusta's body, not yet cold, must be laid out, and mourning garb must be pulled from storage for cleaning and pressing. Food must be prepared for the mourners, details made for the funeral—and now, there were five extra guests.

Brigitta feared Devon might crack under the

stress. To have to deal with Roger's legal advisers along with his mother's death was a great burden to carry, but with a dignity she admired, Devon surprised them all by appearing downstairs in the great hall, prepared to meet with counsel.

There would be no lengthy court hearings, for Devon's proof of his legitimacy, his father's signet ring, was the only evidence needed for him to regain Courtenay. Michael's will had been very specific. He'd stated, on his deathbed, that years ago he had married a Swedish lady-in-waiting, had given her the signet ring to be in turn given to their first-born child. This child, whether male or female, was to be sole heir of Courtenay. Having believed Augusta to be dead, Michael had made no provisions for her. Neither were there provisions made for Roger. It was unclear why Michael had left Roger from his will. Some whispered Roger was an ugly reminder of a regretted moment of weakness.

The lawyers, all bewigged and looking resplendent in varying shades of crisp velvets, conducted their business quickly and efficiently. All but two had served Michael Courtenay for many years. They'd viewed the signet ring firsthand, having been present when King James had bestowed the ring and Courtenay and its vast lands on Michael, so there was little doubt as to the validity of the ring. Also, the resemblance between Devon and his deceased father could not be denied. Devon had inherited Michael's dark coloring, classic features, and even the Courtenay birthmark, a dark coloring of pigmentation on Devon's left shoulder blade. The advisers, having worked closely with Roger for the past three years, now knew where their allegiance lay. No longer did Roger hold the importance he once had. Devon, at last, was viewed as the true and legal heir to Courtenay.

No sooner had the ink dried on the numerous legal documents than word was spread across the lands of Augusta Courtenay's death. As though she had lived at Courtenay all her life, she was given a grand burial. People from nearby estates flowed in to pay their respects to a woman they'd never met and to view the two sons of Michael Courtenay: one the new heir, the other a bastard. Naturally, Devon received their condolences in the same breath as they heartily welcomed him, while Roger was given scant nods. For days, tongues would wag through the lands of the scandal within the walls of Courtenay, while those who'd attended the funeral commented on what a striking pair the new owner of Courtenay and his young bride-to-be made.

Through it all, Devon was unusually quiet. Brigitta, standing faithfully at his side, worried about him. He seemed to have withdrawn within himself, and when she looked at him, she could see that familiar hard glint in his eyes, the same that had frightened her when she'd first met him. It was as though he was displeased with his inheritance, as though he had re-erected once again that unscalable wall around his soul. But of course, she reminded herself, he had just lost his mother, and Brigitta could hardly expect him to be cheerful at such a time. And Roger, she noted, appeared to fare no better. Forever in their shadows, he appeared to be a man haunted, stripped away of all his glory. How cruel that events should have taken such a course, she thought. It was one thing for Roger to be told within the privacy of his home that he had no rightful claim to Courtenay, quite another for all of the countryside to hear of the news, only to gather around and stare at him like he was an outcast.

Brigitta, seeing Roger's withdrawal as only a temporary reaction to the events, found herself pitying her lover's half brother. Every now and then, she would catch him gazing at Devon with shrouded eyes and an expressionless face. Her attempts at engaging him in conversation were futile. Roger, it seemed, would need time to deal with his loss. Once all the commotion had passed, she told herself, Roger would come to accept his lot and then he and Devon could acquaint themselves and work together in overseeing Courtenay. She knew Devon wanted nothing more than to form some sort of alliance with his half brother. A family meant everything to Devon, and Brigitta was determined to help him achieve his goal.

But that night, when Devon came to her chamber and joined her upon the huge tester bed, he was reluctant to speak of Courtenay or his plans for the future.

"I thought you would be happy now that you are recognized as the legal heir to these lands," she said quietly, her head resting against his bare chest. Their recent lovemaking had flushed her skin and had been a tender balm to her grief-filled soul. But she had felt as though Devon were far away, his mind filled with other thoughts.

Devon sighed and brushed a gentle hand across

her chest, lifting the heavy signet ring still afixed to a chain about her neck. The weight of it, and its significance, burned his palm. "I don't want to speak about my inheritance," he replied. He had been haunted the past few days with remembering the words his mother had spoken before she'd died. It had been difficult for him to walk into the great hall and meet with the legal advisers. In fact, there had been a part of him that had wanted to tell them all his sordid story, to admit that *he* was the bastard son of Michael Courtenay, and not Roger. But his mother's death had held his tongue. He would not sully her good name. He would accept the name of Courtenay, would let all believe he was the rightful heir, and he would give his mother the grand burial she'd always wished for. This had been his last gift to his mother. She had been a loving parent, had gone to great lengths to see to his comfort and happiness. Devon would not deny her the right to be buried beside Michael. Her tombstone read: Devoted wife of Michael Courtenay and loving mother of Devon Courtenay. Beneath such an inscription, Augusta would surely rest in peace.

He toyed with the signet ring, gazing down at his lovely wife-to-be. "I think I shall purchase a new ring for you," he said gently. "Something petite and beautiful, a ring fashioned especially for you. Would you like that?"

Brigitta was stunned. Something was wrong, terribly wrong. "But I thought—" she stopped herself. "If that is what you want . . . but what shall we do with this ring?"

He shrugged, his eyes giving away nothing. "I thought perhaps I would give it to Roger."

"To Roger? But why? You've crossed two continents to find this ring! You devoted your whole life to searching for it, Devon. Why would you want to give it away?"

"I think Roger should have it. After all, Michael was his father, too. Roger deserves the ring more than I. He was Michael's first-born son, not me."

"But your father's will—"

"To hell with my father's will." He slipped his hand behind her neck, undoing the fragile clasp that held the necklace together. "Tell me, Brigitta," he said, tossing the chain and ring onto the small table beside the bed. "Would it matter to you if we had not this great estate? Would you love me any less if I was not to be lord of Courtenay?" He settled back against the pillows, caressing her neck with one hand as he gazed deeply into her eyes.

"Devon! Why would you ask such a question of me?" Brigitta replied, concern shading her voice. "You know my love for you has nothing to do with your inheritance or even your name."

"Yes," he said lowly, drawing her face close to his. "I do know. I guess I just needed to hear you say the words aloud." Slowly, as though to imprint the memory of her to his brain, he traced with one finger the outline of her full mouth, lingering for a moment on the pouty bow of her lower lip. "I love you, Brigitta." Tenderly, he touched his mouth to hers, needing her more than he ever had. His kiss deepened, became hungry and searching, and as he drew her slim body atop his own, caressing her torso, he was lost in the provocative scent and feel of her.

For the next few hours, the world was lost to them and nothing mattered but the intimacies they shared. Devon's only regret was that such bliss could not last, for with the rising of the sun the cares he had pushed from his mind would return full force. What he would do then, he did not know.

Roger Courtenay paced briskly back and forth across the two-hundred-foot gallery housed on the uppermost floor of the mansion, his thoughts dark. Brilliant sunshine, the first in days, flowed through the numerous glazed windows to his right, falling like sparkling diamonds atop the Turkey carpet and shining wood floor beneath. The dazzling display, along with the dancing particles of dust twirling in the air, went unnoticed. To his left, framed in elaborate woodwork hung various portraits: a few by Dutch or Italian masters, and one, the most striking by size alone and its prime position atop the main marble fireplace, was of Michael Courtenay. The man in the portrait could have been Roger, or even Devon; their looks were so similar. Roger stopped before the painting, staring up at it with loathing in his eyes.

"Damn you," he hissed, his fists clenching. "Damn you for bedding my mother and then leaving her alone and unwed to care for your bastard son!" His voice shook with a grief too long suppressed. All his life, Roger had clung to the hope that he was not illegitimate, that somewhere there lay papers, dried and yellowed with age, that would proclaim him the legal heir of Courtenay.

But now, with Devon's proof, all of Roger's dreams had been shattered. Courtenay was no longer his. Nothing belonged to him now. Nothing. Bile rose in his throat, nearly gagging him, and he reached into the hidden pocket of his satin waistcoat, withdrawing his gold snuffbox. He took a tiny leaf of the tobacco, known as the "Holy Herb" to the Spaniards, and pressed it between his cheek and gum. The tobacco was Roger's secret elixir for many maladies. Now, as the leaf heated his mouth, he hoped it would cleanse his stomach of the bile threatening to come up.

Looking at the elaborate, tiny snuffbox, once belonging to Michael Courtenay, Roger was again reminded of his precarious lot in life. He could not even lay claim to this tiny box, nor the tobacco within it! No longer could he even order the precious stuff from Spain. Nothing that surrounded him belonged to him; not the vast parklands of Courtenay, nor the treasures filling the home, not even the servants, who now scattered away to safer regions whenever he was near, were beholden to him. Nothing was as it should be . . . nor would it ever be again. He was filled with despair and a jealousy he did not wish to acknowledge. Devon was now the owner of the house, the man to whom everyone turned for answers or orders. Devon. Devon. The name turned over and over in his head. He hated his younger half brother—hated him perhaps even more than he hated their deceased father.

The sound of footsteps came from the opposite end of the gallery. Roger looked up to see the butler walking toward him.

"Forgive me, my—" Geoffery, having been Roger's butler for the past three years, suddenly stumbled awkwardly over his words. Geoffery, who had never been awkward in any situation. Always cool and precise, knowing exactly what his duties were and carrying them out impeccably, Geoffery was now uneasy and inept, confused as to how he should approach Roger.

Feeling sick again, Roger took another leaf of tobacco. He waved one hand in the air. "Just tell me what you want, Geoffery, and then be gone."

"I, uh, this message just arrived for you . . ." Again he faltered, not knowing how to address the man who had until only a few days ago been his employer and master. He held out a sealed piece of parchment, relief showing in his aged face when Roger took the note and then bade him to leave.

Alone again, Roger stared down at the familiar, impressive royal seal. It was that of Erik Bjord, the great Swedish general who had wed the sickly Princess Thora-Lisa. Roger and Erik had on occasion done business together. Soon after settling within Courtenay, and learning of Michael's will, Roger had met the very political-minded general. Roger had been impressed by the general's business sense, and so sought him out more and more often in hopes of learning from him. Roger had desperately wanted to prove himself to his father. Erik had a keen interest in shipowning and had merged his wealth and power with shipowners in Stockholm and Göteborg. Erik had traveled to England to strengthen mercantile bonds and create new ones, he'd explained to Roger, and upon learning Roger had only recently moved into Courtenay, Erik was more than eager to strike a deal.

After lengthy meetings in which Erik took great interest in hearing all Roger had to tell about Courtenay and its lands, Erik had made several promising business propositions to Roger. But time and again, Michael had turned away all of Roger's ideas. Soon, it became apparent to Roger that Michael would never listen to any of his suggestions. And so, allowing Erik Bjord to sway him, Roger had devised a plan to end Michael Courtenay's life. With Michael gone, and with no heir showing up at Courtenay with the precious signet ring, Roger had total control of Michael's estate.

Having only just acquired his position at Courtenay, Roger had been anxious to delve into the running of the estate and also to invest in mercantile adventures. With Erik's lead and guidance, Roger began to take interest in putting his monies into the buying of goods from Sweden. With the help of his legal advisers, Roger was soon doing a regular business with Erik's burgher associates in Göteborg. He purchased high-quality Uppland ore, nicknamed oreground iron, and also copper, which was essential for the making of armaments and coinage. His investments paid off and so he continued with his trade, reveling in the fact he had done all of this on his own and had nearly tripled the monies he'd invested. How proud Michael Courtenay would be, had been his first thought. And that had been Roger's bright and burnished goal of his life, to rule Courtenay and make it more self-sufficient than before, to make the Courtenay name one people would never forget. How exciting the three years had been for him! Every day had been a new adventure, every step forward a remarkable experience—and every night he'd come upstairs to the gallery and had stood before his father's portrait, telling the handsome, distinguished-looking gentleman in blue satin all about the day's business dealings, of all the money he'd made, of all the clever investments. . . .

But now, Roger thought as he stared blankly down at the bold handwriting of Erik Bjord, there would be no more exciting adventures in the business world. No more traveling to Dover to watch as the ship carrying his Swedish goods made port. All of the fervor and excitement would now be Devon's. . . . And also there was the horrid fact that now, with Devon's proof of parentage, Roger did not care whether or not his deceased father would be proud of him. The glory was gone. The grand adventure he'd waited for all his life had come to a heart-stopping end. The celebration had ceased, all the risk-taking, all the exhilarating highs and lows, gone, forever.

And it was Devon's fault.

Looking back up at his father's portrait, Roger let out a loud wail of protest. "I hate you both!" he yelled, and flung the delicate snuff box at the too-handsome face. He watched through blurred eyes as the lid snapped open and tobacco fluttered down to the wood floor, landing silently beside the box, which had jangled to a stop. "I will get even," he vowed. "Somehow, I will get even with the both of you."

Turning his back on the portrait, he strode deliberately toward the far end of the gallery. He had a meeting he would not miss. Surely, after all the guidance Erik Bjord had given him into the breathless realm of foreign trade, Erik would have some advice as to how to deal with Devon.

Together, Roger thought, perhaps he and Erik could devise a plan to see Devon's downfall, no matter if that meant seeing Courtenay and all its lands go down with him.

Chapter Twenty-two

ROGER STEPPED INSIDE the dimly lit interior of the Ship at Dover, an establishment frequented by both the local folk and travelers to and from the Continent, and let his eyes adjust to the darkness. Before him, spread out on the first of three floors, was a huge common room filled with sailors, workers, and a few harried barmaids. Owned by a gentleman who was noted for collecting furniture cast off by the gentry, the place was adorned with an odd assortment of tables, chairs, and benches. From the two heavily embroidered chairs flanking the cavernous hearth all the way to the gold candle holders, the room was decorated with a sort of hodgepodge flair that Roger found distasteful. The noise of the smoke-filled room was loud, causing the ache in his head to increase tenfold, and the way the serving wenches hustled about and tossed out playful banter with the patrons caused the hairs on the back of his neck to stand on end. His reaction to the scene surprised him and brought home the fact of how much he'd taken for granted since moving into Courtenay. There had been a time in his life when this scene would not have bothered him, in fact, he would have found himself very much at home. But not now. Socially, he was above every person in this room, but because of Devon, he could not lay claim to the vast fortune he once had—nor could he even lay claim to the name of Courtenay. The realization galled him.

In the corner of the room, near the bay window that overlooked the mast-choked harbor of Dover, sat a lone man. Dressed in wine-colored breeches, a matching coat, and a heavily bleached linen shirt beneath, he appeared to be a man above the humanity which surrounded him. About his waist, secured to an embroidered sash, hung a thin rapier, the handle of which rested readily beside the man's large right hand. Atop his long, flowing blond hair perched a low-crowned hat adorned with white and wine plumes that was cocked to an acclivous angle, shadowing one of his lazily-hooded eyes. The way he sat, with his long, powerful legs stretched out before him, his feet encased in expensive bucket-top boots, and the way he gestured to a passing bar maid, made him appear like a king before loyal servants. Clearly, he was

at home among this reckless lot just as he would
be at ease before a huge congregation of rapt lis-
teners, their faces all turned to adore him. His
bearing was not quite regal, but held the air of
one who expected subservience of those around
him. His blue eyes, startling within the fair and
ruddy facial skin, roamed across the rooms once
and then settled on Roger.

Roger immediately recognized Erik Bjord.

At the blond giant's nod, Roger moved forward.
"General Bjord," he said, feeling dwarfed by the
man even though he remained seated. "I—I came
as soon as I received your message."

Erik Bjord glanced up, a tolerant expression on
his face. "How good of you," he replied. He did
not bother to extend his hand in greeting, nor did
he bother to stand. After all, he'd married a princess. He'd come up in the world since his last
meeting with Roger Courtenay. He nodded once
toward the chair opposite him and waited until
Roger was seated and a nervous serving-wench
had set a tankard of ale on the table, before he
spoke. "Tell me, Roger, how do you fare at Courtenay? Was the last shipment of iron ore to your
satisfaction? I was in Göteborg to personally oversee the loading. I wanted to be certain you had the
finest Sweden can offer, my friend."

"The last shipment was very satisfactory," Roger
began. "In fact, I had intended to place another
order—" He stopped himself abruptly. For a moment, the usual breathless excitement of foreign
trade had snuck up on him and he had been swept
away. But now, he remembered that he could not
place that order for more ore, or anything else.

That privilege now belonged to his half brother. He fell silent, toying stupidly with the wet handle of his tankard.

Erik took note of Roger's actions. Leaning back in his chair, taking a healthy swallow of English ale, he looked over the table at Roger's drawn features. "Tell me," he coaxed. "Something is wrong. What has happened, old friend? Have you perhaps invested unwisely in a venture that has not been profitable? Please, you have no need to fear I will repeat the story of your failures. I know it has been a long time since we've met, but I had hoped the bonds of our friendship would not weaken with the passage of months, or even with the distance that normally separates us."

Roger found himself relaxing with the even tone of Erik's deep voice. There had been many times in the past when Roger had turned to Erik for advice and now, he realized, Erik Bjord was probably the only man of such high rank who would even consider speaking to Roger. Without the Courtenay name and wealth behind him, Roger was little more than a beggar to men who had very recently considered him one of their own.

He decided he had nothing to lose—and quite possibly, everything to gain—by taking Erik into his confidence. After all, isn't that the true reason he had kept this meeting?

"I, uh, there has been a bit of a scandal at Courtenay," he began, moistening his lips. "My half brother, Devon, has returned from abroad and . . . and he brought with him the signet ring mentioned in my father's will. He—he found this ring at Vardighet, I'm told."

"Oh?" Erik asked, his eyes giving away nothing. "And who told you Devon found this ring within my home?" He reached for his tankard of ale, taking a long, healthy swallow.

"Brigitta. Brigitta Lind. She is soon to be Devon's wife."

At this, Erik went totally still. His hand, still holding the mug, stopped in midair. "What?" he demanded, his smooth voice suddenly going harsh. "What did you say?"

Roger blinked, startled by the transformation in the man across from him. "I said Brigitta Lind told me my half brother found this ring within the walls of Vardighet. It—it seems Augusta and Michael had been legally wed after all and that Michael left this ring with Augusta. He—"

"I don't care about Devon's foolish old mother!" Erik hissed, slamming his tankard on the table and leaning forward. "Tell me about Brigitta! What do you mean she is soon to be Devon's *bride?*"

"Why, it is just as I said—they plan to be married in a fortnight. The preparations have—have already begun. Devon is sparing no expense, I can assure you."

"No!" Erik boomed. "This cannot be!" He pushed back away from the table making a sort of tent with his hands as he tapped the tips of his forefingers against his nose. Pure hatred flashed in his narrowed blue eyes as he stared straight at Roger without really seeing him.

"Do—do you know this woman?" Roger ventured, extremely uncomfortable with the seething blond giant of a man.

"Know her? Yes," he breathed lowly. "I know

her. Very well, in fact." He fell silent for a moment longer, his face harsh in the pale light of day that streamed across him from the massive bay window. "So, Devon has returned to Courtenay to claim his inheritance . . . and to wed the woman he loves. Ha! What a fool he is!" He blinked, focusing his gaze once again on the man opposite him. "Am I correct in assuming Devon has tossed you out of your home now that he has returned?"

Roger shook his head. "No, not yet, he hasn't. But I've no doubt that he will as soon as he and Brigitta become man and wife."

Erik's lips sneered into a thin line at mention of Brigitta. "Perhaps I can help you then, old friend. Perhaps I can help you rid yourself of your half brother. Forever."

Roger had been thinking the same, but now that the moment had arrived to actually put into words what he'd been hoping for, he didn't know what to say. "Short of murder, I don't know how I'll ever regain Courtenay."

Erik said nothing, just looked at him with those expressionless small blue eyes. Roger felt a chill course up his spine. Surely, the general could not be considering murder? Could he?

"There is another way to get to your dear half brother," Erik offered. Roger said nothing, he only listened, so Erik continued. "All of us harbor secrets about ourselves, do we not? And Brigitta Lind is no exception." Still, Roger said nothing, and Erik became impatient. Very well then, he would be blunt. "Brigitta cannot marry your half brother. *She is already the wife of another.*"

Roger blanched. Brigitta married to another

man? How could it be? She was so innocent and beautiful, so very sincere in all she did! Roger had seen firsthand the love in Brigitta's eyes whenever she gazed at Devon, had seen her devotion for his half brother in every move she made. He measured the man across from him. "I—I find this difficult to believe."

"She is, I assure you."

"But—to whom is she wed?"

"*To me.*"

"You? But I thought—"

"You thought I had wed a princess," Erik cut in, and then gave a harsh laugh. "So did I, old friend. Brigitta Lind murdered the Princess Thora-Lisa and then took her place at the altar. Had I seen through her disguise earlier, our fair Brigitta would now be dead, but . . . like a slippery fish she slipped away with her lover." He leaned forward once again, leaning his elbows on the scarred tabletop. "What I'm telling you now must never be repeated, do you hear? No one must know of this conversation."

"But if Brigitta murdered your princess then she must—"

"You tell no one!" he repeated harshly, then waved one hand in the air. "Thora-Lisa was sickly, soon to die of her maladies anyway. She did not interest me when she was alive and so avenging her death is something I care not to do. It is Brigitta who has captured my interest. I believe she would be a fine princess for Vardighet. She is young and healthy and can give me the sons Thora-Lisa never would have been able to bear. *I want Brigitta Lind for my very own.*"

Roger was stunned into silence as he tried to absorb all the blond giant was saying. "But how?" he muttered. Deceit and treachery had never interested Roger. The only thing that had ever interested him had been Courtenay, and now it seemed the only way he could have his home and lands was to fall in with Erik Bjord. He felt cornered.

"It is simple. You bring Brigitta to me. Where Brigitta goes, Devon will follow, I am certain. You need never see the two of them again. I will take care of everything."

"But the ring . . . Devon is the one who brought the ring to Courtenay and now he is the legal heir."

"I will take care of it," Erik said easily, forming his plans even as he spoke. "Devon will do anything for his precious Brigitta. Believe me, I know. I will simply inform Devon that he will never see his precious Brigitta again unless he relinquishes his title and lands to you. Courtenay will once again be yours . . . and Brigitta will be back at Vardighet where she belongs."

"And Devon?" Roger asked, dreading the answer. After all, they shared the same father, and Devon had not tossed Roger out of Courtenay yet. In fact, Devon had not even made any advances in that direction.

"I will take care of Devon."

Roger didn't like the sound of Erik's voice, nor did he trust the gleam he now saw in those small blue eyes.

"Return to Courtenay," Erik instructed him. "I will follow at a safe distance. Lure Brigitta away from the main house, somewhere on your lands, and then leave her there. I will take care of her. My ship leaves for Sweden soon, and Brigitta will be on board."

Roger hesitated. It was one thing to contemplate revenge and quite another to actually act out his thoughts. "I—I don't know," he began.

"What do you mean? Of course you will do this!" Erik thundered. "Or you will never live to see Courtenay again. Do I make myself clear, Roger?"

Roger swallowed, and felt the terrible bile rising once again in his throat. He wished he had his tobacco. "Yes. I understand." Slowly, he stood. Erik remained seated, reaching for his tankard and finding it empty. Scowling, he roared for more drink, waving Roger away.

"Go," he ordered. "You've much to do."

Roger did as he was told, not looking back. Once outside the Ship at Dover, he stood beneath the blinding sun as he tried to sort out his thoughts. Dover was alive with hustling people and moving carriages. Behind him, in the harbor, were ships whose masts reached upward to staggering heights, towering above the rooftops and scraping each other's sides. There was cargo aboard those ships. Cargo from all ports of the world. Vast sums of money were being made and lost this very minute, ships leaving for faraway lands, the holds bulging with merchandise that could belong to Roger . . . but only if he could reclaim his title and wealth. Without Courtenay, Roger could not be a part of this bustling seaport, could not be an integral part of any seaport.

He *needed* Courtenay, for his pride, for his salvation. And, by God, Courtenay belonged to *him*, he thought bitterly, not Devon. It had been Roger who'd made Courtenay what it was today. Roger had toiled on the lands, had whipped the servants into shape. Roger deserved Courtenay, not Devon.

Whirling away from the inn, he turned his face toward the north, toward his home, his decision made.

BOOK V

❧

The Hunted

Chapter Twenty-three

Brigitta stood upon a low footstool, enduring numerous pricks of stray needles that jabbed into her delicate skin as a fussy tailor moved about her, his small, beady gray eyes staring down across his sharp, beaklike nose at every seam of the gown that was to be her wedding dress. Tall and much too thin, he wore a huge white wig that was often askew and needed a thorough brushing and cleaning, while the rest of him was clothed in the finest scarlet silk, the jewels of his doublet flashing like a mirror coated in sunshine. Brigitta decided she liked the man, although at first his feminine mannerisms had shocked as well as amused her. He had long, tapered fingers, each adorned with glittering rings, and his hands were thin and soft looking. Brisk and efficient, the man knew what he was about, she had to admit. The gown she wore was absolutely exquisite. Instead of the blue she had thought she'd wear, Brigitta now chose to wear white.

Fashioned of white, light-weight brocade, the neckline of the dress left her shoulders bare, showing to advantage her creamy white skin which glowed like alabaster. The sleeves were puffed, and ended just below her elbow in a frill of snowy white. The skirt was full, gored in the front and gathered in the back, and flowed out from the tight bodice in gleaming, rich folds. Brigitta felt positively beautiful in such a creation and she said as much to the tailor.

"Of course," Hobson Appleby merely replied. He sniffed, a nervous habit, Brigitta decided, and then took a step back, placing his hands on his narrow hips as he appraised her. "Just a tuck there, I think," he mumbled to himself, turning his head this way and that. "And perhaps there." He brought one hand up to tap his forefinger against his too-full, red lips. "Hmmm. Splendid! Perfect! Turn about now, would you?"

Brigitta lifted one brow. Turn about on this stool? The man was mad, but she did as she was told, turning slowly. He spoke to her as though she were his equal and not soon to be the wife of the heir to Courtenay. Brigitta didn't mind, though. His subtle way of ordering her about was refreshing. She had enjoyed their chats during the numerous fittings in the past few days and admitted to herself that she would indeed miss the gay Hobson Appleby when the dress was finished, which, by all indications, would be soon.

"Wonderful!" he exalted, more to himself than to Brigitta. "I must say I've enjoyed this experience," he went on. "It is only a pity I will not be able to serve Roger any longer—" He stopped himself, as though he had said too much.

"Go on," Brigitta coaxed. After all, he'd not bothered much about propriety in the past. Why should he start now?

He helped her off the small stool, bending down to fuss with the train of the gown. "What I mean is since Roger will no longer be living at Courtenay I'll—"

"And who told you Roger will be leaving Courtenay?"

He looked up, surprised. "Why, no one, I just assumed . . ."

"Yes, I suppose everyone has assumed Devon intends to toss his half brother out the door. Well you can rest assured that Devon has no such intentions. His only wish is to have his half brother at his side. There is no reason whatsoever why the two of them cannot manage the affairs of Courtenay together."

"And does Roger know this?"

"I've no idea what Roger knows." It was true, she didn't. She'd not seen him in a number of days, and since the night she and Devon had talked of giving Roger the signet ring, the two of them had not mentioned the subject of Roger. "But surely he cannot expect Devon to be so cruel as to banish him from Courtenay."

"Stranger things have happened," Hobson quietly replied, but then brightened. "But of course Roger will be delighted when he hears this. He told me so himself he feared Devon would want him to have no part of Courtenay."

"Roger told you that?"

Hobson nodded. "Roger and I are . . . close. I've known him for three years and have dressed him ever since we met. He is the grand sensation of London whenever he travels there, did you know? He takes great pride in his appearance and it is my delight to dress him in my finest creations."

"And you can continue to create for him," Brigitta said. "You needn't fear you'll be losing your employment simply because Devon has arrived."

Hobson sniffed, clearly affronted. "I'm not in Roger's employ," he said, suddenly full of haughty air. "He and I . . . we have a sort of partnership . . . do you understand?"

Brigitta's eyes went wide, and then she smiled. "Yes," she said. "I think I do."

Elise stepped into the chamber then, ready to help Brigitta out of her gown. Since Augusta's passing, Elise had taken it upon herself to cater to Brigitta in every way she could. Brigitta allowed the older woman to fuss over her, knowing Elise needed something to occupy her while she grieved for her former employer. Devon had given Elise a tidy sum of money and had even offered an escort for the woman so she could return to her home town of Kent, but Elise had waved away the gesture, telling them she wished to stay at Courtenay and work.

"Would you care for some tea, my lady?" she asked once Hobson was gone and Brigitta was once again dressed in her simple gown of pearl gray. Elise had taken to addressing Brigitta as "my lady."

"Elise, you needn't call me 'my lady.' 'Brigitta' will do nicely."

"Oh no," Elise quickly replied. "I cannot call you 'Brigitta.' Soon enough you'll be the lady of this grand house."

"Very well," Brigitta said, smiling. "And yes, I think I will have some tea. I'll be in the summer parlor. Have you seen Devon this morning?"

"No, my lady. I believe he is surveying the grounds. He said something about necessary repairs to the garden walls."

"And Roger?"

"I don't believe he's yet returned from his journey to Dover, my lady."

"I see. Very well, Elise. That will be all."

"Yes, my lady. I'll bring your tea right down."

Brigitta watched Elise bustle out of the chamber. She'd forgotten what it was like to be catered to and addressed so formally. Once she and Devon were wed her status would rise even more, she knew, but the thought did not frighten her. Thora-Lisa had taught her well.

Thora-Lisa. Even now Brigitta missed her dear, gentle princess. Lisa would have been so pleased knowing Devon had finally come home to Courtenay . . . *but would she be pleased knowing Brigitta had fled from Vardighet . . . from Erik?* A chill settled over Brigitta as she thought of Erik Bjord. How long had it been since she'd thought of that horrid man? His name had not even entered her mind since Copenhagen, not since Devon had told her he loved her and didn't care that she had walked to the altar for another man. But now, all her fears were suddenly beginning to crowd in around her. In just two weeks she would be Devon's wife—but wasn't she *already* someone's wife? *No*, she thought, *I won't think of Erik, never again. He is far away and cannot harm me now.*

But even as she left the upstairs chamber and headed down the front staircase toward the summer parlor, a chill crept up her spine, wrapping insidiously around her heart. Alone and in the parlor with its handsome furnishings and bold tapestries, she crossed her arms and ran her hands up to her shoulders and down again as she paced the room. Why did she have to think of Erik now? Why?

Because I am married to him!

No, you're not! Thora-Lisa was his wife!

No, I married Erik, not Lisa. Oh, Lisa, I miss you. I wish you had lived. I wish you had married Erik!

But no, she didn't wish that. Erik Bjord was a heartless, cold man. He cared only for one person: himself. Thora-Lisa would have been dreadfully unhappy with him.

There came a sound behind Brigitta, and she whirled around, coming face to face with Roger.

"Hello," he said, his face, so like Devon's, expressionless. "Elise said I might find you here. I thought I'd join you for tea. That is, if you don't mind."

"Roger! No, of course I don't mind. Please sit down. I didn't know you'd returned from Dover."

"I just arrived," he answered, moving uneasily across the room to take a seat. "I—I had some business to finish there."

He is nervous, Brigitta thought. *Perhaps he doesn't feel Courtenay is his home any longer.* She felt miserable as she watched his dark face with its sharp angles. He had been destroyed when he'd seen the signet ring, and now he had traveled to Dover to "finish some business." Brigitta wished Roger and Devon would soon talk about Courtenay and how it would be managed. But she knew Devon had hesitated to approach his older half brother, although she didn't know why.

"Business?" she asked.

He nodded. "I have invested heavily in foreign trade. I've a ship heading for the New World in two days' time."

"America. How exciting for you."

He looked up, his black eyes tired. "Yes, it was exciting, at one time. But now . . ." He let his words trail off.

Brigitta's misery increased. She wished she could tell Roger how Devon felt, but it was not her place to discuss Devon's hopes and dreams with Roger, she sternly reminded herself. Devon had to be the one to broach the delicate matter of sharing ownership of Courtenay.

Elise entered the parlor then, teacups rattling as she waddled over to them, her face beaming. "Ah, I see you've found each other," she said, setting down her tray that was covered with a highly polished tea set, two delicate porcelain cups and saucers, and a platter of pastries still warm from the oven. She poured their tea, handed them each their cups, and then waddled back out of the room.

"She's very efficient," Roger commented after Elise had closed the door behind her. "But she needn't serve us. There are others who are quite capable."

"Yes, I know, but Elise needs something to occupy her time. You don't mind, do you?"

"Me? Why should I mind? You are the one who will soon be delegating orders to the servants—but here now, I did not come in here to discuss Courtenay or the hired help."

"What did you want to discuss?"

He paused for a moment, taking a sip of hot tea. "You and Devon, and your upcoming marriage. I, uh, I wanted to give Devon a wedding present, something rare and different, and I was hoping you would help me choose the perfect gift."

Brigitta found herself warming to the man opposite her. "Roger, how very thoughtful of you. Of course I'll help you choose a gift. Had you something particular in mind?"

"Yes . . . a few different things actually. You see, since I've been at Courtenay I've begun a small collection of paintings by various masters. I've hung my favorites in the gallery, but the others I keep in a small cottage on the northern end of the estate. Since the weather has been so wretched I have been unable to give you a tour of the grounds, so you've not seen this cottage. It is sort of a private sanctuary for me. I don't even allow the servants there."

"And you were thinking of giving Devon one of these paintings?"

"Perhaps. I—I haven't decided. I've other treasures there as well. I—I was hoping you might go to the cottage with me and help me choose something suitable, since you are more likely to know Devon's likes and dislikes." He looked down at his tea, unable to meet her eyes.

He's nervous, Brigitta thought again. By wanting to give Devon a wedding present he is trying to bridge the gap between them. *How pleased Devon will be*, she thought.

"I would love to help you choose a gift, Roger. And I'm certain, whatever you decide, Devon will be delighted."

"Wonderful. Shall we plan on tomorrow? Say, in the morning sometime?"

She nodded, smiling. Finally, it appeared as though Devon would have his wish: that he and Roger become the family they never had.

Brigitta was up early the next morning and already dressed by the time Devon awoke. She watched him, smiling, as he sat up in bed and fluffed the pillows behind him, leaning back to gaze at her affectionately. Since his mother's death, he now did not bother to leave Brigitta's bed before dawn. Brigitta did not mind. Since Augusta's passing, there'd been a marked change in Devon, and Brigitta's only thought now was to see him happy. He looked very handsome sitting there, his bare chest rising above the linen in well-defined lines. His ebony hair was tousled from sleep and his eyes were slumberous.

"You are up early," he commented.

"Yes, I've a great many things to accomplish this day." There was a twinkle in her eyes as she sat on the edge of the bed and slipped a pair of blue satin slippers on her feet. Decorated with tiny seed pearls, the slippers matched the ice-blue satin dress she'd chosen to wear. "Do you realize we will be married in a few short days? I had no idea there was so much to do in planning for a wedding!"

"You needn't do anything at all, if you don't want to," Devon replied. "You know I don't care if our wedding is a grand affair or a simple one—I only care that it is legal and performed as soon as possible."

"I know that," she said softly. "But since you are now the owner of Courtenay you should have a wedding befitting your title. And truthfully, I do not mind all the excitement . . . it helps to keep my mind from dwelling on the past."

Devon's hand clasped her arm then, drawing her up beside him upon the bed. Welcoming his touch, Brigitta laid her head against his bare chest. "Think no more of the past, sweet Brigitta. It cannot touch us here. Believe me, I, too, am tortured by remembering events I cannot alter . . . but we must look to the future now. We—we must do what we can to make our world as safe and secure as possible for our children."

She was quiet for long moments, listening to the steady beat of his heart beneath her ear. He was right, she knew. She musn't think of Erik Bjord. She could not let memories of that frightening, evil man cloud the happiest time of her life. "Very well," she whispered. "I shall do my best to put the past behind me. We are at Courtenay, where you've always longed to be, where you *belong* . . . and soon we will have a tiny babe, born of love and deep commitment." She tipped her face upward, her eyes shining with tears of happiness. "My heart is full, Devon, and you have made it so. I love you."

His breath caught with her words. Voice husky, he whispered, "And I love you, my sweet . . . forever, without end." His mouth covered hers then in a whispering kiss, gentle and soothing, a balm for all time.

Nearly two hours later, his body sated and his heart near bursting with the love of a beautiful woman, Devon watched with appreciative eyes as Brigitta walked toward the chamber door, her skirts swaying provocatively for his benefit. "Keep that up, wench," he teased, "and I will pull you back into my arms and never let you go."

She laughed, a light tinkling sound. "But then we would never be wed, would we?"

He shrugged, a devilish gleam in his eyes. "Oh, I don't know, I imagine I could urge a man of the cloth to enter our paradise and perform the ceremony right here. We need not ever leave these chambers again."

"You are forever a rogue, Devon Courtenay. Now up with you and get dressed. I shall see you at noon for our meal."

"I don't know if I can wait that long," he replied, his lips spreading in an outrageous grin.

Brigitta shook her head, then stepped lightly out of the chamber, shutting the door before he could attempt to woo her back into his vital embrace once again. Already she was late for her meeting with Roger. She only hoped he hadn't left for the small cottage yet. She looked forward to helping him choose a wedding gift for Devon.

Devon watched as Brigitta shut the door behind her. The air stirred in the chamber, wafting about him with the heady scent of her. Sitting atop the crumpled linen of the bed, the early morning sunlight filling the room, Devon let his thoughts drift back to what Brigitta had said about being haunted by the past. He knew she was thinking of Erik Bjord, of the wedding vows she'd spoken in the name of Thora-Lisa.

How long would it be, he wondered, before both he and Brigitta could forget the past? He knew for himself that as long as he lived within the walls of Courtenay he would be forever reminded of his father and of the fact that he was not truly the legitimate heir to these lands. The thought galled him, even the title that had been placed at his feet the day his mother passed away no longer interested him. He didn't want Courtenay, not like this. This home, these lands, they belonged to Roger, not to him.

Throwing the covers from his body, Devon rose and quickly began to dress, his features grim. He knew what he had to do; he'd known since that fateful day Augusta had spilled her secrets while on the threshold of death. He had only accepted Courtenay because he wanted his mother to have a decent burial. Now, there was no reason to keep his sordid secret to himself.

Leaving the warm chamber behind, Devon moved at a brisk pace through the winding passages of Courtenay, not stopping until he came to his half brother's door. He knocked on the portal once, and then again.

"Roger!" he called out. "It is Devon. I wish to speak with you."

The door swung open and a pale Roger, dressed in rich, deep black, unrelieved except for a froth of snowy white at his throat and cuffs, peered nervously at his younger half brother. "What do you want?" he asked in a flat voice. "Has something gone wrong?" When he spoke, his upper lip twitched in an unbecoming way, and it wasn't until Devon stepped into the elaborate chamber that he noticed Roger wasn't himself this day. Indeed, his half brother appeared nervous and . . . afraid. Yes, that was what caused his black eyes to search the passage before he closed the chamber door, Devon decided.

"Nothing is wrong," Devon said, watching his brother intently. "In truth, one could say there is a great deal *right*—for you anyway."

"Wh—what do you mean?" He withdrew a tiny gold snuffbox from within his coat, taking a pinch of the stuff to place between his cheek and gums. As he did so, his hands shook nervously and he nearly dropped the box, fumbling clumsily with the thing before it disappeared again within his coat. His brow creased with a deep frown; he stared at his brother, waiting for an explanation of this unexpected meeting.

"Perhaps I've caught you at an inopportune moment. You look . . . preoccupied."

"Preoccupied?" Roger parroted. "N—no, not—not at all. I—I've business on my mind is all. I'm doing my best to have all in order for you. Now that you are the owner of Courtenay and I . . . I am not, I—"

"That's what I wanted to talk to you about," Devon interrupted, hating the pain that shot through Roger's eyes with his words. "I've something that belongs to you." He lifted his hand and in the palm of it lay Michael Courtenay's gold signet ring, the ruby flashing brightly. Lowly, he said, "This is yours, I believe, by right of birth."

Roger looked down, his breath leaving him in a rush. "Wh—what do you mean this is mine? Is this some cruel trick, *brother?*" His face was dark as he lifted it from the ring to Devon's face.

"The cruel joke was on me, Roger. Not you. The day my mother died, she made a confession: Augusta and Michael were never wed. Michael could not marry Augusta, for he was already wed to another. Your mother. I am not Michael's legitimate son. You are, dear brother. And so, this ring is yours." He pushed his hand toward Roger once again. "Here. Take it, and all that goes with it; this home, these lands, all of Michael's wealth, and even his title are yours. I want no part of them."

"I—I cannot believe this."

"It's true."

"But . . . but why? If you knew you, and not I, were Michael's bastard son, why did you allow me to be stripped of my position? Why didn't you tell the legal counselors the truth?"

"Because I had only just heard the news from my mother's lips . . . because I wanted to see my mother buried beside the man she loved more than life itself. Had I told what I knew, my mother would never have been laid to rest here at Courtenay. But it doesn't matter now, Roger. What does matter is that I am willing to leave Courtenay and all its riches to you."

Roger stared at him, his eyes misting. "You would do this—for me?"

Devon nodded once, pressing the gold ring into Roger's shaking hand. "I would," he said quietly. "I have." He turned away then, ready to leave. He would summon Brigitta and tell her the truth. She must know he was not the legitimate son of the dead Michael Courtenay. She would understand his reasons for not wanting to live at Courtenay, of course she would.

His hand was on the latch of the portal when he heard Roger's voice behind him.

"Wait!" Roger cried. "I—I cannot let you do this, Devon. I don't deserve this, not at all!"

"And why not?" Devon turned back toward his half brother, confused by Roger's reaction to having his grandest dream once again in his custody. "You've the legitimacy which grants you inheritance, whereas I do not. Courtenay is yours. You are once again the owner of Courtenay, as you have always been since the death of our father."

"No!" Roger cried, flinging the precious ring across the chamber as though it were on fire and had scorched his hand. "You don't understand! I—I don't deserve your honesty, Devon! I—oh, God," he cried, reaching out to grab Devon roughly by the shoulders. "I have wronged you, brother of mine . . . I have—I have sent Brigitta to her death!"

Devon went totally still, shocked by Roger's words. "What?"

"Brigitta . . . I—I penned a note to her, telling her to meet me at the small cottage near the north border. You know the one, it is unoccupied, it has been for years." He shook his head, crying and shaking all at once. Terrified by the dangerous light in Devon's eyes, Roger stepped back, dropping his hands from him like a bird brought down by a hunter's gun. "Forgive me, Devon. Please—"

"What have you done?" Devon demanded. "What do you mean you've sent Brigitta to her death? Tell me, man!" He advanced on Roger, then grabbed him by the sleeve and shook him so hard Roger's teeth clacked together.

"I—I sent her to meet with Erik Bjord . . . I know she married him in the name of another. I—I know her secret, Devon . . . and I told Erik where he could find her, alone and unescorted."

Devon's face went white with rage . . . and fear. Erik, here, in England? And Brigitta, his beautiful, loving Brigitta, a child—their child—growing within her, might very well be at that blackguard's mercy. Immediately, he released his death-grip on Roger and then swung around, heading out the door. Brigitta! He had to reach Brigitta before it was too late!

Chapter Twenty-four

AFTER LEAVING DEVON alone in her chamber, Brigitta headed downstairs to the great hall where she and Roger were to meet. She was tardy, she knew, for her blissful dalliance with Devon had kept her from being on time. She could only hope Roger hadn't taken her lateness as a personal affront. Roger's acceptance meant a great deal to Brigitta. Moving about the hall, filled now with morning sunlight that spilled through the low bay windows, she paced idly until she spotted a square of paper upon the high table. She reached for the note, penned with a hasty hand by Roger. *I waited for you for over an hour*, the note read, *but could tarry no longer. I will be at the cottage for the remainder of the morning. Please come when you are able. R.*

Well, this is a good sign, Brigitta thought, tucking the note into a side pocket as she scurried out of the hall. Confident she could find the cottage on her own, Brigitta passed through the wooden screen entranceway and stepped out into the warming, late spring day. Her feet scarcely seemed to touch the ground as she moved atop the budding lawns of Courtenay toward the northern regions. The air was filled with the gentle trills of songbirds, cuckoos, buzzing bees, and the fresh scent of a new day. Oxeye daisies stirred in the gentle breeze amid a carpet of deep green grasses, and wild irises could be seen poking up, their petals opening to the life-giving sun.

As she walked, humming softly to herself, Brigitta let her mind wander to thoughts of her upcoming wedding. She decided that the great hall should be filled with wild flowers, and with flowering boughs adorning the doors and windows. It would be fun for her to walk about Courtenay and pick the flowers herself. It had been a long and dark winter for her and now, with summer approaching, Brigitta looked forward to settling into Courtenay and preparing for the arrival of their child.

Before she knew it, her idyllic walk came to an end as the small cottage Roger told her about sprang into view. It was a quaint structure, set against the backdrop of towering oaks that lined the beginning of the forest beyond, and was built of honey-hued stone with circular windows. Made gay by bright splashes of vivid wild flowers growing in profusion along its sides; nevertheless, the building showed signs of neglect in that the lawns surrounding it had been allowed to grow unattended—but the overall effect was one of privacy. She could well understand why Roger would have chosen such a spot to be his little hideaway.

The door was ajar, left open, she assumed, to allow the fresh breeze to steal inside. Stepping up to the portal, she called out for Roger. There was no answer, so she went inside.

The front chamber was filled with odd pieces of furniture covered over with great squares of linen. A faint musty smell met her, and she could see the uncovered floor had not been swept in quite a while. A bevy of spider's web clung to the insides of the circular windows as well as the corners of the room.

"Roger?" she called again. "Roger, are you here?"

There came the sound of booted feet from the next room, and she turned. "Roger, I—"

Her voice caught in her throat as she froze in place.

Like a haunting nightmare creeping upon her, Erik Bjord walked into the room.

"No, not Roger. It is I. *God dag, kära Brigitta,*" Erik said in a low, frightening tone. "Or should I greet you in the English language? After all, it has come to my attention that you are planning to wed an Englishman. . . ." He laughed then, though the sound was without mirth. "And to think the English have been known to view the Swedish people as being barbarians. I wonder if bigamy is a punishable crime in this land . . . believe me, it is in our kingdom, dear Brigitta."

Stunned, she stared at him, open-mouthed, for a full second. He had followed her! Why, oh, why had she thought he would not? "Wh—what are you doing here?" she whispered, a terrible fear gripping her entire body. "I—I thought—"

"You thought what? That the powerful Jorgen had taken care of me? Oh, please, surely you do not believe that I could have been so careless as to have walked directly into his trap? Jorgen was never my equal, though he liked to believe that he was. When I received word that he had my 'princess' in his clutches, I did not head blindly to Denmark as he had thought I would. I was well prepared to meet Jorgen, as were my loyal soldiers. It was a bloody battle, but quick, over in moments. We took his lands by storm, destroying everything. Your lover is dead, Brigitta, killed by my own sword."

"He was never my lover!" she spat, but then felt herself grow dizzy with the news. Jorgen. He'd met his death because of her. An involuntary shiver coursed through her body. "You're disgusting," she breathed. "I want you out of here, out of my life."

"I do not think you are in any position to give me orders. You see, Brigitta, you are my wife, my property. I can do anything with you that pleases me."

"I am not your wife!"

"Oh, but you are. Was it not you who walked to the altar where I stood? You took the vows of matrimony, Brigitta."

"No! I—I said those vows in the name of Lisa, not Brigitta Lind!"

He nodded once, standing like a sentinel amid the bright flow of sunshine behind him. "Yes, and that is just another bit of unfinished business between us. I still have not decided how to deal with you. Should I alert the court of Sweden to your treachery, tell them you murdered their poor princess only for the wealth and title she held?"

Brigitta pressed the palms of her hands to her ears, hating the sound of his cruel voice. "Stop it!" she screamed. "I didn't murder Lisa . . . she—she died a natural death."

"And begged you to take her place beside me at the altar?" he finished for her. His blue eyes turned cold, boring down at her. "Lies," he breathed. "All lies. Every word that has ever come from those beautiful lips of yours has been a lie. You think I would believe that Thora-Lisa would want you assuming her title? That woman adored me, she would never have wished another to take her place in my bed. From the time she was a child, she worshipped me. *I* was the reason she lived as long as she did! She wanted nothing more than to be my wife, to give me children, and to grant my every wish. How dare you stand there and tell me Lisa wanted you to take her place!"

"But it's true!" Brigitta insisted, hating the fact

that she must now stand here and explain her actions to this heartless murderer. "And you are correct when you say Lisa adored you. She did, in fact, she cared so much for your happiness that she begged me to take her place at the altar should she pass away before her wedding day. She—she wanted you to have a healthy wife, she wanted all of Vardighet to enjoy the reign of a healthy princess." She stopped then, unable to continue as memories of Thora-Lisa filled her mind. Sweet, gentle Lisa, with her kind and giving ways. Poor Lisa, condemned to a life of misery and to her own fragility in wanting a man as loathsome as Erik Bjord. "*I* did not murder the princess, Erik, *you* did just as surely as if you had put a knife through her heart. You and your careless ways. You ignored her needs, poked fun at her disfigurement, you and all of Vardighet killed Lisa!"

Erik, silhouetted in the room by the bright English sun streaming in from the small circular windows, held up one hand, his face hidden in shadow. "Enough!" he roared. "I have heard enough. I did not come here to listen to more of your lies. I have come to take you back to Vardighet, for that is where you belong. I do not care how Lisa died. She meant nothing to me, she was merely a stepping stone to a higher place. But now, since all of Vardighet believes you are their princess, my plans can continue, unimpeded. In fact, having you by my side will reap me even greater rewards—in bed and out. You will come with me, now. Our vessel, bound for Sweden, leaves soon. You will be on board, lovely Brigitta, and you will continue to walk in Lisa's shoes. You will stand by my side at the court of Sweden and be the adoring wife Lisa always wanted to be. You will bear me sons, healthy young males who will take my place. Together, we will form our own dynasty, one that is even more powerful than that of the Vasas."

He was mad. She could see it clearly now as he stepped toward her. His blue eyes were filled with a cold, frightening calm as he advanced upon her. Erik Bjord was a man beyond reason, a man blinded by his own ambitious nature.

"Stop!" Brigitta demanded. "D—don't come any closer. I will go nowhere with you, Erik. I am not your wife and I don't care what you believe. It—it was not you to whom I spoke the holy vows of matrimony. Devon Courtenay is the man for whom those vows of love and fidelity were meant—not you, never, ever you!"

"Do you think I care, fair Brigitta? It is not your love I seek, but your . . . charms." His heavy-lidded gaze slipped once down her slim form, then back up to meet her wide eyes. "I want sons, many of them and you will bear them. I want a woman who will shine in our court, a woman who will dazzle the burghers with whom I do business. Outside of Vardighet, you can go unveiled, traveling with me to Göteborg and Stockholm while I see to my shipping investments."

"I won't," she breathed. "I—I won't go back to Sweden with you. My place is here at Courtenay with the man I love. Devon will never let you take me away!"

He laughed, still advancing as she scurried behind a cloth-covered settee. "And do you truly believe Devon can save you from me? I've crossed one continent and the North Sea to find you, Brigitta. No man has the power to keep me from you now."

"Devon does! He—he is the lord here. He will stop you."

"But you are my wife. There were hundreds of witnesses at our nuptials. By law, there is no one to stop me from taking you back to Vardighet. And when I'm through here, Devon Courtenay will not even be alive to defend your dubious honor." He stood before her, the settee the only barrier between them.

Suddenly, his plans became crystal clear in her mind. Erik did not intend to leave England without killing Devon first. Her knees threatened to give way beneath her as the realization struck home. Groping for the back of the settee near her, her hands clutching the cool cloth with a death-grip, she stared at the man she had come to hate. "You're a heartless human being," she whispered, tears of pure fear clouding her eyes. *Oh, Devon, my love, what will become of us?* "You cannot truly mean to harm Devon?"

"I mean to kill the bastard."

"He is *not* a bastard! He is the true heir to Courtenay. He owns this land and everyone here bows to his rule! How you have come to be here, I know not, but you'll not be leaving as easily as you arrived."

Erik shook his head, smiling. He was enjoying watching her squirm, she thought. She heard his voice as though it came from a league's distance.

"So, Devon has you believing the grand fantasies his mother passed down to him. How quaint

. . . and how unfortunate. As for my presence here, you can thank Devon's half brother." He saw her eyes widen in surprise. "That's right, Brigitta. Roger is the one who led me here. He wants Devon out of his life almost as much as I do. Once I've . . . taken care of Devon, Roger will be free to run Courtenay as he has these three years past. In the end we will all profit."

"Everyone but Devon and myself."

"Precisely."

She shook her head, trying to clear it of the mind-numbing fear and to make sense of all Erik was saying. She couldn't believe Roger was involved in all of this. Not Roger. He had been so sweet during their last conversation . . . and yet, it was Roger who had posted the missive that sent her here to this small cottage, alone and unescorted.

"Shall we go now?" Erik's hateful voice sliced through her thoughts. "I wish to make it to Dover as quickly as possible."

The man was abominable. His vanity galled her. That he could stand there and so deliberately explain his plans of murdering Devon and then spiriting her away to Vardighet sent chills of revulsion through her.

"I'll go nowhere with you," she breathed. She had to do something, anything to get away from this madman. Stepping quickly to the right, Brigitta pushed off from the settee and lunged for the open door. But even before she could gain a foot or two, Erik shot out one muscular arm, catching her around her waist. With a low laugh, he yanked her lithe body toward him, bringing her flush against his chest, her hands trapped between their bodies.

"Do you think you can outsmart me, Brigitta? What a beautiful little fool you are." He held her so tightly that she could barely breathe. His face was close to hers, nearly touching the cheek she'd turned toward him. "You are my property, Brigitta. I can do with you whatever pleases me. If I wanted, I could carry you into the adjoining room and consummate our marriage. You eluded my bed once, don't believe I'll let you do so again."

Her palms were flat against his hard chest, the buttons of his saffron coat digging sharply into the tender skin of her hands. She pushed, but to no avail. His hold on her was tight and he was much too strong for her to overpower. But she struggled anyway, unwilling to be his prisoner or anything else.

He laughed at her feeble attempts to free herself. "Have you forgotten that I love a challenge, Brigitta . . . or is it that you *want* to incite me?" His eyes roamed down her, lingering for long moments at the rounded curves of her breast and then her waist. "You have bewitched me, you with your lovely face and lush curves," he whispered, his lips brushing her cheek. "Had it been anyone else who took Lisa's place I might have had them put upon the rack, but not you, *kära* Brigitta. In truth, I am glad you rid me of Thora-Lisa. The thought of marrying her was repulsive, but now, with your deceit, you have given me a boon. Not only can I now claim a princess as my wife, but I will know what beauty you hid beneath Lisa's veils." His large hand covered her bottom, pressing her to him. "Yes," he breathed. "I am quite pleased with the turn of events."

Brigitta leaned back, pushing at his solid chest with all her strength. "I hate you, Erik! I would rather die than live a life with you!"

Those were not the words he wanted to hear. Like a frost settling atop a field of flax, his blue eyes turned cold, a frightening gleam covering them. "You have no choice—no choice at all."

With a swiftness he had not expected, Brigitta whipped one hand free of his imprisoning hold and slapped him hard across the face. The sound of flesh hitting flesh filled the air for a split second, and then all was quiet. Erik, stunned for a moment, could only stare down at her incredulously. And then, a mask of deep rage settled over his harsh countenance.

"You will regret that," he hissed, giving a vicious shove that sent her sprawling backward. She tripped on her own skirts, struggling to maintain her balance, but Erik lunged forward, shoving her again so that she fell back onto the cloth-covered settee. He was beyond coherent thinking now, filled with cold fury that she should dare to strike him. He advanced upon her, his features hard, ungiving. Brigitta saw him lift his right arm, saw through a haze as he brought his hand down, slapping her viciously across the face. Her head snapped to the left as pain and anger exploded in her brain. White light burst in front of her eyes. Her skin and the muscles of her neck burned from the force of his blow.

Groggy now, her head swimming, Brigitta tried

to sit up, raising her hands up in defense should he strike her again. "Stop," she tried to yell, but her mouth filled with her own blood that oozed through a cut to her lower lip. She thought of her baby then, the tiny form of life even now growing within. If she stood, Erik might very well direct a brutal hit to her midsection. Brigitta would do nothing to harm Devon's baby—their baby—and yet, she must get away from him. She doubled over, bowing her head, rolling to the side of the settee. But Erik was not about to let her free just yet. With savage intensity, he reached out one arm and latched his hand tightly to her long hair, yanking her head up. He intended to strike her again. Unable to free herself, she saw him raise his left arm, saw the madness in his hateful blue eyes . . . and then the sound of steel whispering through a scabbard filled the air. Erik froze.

"Release her, Bjord . . . and then turn and face me like a man."

Devon's voice, filled with lethal calm, came to Brigitta through the haze. She looked up to see him standing on the threshold of the door, feet planted wide, his long dark hair tossed about him. Dazzling sunshine framed his tall, muscular frame as his loose shirtsleeves billowed in a vagrant breeze that rushed in through the portal.

Slowly, Erik released his hold on Brigitta, turned toward his adversary. "So, you came. I knew you would."

Devon ignored the blond warrior for only a moment as he stepped inside the door, a sword held ready in his right fist. "Brigitta, step away from him," he told her. She sat up, dizzy, disoriented.

"Are you all right?" she heard Devon ask. She could only nod as she pressed trembling hands to her stinging face.

"Y—yes. I—I am all right."

"Then come to me, Brigitta. I want you to go back to the main house. Stay there, do you hear?"

She stood up, the world tipping crazily in front of her eyes. She took an uneasy step forward, and then another, but Erik Bjord was not about to let her go.

"She stays," Erik ground out, and grabbed her by the arm, stopping her flight. She flinched at his touch.

"Let her go, Bjord. The vendetta you have is with me, not Brigitta."

"But you are wrong, Devon. Brigitta is my *wife*. She stays."

Devon's black eyes moved to look quickly at Brigitta who stood shaking beside Erik. Her lovely, heart-shaped face was covered with a red welt left by Erik's hand and her mouth bled freely from an open cut. Devon felt his stomach churn with hatred. He would kill the bastard for striking the woman he loved. "Then we shall match swords for her, Erik . . . to the death."

The blond campaigner nodded, a chilling smile taking over his lips. "Of course," he replied, his eyes taking on an unholy gleam. "That was my plan all along." In one swift motion, Erik shoved Brigitta away from him and then unsheathed his own sword that hung from the sash about his waist. *"En garde!"* he breathed.

Brigitta scurried toward the door and Devon

eased in front of her, shielding her. "Go back to the house," he ordered, his gaze fixed on Erik.

"No! I—I want to stay. I won't leave you here alone, Devon."

Had there been more time, Devon might have argued, but Erik was advancing, his rapier held in front of him, ready to pierce Devon's skin. Devon had no time to think of anything but his opponent. As a young lad, he and Erik had clashed swords on many occasions, and even though Erik had been older than Devon, Devon had been a formidable match. But since that time, both men had grown and had had considerable time to hone their skills.

Devon remembered back to the time in Thora-Lisa's apartments when he and Erik had clashed swords for the first time in years. He had gauged Erik's weaknesses then, had relearned Erik's reactions to his actions. Such swordplay was very much like a game of chess, but played at lightning speed. Cool, thought-through tactics were the key to success, and that was Erik's weakness. Erik, ever impatient, did not take the time to think through his opponent's next move. He wanted to lunge in for thrust after thrust, leaving himself unprotected between maneuvers. Erik cared little for the skillful art of swordplay. Time, that was all Devon needed. He would wear Erik down with parry after parry.

Leaving Brigitta standing near the door, Devon stepped into the middle of the room. The two men circled each other warily, each waiting for the other to make the first aggressive lunge.

"As a lad, I could best you," Devon taunted. "I can best you still."

Erik smiled, coolly confident, and then he made his move. Lunging, he went forward for the first draw of blood. Devon was ready. Alert, totally in control of his body and weapon, Devon executed a perfect parry followed by a smooth riposte. This is what he wanted, for Erik to be the aggressor, to set a quick pace that would soon tire him and dull his sharp reflexes. Matching Erik's gusto, Devon glided nimbly about the floor, feinting and parrying, repelling every one of Erik's quick counterripostes.

The sharp, musical chiming of metal against metal rang in the air as the double-edged blades flashed in sunlight that spilled through the uncovered windows. The men moved across the floor, both nimble and quick, both measuring each other. Their wrists flicked, their blades engaged, scraping, ringing. They parried and feinted, attacked, retreated. It was a dance of death they enacted, an artful meeting of keen minds and agile bodies.

Brigitta, her back pressed against the door jamb, watched in horrified fascination as the two of them shifted back and forth with liquid ease. Both were sweating openly now. Devon's black hair was pressed tight against his forehead, where his brows were drawn together in concentration, and his loose white shirt clung to his broad shoulders, showing the bunching of his muscles as he lifted his heavy sword for yet another clash with Erik's blade. His black breeches, tight against muscled thighs, showed clearly how trained his athletic body was. But how much longer could they continue with this pace? Erik appeared to tire momentarily as he made a thrust at Devon's midsection.

Devon easily sidestepped the lethal point of the blade, meting out a riposte that nicked Erik's left arm. The blond warrior shuffled back, surprise capturing his countenance for a flash of a second. He looked down to see a dark crimson stain spreading atop his saffron coat sleeve.

"I have first blood," Devon said. "Were this a contest of honor, I would ask if yours is yet satisfied."

"This is no contest of honor," Erik hissed. "And well you know it. You may have drawn first blood, but *I* will draw the last. Now, *en garde!*"

And once again, their furious swordplay resumed. Devon moved forward in an unrestrained show of superb skill, the double-edge of his blade driving relentlessly against Erik's guard. Metal clanged, sparks igniting briefly, showering into the air, as the men moved across the floor in a passionate, deadly ballet.

"You have become a competent swordsman since your youth," Erik said, parrying Devon's thrust. "I am impressed."

"Not as impressed as you will be when I drive this blade through your heart."

"Ah, such bold words . . . and from a bastard at that. Be careful, Devon. You forget you are addressing a general. Do you think I care about your idle threats? If I recall, your own dear father once issued such threats to me."

"My father?" Devon replied, disbelief shading his voice. They shuffled across the floor, wrists flicking as their blades flashed like sunlight atop water. "What do you know about my father?"

"A great deal, it would seem. For one thing, I

know he never married your mother as Augusta led everyone to believe—including you." He noted the grim lines of Devon's face, and continued, satisfaction lacing his tone of voice. "I also know how your father met his, shall we say, untimely demise." He feinted to the right then, but struck to the left.

Devon was ready. The hilts of their weapons clashed, locking. "What do you know about my father's death?" Devon demanded, his black eyes clashing with Erik's frosty blue gaze. "Tell me!" In a surge of great strength, Devon brought his arm up, swinging his blade free, then stepped back, his stance ready.

Erik, grudging admiration coloring his eyes, smiled, advancing once again. Above the clink of tapping sword tips, he said, "Surely, you of all people should have by now deciphered the puzzle of who murdered your father."

Devon said nothing, his concentration centered on the double-edged tip of Erik's blade.

Erik, in his vanity, was only too eager to explain. "It was I who did the deed, and with the greatest pleasure, I might add. Your father was a thorn in my family's side ever since he sailed into the Baltic Sea. The bold Michael Courtenay, believing he could stamp out all that my father and grandfather before me held dear, thought he could sail into our waters and take what was ours. I was raised during the reign of the great Gustavus Adolphus, and under his supreme rule we Swedes were the masters of the Baltic, holding all of the great ports from the mouth of the Weser to the Gulf of Finland. Your father was a fool to think he could undo all we had achieved."

As he spoke, Erik's concentration wavered. Off guard, his defense that up until this point had been faultless now slipped. Brigitta watched as Devon gauged this weakness, clearly planning his offense. Her heartbeat quickened, anticipating the final thrust of Devon's lethal sword. Soon, she thought. Soon.

But the sounds of running feet outside the small cottage came to her ears. She whirled in the doorway to see Roger flying toward her.

"Roger!" she gasped as he came to a halt beside her. "What—"

"Don't say a word please," he said in a rush. His face was a mask of rage and pain all at once. "Just give me a chance to explain myself, Brigitta." He looked her directly in the eye and flinched at the sight of her cut lip. "I—I'm sorry," he breathed, reaching out to touch her face.

Brigitta turned away, fear filling her once again. "Don't touch me!"

"Please, Brigitta, I didn't mean for Erik to harm you. I—" But his words were cut off with the sharp ringing of steel from the middle of the room. Devon and Erik were still engaged in their odd dance, both of them growing tired from the physical exertion. Roger turned his attention to the two of them. "Damn! I didn't mean for this to happen, not at all!" In his shaking hands he held a wheellock pistol, cocked and primed.

Fearing he meant to shoot Devon, Brigitta blindly reached for it. "No! I won't let you shoot Devon!"

With surprising strength, Roger stayed her hands with one of his, his eyes boring down at her. "You little fool! I wouldn't shoot my own brother! It—it is Erik I mean to kill." He stepped away from her then, moving inside the cottage, listening intently to the exchange between his half brother and Erik.

"*I* killed your father, Devon," Erik was saying, exalting in his story. "I was the one who put a sword through his pirate heart, and I'd do it again! Your father had too many political contacts for me to ignore him. He wanted the Baltic opened to free trade, he wanted to eat away at the power the great Gustavus had worked so hard to gain for Sweden. I couldn't let him live, for he would have incited others to help him fight against dominance in the Baltic."

Devon heard Erik's words. He had known Erik had played some part in his father's death, but he had not guessed it had been Erik's own hand that had drained the blood from the father he'd never known. His breath left him in a silent rush. Finally, all the truth was out. In just the span of a few short weeks Devon had learned he was truly a bastard, born of an affair between his dear mother and her English pirate lover, and now he knew how his father had died. Suddenly, it was too much to bear. With a fury born deep within, brought on by all the grief he'd held inside for so long, Devon lunged at Erik, surprising the blond giant with a furious advance of steel. Erik, so caught up in telling his story, was unprepared for the attack. His guard was down. In a swift, fluid movement, Devon thrust his sword upward with superhuman strength, sending Erik's weapon flying from his huge hand. The sword flew through the air, twirled, and then skittered across the hardwood floor. Erik, stunned, his eyes wide, could only stare after it. In a fraction of a second, Devon lunged forward, pressing the tip of his blade directly against Erik's throat. He gave it a gentle push and a trickle of dark blood seeped from broken skin.

Erik trembled involuntarily, suddenly unable to meet his own death as boldly as he had sought it upon numerous battlefields.

"Send the blade home, Devon," he gasped. "Do the deed! You've wished for this moment for years, we both know it. Ever since the night I stormed into your precious mother's chambers and stripped her of her pride, you have wanted to kill me. Here is your chance. Make use of it, or you'll regret this moment, I swear to you."

Devon, his breathing heavy, his muscles burning from the strain of their confrontation, hesitated for a moment. He should kill Erik, he knew. He must, for the death of his father, for Brigitta's sake. Before him, at the end of his sword, stood the man who had murdered his father, the only man who could see to it Brigitta and Devon never married. Here was Brigitta's legal husband, a man with whom she had shared vows of matrimony. Devon felt his hand tighten on the hilt of his sword, felt himself lean forward. Now, he thought. Now!

Behind him came an animallike cry of rage. "You murderer!" Roger Courtenay cried. "How could I have been so blind? I allowed you to let me believe I should reap revenge on Michael Courtenay! You blackheart!" Roger yelled, wild with his rage. "I helped you murder my own father!"

Devon looked over his shoulder to see his half brother lift the eighteen-inch wheel-lock pistol, filled with a pound of lead, and point it straight at Erik Bjord's head. Seeing what would come next, Devon immediately dropped the tip of his sword, twisting out of the line of fire just as Roger pulled the trigger. A loud *crack* followed by a small, billowing cloud of acrid, blue-tinged smoke filled the air.

Brigitta, fearing Devon had been hit in the melee, scrambled forward, directly into the haze of smoke. "Devon!" she screamed. "Devon!"

And then he was there, stepping out of the insalubrious fog to wrap warm, strong arms about her. "I am here, Brigitta," he said, his voice low. Trembling uncontrollably, she clung to him, pressing her face against his chest. He allowed her a moment to gather her wits, stroking her back as he turned her away from the ugly sight of Erik's bloody body sprawled atop the floor.

A few feet away, Roger lowered his arms, shocked by his own actions. "Oh, sweet heaven," he murmured. "What have I done? What have I done?"

"The only thing you could do," Devon replied, but Roger wasn't listening.

"I've killed him," he continued pathetically. "I— I killed him! I am ruined . . . all my hopes and dreams shattered beyond repair. What will happen to me now? I've no home, no wealth, nothing— and now this! I've murdered a Swedish general, a man respected and adored by his people. There shall be no peace for me, ever." He looked up then, the smoke clearing as his black eyes, filled with grief, fixed on Brigitta and Devon. "And our father," he whispered. "I killed him as surely as if my own hand had driven the blade through his heart."

"No," Devon said softly, as though speaking to a lad. "Erik murdered our father, not you, Roger."

"I did, I tell you! I—I lured Michael away from Courtenay. I—I sent a missive telling him I wished to meet him in Dover. You see, I didn't want his blood spilled upon the lands I would soon own. And he came, of course he would come, for we had just had one of our numerous arguments. He must have been feeling the weight of his guilt. But it was not I who met him—it was Erik! I let Erik Bjord murder our father!" In shame, he bowed his head, sobbing openly, his shoulders sagging.

Brigitta glanced up at Devon, tears, not caused totally by the gun powder, filling her eyes. Gently, he released his tight hold on her, and she stepped aside, knowing better than to interfere in the moment. Devon moved slowly toward his half brother. Carefully, he pried the wheel-lock pistol from Roger's tight grasp and tucked the thing into the waistband of his own breeches.

"Don't do this to yourself," he said, his voice low. "You didn't know, Roger. You thought—you thought Michael had forsaken you, and he had in a way. He let you grow to manhood alone, knowing very well he was your true father. It was a cruel thing to do. No one can blame you for being bitter. If not for Erik's intervention, I am certain you would never have thought of reaping vengeance on the man who gave us both life. I will not stand in judgment of you, brother." His voice caught, and he took a second to draw in a deep breath before he did something he would have never thought possible before this moment; he clasped his half brother on the arms and then drew him to his body in a tight hug.

The embrace was quick, but heartfelt. Roger straightened, his black eyes, so like his younger half brother, filling with love. "I am sorry we never had a chance to know each other," he said thickly. "And it is my deepest regret that I have now sullied the Courtenay name by taking the life of a Swedish general. There—there will be questions, you know. Many of them. As owner of these lands, you will be responsible for explaining this—this murder. All of the trade I've created between Göteborg and Courtenay will be lost. I've invested a great amount of money, Devon. In fact, what comes of this might very well be Courtenay's downfall."

"Stop," Devon said. "You needn't continue. I can imagine what the consequences will be."

"But I will admit to the murder," Roger added. "I will not run away from this."

"I don't expect you to."

"The Courtenay name will be ruined, discredited. No man of any great standing will conduct business with a Courtenay after this scandal."

"It needn't be that way, not all."

"But how—"

Devon's black eyes were hard, filled with stony

determination. "You could continue your international trade if no one knew you were the one who shot the general," Devon offered. "Your life could continue as it had before Brigitta and I arrived if you tell no one the truth."

"But Bjord is dead! His . . . his body must be returned to Vardighet, questions must be answered. I—I don't understand."

"It is simple. Courtenay rightfully belongs to you, Roger. You are the legitimate heir, not I. It is you who deserves to preside over these vast lands. You are the one who has made Courtenay what it is today. I see no reason why you should not stay here and live the life you've come to enjoy."

Roger shook his head. "But I've just murdered a man!"

"And the only witnesses to the scene were Brigitta and myself."

Brigitta stepped forward, touching Devon's sleeve. "What are you saying, Devon? Someone must answer to this murder."

"And someone will," Devon replied, not taking his eyes from his brother. "*I* will be the one to take the blame."

"No!" Brigitta cried. "I won't let you! Are you mad? They would hang you for such a crime!"

"Only if they can find me," Devon said darkly, turning his face toward her. His features were hard, filled with implacable will, and she knew then he would not be swayed from his staunch but foolhardy decision. "What Erik said is true, Brigitta. I am not Michael Courtenay's legitimate son.

Michael never married my mother, he could not, for he was already wed to Roger's mother."

"What?" she breathed, unable to believe him. "But Augusta said—"

"Lies, all lies. It . . . it was her greatest fantasy. She wanted all to believe Michael had married her before bedding her. But it wasn't so."

"But the ring! You have the ring Michael left with Augusta. Michael's will stated that whoever carries his signet ring should be sole heir to Courtenay."

"Yes, this is true, and I don't know why Michael made such a request, especially since he'd allowed Roger to move into Courtenay. I guess he must have loved Augusta as much as she claimed he did." He shook his head. "I don't know why Michael denied Roger his birthright, but I do know that I will not live at Courtenay. It isn't my home, Brigitta. It never was. I hope you can understand this, my darling, but I want nothing to do with these lands and Michael's wealth. I want no part of it at all."

"But to take the blame for Erik's death?"

"And why shouldn't I? Another moment and I would have run the dog through with my blade. He deserved to die, for killing my father and for all the pain he caused our dear Thora-Lisa."

Yes, she thought. *Erik did deserve to die. But why you, my love? Why should you carry his blood upon your hands?*

"Don't you understand, Brigitta? You and I, we can make our home anywhere in this vast world. We have each other, Brigitta, and our unborn babe. That is enough."

Roger stared incredulously at his younger half brother. "You would do that for me?" he asked. "You would let all believe you murdered Erik?"

Devon nodded, once. "Yes, for you, brother, I will. Brigitta and I will leave here, today, now. You need give us only enough time to be clear of Courtenay before you summon the alarm. Tell the authorities what you will. Tell them I lured Erik here and then shot him. There are those at Vardighet who remember me, I know. They will not find it unbelievable that I could have killed Erik. Lord knows I had reason enough to hate the man. I will even put in writing that I am not the true heir to Courtenay. Once Brigitta and I leave, you will be the sole owner. There will be no one to threaten your position ever again."

"But where will you go, Devon? Where will you and Brigitta flee?"

"I don't know," he answered truthfully. "The New World, perhaps. That is, if Brigitta is willing to go." He glanced over at her, posing the unspoken question. Did she still want to share a life with him, a life without the riches of Courtenay, a life with a man who was truly a bastard?

Brigitta met his gaze and saw behind the brave front he upheld for his brother, saw the desolation and uncertainty that lay just beneath the surface of those black orbs. The sacrifice he was offering for Roger was great, far greater than Devon need make, but she knew very well he had to do it. The revelations Devon had met with in the past hour were staggering. Her heart went out to him.

Softly, her eyes shining with her love, she said, "I told you once I would go anywhere with you—

even to hell. Wherever you lead, I will follow. Whatever hardships you face, I will face them, too. I am a part of you, Devon, and you of me. In Denmark, amid a wild thicket filled with early morning fog, I pledged my troth to you. I care not for wealth or titles . . . I care only for you, my love. We've a babe to raise, and we will, together."

Devon felt his heart turn within his ribcage in a tumble of joy and love. His Brigitta, so brave and strong, so steadfast. He loved her with all his body and soul. She was the brightness of his days, the highest pinnacle of his dreams.

A smile split his mouth, the first in days, and he wrapped one arm about her slim shoulders, giving her a tight squeeze. Turning back to his half brother, he said, "Then it is settled. The murder of Erik Bjord will fall on my shoulders, and with your help, Brigitta and I will be away from Courtenay. You will have your dream, brother . . . and I will have mine."

BOOK VI

The Bride

Chapter Twenty-five

THE HUGE MERCHANTMAN, just out of the English Channel, sliced through the choppy waters of the North Atlantic Ocean, leaving in its foaming wake the land of England and all its turmoil. Brigitta, wrapped in Devon's strong arms, her back pressing against his chest, stood aft near the rail, the salt spray whipping up from the waters to brush atop their skin with a cleansing breath. She breathed deeply of the fresh air, tipping her head back to capture the rays of a brilliant sun upon her face.

"Happy?" Devon inquired, giving her a gentle hug.

"Forever," she answered, "as long as you are by my side."

"And I will be at your side forever, *kära* Brigitta. Never doubt that."

"I don't. Not now." She allowed him to plant a soft kiss to her temple, her ungloved hands entwining with his. "That was a very noble thing you did for Roger. He . . . I am certain he will be forever in your gratitude."

"It was not his gratitude I sought."

"No," she answered thoughtfully. "Absolving him of the blame for Erik's murder was something you felt you had to do. I understand that, Devon. I believe you felt you owed Roger something, on behalf of your father. I—I know you don't want to talk of this anymore, and I will respect that wish, but I just want you to know that I understand. You are a man motivated by deep-rooted responsibilities, and I admire that characteristic in you. You knew your father had wronged both you and Roger, and knowing Roger was the first-born son, you wanted to give him Courtenay."

Devon stared sightlessly at the endless horizon of blue on white-capped sea-green. "I never truly felt at home within the walls of Courtenay, Brigitta. Even when I thought I was the sole heir, I did not feel as though the place was mine. There were . . . there were too many ghosts lingering about."

"Yes," she said softly. "I felt it, too."

"Then you do not regret my actions?"

"Not at all. In fact, I am looking forward to building a new life in America. Roger's wedding gift of gold will see us through the coming months. I am certain we can forge our own place in this land they call the New World. Who knows, perhaps we can even form our own mercantile empire, even trading with Roger in England."

Devon chuckled. "Roger would be elated," he replied. Turning her slim body about in his arms, he held her loosely by the shoulders, and said, "Do you know, Brigitta, how much I love you? For all of my life I have been searching for something, forever chasing after some elusive dream. There was a time when I believed having Courtenay and all its wealth, along with my father's name, was all that mattered to me. But I was a fool, for what I had truly been seeking was always here, inside of me." He brought her right hand up and placed it above the spot where his heart beat a steady rhythm. "What I'd actually been searching for was love, a love so bright and blinding it obliterates all else . . . and this is what you have brought me. I don't need riches or titles, I don't need anything or anyone but you, Brigitta. You are the soul my heart has been aching for all these years. *You, my sweet, are the end of my rainbow.*"

His words, straight from the heart, swirled around her, cloaking her in a warm shield of protective ecstasy. "And you are mine," she whispered, her undying love shining brightly in her summer-blue eyes. She stepped into his warm embrace, allowing him to wind his strong arms about her as the deck heaved beneath their feet.

Together, beneath a dazzling sun that showered its warming rays atop a churning sea, they clung to each other. And the world, with all its challenges and wonders, spread out before them, beckoning them.

They were ready, she thought, finally ready to meet the future head on, for theirs was a wild love, challenged by fierce odds and tamed, in the end, by their own kindred spirits. Together, there was nothing they could not face.

Reading—
For The
Fun Of It

Ask a teacher to define the most important skill for success and inevitably she will reply, "the ability to read."

But millions of young people never acquire that skill for the simple reason that they've never discovered the pleasures books bring.

That's why there's RIF—Reading is Fundamental. The nation's largest reading motivation program, RIF works with community groups to get youngsters into books and reading. RIF makes it possible for young people to have books that interest them, books they can choose and keep. And RIF involves young people in activities that make them want to read—**for the fun of it.**

The more children read, the more they learn, and the more they **want** to learn.

There are children in your community—maybe in your own home—who need RIF. For more information, write to:

RIF
Dept. BK-3
Box 23444
Washington, D.C.
20026

Founded in 1966, RIF is a national, nonprofit organization with local projects run by volunteers in every state of the union.

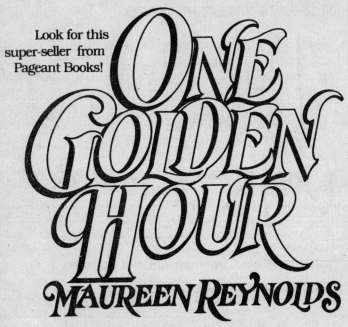